WILD FIRE

She felt his lips on her eyelids, one then the other, and opened her eyes to his, to the sight of his pupils dark as onyx, reflecting tiny images of her face, their wells filling with smouldering desire. A shaft of sunlight drove downward from the top of the calico curtains drawn over the high window, a golden broadsword thrusting its point into the floor out of sight beyond the foot of the bed. And halfway down its edge dissolved, settling a slender arc atop his hair, a cap of gold.

'My darling, my darling,' she whispered huskily . . .

Wild Fire

BARBARA RIEFE

SPHERE BOOKS LIMITED
30–32 Gray's Inn Road, London WC1X 8JL

First published in Great Britain by
Sphere Books Ltd 1983
Copyright © 1981 by Barbara Riefe
Published by Sphere Books Ltd
Published in the United States of America by
Playboy Paperbacks 1981

TRADE
MARK

Set in Plantin

Printed and bound in Great Britain by
Collins, Glasgow.

This book is dedicated
with love and affection
to my mother

He's a fool, who thinks by force, or skill,
To turn the current of a woman's will.

– Henry Tuke, 1755–1814

1

Her hair was a profusion of cinnamon waves unable to decide on pattern or direction of fall; 'as untamable as a wolf,' complained her mother. There were those who observed that her dark eyes were too dark, as black as Trincomalee ebony. Others complained that her lips were overly full, lending her mouth a determined look that bordered on pugnacity, even insolence. Her cheekbones were described as being as high as an Osage squaw's by one close friend of her father's. Someone else noted that her skin was insufficiently pale for a young woman of breeding and quality and that in candleglow it even assumed a sheen resembling polished bronze. And nearly all who knew her agreed that she was much too tall, though not at all statuesque, and guilty of the annoying tendency of looking over people's heads instead of down at their eyes when they were addressing her. As if all of these imperfections were not burden enough, anyone could see that she was painfully slender and too full-busted for it. And she had the habit of standing with her weight balanced on one leg, the knee of the other bent at an angle, an awkward posture most apparent when she was in the company of other girls who carried their persons properly.

Older women with no axe of envy to grind lamented that she seemed content to wear the loveliest gown with the studied indifference of a beggar for his rags. Men invariably glanced at the poor girl, looked away, then looked back to see if their eyes had deceived them. Endeavoring to offset these all too conspicuous inadequacies of feature and structure was but one asset worth noting. She was beautiful.

Like all so endowed, Tawny had been aware of the changeovers in her life, from beautiful baby to pretty little child to ungainly girl to enchantingly lovely woman. Nor was she indifferent to her appearance – the admiring stares of men and the looks of something other than admiration of their women reminded her all too frequently that she was worthy of attention. But then, aunt Lydia Rampling Cutshaw had been described as a beauty in her day. Tawny's eyes drifted from the rain-thrashed woodland rushing by the crack in the coach's canvas curtain to her aunt, seated diagonally opposite her, her heavily powdered, puffy face hovering over *Godey's Lady's Book, The Drawing Room Companion,* her pink-rimmed hazel eyes embedded in the flesh like raisins thumbed into dough, her classical bow lips laboriously forming one word after the other. Lydia Cutshaw was in her middle fifties, but life in western Missouri along the untamed edge of a nation little more than thirty years old had early taken its toll. The omnipresent dangers, the hardships, and the demands of daily toil had conspired to ravage her beauty and steal her pride in it. Her face was sapped of vitality, the skin as ruddy as King's Evil. Her neck was laddered with lines, the flesh beginning to welt and wattle. Her eyes, once bright and twinkling, had assumed a dull cast, as if the mind behind them had lost all zest for life, all interest in the living world. She wheezed when she breathed, rising from her chair, climbing stairs with the difficulty of a woman twice her size and twenty years older. Tawny felt a warmth and affection for her – she admired her vibrant personality, her grittiness, her sincerity and genuineness – but, recalling how she had looked ten years earlier and seeing her now, it was all she could do to keep from sighing aloud in pity.

Sharing Lydia's bench seat were her daughters, Tawny's cousins – Emily, nineteen, the pretty poser, as well scrubbed and shining as a new pan, picture-perfect in every detail in her bunched-up brown pipe curls, her lightly rouged cheeks, and her rosebud print dress with a trifle too much lace at cuffs and collar. And Priscilla, two years younger, as scrawny as a fawn, her wide and wondering watery eyes forever blinking, her conch-pink nostrils harboring perpetual sniffles. Priscilla, as clumsy as a marionette in unpracticed hands, the whole of her homeliness surrounded by a bonnet of Neapolitan straw gaily decked with bows of corn-colored ribbon rushing the summer, it being not yet May.

A bullying downpour slammed against the coach roof,

and the vapor gathering within assaulted Lydia's face powder and Emily's curls, dampened everyone's hanky, and, clearing breathing passages, permitted incursion of all sorts of disagreeable odors dominated by that of the old leather interior paneling.

Like her mother alongside her, Priscilla was captive to a book, her constant companion, studied and restudied by the hour until it had swollen to twice its bulk: *Trotter's English Dictionary*, in which Dr. Trotter offered not only words and definitions, but examples of usage.

'Lord help us if this rain keeps up all the way to St. Louis,' observed Lydia without raising her eyes from her book.

'I don't believe it will, Mother,' said Priscilla, emulating her. 'I am sanguine about it. I have no trepidations.'

Emily smirked and winked at Tawny, and Tawny winked back. The coach lurched violently, raising bandboxes from laps, rattling the trunk on the roof, the candle lamps inside, and the dead coals in the foot stove in the center of the floor, and throwing Priscilla against Emily and Emily against Lydia, crushing her bulk into the corner. The vehicle then settled back into its ruts and scordatura of sounds – the drilling rain, the steady thump of mud gobs propelled against the dashboard and undercarriage at the front by the horses' hooves, the pounding hooves themselves, and the occasional crack of the driver's whip.

It was the worst time of year for coach travel. In winter the Missouri ground was like stone, in summer – during dry weather – equally hard, with dust the only additional discomfort. But now, as in the fall, the way was a quagmire. It was no real road to begin with, but a corrugated swath peeled by a dragged log across the heart of the territory at a right angle to the Osage Boundary Line, a stripping become a shallow canal of earthy mucilage capable of sucking wheels hub-deep in certain spots and rinsing the floorboards in others, a boggy interruption in the north-to-south land-scape where anything springing from seed was crushed by hooves and wheels before it grew large enough to green. Sharing the pole, neck yokes, and whiffle-tree in valiant challenge to the two hundred miles of mire were four overworked, undernourished bays reined to the hands of a blowzy-bearded driver wearing a filthy flannel shirt, corduroy breeches stuffed into high boots, a scarlet crown hat, and a shabby, holey leather coat buttoned up to his foul mouth against the merciless rain. The seat Tawny occupied was velvet, upholstered with hay, she fancied, so hard was it. And every jar, every jounce, every jolt tested the twin leather throughbraces cradling the coach, wrenching all four passengers' spines, prompting sighs and grimaces.

Three other passengers had shared the seats, boarding at Lexington, but had disembarked at Fayette, leaving the Cutshaws and Tawny in privacy. The fare was five dollars per passenger one way from Titus Forks to St. Louis – extravagant but, without any alternative travel, unavoidable. They would be staying a week, seven days filled with festivities, merrymaking, and excitement – lavish dinner parties, cotillions, and balls by night, riding and racing and sight-seeing down the Mississippi by day, wedding preparations and rehearsal, all culminating in a Grand Ball the night before cousin Marcy Rampling's wedding.

'To a Mr. Boyd Chevrier,' Lydia had told them. 'Tall, dashing, sinfully handsome, so they say. And we are all invited. Isn't it exciting, little chicks?'

Immensely exciting to Tawny, filling her heart with flowers and her mind with delicious anticipation. But at the same time it was also disturbing. Marcy's father had invited George Cutshaw, Lydia's husband, who had 'respectfully and with regret declined,' being in the throes of recovery from a broken hip. No invitation had been sent to Tawny's father. Disturbing, but not surprising. Jack Kinross and Aldous Rampling disliked each other with a passion, a simple case of opposites repelling. Aldous was educated, esteemed as a man of breeding and bearing who had become extraordinarily successful in shipping – so successful that some St. Louisians had begun calling the Mississippi the River Rampling. In contrast, Jack Kinross had been schooled in the wilds of Virginia, Louisiana, Texas, and Missouri, a rambunctious, bourbon-loving backwoodsman not unacquainted with blood, mud, and most of the seamier aspects of life on the frontier. A 'horse-swopper' by trade, he had wooed and won Miriam Rampling, Aldous's youngest sister. In time a daughter, Crystal Taunton (after her mother's maternal grandmother's family), had been born, growing up the only child in what Tawny earnestly believed to be the happiest home in the world. Until her beautiful, doting, happily married mother took leave of her senses and put a ball from her husband's favorite pistol through her temple. It was this painful event that had created the unbridgeable breach between Tawny's father and her uncle. Aldous openly blamed his brother-in-law for Miriam's untimely death and 'the manner of it'. Friction between the two almost reached the stage where pistols alone would settle matters, but cooler temperaments had prevailed.

Aldous's rage and resentment might have endured, but Tawny knew him to be a decent man, and after the initial furor had blown over, as she expected, he had let the sleeping dog lie. Welcoming her into his home, he would politely inquire after her father's health and the state of his business. And mention him no further. Still, Aldous's presumption in blaming Jack Kinross for the death of the woman he worshipped, the woman he would have given his own life to save had such been possible, would always nettle Tawny. In her view no man and woman had ever loved each other more than her father and mother. She could cite a thousand examples of their devotion. That any outsider could persuade himself that Jack Kinross had failed to do everything in his power to help save her from herself, or, worse, had actually driven her to suicide, was unthinkable.

But Tawny cautioned herself against letting that old dog's shadow fall over these seven days. If Aldous could keep his sentiments to himself, she could hold her tongue. She had last seen her uncle and her aunt and Marcy three years earlier, when they had come to Titus Forks to visit the Cutshaws. Tawny remembered Marcy years prior to that visit as a pretty and precocious child of eleven tossing her lovely blonde curls about, demanding and gaining everyone's attention, but nevertheless vivacious, exciting, and bright as a new shilling. Tawny had taken to her the moment they'd met, so much more interesting and alive was she than either Emily or Priscilla. But this precipitate fondness was not reciprocated. Marcy was so concerned with showing off she scarcely spared her taller Kinross cousin as much as a passing glance. And yet when the two had met more recently they had hit it off uncommonly well, babbling on for practically the entire visit, all but ignoring the Cutshaw girls, both of whom seemed content to watch and listen.

Three years was a long time, more than enough for a girl to mature into womanhood. Tawny wondered what Marcy looked like. Aldous was handsome, and she resembled him – the identical green eyes, the flawlessly sculptured features ... She would be beautiful, her blonde hair likely long and lovely and still her outstanding feature. She was twenty now, eighteen months younger than Tawny, and, having 'landed the big fish,' as George Cutshaw put it, would be married within a few days. As if pricked by a needle, Tawny felt a twinge of envy. Marcy might as easily be coaching across Missouri in the opposite direction, to *her* wedding, but she wasn't. One had to have a beau to entertain prospects of marriage. Tawny had none. Geography was the culprit. There were fewer than fifteen homes in Titus Forks, while nearly two thousand people resided in St. Louis, with dozens more arriving every week. Young people couldn't avoid meeting young people. And thanks to her father's success, Marcy Rampling would have to be among the most admired and sought after. Only last year, according to Lydia, Aldous had finished building the biggest, most beautiful, most impressive home in town, if not the entire Territory. A worthy symbol of his wealth and position, and not likely to discourage prospective suitors for his daughter's hand.

Tawny was dying to see the house; she had never been in any house that wasn't built of logs laid horizontally, frontier-style. It was said that even back before the War the French in St. Louis were building their homes with logs set up vertically, and the more prosperous among them were erecting the first stone houses. And within the past twenty-five years St. Louis had grown into a city of no fewer than fifty blocks, with more than two dozen fine stone mansions along its three main north-south streets – the Rue Royale, the Rue de l'Eglise, and the Rue des Granges.* The more than one hundred frame buildings boasted elaborate verandas and lovely flower gardens, cultivated fruit trees,

* These three streets no longer exist, having been replaced by a riverfront national park.

and *potagers*. Indeed, St. Louis in 1808 would have resembled a little town in Brittany had it not been for the Indians wandering about.

Lydia had gotten all her information from Aldous and Marcy and in passing it on had no doubt embroidered it skilfully, but the pictures that she painted flitted across Tawny's imagination, raising her expectations far beyond the bounds of reasonableness.

Lydia wearied of reading, closing her book in her capacious lap, closing Priscilla's for her and resuming her lecture on the proper conduct required of young visitors to St. Louis, a lecture begun shortly after the invitations had arrived and, reflected Tawny, certain to be continued long after they got there.

'Emily, when you are in the company of others and a humorous story is told, you are expected to laugh, of course, but you must not shriek. No matter how hilarious the story. Priscilla, when a boy asks you to dance, you are not to blush, stammer, and cover your mouth with your hands. Tawny, you are not to dance with boys a foot shorter than you are. Decline gracefully, my dear, so as not to injure their feelings. None of you are to wander about the house or grounds unescorted. You are not to pick up vases or bric-a-brac and the like to examine them. You'll only leave fingermarks, and if dropped, whatever it is may dent or, bless my stars, break. You are not to lie in bed babbling to each other all night. You must be rested and clear-eyed every morning, not yawning over breakfast. Since all three of you are to be bridesmaids, you must be prepared to learn your duties, practice them diligently, and execute them flawlessly. God forbid any of you trip and fall going down the aisle.'

Thrusting her hand into her reticule, she brought out a small brown bottle, uncorked it, swigged, recorked it, and put it back. Her medicine for her rheumatism, so she claimed. Whether it was medicine or gin taken from the quart bottle behind the sugar sack in her kitchen cabinet was questionable, but tasting it did remind her of some advice she had overlooked.

'And no one is to take alcoholic beverages at any time, even you, Tawny, though you're older.'

Tawny reflected on this. 'What if they serve wine at dinner?'

'Wine everyone drinks, except Baptists, of course,' replied Lydia. 'I'm talking about bourbon whiskey, barrel whiskey...'

'Gin?' asked Emily with a devilish look.

'No gin, nor even flip.'* Lydia continued detailing the rules until she mentioned Marcy and Priscilla interrupted.

'She's such a lucky stick,' she lamented, pouting. 'I wish I had a beau!'

'Don't be silly, child!' snapped her mother. 'You're barely seventeen.'

'Jennifer Spence is only sixteen, and she and Ralph Twining have been ambulating together for months!'

'Jenny Spence has "ambulated" her way into a reputation as unsavory as a delta doxy.'

'Mummy, why is it all the bad girls have beaus and all the good girls sit home dreaming and wishing?' asked Emily slyly.

Lydia sniffed. 'If you don't know the answer to that, I heartily fear for your future. Besides, you've no cause for complaint. Richard Hanley danced with you four times at his sister's birthday party last week, Priscilla told me.'

'Ugh, I can't stand the cloddy thing. He's a toad. His breath reeks, he's clumsy as a plow horse, and his nose is always running... He's disgusting.'

'Be quiet!' burst Priscilla in a hurt tone, wiping the wetness from her nose with her sleeve and getting a slap on the forearm from her mother.

Tawny leaned into her corner and closed her eyes to envision the rain parting like curtains to reveal St. Louis neatly clustered at the river's edge, bright with lights under a woolly blue blanket of darkness. A barrage of skyrockets began shooting up from Aldous Rampling's house, standing five times as high as those around it. The colors exploding against the night spelled out 'Marcy' in letters a hundred feet high. And as the word began to drip and die, the scene vanished, replaced by a view of the aisle in the church, the

---

* A mixed drink made with liquor or wine, sugar, and egg, powdered with nutmeg.

8

procession moving slowly up to the waiting minister and groom and best man, Marcy on Aldous's arm radiant in her satin dress and tulle veil. And her ring, a diamond as big as a pigeon's egg, dazzling all eyes.

The coach wheels struck something in the road, the left front wheel bouncing high, the rear following, the coach coming down once, twice, shaking the four of them like rag dolls in a basket and continuing on its way.

2

The rain leaking in ran slender trails down three of the four corner pillars, deepening the dampness pervading the interior of the coach. Against it the foot stove offered little defense, although the coals vigorously stirred now and then by Lydia continued to glow. It had been raining every turn of the wheels since Titus Forks; one would have surmised that by now the four passengers would have accustomed themselves to the discomfort. But since the weather worsened noticeably as the hours dragged by, this was not to be. Twilight only deepened the gray of the day within them, and without, the storm clouds lowering ominously over the land.

The horses were slowing now, the driver yelling, 'Geer there,' above the insistent rattle of the rain. 'Whoa-who-oof' and the coach veered sharply to the right as he pulled to a stop. The four exchanged inquiring and worried glances as they heard him climb down and swing to the ground. Lifting the leather window cover, he presented his comically ugly face, his forefinger touching the brim of his hat in salute.

'Excuse me, ladies, but the road's getting stickier and stickier. The horses are tired and at this rate we'll not be reaching the river until well after nightfall. I would prefer to cross during daylight, with the water a mite less ferocious than it's sure to be this night.'

'And what are you suggesting, driver?' asked Lydia.

'I'm suggesting Matthews' Inn, about a mile up the way – a rest for the team, a hot meal for us, a chance to dry out a bit, and a warm bed. We can breakfast and be off again before sunup, with hopes that the rain will have stopped by then.'

'Matthews' Inn, you say?'

'A first-rate place, ma'am. Separate rooms and everything. Everybody stops there.'

'I can imagine . . .'

'We'll never get across the Missouri tonight, Mummy,' interposed Priscilla. 'We'd surely fall off the ferry and drown ourselves for such precipitancy.'

The driver gaped, and Lydia smiled. 'Hush, child.' She pursed her lips, a tight little red button. Crimpling her brow, she weighed her decision. 'Very well, driver. Matthews' Inn it shall be.'

Again the man saluted. He climbed back up, whirled his whip – twelve and a half feet from butt to point of lash – snapped it with a crack like a pistol shot, and bellowed, 'Whoo-up.' Up and free of the slough's grip rose the coach. The horses' hooves resumed hurling mud lumps, as if retaliating against the coach for its burdensome weight and the consequent drain on their strength. Presently they began climbing, slowing as they did so, the whip cracking above them rapidly, the driver urging them on with a shout. Topping the rise, they thundered down the last hundred yards to the inn with a blast of his horn announcing their arrival. The coach shuddered to a stop, flinging the water running down the pillars over the occupants. The hosteler's bell clanged loudly; he appeared, the horses were relieved of their shafts and stabled, and, clutching their carpetbags, Lydia and the girls were helped to the ground, shielded from the torrent by capacious umbrellas. Picking their way gingerly between the puddles, they were greeted at the door by the Matthewses, husband and wife, and entered the inn.

Elias Matthews was a wide-shouldered man with restless blue eyes and a voice that rumbled from his throat like mild thunder from the pit. Mrs. Matthews was a plump woman with a stacking of chins supporting her small pink mouth. On her lawn cap, tied under her lowest chin, a narrow frill encircled her beaming smile. Her dress was a mauve-and-white print, with a bell-shaped skirt peeking around the edge of her apron.

Like every other building Tawny had ever seen, the inn was constructed of logs seamed with clay, this one two stories rising to a roof of shakes painstakingly hewn one by one from the heart of the red oak with froe and mallet. The puncheon floor – split tree trunks sixteen to eighteen inches in width and faced with a broadaxe – was polished to a shine. At one end of the public room a cat-and-clay chimney constructed of sticks and mud rose above a roaring fire, the flames licking at a cast-iron kettle suspended from a hook close by the throat of the fireplace. Three tables made of puncheon cleated together on posts and one fashioned of boards dominated the room, each one attracting a covey of three-legged stools, most of them occupied by earlier arrivals, a quiet, mannerly-appearing, self-disciplined group sitting in patient expectancy at their plates and utensils. As one they turned to gape and appraise the newcomers. Tawny noted that they were mostly rough-looking, unshaven raftsmen, better and more expensively dressed travelers, professional men, and a couple of peddlers passing through, their tinware, calicoes, laces, ribbons, and linens laid out on the table in front of them for inspection by Mrs. Matthews. There was in addition a parson, his collar encasing his skinny neck, his spectacles balancing on the bridge of his nose precariously, his elbows on the table flanking his plate, his slender hands folded in front of his face as if he were preparing to call the company to prayer.

A veil of smoke hung from the rafters, all but obscuring them and the pewter mugs and bunches of drying corn festooning them, so thick was it. Better than half of the men were puffing on pipes, raising bluish-white screens partially concealing their curious stares. There was no dampness here but a cheery warmth, a recognizable effort at hospitality for this gathering of strangers grateful for refuge, eager to appease hunger and thirst.

In spite of her concern as to where she stepped walking from the coach to the door, Tawny's slippers with their thin flat soles were soaked through to her stockings, and her dress of yellow linen with narrow stripes of black edged with amber hung upon her like a flag at rest.

A serving girl was bringing food in from the kitchen, lifting the door curtain with her shoulder, her tray weighed down with steaming bowls of beets and cooked cabbage, beef and pork, fish and cheese. The tray set down on the far corner table and the bowls set out, the men, picking up their whiskey and rum mugs to make room, then seized their steel knives and two-tined forks and dug in. The chorus of approval that had greeted the tray's arrival mellowed into hushed conversation accompanied by the clinking of utensils. In seconds the food had vanished from the bowls, faces were lowered to plates, and everything appropriated was hastily scooped into them. To Tawny, looking on along with the envious occupants of the other tables yet to be served, it was like a pack of starving wildcats tearing apart the carcass of a sheep, every man for himself and the devil take his slower neighbor.

The scene repeated itself with the reappearance of the loaded tray. In the meantime the Matthewses had seated the four of them, and when their table was served the men sharing it bridled their voracious appetites long enough to make sure that the ladies' plates were filled before they themselves attacked the bowls. In addition to the food brought in from the kitchen, a second serving girl, bowl in hand, stooped by the fire and with a pointed stick fished baked potatoes out of the ash bed on either side of the blaze.

The meal was delicious, as well as giving Tawny a chance to practice her table manners for St. Louis. Cold milk was brought for the three girls, in preference to the customarily atrocious coffee, while Lydia and Mrs. Matthews shared a pot of tea and conversation. Sitting opposite Emily, Tawny ate slowly, taking small portions onto her fork, her eyes lowered to her plate. Gradually, though, she began to feel other eyes upon her, an uncomfortable sensation that worsened progressively as she continued eating. She dare not look up, she thought, until she reached a point where she could no longer resist doing so.

Bearded, ruggedly handsome, and patently brimming with self-assurance, the raftsman leered at her as their eyes met. Then he winked. Looking back down at her plate, she could feel her cheeks redden and his eyes continue to burn into her, peeling her dress and chemise from her body, baring her breasts, drawing, she fancied, every male eye in the room to her nakedness. She couldn't have been more grateful when Mr. Matthews broke the spell, clearing his throat and to the parson beside him announcing his concern over recent deliveries of his barrel whiskey.

'Jim Higam brings a thirty-gallon barrel once a week, he does, delivered right to the door. Sealed as tight as a trivet, top, bottom, and sides. But this is the mystery. When I roll her to the pantry and open her up, more often than not she's down a good two gallons.' He measured with his fingers in the air, his broad brow knit in perplexity. 'How can that be?'

'The fairies steal it in the night,' said one of the peddlers. Everyone laughed except the host.

'It's no joke to me,' he said, 'it's money down the drain. I've complained to Badger and Son, my suppliers up in Abington, but they insist that when the barrel leaves the distillery it's full to the top.'

'Maybe it evaporates,' suggested another.

'How?' asked Matthews. 'It's not boiled.'

'There's a very simple explanation,' said a tall sallow-faced man with a square of court plaster fastened to one cheek. 'It's drained on you.'

'I tell you, sir, the barrel's airtight. It's got to be, I roll it from the front door clear to the pantry out back without so much as a single drop spilling.'

'It's drained, I tell you.'

'Nonsense, from where? Where's the hole?'

'It's drained. You have the barrel out back?' Matthews nodded. 'Fetch it in, I'll show you.'

Matthews rose, tossing down his crumpled napkin and eyeing the man with a glint of suspicion. But he complied. Vanishing behind the door curtain, he soon reappeared, placing the barrel in the center of the table and challenging the man to prove his opinion. Reaching into his vest pocket, the stranger brought out a pocketknife and proceeded to loosen and remove the brads holding the lower hoop in place.

Matthews and the others at the table, at all four tables,

looked on in silence. The hoop dropped to the table with a soft rattle. Bending, the man closely examined the area exposed.

'There we are . . .'

'There we are what?' asked Matthews, mystified.

'See for yourself. See those two plugs? No bigger round than Osage arrow shafts, but there they are, plain as day. Your delivery man is the culprit. He loosens the hoop, drills one hole for air pressure, another right alongside it . . . there, drains off a gallon or two, plugs both holes, replaces the hoop, and puts back the brads.'

'Well, damn me for an Injun,' growled Matthews.

'Elias!' snapped his wife.

'Excuse me, ladies. Of all the thieving blackguards. Oh, just you wait till Higam shows his face and his barrel at my door Tuesday next. I'll punch him 'cross the road, I will!'

Once more everybody laughed. And Tawny's admirer resumed staring at her.

3

Lydia and Priscilla were to share a room, with Emily and Tawny two doors down, the two rooms separated by the parson's and peddlers'. The beds were typical of those found in the wayside inns scattered about the Territory. Climbing the ladder to the upper floor, venturing down the hallway directly above the public room all the way to the far end, the girls were stopped by Lydia and issued their instructions.

'Keep your candle burning if you wish, my chicks. Make certain your bed stick is straight before you climb in, and the instant you enter, latch and bolt your door.'

Emily and Tawny nodded and kissed Lydia and Priscilla good night. Opening their door, they discovered a discouragingly tiny room, barely large enough to accommodate one bed. It stood with its head touching the window wall, its foot scarcely two feet from the door. Against the

14

wall to the right stood a washstand with a bowl with a large chunk missing, a pitcher of water, a chair, and a small Franklin stove.

The ends of the rails supporting the tick stuffed with marsh hay were inserted in the logs of the wall, thereby making a single stout stick adequate to hold up the foot of the bed. Cords were tied from side to side on the frame rails, the cords running backward and forward around short upright pins inserted in the rails. This created a webbing of nine-inch squares. Upon this was laid the tick. The solitary stick supporting the foot of the bed looked as if the slightest jounce would send it clattering to the floor, the bed with it, but the two head corners connected to the wall prevented this. The only problem with corded beds was the inevitable sagging toward the middle, which would bring Emily and Tawny together regardless of how many times they rolled over to avoid contact.

'Like two piglets at a sow,' complained Emily, setting the candle on the stove. Tawny latched and bolted the door, setting her carpetbag at the foot of the bed and taking out her flannel nightgown. They undressed, Emily commenting on the good-looking peddler, a tall blond-haired Scandinavian, who had smiled at her during dinner. Tawny made no mention of the raftsman. Now that she thought about it, she was grateful that she had had the presence of mind to show no reaction whatsoever to his smile and wink. Thank God he hadn't approached her when they got up from the table.

They were preparing to lie down when Emily wandered to the window and, pressing her nose to the glass, cupped her eyes with her hands, squinting out into blackness.

'It's stopped raining.'

Before Tawny, standing at the foot of the bed, could move to stop her, she pulled open the window. In rushed the breeze, playfully tousling Emily's curls, filling the room with a damp chill, and blowing out the candle, plunging them into darkness.

'Oh drat!' cried Emily.

'Close it, dear, please.'

'I can't sleep in this, Tawny, I never can sleep in the dark. Besides, Mummy did say to keep the candle burning...'

'Don't be upset,' said Tawny. 'I'll go and get a light.'

'Downstairs in the fireplace.'

'Bolt the door after me.'

'I will ...'

Groping for the candle, Tawny knocked it to the floor, retrieved it, and went out into the hall. At the far end the faint glow of the downstairs fire ascended the ladder and flung itself against the face of the wall, forming slender black wraiths that seemed to dance. She could hear the crackle of the fire interspersed with the snoring coming from behind locked doors. Making her way down the hall, she was within a few steps of the top of the ladder when a door opened behind her. At the sound she turned instinctively. A raftsman fully dressed, his open shirt collar revealing the V of his tanned and hairy chest, smiled at her amiably and held up his candle.

'Looking for a light, miss?'

She hesitated. 'I ... yes.'

'Here we are.'

Turning back, she walked toward him, her candle held out in front of her, preparing to touch the wick to his flame. To her surprise and horror, the instant she reached him he tossed his lighted candle into the room and grabbed both her wrists with one hand, fastening the other over her mouth and dragging her bodily inside. Easing the door closed behind him with the sole of his boot, he pulled her, kicking and wriggling, over to his shakedown. So firmly was his hand pressed against her mouth, she feared he would dislodge her teeth. Her heart beat wildly at the look of lust in his enormous eyes. There were others in the room, four, possibly five men, but she was only dimly aware of them, her mounting terror fixing her gaze upon her tormentor. He freed her mouth, but before she could utter a sound a knotted handkerchief was jammed between her lips and tightly tied at the nape of her neck.

Pushed down onto her back, she watched, horror-struck, as the others gathered silently about her. Then her wrists and ankles were slammed to the bare floor and held in place.

'Me first, Jason,' whispered a voice.

'To hell with you, man, she's my catch.'

'Rip off her nightdress,' said another. A candle was

brought into the circle and held aloft as hands clutched her clothing and tore it from her. She began writhing, struggling to cry out, prompting a burst of laughter at the sight of her abject helplessness.

'Here we go!' snapped the one who had pulled her into the room. 'My God, will you look at those breasts. Ever see such beauties in your life?'

Like a hammer striking, a head lowered, a hot mouth working over one exposed breast. Striving to get it all in his mouth, unable to, he began cursing softly, then sucking. Too hastily, too hard: the pain raced down from the nipple into her heaving chest. A fist shot out of the circle of candleglow, striking her attacker full in the temple, knocking him away. He and the one who had pulled her into the room began to argue, but were speedily silenced by the others. Now the first one had lowered his breeches, exposing his rapidly hardening member. Grinning sadistically at her, he spread her thighs with his bare knees, then barked at the two gripping her ankles.

'Let her go, damn you, she's got to move to make it good . . .'

Gritting her teeth, she braced herself, continuing to writhe and struggle to avoid his thrust, to pull her wrists free and push him away. She was unable to. His member, now fully erect and throbbing, drove between her trembling thighs, a knife stabbing hilt-deep sending a shriek up her throat, stopped by the gag knot and spreading upward into her brain. And ringing silently in her ears as he began probing and thrusting . . .

The relentless horror of it, the excruciating pain driving and driving again, ripping her mercilessly, the weird shadows spread across the rafters and down the walls by the candle, the lust glazing the eyes in the faces circled above her wrenched her pounding heart within. She shuddered and closed her eyes to his bestial face, a mask of mingled fury and overmastering hunger to possess her, as if nothing would serve his gluttony but to break her body and soul.

In the interlude of stark unreasoning terror that followed, with each new attacker entering and violating her, she died and died again. The painful stabbing repeatedly lanced up into her belly and spread throughout it like a torch thrust into her. Becoming sharper, more acute, more agonizing, it touched her heart, a tongue of raw flame flicking, searing . . .

At length, wearied with their efforts, they turned one by one to other abuses, too bizarre, too cruel and humiliating to be described. Her body became a vessel besieged by members and mouths, its most intimate areas assaulted and degraded. She prayed to heaven for release. It came at last, a thick curtain enveloping her consciousness, suffocating the fire of her agony, draining awareness from her mind.

4

'Easy, little chick, precious darling. Don't move, there's no need.' It was Lydia's voice, the tone heavy with sympathy, the words so softly uttered as to be all but inaudible. As if she were whispering from the other side of the room. But when Tawny's flickering eyelids parted and she focused upon her aunt, she saw that she was directly above her.

'Poor darling . . .'

Recollection of the nightmare exploded in Tawny's mind, overrunning it with visions of leering faces, the rapists down on their knees one after another, the pain of entry, the act, the terror that had seized and held her in its thrall. She shuddered and almost without being conscious of it moved her thighs, activating a dull ache. For an instant she fancied she had been lying abed for a week, giving her battered body sufficient time to recover. The aching was tolerable, but would she ever recover from the wound in her heart? Reflecting upon this settled her into an all-enveloping numbness, a shroud of despair.

Mrs. Matthews stood on the opposite side of the bed, her lower lip trembling slightly. She too wore a look of well-intentioned sympathy.

'How do you feel, my dear?'

'I'm all right, I think. If I can walk.' She imagined she was still wearing the gag, feeling the knot at the nape of her neck.

'There's no rush,' said Mrs. Matthews. 'Dr. Herrick's

been sent for. He should be here shortly.'

'What time is it?'

'A little after eight,' said Lydia.

Tawny pulled herself upward, bringing her shoulder blades onto the pillow and prompting both women to hold her down. 'I should be up and dressed. The coach...'

'The driver will wait as long as necessary,' Lydia said.

Tawny's hand slid over the coverlet, over her face to her forehead. 'The last thing I remember, they were coming at me again... I fainted. What happened then?'

'You may thank your cousin Emily for what happened then.' Lydia struggled to smile. 'When you didn't come back to the room, she tried to wake me, poor chick.' Lydia turned to Mrs. Matthews. 'To wake me or Priscilla would take a cannon barrage.' She smoothed the hair back from Tawny's forehead and went on. 'She went straight to the Matthewses' room and roused Mr. Matthews. He listened at the door, broke it down, and clubbed two of them senseless. The other two got away out the window.'

'I must tell you, miss,' said Mrs. Matthews, 'nothing like this has ever happened before. Our door has been open six years now and we've never had any trouble, not a smidgen, not of... this sort, that is.'

'It was my fault,' said Tawny with a sigh. The two women started and glanced at each other. 'I was on my way downstairs to get a candle light. One of them came to his door with a candle. He offered me a light. I... couldn't see bothering to climbing down and back up the ladder if...' Again she sighed. 'You don't understand.'

'It's not your fault, little chick,' said Lydia reprovingly, 'not a bit of it. Accepting the offer of a light out in the hallway – how can you possibly blame yourself for that? If anyone's to blame it's your Aunt Lydia. I never should have agreed to split the four of us up into two rooms.'

'Then it's my fault,' interposed Mrs. Matthews.

Lydia snorted. 'Stuff and nonsense. Besides, what matter now where the blame lies? We can't undo what's been done. Tawny, I'm so dreadfully sorry, you can't imagine how awful I feel. What on earth will I tell Jack? I wouldn't blame him if he never speaks to George and me again!'

Tawny succeeded in allaying Lydia's concern in that

regard. The doctor arrived, a ponderously massive individual with hair in need of brushing and combing. He wore a linen suit wrinkled from his shoulders to the knees of his breeches. Shooing Lydia, Mrs. Matthews, Emily, and Priscilla, who had entered the room shortly before he'd arrived, out the door like bothersome cats off a carpet, he examined his patient, pronounced her 'passably fit,' but for bruises on her breasts and thighs along with a few scratches, gave her a headache powder and two additional ones to see her to St. Louis, and departed. No sooner was he out the door than in came Mr. Matthews with word that the two men he had succeeded in capturing had been turned over to the constable in nearby Sawyerville.

Able to walk and dress herself, Tawny joined the others for late breakfast, bacon and eggs, bread and coffee. They boarded the coach and resumed their journey to the river and beyond it more than a hundred miles, St. Louis.

She felt some physical discomfort. But the primary pain afflicting her was anchored in her pride. Sitting in the coach, her eyes fixed on the dense congregations of hickories, sweet gums, chestnuts, hard maple, and short-leaf pine drenched by the bright morning sunlight, she could feel her aunt and her cousins sneak occasional glances at her. She imagined their minds at work generating pity, curiosity, and something akin to fascination, at least on the part of Emily and Priscilla.

Tawny hated this. It made her feel dirty inside, indelibly stained, her virginity so brutally stolen by the animals in the room, her innocence utterly destroyed, her body abused and now healing, but never to heal completely, not really. The scars would always be there, and embedded forever in memory would be recollection of the sheer terror of her time in hell.

Like the loss of a limb or the use of an eye, it was something she would have to learn to live with. Lydia's stern injunction to both Priscilla and Emily never to breathe a word of what had happened was well intentioned, to be sure; the trouble was it *had* happened – she knew, and so did they. Her father would know as well. Getting dressed, Lydia helping her, she had begged her aunt to keep it from him. But Lydia would have no part in deceiving him. However reluctantly, Tawny could understand this: telling Jack Kinross would in some measure unburden Lydia's own guilt in the matter. She might even be hoping he would upbraid her, accuse her of being responsible, and vent his anger on her.

On the bright side, no one in St. Louis would have to know, least of all Aldous and Marcy. If it got out she'd be mortified to tears; she would hide her face in her muskmelon bonnet and never show it to either of them again. Such a tawdry business had no place in the purity and gaiety and celebration of Marcy's nuptials, surely the happiest week in her life.

The coach bounced, wrenching them about in their seats, all four gradually settling back, Lydia tilting her head and smiling affectionately at Tawny. Dear God but she hated this, this uncleanness pervading every inch of her body and mind. Would she become pregnant? she wondered. Heaven knows she could. That would be marvelous; she'd never be able to hold her head up in Titus Forks again. Poor Daddy, how would he think of his darling daughter? The whispering, the gossip if it should ever leak out. It was so cruel, so monstrously unfair. What a life this was, everything singing along just beautifully and suddenly the whole world dashed to pieces!

'We should be reaching the river shortly, chicks,' said Lydia with affected brightness. 'And in St. Louis by dark. Isn't the scenery beautiful, though, just lovely!'

Lovely, lovely, reflected Tawny, turning her glance from the open window and letting it fall to her fingers twisting her hanky in her lap.

5

It was the largest building Tawny had ever seen, a three-story stone mansion trimmed with oak painted white, a Grecian temple – at least at the front it resembled one, displaying massive fluted columns of marble with intricately carved Corinthian capitals. The two inner columns framed a double door fashioned of inlaid oak, with shiny brass knobs, knockers, and hinges, each door so heavy it must have taken six men to raise and hang it, she thought. The doors opened on a wide hall, its pegged floor overlaid with a carpet, depicting scenes from Greek mythology. In the center of the floor was a large round mahogany table, upon it a lamp with a yellow silk shade. The hall led to two enormous rooms left and right, drawing room and dining room, each lavishly furnished and with its own exquisite period Italian brass-and-crystal chandelier. And opposite the front doors a winding staircase carpeted full length rose to the second and third landings.

Bandboxes, bundles, and bags in hand, they were greeted at the door by Aldous, as warm and gracious as Tawny remembered him, and even more distinguished-looking. By his side was Helene Rampling, a plain but gracious and generous-hearted woman, who began fussing over them even before they had set foot through the door. Marcy was overjoyed at sight of the girls, and at her insistence they followed her up the stairs at a half run. All three were to share a large corner bedroom at the end of the hallway overlooking the garden, overlorded by two tall walnut trees, their branches reaching for the house and sky and the imposing wrought-iron fence beyond.

A rectangular version of the hallway carpet, its colors reversed, covered the floor in support of a double feather bed with posts that threatened to push its glazed chintz canopy through the ceiling. There was also a single bed, lower and less imposing in appearance, which had been brought in and set under the windows. An armoire sufficiently capacious to hide a coachful of people, a full-length gilded mirror (which Emily insisted was solid gold), an easy chair that practically swallowed Priscilla in a billowing cloud of maroon velvet when she plopped down into it, a marble washstand, and a vanity with a mirror of its own completed the furnishings. And the room was filled with the scent of lavender. As sights and scent assaulted her senses, Tawny could only gasp in admiration, eliciting a laugh from Marcy.

She had begun chattering like a magpie at the door,

continuing all the way up the stairs and into the room. Throwing herself down upon the bed, she stretched and went rattling on as the girls filled their eyes with their surroundings.

'You're the first, but positive scads of guests are coming, and not all relatives. The Wintons, all the way from New Orleans. And Grandmama and Grandpapa Bascomb from Kentucky, and Mr. and Mrs Carpenter with Lawton... ugh, I can't abide Lawton Carpenter. He's skinny as a rake and his hands are always damp and cold and he hangs over you when he talks. Last time they were here he asked me to marry him, begged me! La-de-da, it was all I could do to keep from laughing in his face, the poor simp. Of course, I daren't do that, his daddy and Daddy do business together. Most boys are simps, but not men... my dear darling Boyd is beautiful. You'll all three positively faint dead away with envy when you see him. Every girl does. I call him my warrior prince. He has tight little black curls all over his head like Alexander the Great. I think it was Alexander the Great. Boyd was a lieutenant in the army, you know, but he resigned his commission. La-de-da, was I ever furious when he told me! He looked so dashing, so sinfully handsome in his blues, his brass buttons shining so, just absolutely scrumptious. Still, being an army wife is no fun, the way they push you from pillar to post. Unless, of course, he could have made general. My, I do prattle on so, don't I? But it's been years and years since we've seen each other and there's so much to talk about. And Daddy's gotten rich, we're rich, rich, rich!' She flung out her arms, taking in the world as if it were hers. 'Boyd works for the Excelsior Fur Trading Company now. Daddy wanted to put him in charge of the warehouse, but he doesn't want to leave Excelsior because he's a partner or something. He likes fur trading. I don't care what he does, the dear darling, as long as he loves me forever. And he does. I've never been so happy in my life. Every morning I wake up and pinch myself to make sure it isn't all a dream. I mean my Boyd is so beautiful and so adorable. And he worships me; la-de-da, he's simply mad about me! And insanely jealous if another man so much as looks at me. I wouldn't be surprised if one of these days he fights a duel over me. We're going to have two children, a boy and a girl, Boyd Junior and Helene, after my mother. I shan't want more than two because I don't want to ruin my figure. And if having the first one hurts terribly I'll stop right there. Just wait till you meet my dear darling ... all my friends are shriveled up like peppers, green, they're so jealous.' She thrust her hand in Tawny's face, rising to sit on the edge of the bed. 'See my ring? It's half a full carat. Isn't it beautiful? I picked it out.'

'It's lovely,' said Tawny quietly.

'Try it on, do,' insisted Marcy. Jerking it free of her finger, she pressed it upon Tawny, who slipped it onto her own ring finger. Priscilla and Emily oohed and aahed. It was pear-shaped in a setting of white gold and was indeed beautiful.

'Marcy...' Her mother and Aunt Lydia stood in the doorway, beaming. 'My dear,' said her mother, 'you must give the girls a chance to get out of their things and relax from their journey. There'll be plenty of time for chitchat at dinner. Besides, the Carpenters have just arrived and Lawton is asking to see you...'

'Ugh!' Marcy made a face, kissed Tawny, Priscilla, and Emily, in turn, and clapped her hands. 'I'm so glad you've come. La-de-da!'

Tawny returned her ring. Instead of putting it back on, Marcy held it high with both hands, whirling about under it.

'Beautiful, beautiful, beautiful,' she sang, and ran out the door.

'La-de-da, what a silly stick she is!' exclaimed Priscilla, unable to conceal the envy in her tone.

Tawny laughed and, dropping into the velvet chair, began removing her shoes. 'She's all right, she's just walking on air and bubbling over. You'd be too if you were about to take the big step.'

'I'll bet he isn't sinfully handsome, I'll bet he's not at all,' persisted Priscilla. 'He's probably no better-looking than Lawton Carpenter!'

'Why should you care?' asked Emily. 'She didn't steal him from you.'

'The lucky stick!' Priscilla pouted. Jumping onto the bed, she began kicking violently.

The week-long celebration began that evening. By the

24

dinner hour most of the houseguests had arrived and, joined by those from town, brought the mansion to life with noise and laughter. Every room was lit up, every bottle pouring while the insistent scraping of a fiddle band filled the drawing room and filtered through the halls. Never had Tawny seen so many illustrious and prestigious-looking older and middle-aged men, handsome, charming, and beguiling, even fascinating-looking young men, cultured-looking, richly attired ladies – the dignified, the pompous, the gallant, the speedy and slow of wit – people with obvious wealth, people with obvious pretensions to wealth, and those without pretense to anything but hunger and thirst, all come to pay homage to the king and queen and princess. And the wedding gifts giving promise of growing into a steady stream came purling through the door.

The warrior prince arrived. Tawny watched Marcy run to greet her Boyd Chevrier. Handsome he was, though not sinfully, whatever Marcy meant by that. His jet-black curls were strikingly attractive. At a distance Tawny could not make out the color of his eyes, but what she could see of the rest of him impressed her. He was well over six foot, strong-shouldered, a bit stiff in posture – too many formal inspections, she surmised – well built and muscular-looking under his dark suit. She liked his face, though his nose was a trifle small, and perhaps his mouth might have been wider and the lips firmer-looking. Still, it was an honest, open face, a face that declared that Boyd Chevrier's mind was his own, with no part of it subservient to Marcy Rampling's or anyone else's domination. The rigid set of his jaw confirmed it. Where, thought Tawny, were the Boyd Chevriers in Titus Forks? Why did the St. Louises and New Orleanses have to claim and covet them all?

She watched as Marcy appropriated his arm and began pulling him about, introducing him to the guests. Emily and Priscilla came sidling up to Tawny.

'He *is* handsome,' said Emily, a trace of regret in her tone.

'Not awfully,' Priscilla said, sniffing. 'Not in a plain old suit like that. It's so . . . so venerable-looking!'

Marcy spied them and came barging through the crowd, towing him after her.

'Tawny, Priscilla, Emily, this is Boyd. Boyd, darling,

these are my cousins come all the way from Titus Forks.'

Tawny smiled inwardly. From his reaction he had never heard of Titus Forks. He shook hands with each in turn, mumbling something about what a pleasure it was to meet them, but obviously not as interested in the event as either Priscilla or Emily.

That, for what it was worth, was Tawny's introduction to Boyd Chevrier.

The next day was spent at horse races and on Aldous's boat on an excursion upriver to Mosenthein Island, where the warehouse was located, not one warehouse but actually a half dozen or more grouped in a complex, with fifty or sixty workers bustling about loading and unloading large keelboats.

Tawny was standing at the rail with Lydia as their vessel turned toward the dock. Aldous approached them.

'How is George's hip getting on, Lydia?' he asked.

'I keep telling you, dear, it's mending. But slow as cold molasses in January. To tell the truth, it's a pleasure getting away from the grouchy old thing. I'll be so delighted when he's up and out of the house again.'

'A pity he couldn't make it, though. And, Crystal, my dear, how is your father?'

'Fine, thank you, Uncle Aldous.'

'How is the business?'

'All right, I guess. He doesn't tell me much about it.'

'No need to clutter your pretty little head with talk of horses and harnesses, eh?'

'I guess.' He made her feel as if she were seven. And the way he stared made her uncomfortable. When moments later he excused himself in response to his wife's summons, Tawny mentioned how she felt, her uncle's effect upon her.

'Nonsense,' said Lydia with attempted conviction, despite a look of concern. 'How are you feeling?'

'I'm all right. Please don't change the subject. It's true, you know, and it's only when he mentions Daddy. He hates him so it's enough to make me sick to my stomach!'

'"Hate" is a very strong word, Tawny.'

'It's what it is.'

Lydia sighed and, taking Tawny's hands, searched her eyes. 'My little chick, I've never said two words to you about your mother and father and Aldous, have I?' Tawny shook her head. 'I imagined you'd think it wasn't any of my business. But we are all family and you're older now, and there's something you should get clear in your thinking. You believe your father loved your mother, don't you?'

'Of course...'

'I couldn't agree more. But, and you must take my solemn word for it, Aldous loved her just as much. In a different way, of course, but just as deeply. I never told you, but it was I who broke the news to him. My dear, he took it mortally hard... I could see how crushed he was, how frustrated and helpless he felt, and how quickly he filled up with regret at having failed in his duty.'

'What duty?'

'Failed to prevent such a needless calamity. As if he could have. Unfortunately, at the same time he began reaching out for someone to blame.'

'Daddy, naturally.'

'Exactly. His whole life poor dear Aldous has been hagridden by the self-assumed responsibility to protect his little sister from those outside the family circle, including your father, however honorable his intentions.' Turning to the railing, she grasped it and stared off downriver at the sunlight gilding the placid water. 'When the three of us were young Aldous was always protecting and shielding your mother and me. Miriam used to call him Sir Aldous, the fearless knight in armor sworn to watch over his ladies fair. Our daddy used to tease him about it, but it didn't embarrass Aldous. He was proud of it. What I'm trying to say is it's not that he hates your father so much as that he hates what happened and his own failure to see it coming. As if he'd been derelict in duty. His conscience has treated him unmercifully...'

She was rationalizing, thought Tawny, groping for excuses for him, spurred by the loyalty of blood.

'Aunt Lydia, he's a fool,' she said quietly. 'Anyone who hangs on to a "need to blame"... It's been nearly six years, why can't he let go of it? If time can heal wounds, why doesn't he let it?'

'I don't know the answer to that, child. Perhaps it's simply not within his power to. Wounds to the heart can be perilously deep and lasting. All the years of one's life aren't enough to banish the pain.'

'Well, it may be a good thing Daddy didn't come, but it's no credit to Aldous. He could at least have given him the chance to refuse an invitation.'

'And what if your father refused to refuse? What if he came?'

'They'd be at each other's throats in ten minutes.'

Lydia nodded and smiled. 'Perhaps Sir Knight prefers to stand his armor in the living room instead of girding it on for the fray.'

That night there was a dance at the Washington Meetinghouse. A dance with a cotillion led by Marcy and Boyd, and halfway through the first hour the new waltz, just arrived from Germany, a three-step dance based on the *valse à deux pas* of France purportedly spreading throughout Europe, was requested of the orchestra leader. Tawny, Emily, and Priscilla had been practicing it at home ever since the arrival of their invitations, but none of the three had ever danced it with a man.

They were standing in nervous anticipation under an archway watching the more adventuresome couples, among them Boyd and Marcy, swing smoothly around the floor when they overheard a conversation, a man and two women seated behind a jungle of ferns and other large green plants. From where they were standing it was impossible to see the speakers, but their comments were all too audible.

'My dears, have you seen the three bumpkins from out in the Indian Country? Aldous's sisters' daughters ...'

'I've seen them, with hay in their hair, eyes like saucers, and homemade dresses you wouldn't catch a nigger child in!'

'The poor creatures must feel outrageously self-conscious.'

'Like they say, you can pick your friends but you can't pick your relations. Poor Helene, she must be mortified to tears.'

'Good enough for her. The way she and Aldous flaunt their money is positively indecent. I'll wager this wedding is costing them a pretty penny.'

At which point the music stopped and Marcy came running up to them, towing her Boyd as usual.

'You must all three dance the waltz with Boyd. You first, Tawny!'

Tawny looked at him and looked away. 'Marcy...'

'Miss Kinross, may I have the pleasure of this waltz?'

Tawny was dying to dance with him, but embarrassed to tears at the thought of putting the country bumpkin on display. Sensing her hesitancy, he smiled warmly, took her hand and waist, and swept her away. Behind her Tawny could hear Marcy.

'You're next, Em, and then you, Silly.'

'Don't you call me Silly, Marcy Rampling!' burst Priscilla.

Boyd heard and laughed. Tawny's eyes darted left and right. Why was she suddenly so nervous? And so self-conscious over her new sapphire-blue ball dress, her kerchief with the starched, standing ruffle, and the new drooping puff sleeves of taffeta, which she detached and was wearing for gloves. It was the latest style, and the prettiest dress this country bumpkin had ever owned. She did wish she had a cameo of some sort around her neck instead of a plain old black ribbon. Better than a cameo, a necklace of golden harps like those Marcy and so many of her friends were wearing, all the rage according to Marcy. Thank goodness the floor was now filled with dancers. Once into the thick of them she would escape the critical stares of Aunt Helene's friends, and if she did trip at least nobody sitting on the sidelines would see her and burst into laughter.

He was a surprisingly good dancer, completely relaxed, swinging her easily about, her ribbon sash flying, her skirt rustling loudly. How heavenly, she thought, so much fun, so easy and fluid; it was all she could do to keep from bobbing her head in time with the music.

'So you're Tawny. That's a new name on me.'

'Short for Taunton. It's a family name.'

'Is it? I would have thought it was because of the color of your hair.' Her hand fled his shoulder to touch her hair self-consciously at the chilling thought that it might be in disarray. His whispered comment assured her it was not. 'It's beautiful.'

'It's . . . thank you.'

'I mean it.'

Round and round they whirled. She speedily found herself hoping that the music would never end, that he would guide her round and round and round and round until they both collapsed in exhaustion. And not the least of her delight came from being able to dance with a man she could look up to instead of down upon. Talking to one's partner's hair or his upturned face was so depressing, no fun at all. Particularly in knowing that onlookers were snickering, whispering 'beanpole' and similar snide allusions to her height, which stooping only drew attention to. But this, his left hand holding hers, his right encircling her waist holding her close to him. A tremor raced through her body and her cheeks tingled. He was enjoying himself as much as she, she could see it in his face.

'So you've come all the way from the other side of Missouri. You must have a very close family.'

'Not terribly, but I wouldn't have turned down this invitation for the world. If you were I and living in Titus Forks, would you?'

'Is it that small?'

'It's tiny, only a few families clustered together – mutual protection against the Osage.'

'Do they give you much trouble?'

'No, but the flintlock over the fireplace is always loaded.'

'What do you think of St. Louis?'

'It's fabulous, it's another world.'

'Is this your first visit?'

She nodded and lowered her lashes. 'First anywhere . . .'

They talked about the river and the levee, which she'd only managed a glimpse of when boarding Aldous's boat.

'You must see it at night. It's all lit up like a Christmas tree. A mile of boats, up from New Orleans and down from points a thousand miles north. But you have to mind the mud, it's a foot deep this time of year.'

'I'd love to see it, and the town.'

'You'd better see St. Louis first, it may not be here next time you come.'

She tittered. 'Where is it going?'

'I'm serious. The river keeps changing direction. It

shortens itself and lengthens itself and creates big chunks of land and washes others away. There's a settlement that used to be located three miles below Fort McHenry. Now, would you believe it, the same spot is two miles above it.'

'No, I don't believe it!'

'It's the gospel truth.'

The music stopped with the suddenness of a door slamming. Everyone applauded enthusiastically. Cries of 'more' were heard, and the orchestra struck up 'The Penny Waltz'. Boyd escorted her to the sideline, thanked her with a bow and a grin, and exchanged her for Emily.

She watched them glide away, Boyd in his blue coat and buff breeches, his sleek-fitting boots polished to a glassy shine. Marcy edged up to her.

'Now what do you think of my Boyd?'

'He's very, very nice,' said Tawny quietly. 'You're very lucky, Marcy.'

'Aren't we, though? La-de-da...'

She began about Boyd and herself and her father and her wedding and money. Seemingly everything in her world could be seen only through the glass of money, assume value or importance only within the context of its cost. It rapidly became boring to Tawny, apparent as it was that her cousin's only real interest in life lay in flaunting her wealth and the advantages it ensured. Again the music stopped, and Boyd came over to dance with Priscilla. Marcy turned her attention to Emily, and began repeating the same opinions and observations to her all but word for word. Tawny excused herself and went outside for a breath of air, pulling her shawl tightly about her shoulders to ward off the chill. The scent of dogwood was in the air, and when the breeze died the coolness vanished. Spring was gradually arriving in all its promised glory. Leaning against the porch railing, she watched a cardinal, a splash of scarlet, wing across the yard to the sweet gum tree standing at the corner of the building. Then a quiet laugh drew her attention to the opposite end of the porch. A couple was standing in the shadows, the boy kissing the girl on the neck, she appealing to him to stop, but making no effort to discourage him. Pulling her tightly to him, he began kissing her on the mouth with uncontrollable passion. Tawny turned her eyes away, suddenly deciding

31

that she had had enough of people and conversation and dancing for one night, that she was tired and the sensible thing to do would be to walk the three blocks down the street to the house and retire.

After all, one really had to be in the mood to enjoy oneself.

6

There was a dinner party the following night, held at the house and attended by no less than forty people. Tawny was already seated when Boyd took his place beside Marcy, diagonally opposite her. Tawny glanced at him and he smiled, but moments later when their eyes met he had a curious expression on his face, as if he'd just thought of something and wanted to discuss it with her. But even had this been so, under the circumstances it would have been impossible, for as usual Marcy was tying him up with words. He was a good listener, Tawny reflected; any man who married Marcy Rampling would have to be. She studied her. Marcy was beautiful, her full lips lightly salved, her face gently dusted with pearl powder, the peony rouge on her cheeks dexterously applied with a rabbit's foot, her lovely blonde hair resting on her creamy shoulders. A handsome couple.

The dinner was superb, tom turkey with stuffing and vegetables and a delicious sherry 'from the Jerez de la Frontera region of Andalucía, Spain. Near Osuna', according to Aldous, who obligingly sampled it for everyone's taste. The crystal and china and mile-long *point de Venise à réseau* lace tablecloth were beautiful, and the candles glowed almost as brightly as Marcy. The Princess Rampling was the center of attention, the recipient of enough flattery to satisfy a dozen brides. But after the dinner, when the ladies retired to the upstairs salon for tea and cookies and the men drifted to the drawing room for brandy and cigars, Tawny watched the happy couple flee the house for the garden in what appeared to be a not-too-pleasant mood. Whatever the difference of opinion, it had developed just as the dinner concluded and the guests were rising from the table. The two of them had lowered their voices, so Tawny was unable to hear what they were saying, but that it was a disagreement of some kind was obvious from their faces. When they retreated out of doors, although they were visible through the French windows, the discussion could not be heard. But by now it had clearly become a serious, even somewhat heated argument.

'What do you suppose is the matter?' asked Emily.

'I haven't the faintest idea,' said Tawny, 'but Marcy seems to be doing most of the talking.'

'As usual.'

'We shouldn't be staring at them...'

'Can't we open the windows for some fresh air, it's so stuffy in here...'

'Emily, you're priceless. I'm sure it's nothing. You know very well when it gets this close to "I do" sometimes the bride and groom get a bit nervous.'

'She's a good deal more than nervous,' said Emily, 'she's reading him the riot act. You'll think me awful, Tawny, but in these three days I've decided I really don't like her, not at all. She's so mouthy and spoiled and vain and arrogant. And such a showoff. Just like she was when she was little, only worse. What on earth he sees in her I'll never know!'

'She's not that bad, she's just all wound up and walking on air.'

'You keep saying that, but it's no excuse for the way she behaves.' Emily paused, tilted her head to one side, and narrowed her eyes at the unhappy couple outside. 'She doesn't much look like a bride, does she? She looks more like an old married shrew.'

Whatever the subject of disagreement, it was settled a few moments later and the two returned, Marcy clinging tenaciously to his arm, all smiles, as if nothing untoward had passed between them. But one look at his face and Tawny concluded that she had never in her life seen anyone so angry and doing such a laudable job of controlling it.

Two nights later the wedding rehearsal was held in the new, actually not-yet-completed, Methodist Church on the other side of the town. To Emily's surprise and elation,

Marcy announced that she was to be her maid of honor, 'since Ellie Hampton and her mother have sent their regrets, the silly things. My best friend and she can't even come to my wedding!'

The rehearsal was dull and routine, the most enthusiastic participant being the minister, a hawk-faced older man with a stomach as round as a stove belly and a lisp that set Priscilla giggling and hiding it behind one hand while her mother glared daggers of disapproval at her from a box pew.

There appeared to be no residue of ill-feeling between bride and groom; he was properly attentive and she as loquacious and as demonstrably adoring and possessive as ever.

The night before the wedding was *the* night of the week, and in step with the ascending order of lavishness, the next-to-the-top event was to be a Grand Ball held in the most spacious hall available, nearly twice the size of the one in which practically every eligible female had danced the waltz with Boyd Chevrier. It was a memorably enjoyable evening: Tawny was introduced to and danced with old men and young men, middle-aged men and a boy barely sixteen, despite his insistence that he was twenty. He introduced himself as Henry Jefferson Mott Coldridge III. Henry stepped on her toe and tripped over his own; he was pale with nervousness, his breathing as rapid as a consumptive's and his hands clammy. Dancing on tiptoe he barely came up to her chin, but he accepted the challenge with an aggresive abandon and a devoted attention to footwork that would have won the plaudits of a dancing master. When the music ended and he bowed and thanked her for the turn, she watched in amusement as he rejoined his waiting friends and began collecting coins from one after the other.

Halfway through the evening, in the middle of a reel, Marcy suddenly broke away from Boyd, rushing to the door and out into the night, leaving cloak and fiancé behind. As her father helped her into her carriage she dramatically voiced the wish that her guests should not let her departure deprive them of a good time, that they should continue to enjoy themselves as long and as late as they pleased. Outside on the lawn Tawny joined Lydia in looking after the carriage jouncing away toward Rampling House carrying father and daughter.

'I wonder what that was all about?' asked Tawny, thinking aloud.

'Something about a queasy stomach. Night-before-the-nuptials butterflies, if you ask me. She'll be all right in the morning. She does have a flair for the theatrical, though, wouldn't you say?' Lydia laughed and, reaching into her bag, took a hasty swig from her bottle. 'This night air plays hob with my joints. Coming?'

'In a little bit.'

'Don't stay out too late without your cloak, Tawny.'

'I won't.'

Lydia rejoined Priscilla and Emily in the hallway, and Tawny walked to a tall cottonwood with a swing suspended from its largest bough. Marcy hadn't looked 'queasy' leaving: she'd looked upset, the same pink cheeks and stubborn set to her features Tawny had seen through the French windows at the house after the dinner party earlier in the week.

Holding the ropes of the swing by crooking her elbows, Tawny began pushing easily with her heels, the hem of her beige taffeta dress swishing softly, her fan folded and gripped in her left hand. A harpsichord was carrying the melody for the dancers inside, jangling spiritedly, as crisp and sharp as crickets. The smoke from the maple logs crackling in the fireplace came wafting down from the chimney top in a gossamer plume, adding its own perfume to the air. Tawny began humming with the music, wondering about Marcy, curious to know what had caused her sudden departure, certain it wasn't anything as commonplace as a stomachache.

'Isn't it a bit chilly?'

Tawny braked to a stop with her heels and turned. Boyd was standing behind her holding her cloak, draping it over her shoulders. He was smoking a cheroot, the light of its ash setting his dark eyes gleaming when he drew on it. He managed a smile, but it was not his usual friendly grin. There was something uncomfortable in it, strained, as if in his embarrassment he were forcing it for her benefit.

'What are you doing out here?' he asked.

'Hadn't you noticed, I have a habit of slipping away by myself.'

'Mind if I join you?'

'Marcy might...'

'Marcy need never know. Not to sound like a conspirator, but right about now I imagine she couldn't care in the least what I do or who I do it with.'

'That does sound conspiratorial.'

He cupped his hands to his ears. 'They're broiling. I believe she's saying some very unflattering things about me as she throws herself into bed.'

'I'm nosy – what did you do to her in there?'

'A terrible thing, outrageous.' He began pushing the swing gently, Tawny's cloak rippling softly behind her. 'I should be drawn and quartered – I had the gall to remind her of a promise she made me. She had given me her word and now she's gone back on it. Reversed herself completely.'

'Word on what?'

'It's a long story, I'm afraid, and fairly boring.' Taking hold of the ropes, he stopped her suddenly, so abruptly she nearly fell over. 'Say, I just thought, you haven't seen the levee by night, have you?'

'No...'

'Come.' Seizing her hand, he ran with her to his carriage, parked in among the others in a large open area at the side of the building. Moments later the whip was snapping over the sorrel mare, the carriage lurching forward down the narrow road heading eastward toward the river.

The levee was indeed lit up like a Christmas tree, lamps and lanterns and naked torches puncturing the blackness, revealing a line of keelboats, packets, and smaller craft spreading up and down the river as far as Tawny could see. In the aftermath of an unusually severe winter, the wooden sidewalks were in disreputable condition, and the recent heavy rains had created a layer of mud running more than a foot deep in some places, a long narrow slough paralleling the riverbank, through which those boarding and debarking the boats anchored at the edge were obliged to slog. Here and there loose planks had been laid across the morass to keep shoes and skirt hems above its grasp, but as often as not they had vanished beneath the foot of the first person stepping upon them.

The cheerful voice of a concertina floated melodiously down the night, coming from a dimly lit shack upriver, while a harmonica being played sadly out of tune tried valiantly to compete with it some fifty feet away. Gangs of men passed back and forth, singing loudly and yelling at one another, weighted down with rope and sacks, baskets of fruit, huge watermelons, baggage and crates. Mingling with them were trappers and transients, Indians, slaves, and Creoles. Other men sat in their boats dozing, drinking or smoking, laughing, arguing with their neighbors while they worked at tightening and repairing nets and sails and ropes. And witnessing the whole colorful panorama of raucous, unrestrained activity like a great prehistoric creature indulging the antics of insects by its side, the river eased silently by, heading for the Gulf, seven hundred miles distant, a dark, flat-backed monster undulating sluggishly toward its own mouth.

Driving up and down alongside the dilapidated walkway, Boyd pointed out everything there was to see, including a battered-looking packet, partially sunk, in the process of being raised between two other boats.

'It's fascinating,' said Tawny, 'but we really shouldn't have come away like this.'

Reining the sorrel to a stop, he stared at her. 'Why not? Who's to tell us when and where we can't go? Besides, I doubt if anybody saw us.'

'It just doesn't seem right.'

'Perhaps not, but I've got to talk to you. I've got to talk to somebody so I can know whether she's wrong or I am or what. This whole mess has gotten me so muddled...'

'What "mess"?'

He sighed. 'Lady, would you please be so charitable as to permit me to tell you the story of my recent life?'

'I'd be delighted.'

'I'm sure.' He smiled grimly, and sympathy like a pick flicking the string of a mandolin touched her heart. 'Seriously, you knew of course I was in the army.' She nodded. 'I got out because the Excelsior Fur Trading Company offered me a job and a full partnership. It looked

37

like a great opportunity in something I'm fond of. Now, after the first year, it's still a great opportunity. Still, what is any opportunity if you don't take advantage of it?'

'I'm afraid I don't follow you.'

'Remember last year when Governor Lewis and Billy Clark got back from their expedition?'

'Up the Missouri River, west to the Columbia.'

'A tributary of the Columbia. Tawny, what that handful of men accomplished was downright incredible. They traveled nearly four thousand miles round trip. They found Indian tribes no white men had ever seen before. They were the first explorers to reach the Pacific crossing the continent north of Mexico. They beat about the entire northwest corner of the Territory.' His voice sobered and his eyes caught fire as he went on. 'They found a valley out there, the Willamette. It lies between two mountain ranges, and Wells Whitfield, who was with the expedition and has seen it, says it's the most beautiful strip of land on God's green earth, lush fields and forests curling from north to south nearly two hundred miles into the foothills on either side.'

Slapping the horse's flank lightly with the reins, he started her up, pulling away from the levee, the lights and the noise, the smell of fish, the mire, and the great river surging past the file of boats nosing the wharves. 'My company, Excelsior, wants to establish a trading post there; up near where the Willamette River joins the Columbia is the likeliest spot. The board of directors wants to put up the money for a train, a big one, maybe fifty or sixty wagons to head out along the Missouri across the Rockies, up to the valley. Tawny, they've asked me to lead it, to be in full charge.'

'Oh, Boyd, that's marvelous!'

'Is it?'

'Of course, it's such a challenge. Just thinking about it I get gooseflesh all over.'

He eased the horse to a stop near a grove of walnut trees standing stark and leafless, their branches rising in tall tones. The full moon cleared a cloud, and the air was suddenly redolent of wildflowers, the vanguard of spring's colorful carpet soon to cover the forest floor and the fields surrounding the town.

'You're so right, it's more than marvelous, more even than a challenge. It's . . . the chance to conquer a whole new world.' He paused, his face darkening. 'Only . . .'

'Marcy disagrees.'

'I told her about it two weeks ago. Her father had offered me a job, pretty much what I'm doing for Excelsior, seeking out the independent trappers and working up agreements with them for what they bring in. I asked for time to think it over and I decided I'd be better off staying put. I'm a partner, Tawny. If Excelsior is a success, as big as we hope, I can do very well. With Aldous, well, he's already successful. I wouldn't be building anything there, not for myself, only enlarging what already exists. In this job I've got a feeling of independence I could never have with him. Not that he wouldn't be good to work for, or wouldn't be fair with me. That's the trouble – he'd probably bend over backwards to make me happy. I wouldn't want that. Who would?'

'You want to make it on your own.'

He nodded vigorously. 'Without his or anyone else's boost. Then too, if I worked for him I'd be Marcy's husband, the fair-haired boy, everybody else looking at me out of the corner of their eye. That I'd really hate.'

'She accepted that, didn't she, I mean your staying with Excelsior?'

'She did, begrudgingly. Every concession Marcy makes is begrudging. She's beautiful, she's good-hearted, she's loyal, and a dozen more things you can admire and respect, but God Almighty is she spoiled! She's like a lot of people – they go whole hog for an idea, but then the next morning when they've thought it over they're not so sure. Right before your eyes they change their minds completely. Do you know, I practically pleaded with her on bended knee to think the thing through completely before she gave me her answer . . .'

'On going to the valley?'

He nodded. 'I told her how hard it would be, the weather, the Indians, conditions in general just getting from point to point. Not only dangerous but uncomfortable and exhausting, as rough as rafting from start to finish. Marcy's not good at roughing anything, because she's never had to. I was honest about it, but to my surprise she went for it whole hog.

Fell in love with the idea – the challenge, the wide-open spaces, a new land, new people. You never saw such enthusiasm. I was so proud of her, and so relieved. The thing is, it's not the danger or any of that that makes it attractive, at least to me, it's the golden opportunity, the chance of a lifetime. How could I face the other chaps at Excelsior if I turned it down? How could I face Mr. Prescott, who singled me out and offered it to me? In ten or fifteen years settlers will be pouring into that whole area, all down the coast. To be among the first ones there, to be already settled, in business, trading with the Indians, even the ships landing on the coast, traders coming up the rivers, it's just so fabulous...' He held one hand out, cupping it. 'My chance, Tawny, right in my hand, the chance to do something with my life, to go out and slay the dragon. Either that or stick here in St. Louis and grow old and fat and rich watching the town grow up around me. It's already too big for my liking. Out there...'

'It's another world, as you say.'

'It is. So what does she do but change her mind. Now she absolutely refuses to even consider going. She sees my dream as her nightmare. You want to know her biggest reason for not wanting to go?'

'She doesn't want to leave her mother and father?'

'That's only part of it, her parents, her friends, everything near and dear. But her biggest complaint, Tawny... she doesn't want to leave her bedroom! She claims she's finally got it decorated exactly the way she wants it and she's not about to trade it in for a wagon and sixteen hundred miles of rocky trails.'

'Boyd, she's a woman. If that's how she feels...'

'Then why in hell did she tell me she'd go in the first place? Like I say, I tried my damnedest to talk her out of it. She wouldn't listen, she insisted on going. "To the ends of the earth with you, my dear darling..." I told the directors, Prescott; everything was set.' Tawny smiled thinly. 'It's no joke. Here I was thanking my lucky stars. I want to head out there so badly I can taste it. The future's out there, Tawny, our future, hers and mine.' He shook his head. 'Why bother going on and on about it. As you say, she's a woman. I expect no woman can see it the way a man does.'

40

'Doesn't that depend upon the individual?'

'You'd go, wouldn't you? You wouldn't be afraid.'

'I don't have a beautiful bedroom. It's nice, comfortable, but not something I'd want to take with me. Seriously, the whole idea does sound exciting, fascinating. Maybe because I've never been more than ten miles away from Titus Forks before coming here.'

'I'm not the least surprised.'

'What?'

'You two are as different as night and day. You haven't a spoiled bone in your body.'

'Don't fool yourself, Mr. Chevrier, I could learn to be spoiled very easily. If ever the chance came my way.'

They talked the night away, leaving Marcy out of it from that point on, turning their attention to the projected expedition, which he no longer considered himself part of. His acceptance of this was painful to see. All his considerable enthusiasm seemed to seep out of him, leaving him downcast and defeated. It was so unlike him it disturbed her. She could agree that it offered the chance of a lifetime, and could understand why watching it slip from his grasp would hurt so, and her sympathy for him was hard to conceal. At the same time, a strange feeling came over her, covering her like a velvet curtain, capturing her in its folds: a warm affectionate feeling for this unhappy, this bitterly disappointed man, this man who was obviously so fine, so decent and deserving, so very human, and who had been so open and honest to Marcy regarding the expedition. She thought of her father and all the many ways he and Aldous were in opposition. Like Jack Kinross Boyd Chevrier did not fancy picking at the bird of life, seeking out the easily removable parts with knife and fork, the tastier morsels. No, her father and this man would seize it in both hands, attack and devour it.

Still, knowing Marcy as she had come to, she could understand why she had had second thoughts beyond sacrificing her bedroom. It wasn't the danger, the hardships, the inconveniences, the distance from her father and mother and all the joys and comforts surrounding her in Rampling House; it was a prospect far more terrifying – the need to cast aside the role of princess she and her father had worked so hard to create and perfect. Princesses simply did not ride covered wagons over unmapped trails, did not beat a team over a precipitous mountain ridge with chasms a thousand feet yawning on either side, did not bathe out of a bucket, burn with the heat of day, freeze with the cold of night, swallow hard and repeatedly to keep their hearts down in their breasts when the bloodcurdling howls of the Cheyenne, the Crow, and the Blackfoot pierced the dusty air. Princesses did not rub down their arms, backs, and buttocks with horse liniment to chase the aches of the daily miles, nor shoot at snakes, wolves, cougars, and bears in defense of their lives. Princesses did not run risks and court injury and death through choice. Tawny suppressed a smile. She could just see Marcy's beautiful walnut tester bed fetched all the way from England sitting in the back of a wagon, her lying in it plucking her eyebrows in her hand mirror while her favorite Negress bent over her, breakfast tray in hand.

They talked, about their childhoods and dreams, experiences and people and each other, untiringly, as if in one night to make up for all the years preceding each had been denied the other's company. Then suddenly, like a gust of wind intruding upon absolute calm, they realized that the night was fast disappearing, supplanted by the somber gray of morning fording the river, creeping silently through the town.

'What am I doing?' she gasped. 'I must get back to the house. Where did the time go?'

Taking out his watch, he wound it. 'Do you know we've been talking almost seven hours? I'm really sorry, forgive me.'

'What's to forgive? It's been delightful, the most fun I've had since we got here. But I must get back before the house wakes up.'

'So you shall, Cinderella, hang on to your cloak.'

Off they rattled, dashing over the deserted road, the sun a ghostly white insinuating its presence upon the horizon at their backs beyond the river, the birds chirping to life in the naked trees, and far down at the end of the road Rampling House standing patiently awaiting them. He pulled up at the rear, the sorrel snorting, clouds of vapor rising from her nostrils. Curiously, the back door was locked. Hand in hand, they walked around to the front.

She smiled, suppressing a yawn. 'I'll sneak in, up the stairs, slip into bed, and pretend to wake up half an hour from now.' Again she yawned, talking through it and one gloved hand. 'I think I'm tired. Excuse me...'

'I certainly got carried away, didn't I?'

'Didn't we both...'

He took her by the shoulders, and, unable to control herself, she pecked him fondly on the cheek. It was a mistake. The increasing warmth in his voice, the sober look in his eyes should have warned her that his feelings for her were defining their presence in his heart as surely and as swiftly as her own feelings for him had made themselves known. He tried to kiss her, but she slipped her hand between their mouths. In his arms she felt weak all over, and for a fleeting instant was afraid she would lose all control.

'You're trembling,' he said softly.

'Please, Boyd, we mustn't, it's wrong.'

'How can it be, Tawny? Look at your eyes in mine. It's happened, hasn't it? You know it has...'

Gently she pushed him from her, her heart thundering in her chest. 'Please...'

He sighed and dropped his hands from her shoulders. 'I'm sorry,' he whispered, 'I'm so grateful to you for this night I guess I got carried away.'

She squeezed his hand affectionately and smiled. 'I hope it all works out for you, I really do. You deserve it so.'

'We'll see. Go ahead in. I'll wait a bit until I can be sure you've made it.'

'And if I don't, what will you do?'

'March in and pull them all off you!' He laughed loudly. 'Ssh...'

The door was unlocked. Easing it open, she turned and waved to him, and was starting in when she was stopped abruptly.

'Back at last, are you!'

On the next-to-bottom stair in her nightdress, a stumpy candle sputtering in hand, stood Lydia, glowering fiercely.

'Aunt Lydia, let me explain –'

'Spare me!' Blowing out the candle, she flung it aside.

'I'm not a fool, Tawny. Don't you dare take me for one.' She threw her hands high. 'How could you do such a monstrous thing? Whatever possessed you?'

'Please, I've done nothing, I swear –'

She might as well have been talking to the statue of Aphrodite in the garden. A look of pure loathing seized and held Lydia's features.

'Have you no shame, you hussy? Where did he take you, to some hayloft to romp all night like a levee slut?'

'How dare you! I haven't been anywhere, I haven't done anything. Think as you please.'

Tawny started up the stairs, but her aunt caught her arm, pulling her back.

'You listen to me, young lady. You've brought shame and humiliation down on this house tonight, down on a family that welcomed you openly, with charity of heart.'

'You have a filthy mind, Lydia.'

'If I do it's you who's made it so. Would it interest you to know that Marcy tried to kill herself? Throw herself out the window?'

'As you said yourself, she does have a flair for the theatrical.'

'You heartless Jezebel. Slut! *Slut!*'

'I didn't hear that, Lydia. And for the last time, I have done nothing, nor has he, to be ashamed of!'

'You call carousing about the countryside with your own cousin's husband-to-be nothing? *Nothing!*' She had become livid; Tawny had never seen her in such a state, never imagined her capable of such rage. 'You heartless slut, you've wrecked everything! Marcy's right, you're not fit –'

'Enough!'

It was Boyd coming in, his face black with fury. 'Don't you talk to her like that! Not another word! You keep your filthy accusations, your vulgar insults to yourself, you hear me?'

Lydia glared at him, then shifted her eyes to Tawny, impaling her with a withering stare. 'Go straight up to your room, my girl, and stay there,' she snapped. 'I shall deal with you presently. As for you, Mr. Chevrier, you'd best tuck your tail between your legs and get out of here before you wake up my brother! You do and he'll be after you with a horsewhip!'

'Lydia...'

Standing at the top of the stairs, bleary-eyed and with a look of martyred suffering, was Aldous, Marcy coming up behind him, her eyes snapping, her mouth twisted with rage.

'Never mind, Father, I'll do the talking.' She did not talk, she screamed. *My darling, what have you to say for yourself?* Don't bother saying anything, I'm in no mood to listen. What are you waiting for? You want her, take her – and this!' Pulling her engagement ring from her finger, she flung it at him. 'You groveling bastard, fortune-hunting pig! Take your trash, you river rabble, I wouldn't marry you if you were the last man on earth!'

'Marcy,' began Tawny, 'you don't know what you're saying, you're blowing this up all out of proportion –'

'Stay out of it, Tawny!' snapped Aldous. 'We'll have no twisting the knife in the wound. I must say, I'm not surprised. Blood will tell...'

It was a vile insult. Her patience, bowed like a dried stick, snapped. She became furious, so outraged so suddenly that Lydia stopped what she was about to say and could only stand and gape.

'You insulting soft-bellied son of a bitch! My father is a better man than you could ever dream of being, in every way!'

'*Witch!*' screamed Lydia. 'First Matthews' Inn, now this.'

Tawny gasped, staring at her. 'What's that supposed to mean?'

'You and your innocence. Butter wouldn't melt in your mouth. I actually believed they attacked you. What a fool I was. Why don't you tell us what really happened with the candles in the hallway?'

'Oh, Lydia, thank you.'

'Thank...?' Lydia reacted, completely flustered, her cheeks sagging.

'For making it easy.' A hollow half laugh escaped Tawny's throat. 'Hurting you was the last thing I wanted to do. But now I can thank you for sparing me that concern. Don't bother ordering me up to "my" room. I wouldn't be caught dead under this roof another ten seconds! Burn my things if you like. Good-bye!'

'*Out, the two of you!*' shrilled Marcy. '*Out! Out!*' Snatching up a vase from the stairpost, she hurled it at Boyd, missing him by a wide margin. The vase shattered against the door frame.

They left, the carriage heading down the way they had come. Staring grimly into the pale sun rising, Tawny's face gradually softened until a grin took shape across it.

'You forgot your ring.'

'So I did,' he said in an amused tone.

'You think it's funny?'

'I think it's hilarious!'

'So do I . . .'

They began giggling, then chuckling, then laughing, howling uproariously, lifting the mare's ears, sending birds nervously fleeing their perches, and prompting an old woman opening a window to lean out and stare at them foolishly. One hand gripping the reins, Boyd slipped his free arm around Tawny. She held his hand tightly against her waist.

'This is absolute madness, you know,' she said softly, 'we don't even know each other.'

'We've known each other a thousand years, my darling,' he said and, leaning over, drew her mouth to his, kissing her ardently. She closed her eyes, the whole world turned to jewels, and the music rising in her heart was the most beautiful she had ever heard. She kissed him, soulfully, wholly without reluctance, spared any twinge of conscience by Lydia's outburst.

7

It was not at all as Tawny pictured it would be. It was too hastily and awkwardly come by, wholly accidental, unlooked for, unexpected, a bumping together of hearts instead of the classic meeting and gradual blending; in a way

46

like being tossed into a pit, pushed together by the stupidity, jealousy, and blindness of others. Born in innocence, encouraged by the alchemy of understanding, inspired by need, accomplished in defiance, flaunted with pride. There it was, love!

'This is insane!' she burst as he geed the sorrel off the road and under a tree. 'Absolutely insane. What are we doing?'

'Recovering from the shock. Tawny, we're in love.'

'Heaven help me, we are.' She stood up from the seat and addressed a gray squirrel posed on the branch above their heads, its dark brown eyes twitching about nervously. 'I'm in love. How did it happen?'

The creature blinked, turned tail, and scampered back to the trunk. Boyd pulled her down.

'It didn't, you caused it. You're so beautiful, Tawny, a goddess. My goddess to worship.' He kissed her lingeringly, cupping her cheek in the softness of his palm. 'I love you, my darling.'

'We didn't do this. It didn't happen.'

'I love you.'

'All that screaming, Marcy throwing the vase, Lydia...'

'Forget them, every blessed one, sweep them out of your mind. Do you love me, darling?'

'I do. I do.'

They planned. First breakfast, then to the office of the Excelsior Fur Trading Company on Market Street and a meeting with Mr. Douglas Prescott, Boyd's superior, the man who had selected him to lead the Willamette Valley expedition.

'Then to Titus Forks,' Boyd murmured, squeezing her hands affectionately. 'How far?'

'Two hundred miles.'

'To ask Jack Kinross for his daughter's hand in marriage. What if he says no?'

'I say yes, he'll say yes.'

'He may not like the idea of you traipsing off to Oregon. It's dangerous...'

'Nonsense. Don't be surprised if he asks to come along.'

'If he can drive a wagon, he's welcome.' He sobered and tilted her face upward, kissing her forehead lightly. 'Mrs. Chevrier, are you absolutely sure you want to go?'

'Absolutely, Mr. Chevrier. Darling, we shouldn't dally. I hate to say it, but I don't trust Aldous, not where Marcy's concerned.'

'He can't do anything to us.'

'Darling, he's rich, he's powerful, and he has a vindictive streak as wide as the road. I wouldn't put anything past him.'

'Your Aunt Lydia isn't exactly the forgiving kind.'

Tawny looked glum. 'She's the dearest, kindest, sweetest woman I know. And now surely she'll never speak to me again.'

'Her fault, not yours.'

'Does it really matter whose fault it is when old friends fall out? And we *were* old friends – she was more like a mother to me than an aunt.'

'Darling, there's nothing you can do about it. You tried to explain, she simply wouldn't listen. I'm sure your two Titus Forks cousins will understand.'

'Emily will. I'll bet right now she's jumping up and down and cheering.' She paused and searched his eyes. 'I wonder what Lydia will tell Daddy.'

'I wouldn't worry about that, you'll be talking to him before she gets her chance to. By the way, what was she saying about Matthews' Inn? The hallway, the candles?'

Avoiding his eyes, talking softly to her hands clasped in her lap, Tawny explained, taking pains to delete the more grisly aspects of the episode.

'The bastards, the filthy animals! And Lydia has the nerve to imply that you led them on...'

'She was just lashing out at me, darling. I understand how she feels. Being my chaperone, responsible for me, and suddenly finding herself helpless to prevent my destroying everything.'

'Darling, you didn't destroy anything. If this hadn't happened, if I'd never even driven you to the levee, the wedding still would have been called off. Marcy would never change her mind about going. And she'd never convince me that I should stay!'

'I suppose.'

'It's true. Tawny, there can't be any compromise.' He shrugged. 'How could there be a wedding?'

'All the preparations, all the guests, the gifts, the money, thousands of dollars. I'm amazed Marcy didn't whip out a gun and shoot me.'

'Me first.'

Snapping the reins, he started the mare off onto the road, reaching the corner and heading down Market Street.

8

It was not until they had come within a mile of Titus Forks, shortly before midnight, that Tawny was able to get up the courage to confess her concern regarding her mother's death.

'Daddy and I knew something was wrong. She'd forget things, sometimes right in the middle of the conversation, what she was talking about, where she was. It was as if a piece of her memory had dropped out of place. And she complained of headaches. Dr. Gallagher said that letting things prey on her mind caused that. That and nervous strain; she was a very nervous person. But I always felt there was more to it than that. You don't just kill yourself because you're high-strung.'

'What things preyed on her mind?'

'Mostly money. There was never enough. And Daddy's drinking.'

'Does he carry on when he's drunk?'

'Loud and funny mostly, never mean. He hasn't a mean bone in his body.' She caught and held his eyes. 'We never dreamed she'd kill herself. She never let on how deeply, how terribly her monster was tormenting her.'

'It must have been awful for you.'

'Worse for poor Daddy.'

A slender gray cloud dusted the full moon, sliding across its full face, briefly dimming the eerie glow bathing the thickly wooded land. The mare was nearing the point of exhaustion, her head bobbing to her pace, the strain apparent. They had stopped only once, at an inn outside

Pawling, the halfway point. They had eaten, fed the horse, and rested for an hour.

'Since we're into baring family skeletons,' he began.

Her hand on his arm stopped him short. 'That's not what I'm getting at, Boyd.'

'What then?'

'Darling, none of us, the doctor, Daddy, nor I, ever really knew what brought it on. But Dr. Gallagher mentioned something about it being the sort of thing that's ... in the blood.'

'And you think it might be in your blood? Tawny, that's nonsense!'

'Is it?'

'Absolutely.'

'I wish I could be that sure.'

'You think suddenly something is going to snap and you'll go berserk? Ridiculous, preposterous! You've never shown any symptoms, have you? No suspicious indications, no hints?'

'Nothing up to now.'

'Nothing up to now. So you're patiently waiting for something to show itself?'

'I didn't say that.'

'You're implying it. Darling, put it out of your mind. There's no earthly reason to live in fear of such a thing happening. In the first place, insanity doesn't work that way.'

'I'm sorry, I've read practically everything written on the subject. One of the four proven causes is hereditary predisposition.'

'In congenital idiocy, maybe, but that wasn't her problem. She was no idiot or imbecile, nothing like it.'

'There's no way of knowing now what she was, or what she had. Dr. Gallagher didn't know back then; if he did, he never told either of us.'

'Whatever it was, it obviously wasn't congenital. Did she have any relatives with mental illness?'

'None that we know of.'

'It's likely you'd know if you had, isn't it? Darling, face it, you don't have any more chance of losing your mind than the man in the moon.'

His efforts to persuade her were so determined that she saw little to be gained by prolonging the discussion. Still, there was nothing he was able to say convincing enough to dispel her fears.

They rounded a bend, coming within sight of Titus Forks, lightless and slumbering, sharing the moonlight with the maples surrounding it.

'Our place is all the way down the other end,' she said.

'Here's a thriving metropolis if I've ever seen one. Shades of Chicago. I've never seen such traffic, do we dare try the main street?'

'Clown!'

Jack Kinross's cabin squatted to one side of a corral, a dozen horses standing asleep inside it. Opposite, a log barn with a shake roof uplifted its rectangular bulk against the star-strewn sky. A light inside the barn banded the narrow space between the two doors a pale yellow.

'Daddy's still up,' said Tawny.

Boyd drew up in front of the barn, helped her down, and removed the sorrel's harness. Then he unclasped both trace tugs, slipping them through the trace bearers, freeing her from the carriage.

Tawny opened one door. In vest and shirtsleeves Jack Kinross was kneeling beside a mare. His features appeared exaggeratedly pronounced in the reflection of the solitary candle, the hollows of his cheeks dipping deeply, his eyes buried in their sockets.

'Daddy!'

His mouth fell open with a gasp, his face exploding in a grin.

'Well, will you look at what the cat dragged in. In your best ball gown, no less!'

Boyd appeared in the doorway behind her. Jack Kinross's grin faded, a questioning look supplanting it. Tawny threw her arms around his neck, kissing him loudly.

'Daddy, I want you to meet Boyd Chevrier. We're going to be married. Hush...' She placed her fingers lightly against his mouth. 'I'll explain everything.'

'Hopefully.' He laughed, and the two of them smiled, more, felt Tawny, out of relief than amusement on Boyd's part. She poured out explanation. Her father's reaction took the form of mild shock tempered with pleasure, his eyes twinkling.

'Priceless! You, the groom, and now she, this jingle-headed roughneck tomboy, the bride? It's insane. Where's your Aunt Lydia? What does she have to say about this? What does Mr. Stuffed-shirt Rampling? Helene? Marcy? You're unbelievable, girl. You traipse clear across the Territory to your cousin's wedding and on the very day it's to take place you show up back here with the groom! You're both mad, you've got to be. Wait till old George Cutshaw hears, he'll die laughing. He'll do a damned somersault, busted hip and all!'

'I'm afraid Tawny's jumped the gun on me, sir.' Boyd blushed and fought off the urge to stammer. 'I . . . wanted to ask your permission for her hand . . .'

'My permission?' Jack stared, aghast. 'Brother, you honestly think this spindle-shanked blight of my life asks my permission on anything? Least of all which of the horses she can take out and ride into the ground? Don't be ridiculous, man.'

'Sir . . .'

'Pay no attention to him, darling, he's crude and unmannerly and as insensitive as a goat.'

'I am, am I?' With this Jack swept one hand in a wide arc, bringing it back and slapping her loudly on the bottom.

'*Ow!*'

'Be still! Permission granted, what the hell!' Grasping Boyd's hand, he pumped it vigorously, then went back down on his knees beside the horse. 'Look at this poor girl,' he said soberly. 'She's down with the horse-pox.'

'Horses get the pox?' Tawny asked, kneeling beside him and stroking the mare's head, the one eye in evidence rounding white with fear. 'There's a good girl.'

'Horse-pox, all four legs. She's running a fever, her heels are swollen and tender. Another day or so she'll be oozing fluid and starting to scab.'

'Can't you do anything for her?'

He shook his head. 'Nothing anybody can do, except keep an eye on her. And see that she's comfortable.' Picking up a folded blanket hanging over a nearby stall gate, he spread it over the horse. 'When the scabs start showing they'll dry and fall; the sores'll heal. She'll be all right. All we have to do is keep her clean, and if the inflammation gets worse, bathe it with a weak solution of carbolic acid. Get that candle, Boyd. I'm thirsty, let's get into the house and see if we can find something worth drinking. I'm itching to hear all about you.'

The bourbon bottle waited while Tawny showed Boyd her bedroom. There was no tester bed imported from England, or anywhere else, only a well-worn goose-down tick that looked as comfortable as a cloud. It lay on a frame made of saplings standing on the bare plank floor. Against the far wall was a plain pine blanket chest, beside it a Chippendale chest-on-chest-on-frame, which Tawny explained had been brought by wagon all the way from Virginia. One glance at his daughter's bed prompted a question from Jack.

'When and where did you plan to hold the wedding?'

'Here?' Tawny shrugged and stared at her father.

'Are you asking or telling?'

'Telling. Here, tomorrow morning.' She turned to Boyd for approval, and he nodded.

'I've got a better idea,' said Jack. 'How about tonight?'

'Don't be silly, it's after midnight. Besides, I'm ready to drop. I'm going to bed.'

'Not yet,' said her father, warming to his idea. 'Hear me out. I can go wake up the Reverend Pinchott and his missus to witness. He can marry you in two shakes.'

'What makes you think he'd want to in the middle of the night?'

'He will. He's got his eye on that little mare in the barn. If I agree to swap, he won't mind doing us a favor.' He smiled at Boyd. 'You'll like the reverend. He's a hard-nosed, hardheaded, hard-working Hard Shell Baptist. Besides, if you two don't get married tonight, Mr. Chevrier there'll have to sleep in the barn. You wouldn't appreciate that, it gets as damp as a swamp in there when the air's heavy like it is tonight. First we'll have a little something wet, talk a little, then I'll run over and wake up his nibs.'

There was no arguing with him. Tawny was too tired to start, Boyd too was impressed with his father-in-law-to-be's stubbornness. Jack's inspiration was not without its flaw, however.

'I regret to say I have no wedding ring for you,' said Boyd quietly.

'Tawny!' barked Jack. 'Go fetch your mother's. It's wrapped up in that little square of oilcloth in the bottom of the cedar chest in my room. It'll be too big; you've got no more flesh on your bones than a newly hatched chick.'

Tawny threw her arms around her father's neck and kissed him loudly. 'Daddy, Daddy, Daddy, I love you so!'

'Let go, stop it!' Jack struggled to free himself, feigning embarrassment.

'Tawny,' said Boyd, as she started out of the room, 'before we leave Missouri, I promise, I'll buy you the biggest, most beautiful, the finest diamond I can find.'

'I'll drink to that,' said Jack flatly.

He got a bottle out from the cabinet under the sink pump and two tumblers down from the cupboard, blowing the dust out of them and setting them on the table. Tawny set about brewing a cup of tea, yawning, fighting to keep her eyes open.

'I take it you approve of Mr. Chevrier,' she said, setting the pot on the stove, kneeling, and stirring the coals.

'He looks all right,' her father said, shrugging. 'What do I care, I'm not marrying him. Chevrier, that's French...'

'I'm half French,' said Boyd, glancing at Tawny out of the corner of his eye and inwardly bracing himself for the inquisition. 'My mother was Scottish, my father French-Canadian.'

'Canadian? How'd you manage to get all the way down to St. Louis?'

'I trekked.'

'Daddy, must you know his life history?'

'Ssh, it's proper. Isn't that so, Boyd?'

Boyd was not reluctant to discuss his background. His mother and father had both been killed by Iroquois. This he divulged without bitterness, with an attitude more fatalistic than anything else. In his teens he had made his living trapping 'practically all over the Territory', until he was twenty. Then he had joined the army, rising to the rank of lieutenant and taking his honorable discharge when offered a job by Excelsior.

'Oregon is a long and hazardous haul,' observed Jack.

'Would you like to come along?' Tawny covered his hand with her own. He shook his head.

'Not a chance, missy. It's hard enough keeping body and soul and a business together here in Titus Forks.'

'You're welcome to come,' said Boyd. 'We could use a man who knows as much about horses as you do. A good mount can be the difference between life and death out there.'

'No. You flatter me and I appreciate it, but it's not for me. You two are youngsters, it's time you got your start. Me, I'm too stumped down and settled to pull up stakes for a haul that long. I'd catch pneumonia in the mountain snow and never see the Willamette Valley.'

'Daddy, when we leave who's going to take care of you?'

'Pshaw, as if you ever had to. It's the other way around and you know it. Hell, if it weren't for me you would have wandered off into the woods, fallen down a chuckhole, and busted both legs long before this.'

'Of course.'

Jack emptied his glass, got up, and took his wool sack coat and kettle-finish fur hat down from the wall peg by the door.

'I'll be back in ten minutes. Boyd . . .'

'Sir?'

'See that you don't finish off that bottle, it's the last one in the house.'

Away he went.

'I have to say this, darling,' began Boyd, 'your father is one of a kind.'

'Amen.'

Taking her in his arms, Boyd kissed her eyes, her hair, and her mouth. 'I love you, my darling.'

'I love you, my husband. I must confess I never dreamed it could be this beautiful, being in love, being wanted, needed . . .'

Framing her face with his hands, he kissed her again, soulfully, lingeringly.

*

True to his word, Jack was back shortly with the Reverend and Mrs. Pinchott. There was more mystification than annoyance in the minister's pale and pockmarked face. Tawny couldn't see Mrs. Pinchott's face right away; the woman was too busy yawning and hiding the effort behind both hands. The introductions completed, the preliminary words were spoken, the ring was introduced, the vows were taken, and as the iron case clock in imitation Tennessee marble on the mantel over the fireplace sounded the hour of one, Crystal Taunton Kinross became Mrs. Boyd Chevrier.

9

She felt his lips on her eyelids, one then the other, and opened her eyes to his, to the sight of his pupils dark as onyx, reflecting tiny images of her face, their wells filling with smoldering desire. A shaft of sunlight drove downward from the top of the calico curtains drawn over the high window, a golden broadsword thrusting its point into the floor out of sight beyond the foot of the bed. And halfway down its edge dissolved, settling a slender arc atop his hair, a cap of gold.

They lay naked, the sheet flung to the foot of the bed in a tangle. His hand slipped up her body into her hair, stroking it gently, gradually arousing a delicious tingling sensation in her thighs and lower body, stirring the embers of the passion of the night from their dormancy. His fingers played, losing themselves in the luxuriant and abundant waves. His warm lips deserted her eyes, kissing down her cheek to the corner of her mouth, down her jaw to the pulsing concavity of her throat, exploring it with infinite tenderness, touching as lightly as the silky-down milkweed pod caresses the air through which it falls. Out to the point of her shoulder and down to her breast, rhythmically rising and falling above her pounding heart, his mouth ventured. Gently, ever gently, he ringed the areola with kisses, links of sensuous ardor forming a chain to bind her heart beneath. The tip of his tongue, swollen with the fire of his passion, found her nipples, one then the other, rousing them to steely hardness, causing her to moan softly.

The glorious touchings were coming more rapidly now, concentrating on one breast then the other, traveling slowly under each, then down to the valley of her stomach, outward to her hips and down, down to the soft, smoothly angled planes of her thighs. The fire building within suddenly leaped into flame, licking at every nerve end, every source and oasis of rapture. Like a blazing whip his tongue flicked and darted over her flesh. Now she moaned aloud, which only accelerated the soul-binding, supremely beautiful, magnificent ferocity of his attack. His lips and tongue lay siege to her body, slowly but certainly driving her into a frenzy of passion, of unquenchable desire for orgasm. Oh, to burst the dam of her carnal craving, to feel him enter and fill and swell and probe with his manhood her most intimate parts, to be bound, one body, one heart, one soul . . .

'My darling, my darling,' she whispered huskily.

'Ssh.'

'Now, now, please . . .'

'Soon.'

'Now!'

Never in her wildest dreams, her most inspired fantasies, had she ever conceived of such wanton joy, such incredible pleasure. It was as if all the yearnings of her years, all the sensual fire, the hunger, the uncontrollable lust had been amassed and distilled for this heavenly interlude, their essence reducing to a single burst of flame that must inevitably consume her. Her entire body throbbed and pulsed and writhed, threatening to burst . . .

'Now, Boyd, now!'

As lightly as a shadow he was up and over her, easing his enormous member between her quivering thighs, moving slowly forward . . .

10

Eight days later, Tawny and Boyd joined the Excelsior Fur Trading Company's expedition to the Willamette Valley. The group had assembled at Keys Landing, fifty miles north of Titus Forks on the Independence River. The itinerary called for the train to head out in a northwesterly direction following the Little Blue River to where it began to parallel the River Platte. They would winter, not up north with the Mandan Indians, but west-northwestward in the Rockies, hopefully somewhere just beyond what the mountain men whom the Excelsior executives had consulted called the South Pass. There, long before winter's cold had seized the mountains in its merciless grip they would build log homes for themselves and their animals, buildings well caulked between the logs in defense against the bone-chilling cold.

However, long before the mountains rose to threaten them, the migrants would be obliged to risk the hazards of the Great Plains. Along the flat, dry, and dusty land studded with sagebrush and creosote bushes the summer temperatures regularly rose above one hundred degrees. The storms that occasionally came funneling down from the border were alleged to be the most savage west of the Mississippi, the wind moaning interminably and buffeting every living thing that dared to venture across its path. Once they were forced to cut away from the river to cross the Plains water would become scarce, so precious that men had been known to kill their own flesh and blood to keep from dying of thirst. In the summer heat as in the pitiless cold of winter, oxen, mules, and horses collapsed and died in distressingly large numbers. On the Plains there was no escaping the relentless fire of the sun, no shelter, no shade other than the cotton or canvas covers of the hickory-bowed wagons.

Why then, in the name of all reason and sanity, this long

and treacherous hegira through hell? Why would anyone voluntarily solicit such adversity, such barbarous punishment?

For the vague promise of a new life, a chance to build for one's remaining years and for one's children an existence of substance, of enduring values; this was essentially the only way left the dreamer to eradicate the failures of the past, by challenging and conquering the future. Hope gleamed in the migrants' eyes, excitement and anticipation building by the hour as the time drew near to form the line and whip up the animals for the first long leg to the Bluffs.

To anyone chancing upon the place, Keys Landing itself seemed like the last stop to nowhere. Barely two years earlier the first rough-hewn log huts had been raised, clayed together, and covered with roofs. There were only three clapboard houses along with a grog shop and a few stores. *The* Landing – as the permanent residents called it – would never be known for its size; it was its position that earned it its importance, for it was at the moment the gateway to the West, the staging area that attracted those whose minds' eyes could see over the Rockies and the Cascades to the opportunity beyond. To Missouri they had come from as far away as Philadelphia, New York, and Boston. Recognizing Ben Franklin's maxim that in union there is strength, they were banding together under the aegis of the company for not merely strength, but the advantages of shared dependency and mutual protection – against the elements, the savages and the ill fortune which in a thousand guises lurked along the trail.

No fewer than sixty-six vehicles were to comprise the wagon train, with two hundred and fifty-two people, including a baby born that very morning. Boyd would be sharing overall command with one George Latchford, an Ohioan, an older man whom both Chevriers had met upon arriving and whom Tawny was not impressed by. From the manner in which he introduced himself, his wife, two sons and daughter, it was evident that Latchford enjoyed an astonishingly high opinion of himself and his abilities. His conversation was securely pegged to *I, I, me, me*, and *mine*. He appeared determined to deny anyone else the pleasure of finishing a sentence, his wife not excepted. Pompous, arrogant, self-indulgent, he was in addition a religious fundamentalist who sought solution to all problems in his dog-eared copy of the King James bible. 'The Lord will protect, the Lord will provide, the Lord will guide.' Say nothing, observed Boyd upon their parting with the Latchfords, that the train be well armed, adequately supplied with food and other necessities, and he and Latchford be in possession of accurate copies of Lewis and Clark's best maps.

Tawny had little interest in Latchford Senior. Scarcely had they been introduced before her attention was drawn to Jenny Latchford, a fetching nineteen-year-old. Even before 'Delighted to meet you', Jenny began cow-eyeing Boyd, so obviously and shamelessly that it was all Tawny could do to subdue a gasp. To make matters even more intriguing, she bore a vague resemblance to none other than Marcy Rampling. Jenny Latchford, Tawny decided on the spot, she would be keeping a close watch on for the next four months.

She and Boyd introduced themselves or were introduced to all the hardy souls assembled in preparation for the trek. Tawny had expected that there would be more children, but in the entire party there were only eighteen. Many parents had left their youngsters with relatives back East, planning to settle in the valley first before sending for them. Tawny failed to understand this, but Boyd pointed out that by the time they reached their destination and settled, other wagon trains would be on the trail; by the following spring new settlements would have sprung up along the way, making the journey easier, hopefully less hazardous. Even now there was talk of a fort being erected at Laramie.

If Boyd had made a powerful first impression on Jenny Latchford, a bull of a mule skinner who called himself Telford Ingersoll, whose credentials included a two-year stay in prison in Virginia for unjustifiable manslaughter, all but duplicated it when Boyd introduced him to Tawny. Ingersoll stared raptly, his eyes narrowing evilly, quite like the raftsman's at the dinner table at Matthews' Inn. No sooner had his sweaty hand released her own upon exchanging greetings than she made a mental note to give Mr. Ingersoll the widest possible berth.

Almost from the moment she and Boyd had arrived from Titus Forks it was evident to Tawny that in this gathering of strangers from so many different parts of the East, people of varied backgrounds, education, and bloodlines, so many diverse personalities, disagreements among them would crop up under the best conditions. What, she wondered, would happen under the notoriously difficult conditions which awaited them? Little did she imagine that trouble would start even before the first wheel rolled.

Most of the vehicles were farm wagons light enough so as not to overstrain the pairs of oxen, yet sufficiently strong and durable to carry loads of as much as 2,500 pounds. The majority were fashioned of hardwoods, oak, hickory, or maple. Tires, axles, and hounds – the bars that connected and braced the undercarriage – were made of iron, practically the only metal parts. This helped to keep any vehicle's overall weight at a minimum. There were no springs; the wagon bed, approximately four feet wide and up to twelve feet long, was loaded with necessities, allowing little if any room for passengers. Mindful of what should and should not be taken along, Boyd summoned the heads of all the families to a meeting shortly after the midday meal. He warned them that they must expect their draft animals to grow wearier and weaker as the days went by.

'Which means your loads will have to be lightened. I saw a fine-looking sideboard loaded into one wagon, brass knobs, floral design . . .'

'Mahogany with bird's-eye maple inlay,' interjected a tall bearded man proudly. 'Maw and I fetched it all the way from Albany.'

Boyd sighed, lowering his voice to soften the blow. 'Mister, I'm going to have to ask you to leave it behind. Sell it if you can.'

'Are you crazy? That piece is worth thirty dollars, more! It's my wife's pride and joy.'

'I'm sorry, you'll either have to leave it here and get what you can for it, or take it along and when your oxen are on the verge of collapse halfway over the mountains, dump it along the trail.'

'We aim to take it, and that's that!' snapped the man in exasperation.

Tawny, looking on outside the circle, could see from the look on his face that he knew he was wrong, knew it made sense to leave the piece. Still, how would he explain it to his wife? Others spoke up in defense of the man's right to bring it along, among them Latchford. This upset Boyd.

'George,' said he to the older man as the meeting broke up and the others drifted away, heading back to their waggons, 'you and I are supposed to be pulling as a team, not in opposite directions. I'm not telling that fellow or the little German from Philadelphia with his nine Franklin stoves or anybody else to get rid of excess baggage just to rile them. The thing is, that sideboard and eight too many stoves could be the difference between life and death for both of them and their wives. Whitlaw with his sideboard may just change his mind and decide to dump it, only too late, when his team is done for. Then what does he do, harness up, grab the tongue, and haul his rig over the mountains himself?'

'You're forgetting one thing, young fellow,' said Latchford evenly.

'What?'

'I've said it before, I'll say it again. In time of need, our Heavenly Father will provide. Friends will come to Mr. Whitlaw's aid, friends will lend a helping hand.'

'Latchford, you'd better get this through your head before we start. Out there across the Plains into the mountains the first thing that dries up is the milk of human kindness. The first thing dropped off is a man's fellow feeling for his friend or neighbor. It's a luxury none of us, not you, not me, not Whitlaw or the German, can afford.'

'I'm inclined to doubt that. Under stressful conditions man invariably rises to the summit of his character. You're forgetting your bible, my boy, specifically the Book of John, chapter fifteen, verse thirteen. "Greater love hath no man than this, that a man lay down his life for his friends."'

Tawny could see nothing was to be gained by furthering the discussion. 'Boyd,' she said, 'excuse me, may I speak to you a moment?'

Taking him by the arm, she practically dragged him away from Latchford.

'Did you hear him?' he fumed. 'Did you hear that self-righteous, sanctimonious –'

'Ssh, simmer down.'

'What do you want?'

'Nothing, darling, other than to keep you from locking horns with him. Boyd, you mustn't let him get under your skin. There are going to be no end of days far more trying than today. You two have to share command; how will it look to the others if you're constantly arguing?'

He sighed in capitulation. 'You're right. From now on I'll just smile and nod my head whenever he blurts out his foolishness. Then quietly go about doing things properly in my own way. Darling, will you do something for me?'

'Of course.'

'Go to each wagon in turn and see that their tar and tallow buckets are full. Twice every day the wagon wheels will need lubricating. If anybody runs out of tar and tallow they'll have to shoot a buffalo or a bear and squeeze the grease out of the hide.'

She laughed, patting his cheek affectionately. 'Done.'

'You think I'm fooling? That's exactly what they'll have to do. Another thing, see that the tools in their jockey boxes are clean. If they need anything they should pick it up at the stores before sundown. We roll tomorrow at dawn.'

Off she went while he turned his attention to his manifest, comprised of a long list of necessities and luxuries:

WEAPONS

Rifle
Pistol
Holster
Gunpowder
Lead
Bullet mold
Powder horn
Bullet pouch
Knife
Hatchet

BEDDING AND TENT SUPPLIES

Blankets
Feather beds

Pillows
Ground cloths
Tent
Tentpoles
Stakes
Rope

COOKING UTENSILS

Flint and steel
Dutch oven
Kettle
Three-legged skillet
Reflector oven
Coffee grinder
Coffeepot
Teapot
Ladle
Butcher knife
Tin tableware
Full water keg

FOOD

Coffee
Tea
Bacon
Flour
Sugar
Baking soda
Cornmeal
Dried beans, beef, and fruit
Hardtack
Vinegar
Pepper
Molasses
Salt
Rice

DOMESTIC ESSENTIALS

Needles, pins, thread
Scissors

Surgical instruments
Liniments
Bandages
Cotton
Stools
Chamber pot
Washbowl
Candle molds
Candles
Tallow
Spyglass

CLOTHING

Buckskin pants
Wool pantaloons
Duck trousers
Cotton shirts
Flannel shirts
Cotton socks
Wool sack suits
Rubber coats
Cotton dresses
Brogans
Boots
Hats and bonnets

TOOLS AND ADDITIONAL
   EQUIPMENT

Chains
Heavy rope
Extra wagon tongue
Extra spokes
Extra tires
Oxshoes, muleshoes, horseshoes
Linchpins
Kingbolts
Oxbows
Plow
Axe
Axles

Set of augurs
Spade
Crosscut saw
Gimlet
Hammer
Hoe
Shovel
Whetstone

LUXURIES
Furniture
Iron Stove
Books
Musical instruments
Preserves
China
Silverware
Toys
Dolls
Plant cuttings
Fine clothing
Fine linens
Clocks

While drinking water could pose a problem at one point or another along the trail, food should not. Buffalo meat, cooked and eaten fresh or cooked and dried as jerky for future use, would be available. Rabbit, sage hen, and grouse would help to vary the daily menu. Fried flour cakes, johnny-cake, soda bread, and dried apple pie would also help to augment the emigrants' diet.

Nevertheless, for every promised boon – clean, clear stream water, wild berries, and other examples of nature's bounty – Boyd could cite a dozen dangers and difficulties to be overcome or bypassed along the way.

If only he could count on Latchford's cooperation. But the older man seemed to consider any effort in that direction either a show of weakness or not to be squared with his religious convictions; in short, the making of decisions would be better left to Divine Judgment.

A gig came rattling toward him, its rear wheels raising a great cloud of yellow dust, a little barrel of a man holding the reins of a high-spirited stallion. The new arrival was bareheaded, pink-scalped, and bearded down to the center button of his vest. They hailed each other, waving, and when the horse was drawn to a stop, Boyd helped the man down from his seat.

'Mr. Prescott, I was beginning to think you'd never get here.'

'I wouldn't let you down, Boyd.' Tucking his beard inside his jacket, Prescott buttoned up and glanced about. 'Everything shaping up?'

'More or less.'

'Why so glum, problems?'

'A few. Can I ask you a question, sir?'

'Ask away, the time's getting short. My gracious, what a crowd.'

'Am I wrong or am I supposed to be in command here?'

'Are you having trouble with George Latchford?'

'Who *is* he?'

'Hasn't he told you! A lay preacher from Ohio. He led these folks out here to Missouri, lone hand in command.'

'I'm expected to share command with him?'

'Not exactly.'

'What's that supposed to mean?'

'You're to be in sole charge of the train. It moves when you say, stops when you say; any difficulties along the way, you decide how to deal with them. He and his people are supposed to defer to your judgment.'

'You'd better tell him that.'

'As far as the people's personal needs, personal problems, he's the one they'll turn to.'

'The Great White Father.'

'Something like that.'

Boyd sighed in annoyance, digging his knuckles into his hips and studying the dusty ground. 'I don't think it's going to work.'

'You're going to make it work.'

'Not if we don't get along.'

'Tell him straight out, son. He knows who's responsible for what. You just explain to him what you want to do from one day to the next, hear him out as a matter of courtesy, and do what you think best.'

'At the risk of sounding conceited, you know as well as I do there can be only one man in charge. Committees never work, and two people sharing command can be disastrous.'

Prescott's chubby features softened. 'Would you like me to have a word with him?'

'I'd appreciate it.' Boyd paused and lowered his voice. 'Did you bring it?'

A grin spread slowly across Prescott's face. His bright blue eyes snapped and gleamed. 'You think I'd dare forget it?'

Reaching into his breast pocket, Boyd brought out a folded envelope. 'One hundred and ninety dollars, right?'

'Exactly.'

Prescott produced a small square green velvet box, depressing its lid button with his thumb, opening it and revealing a beautiful blue-white diamond ring.

'Congratulations, my boy, I hope you two will be very happy.'

'We are and we always will be, sir.'

'She's a marvelous girl, pretty special to marry a chap and start a trek with him all the way to Oregon practically the same blessed week.'

'Pretty special is right, sir,' said Boyd, turning the diamond at the ends of his fingers, watching it catch the sun's light in its smoothly polished facets.

11

Nikandr Suverin, subaltern of the Tenth Saint Petersburg Hussars, on detached service to the Russian-American Trading Company and posted to New Archangel* in Alaska, confronted his image in the tin-framed mirror above his washstand and hesitantly examined his tongue. It was furry, heavily coated, and characterized by an oddly metallic taste, as if, he thought, he had been chewing nails while he

---

* Present-day Sitka.

slept. His aching head and queasy stomach and the red blotches staining the whites of his dark brooding eyes, however, confirmed that it was not nails but *ryabinovka** which was the cause of his condition. Why, he asked himself, did he feel it necessary to down the better part of a quart of the filthy stuff every night when the following morning invariably punished the crime in such a disagreeable manner? Why indeed? Only because in the brown depths of the bottle lurked escape from his surroundings, forgetfulness that New Archangel even existed. The mornings after notwithstanding, the *ryabinovka* the nights before rendered life tolerable in the absence of everything that in normal circumstances would have made it delightful. Holy saints, how he missed Saint Petersburg, the court, the glittering affairs, the splendid balls, the parties, the women – the so-desirable ladies with their milk-white skin with a faint pinkish cast, with their great round breasts, the nipples poking against the lace edging of their décolletages, ever threatening to burst free! Colonel Zorodoff's Mazovian wife, who laughed like little bells tinkling, so loved to dance the mazurka, downed *kvass* by the tumblerful, and romped on a certain subaltern's bed like a cat wild in heat in a pen full of toms! Colonel Zorodoff's wife with her alabaster thighs, the tiny, almost invisible blonde hairs overlying the plain of her stomach, the perspiration collecting between their bellies as he drove his manhood into her and she squealed rapturously. Colonel Zorodoff's devoted wife; what was her first name?

Holy saints, what he wouldn't give for two spins around the floor with that buxom redhead who slept with Yermolay Alexeyvich, His Imperial Majesty's chamberlain's nephew. Give this loyal horse soldier five minutes between her thighs and she'd never look at that lucky bastard again, let alone grant him her favors.

Damn the world! Why was he letting his aching head run on so? It was all fantasy, all in the bottle, all fifteen thousand miles away in Saint Petersburg. It might as well be on the moon. It would be the most joyous day of his life when word arrived of his transfer. He had petitioned Colonel-General

*Vodka flavoured with ashberries which have been steeped.

Kropotkin, with his post commander's permission, to be sure; Colonel Luka Poplova understood and was sympathetic to his plight, at least his dumpy little wife, Varya, was. She had promised to persuade the colonel that her dear Nikki was rotting on the vine in this icebox, that the year he had already served had to be equal to ten in the toll it was taking on his *joie de vivre*, not to mention his liver. Colonel Poplova was not the stumbling block, however: it was Headquarters in Saint Petersburg. Requests for transfer, however favorably looked upon and deserved, took eons to work their way through the morass of military machinery. Holy saints, if only he had a voice to pester the colonel-general in his behalf, some loyal friend who might hasten the process.

'Lieutenant Nikandr Suverin, Tenth Hussars, Saint Petersburg, on detached service to the Russian-American Trading Company in New Archangel, is hereby ordered to appear at Third Army Headquarters on Broskya Street at 11 o'clock on the 14th of May instant . . .'

Out. Out of this ice-locked prison, the key turning, the shackles binding his spirit removed. You are hereby set free of this grinding boredom, this vise of soul-pinching monotony, the endless, empty days, the drunken nights, the flat-faced Aleut bitches reeking of sweat and rancid bear grease, their toothless grins mocking you, their gimlet eyes staring blankly as you mount them. They all look alike, the disgusting cretins, like wooden dolls carved by the identical hand. 'Lieutenant Nikandr Suverin, a grateful Mother Russia welcomes you home.'

Sighing audibly, unintentionally aggravating the throbbing between his eyes, causing him to wince, he emptied the pitcher into the basin, thrusting his face into it, eyes wide. Holy saints, it was freezing! Out he jerked, sending water spattering in every direction. His somewhat wasted-looking, though undeniably handsome, face in the glass had reddened perceptibly and was now two shades lighter than the red splotching his aching eyes. Again he displayed his tongue and, bending, gulped a mouthful of water, churned it about from cheek to cheek, and spat it back where it had come from. Bearing with it some of the fur and disagreeable aftertaste of the vodka.

Behind him the simmering pan of water he had set on the stove upon arising began to boil. Tossing the cold water out the door into the yard, waving to Private Golkov on sentry duty on the stockade wall walkway, Suverin seized the pan from the stove and emptied it into the bowl. He then began lathering his face to shave. Moments later his straight razor was gliding over his cheeks, removing his morning stubble. Securing his towel in the neckline of his undershirt and raising his chin, he was preparing to stroke beneath it when a knock sounded at the door, an insistent tapping like a woodpecker attacking a tree.

'Nikki, Nikki, are you awake?'

Varya, one of only two white women in New Archangel, Mrs. Colonel Luka Poplova.

'Coming.'

Once again striding to the door, his diligently polished boots pounding the wooden floor like a sledge, he swung the door wide. The apple-dumpling lady, as he privately described her, filled the lower half of the frame with her shapelessness, her ball head sunk between her round shoulders balanced on her ball body, her little ball cheeks protruding like ripe apples, her hazel eyes beaming with ... motherly pride? She persistently treated him like her son, all but suffocating him with maternal affection, to the amusement of her husband.

'Nikki, get dressed! Quickly! A ship has dropped anchor in the bay.'

'What ship, Varya Mihailovna?' His heart quickened. A Yankee? Or from home? From home! Bringing his precious transfer! Wiping the remaining lather from his partially shaved face, he flung the towel to the bed. Coming into the room, she picked up the towel, folding it neatly and hanging it on the rack alongside the mirror.

'The *City of Kursk*.'

He roared his pleasure. 'From home, yes!' He hugged her so tightly she squealed. Then, grabbing her hands, he danced a jig in a circle, singing loudly.

'Nikki,' she shrilled, 'let go of me! Settle down, hussar. You get your hopes up too high, when they fall they'll shatter to bits!'

Pulling his freshly laundered snow-white tunic over his

head, he hastily closed the three shoulder buttons and out of habit dusted down the three stars of his rank on the opposite shoulder with his fingertips, almost as if to reassure himself that they were still in place.

'They've brought my transfer, Varya, I know it, I feel it! It has to be, I'm already here thirteen months seven days.'

'So? Luka and I and the Prishibeyevs, almost everybody, have been here nearly three years.'

'Ah, but neither Luka nor Captain Prishibeyev has applied for transfer.'

She shrugged reluctant agreement with this, sighing and turning from him. Her tone was restrained, reflective. 'I shall miss you, Nikki.'

'I shall miss you. I shall write you long letters.'

'Liar!'

He kissed her on the forehead, awarding her his most disarming smile.

'You devil,' she hissed, 'what you miss is the ladies at court. Once you're back you had best be on better behavior than you were when they bundled you off here. Or be prepared to catch a bullet in your brisket. Outraged husbands have been known to shoot first and apologize afterward.'

'You misjudge me, Varya Mihailovna. It's true, I would rather be back at court than in this frozen paradise, but not merely for the . . . social advantages. I prefer to be at the nerve center of things, not out at the fingertips. Promotions are given to the qualified you can see, not the ones you hear about in dispatches.'

'Then Colonel-General Kropotkin is not going to meet you at the pier with another star on a stripe? Welcome home, Second Captain Suverin! Ha . . .'

'Now you are laughing at me. So I am ambitious, is that a sin? What would you have me do, sit back and let some chalk-cheeked clerk or some clod of an oat farmer from Nolinsk take my promotion? Don't you think thirteen months out here deserves at least one more stripe? It's very little, Varya Mihailovna.' He measured with his fingertips. 'Only three inches long. And the star is tiny.'

'Silly!'

'I must hurry . . .' He buckled on his sword and, turning

to the mirror, ran his fingers through his straight black hair. Then, with a practiced snap, he twirled the ends of his mustache tightly.

'Relax, Luka and Captain Prishibeyev have already taken the pinnace out to meet her. Unless you prefer to swim for it, why not come back with me to our cabin and let me put some breakfast into you. Something solid in your stomach will cure your hangover and bring the white back into the whites of your eyes, you naughty boy.'

'That's very thoughtful, Varya, but I really should get out to the ship. I'll take one of the quarter boats.' He turned to his mirror, straightening his hair with his fingertips a second time, then jamming on his issue cap. 'How do I look?'

'Half shaved.' Once again he pecked her forehead. 'Put your coat on, you'll catch your death without it.'

Drawing on his otter-skin jacket, he clutched it together at the front with one gloved hand against the morning chill and pushed the door wide. She brushed by him clucking disapprovingly, waving him away. The sun was already as bright as glare ice, bouncing off the bergs in the bay and the winter-capped mountains rising behind the settlement, and smashing against his throbbing eyes. Pulling the bill of his cap lower, he made his way across the yard toward the door in the main gate. Standing at present arms alongside it was a squat-faced corporal squinting into the glare, methodically lifting one booted foot after the other in a steady silent rhythm to encourage the sluggish circulation in his tingling toes. His face, collecting about a nose as round as a mushroom cap, dissolved into a grin at the sight of his commanding officer.

'Good morning, sir.'

'Corporal Zubov. Cold, eh?'

'A day for the seals to stay under water, sir.'

Lieutenant Suverin brushed a bit of some nondescript debris from the corporal's epaulet, a gesture more of affection than to point up his lack of neatness. New Archangel was not Saint Petersburg; laxity in the petty and trivial regulations was indulged, even encouraged. Among the post regulars the conviction prevailed that the civilian governor, Yurii Kuskov, was more a stickler for adherence to the official codes of dress and deportment than was the colonel. Kuskov had been bedded down with a lung infection for most of the winter, however, affording him little opportunity to play inspector general.

As the corporal leaned his flintlock against the fence, preparatory to opening the door, Suverin glanced about the fortress, this islet of Russian military presence in the virtual heart of the Tlingit Indian territory. Thirty months before his own arrival, Yurii Kuskov's predecessor and his men had taken the entire winter, laboring with whipsaw, adze, and axe, to raise the fort. The result was imposing testimony to man's conviction that any effort to survive in alien territory made dependable protection the first priority. The fort itself was fashioned of timbers two feet thick; it measured seventy by fifty feet at the base, with the upper story jutting out two additional feet. High watchtowers were perched at the two bay front corners. Grouped around the structure, like chicks nestling their mother, were the cookhouse, a smith's cabin – as yet to be equipped – homes, and other outbuildings, including sheds for domestic animals. The assemblage was enclosed by the high, solidly constructed stockade. Saint Michael: Archangel's home in the wilderness. The fortress succeeded in impressing the savage Tlingits, whose chief, Ska-yut-lelt, had met with scathing criticism from his fellow chieftains in the Tlingit tribal confederation for permitting the white man to settle on holy Tlingit ground. The guards on duty in and outside the watchtowers, strolling the walkways at shoulder arms, were presumably alert to any threat of Tlingit reprisal for the chief's tactical blunder. The Aleuts who also inhabited the area had proven themselves more peace-loving neighbors, and it was they upon whom the representatives – military and civilian – of the Russian-American Trading Company depended for their peltry. The installation mounted no fewer than sixty guns. The palisade gates front and rear appeared as solid as the fabled Golden Gate of the Starokievskaya Chast of the Old Town of Suverin's native Kiev. Unlike Kiev, however, there was no Saint Sophia here, not even a temporary chapel, much to Varya's and Natasha Prishibeyev's disappointment.

The winter at long last on the wane had been the most severe in anyone's memory, even that of Ankutat, the chief of the Aleuts. Savage gales had lashed the coast from the Aleutians, strung out into the Bering Sea, back eastward to Kodiak Island, and along the crescent coast of the gulf down to Queen Charlotte Island. The snows had been extraordinarily heavy and the cold bone-shattering. Even now, approaching the middle of May, the bay was still choked with massive boulders of blue, gray, and glaring white ice. To any man newly arrived in New Archangel the awesome sight suggested that the full moon, having been shattered by some cosmic force, had tumbled in fragments into the water. It would be the end of July before most of them melted. And six weeks after that, the temperature would once again begin inching downward in anticipation of a new winter.

In front of Suverin a battered, iron-prowed barkentine, the *City of Kursk*, sat rigidly hawsered to the bottom, her ice-covered stays and braces, shrouds and ratlines glistening like crystal in the dazzling brilliance of the sun. Off her port beam a hundred yards to the north, the *Saint Nicholas*, Captain Grigory Prishibeyev's trim little galliot, lay anchored in the ice, angled slightly by its buckling, her bowsprit nudging upward like the tusk of a narwhal. To Suverin's left, beached and securely tied down against the capricious breeze, were two quarter boats, the *Saint Nicholas*es, freed from their davits and brought to shore the previous fall before their double blocks became frozen, rendering them unworkable until the summer sun set them free. Suverin hailed the two men chipping ice from the tholepins.

'Ready the oars, you two, we're heading out to the ship.'

'When, sir?' inquired the taller of the two, an ungainly, too garrulous Muscovite whose tongue Suverin had been obliged to curb on previous occasions.

'At once, Javelov.'

The man to whom he had spoken turned and pointed up the beach. A single file of Aleuts and white trappers, their backs burdened with beaver pelts, was picking its way through the stones toward them. '*Promyshlenniki*, Lieutenant.'

Suverin scowled. 'You, Drzhembitsky,' he said in his most authoritative tone to the other man. 'Take them in. Escort them to the warehouse and present them to the governor's aide. You' – he turned back to Javelov – 'ready the oars and let's go.'

'Me alone, sir, this enormous boat?'

'You alone this enormous boat.'

Javelov shrugged and mumbled to his comrade, causing him to laugh, then quickly choke it back with an embarrassed grin. Suverin prided himself on his excellent hearing; he caught only the first few words, but the comment was not original and its meaning was perfectly clear.

A dulled facet on the jewel of Suverin's reputation was his well-known sensitivity to criticism, even that of the lighthearted variety. Coming from his superiors, it was swallowed and lodged behind his pride; coming from his inferiors, it was impossible to keep it down. Striding up to Javelov, he confronted him with a withering glare, placing one gloved hand against the man's chest.

'Say that again, Private.'

Javelov reddened. 'It was nothing, sir, a joke.'

'Say it again.'

Javelov turned to Drzhembitsky for support, but the latter deliberately and effectively closed himself off from the situation by saluting, spinning about, and marching double-quick toward the on-coming trappers to intercept them.

Javelov swallowed hard, studied the toes of his boots, and repeated the phrase, mumbling it.

'A specialist is like unto a gumboil; his fullness is one-sided.'

'So you consider your superior officers gumboils, do you?'

Javelov blanched, affecting shock, albeit unconvincingly. 'You, sir? You misjudge me, Lieutenant, it was not you I was talking about, not at all. It was the trappers. They are such single-minded clods . . .'

'You are a liar. Take seven nights tower duty, starting tonight. The night air may clarify your thinking, help you remember your status vis-à-vis my own. And while we are on the subject of old proverbs, there is one you might keep in mind. Let me see . . . ah yes, "Keep your clever tongue in your head, and your cleverest barbs unsaid." Into the boat with you.'

Javelov rowed them out to the *City of Kursk*, the bow of the quarter boat bumping against the Jacob's ladder. Suverin hailed Captain Prishibeyev, commander of the ice-locked *Saint Nicholas* nearby, leaning over the *Kursk*'s gunwale and puffing on his pipe. Suverin started up the ladder.

'Wait for me,' he barked down to Javelov. Prishibeyev, a sturdy, thick-necked little man with a cheerful disposition and a complexion ravaged by smallpox, welcomed him aboard, helping him over the rail. Colonel Poplova and a tall, harried-looking bearded man emerged from the forward companionway and came strolling down the deck toward them.

'Nikandr,' boomed Luka Poplova, 'what are you doing here, as if I didn't know...' The colonel held up a large parchment envelope, its wax seal broken, the offshore breeze fluttering its loosened ribbons.

'You've got it!' snapped Suverin, his heart leaping in his breast.

'I've something for everybody in here.' Poplova laughed uproariously, stuffing the envelope in his belt. 'Captain Yankovlevich, may I present my aide, Lieutenant Nikandr Suverin, like myself a refugee from the Tenth Hussars, two Imperial outcasts, if you will. Nikki, Captain Yankovlevich.'

Salutes and vigorous handshakes.

'Where do you come from, sir?' inquired Suverin.

'From old Archangel to New. The colonel has been telling me that the hunting has been excellent in spite of the weather.'

'We can fill your holds from the plate floors to the tie plates. Beaver, sea otter, seal. Blue fox, wolf, even bear.'

Yankovlevich beamed and turned to Luka Poplova. 'Have you heard the latest price on sea otter? The Chinese are offering a hundred twenty-five rubles a pelt.'

'Amazing,' remarked Prishibeyev. 'We pay what, four rubles?'

'Captain Yankovlevich,' began Suverin, 'forgive my curiosity, but what do you bring us besides my transfer?'

Luka Poplova raised both hands and, crossing them, shook his head emphatically. 'Nikki, contain yourself, nobody said your transfer has come. There is no transfer.'

Suverin gasped. 'But you –'

The colonel tapped the envelope in his belt. 'I said I had something for everybody in here. Better than a transfer.'

Suverin groaned inwardly. 'I don't understand, sir.'

'Be patient, my boy. When we get back to shore I will explain.'

It would be out of order, even rude, to press the point further, decided Suverin, suddenly crushed, anger stirring in him, his juices rapidly coming to a boil. *Damn the world! Damn his rotten luck! Damn Kropotkin for a bumbling old fool, so tangled in his own red tape he'd probably buried the request under a mountain of dispatches and reports. Damn! Damn! Damn! So it was to be another three months in this godforsaken hole. Varya Mihailovna was right, get your hopes up too high and crash!*

He only half listened to the others, stewing in his disappointment. They had turned the discussion to what Yankovlevich had brought to New Archangel, in response actually to Suverin's own question. The *City of Kursk* had brought the usual arms, ammunition, cloth, molasses, dry stores, *kvass*, vodka, cigars for Prishibeyev, tools and equipment for the blacksmith shop – a ratchet forge, a ninety-pound steel-faced anvil, bellows, hammers, tongs, tuyere irons – trinkets and junk for trading...

Suverin stared at his superiors. Luka Poplova and Prishibeyev were as delighted as children with new toys, all but jumping up and down and clapping their hands with each new disclosure.

He himself couldn't care a stale fig for any of it. *Damn Kropotkin! At this snail's rate, this luckless dog would be as old as Luka, as old as the colonel-general himself, by the time Headquarters got around to tossing him his bone!*

12

To add to his annoyance, and plunge him deeper into the private pit of his disappointment, the colonel promptly assigned him to work with Yankovlevich's first officer directing the peltry loading. The sun burned brightly, but was too weak to warm the frigid air to any appreciable degree, and the temperature continued to stubbornly resist rising as the morning wore on. Tramping about and barking orders on an empty stomach failed to improve Suverin's disposition. The wind funneling down from the Wrangells and the St. Elias Mountains wailed like an angry phantom, slamming against the vessel, rattling the yards and spars, and sending tinkling showers of ice down upon the decks and the crews transferring the bundles of furs from the quarter boats up over the gunwales down into the holds. Suverin swung his arms to chase the chill, his breath rolling out of him in a cloud, his teeth aching with the cold, his lips cracked and brittle as glass.

The cargo was in, the hatch covers were reset, and the men acknowledged their liberation from duty with an appreciative huzzah. Ten minutes past the hour of noon Suverin returned to the stockade and was informed by Corporal Zubov, still stomping at his post, that the colonel wished him to report to the main house.

The main house was a two-storey cabin located in the shadow of the northwest watchtower. The Poplovas occupied the four rooms which comprised the upper floor; the lower served as a combination dining and conference room. Suverin's knock was answered by Natasha Prishibeyev, a quiet, humorless, once-attractive woman with a seductive glint that leaped to life in her dark blue eyes when they met Suverin's own, and a full-lipped mouth that betrayed the presence of the fire, damped though it may have been, within. In the lieutenant's mental catalogue of conquests and possibilities Captain Prishibeyev's wife was listed under the heading of 'things to do before returning home'. On occasion, the hunger in the woman's eyes was pathetic to behold.

Greeting him with the others present, she smiled, lowered her eyes, and returned to the samovar and her tea. Suverin made his way to the stove, divesting himself of his cap and gloves and rubbing his hands briskly over the partially opened plate. The colonel, Captain Yankovlevich, and Prishibeyev hung over the conference table, absorbed in a large map. The Company governor, Yurii Kuskov, pale and wracked-looking, continuing in the grip of his illness, had deserted his bed to join them. Leaning on the table for support, he spared one hand long enough to wave a feeble greeting to Suverin. Varya sat in her rocker in the far corner alongside the samovar, attacking a hole in one of her husband's socks with a fishbone needle.

'Nikki, over here,' snapped the colonel, gesturing vigorously without lifting his eyes from the map.

It was, noted Suverin as he approached the table, the general territorial map of the Gulf of Alaska and the coastline threading down to Ketchikan. Supplementing it southward, its border folded underneath to enable it to join the lower edge at Ketchikan, was the map of the lower coast down as far as California. Luka sipped his tea and set his glass squarely over Ketchikan, holding one edge upon the other.

'Nikki,' he said soberly, 'you can forget about your transfer, something has come up that's going to be worth ten transfers to you, to all of us. Captain Yankovlevich here has brought us the goose that lays the golden eggs, orders from the Company. We are to mount an expedition with the aim of locating a site for a permanent fort . . .' His stubby finger traced the coastline southward, passing through Puget Sound, stopping beside Cape Disappointment at the mouth of the Columbia River. He encircled it. 'Somewhere in this area. Which will be just the beginning. The long-range plan calls for installations all the way down to California.'

'Holy saints!' exclaimed Suverin.

The others laughed, and the colonel threw a fatherly arm around Suverin's shoulder. 'So now Saint Petersburg doesn't look quite so inviting, eh? All that nonsensical intrigue, the rivalry, the hounds wagging their tails, barking, battling for the bone of royal favor from His Highness, the fickleness of the boyars' wives and daughters, the duplicity of senior officers...' The colonel turned to Captain Yankovlevich. 'He's ambitious, this one, he wants to be a captain at twenty-six, a colonel at thirty, general of all the armies by forty, eh, Nikki?'

'Sir...'

'I'm embarrassing you. Forgive me.' He hammered the map with his fingertip. 'But make no mistake, this is where the promotions are, where you'll be winning your stripes and stars. Here's where you can make yourself a hero.'

Suverin stared at the map, mesmerized by it, his thoughts inundated by the ambrosia of his ambition, his imagination leaping to life, his inner vision picturing himself leading his force into a clearing, planting the Imperial standard, the double-headed eagle fluttering from its staff.

'*I claim this land in the name of His Imperial Majesty, Alexander the First, Czar of all the Russias...*'

'Nikki...'

'Yes. Colonel.' Snapping his heels, Suverin stiffened to attention.

'What about the loading?'

'Completed, sir.'

'What about your precious transfer? You still wish to go through with it?'

'What transfer is that, sir?'

Luka burst into loud laughter, and Varya, still plying her needle, smiled at her favorite subaltern.

'Did I not promise you that the sealed dispatch case contained something for everybody?' continued the colonel. 'Not the least our esteemed associate Captain Prishibeyev here. That is, if he is able to unlock the *Saint Nicholas* from the ice by the first week in June. Eh, Grigory, what do you think?'

Captain Prishibeyev's pockmarked face blushed furiously. 'If the sun does not free her we'll blast her out with black powder. If that doesn't do the trick, I'll chop her out with axes!'

'If I may be so bold, sir,' began Suverin. 'Why not blast her out and get started right away?'

'Ah, the impulsiveness of youth. Business before heroics, Nikki,' replied the colonel. 'Besides, we will have to wait for the Californians to come and do their trading and leave.'

'How large a party do you intend to mount?' inquired Yurii Kuskov, blowing on his tea and sipping it.

'The Company is giving us very specific orders as to that.' Removing the contents of the parchment envelope delivered to him by Yankovlevich, Colonel Poplova flattened the papers on the map and, leafing through them to the third sheet, located what he was looking for. 'Twenty people, with you, Grigory, commanding at sea and Lieutenant Suverin on land. Seventeen men, among them four Aleuts, two Aleut women, and Mrs. Prishibeyev, of course.' Luka nodded toward Natasha, hovering about her samovar like a monk over his favorite monstrance.

'Why the two Aleut women?' inquired Suverin.

'Because the Company says so, Lieutenant.' Luka grinned, stirring his tea with his finger, tasting it with little semblance of pleasure, and setting it back down on Ketchikan. 'Follow me closely now. Saint Petersburg wishes us to start down the coast. Grigory, you're familiar with this area...'

'It's beautiful,' piped up Prishibeyev dolefully. 'The weather is lovely that time of year, fog and rain and rain and fog. And the woods are overrun by our friends the Tlingits.'

'Nevertheless,' continued the colonel, 'you will be trading as you go, at the Queen Charlotte Islands and all the way down to here, Vancouver Island. Nobody is asking you to risk your necks foolishly. Run along as close to the shore as the rocks permit; when you see totem poles showing above the trees, lay to and fire your falconet. They'll be watching you, they'll know what you're there for. They'll come out in their canoes bringing otter pelts. You'll trade the usual junk, and when they have nothing more to offer in exchange, you move on.'

'You say the permanent fort is to be built around the Columbia River?' interjected Suverin.

'That's correct,' the colonel replied.

'An excellent choice,' remarked Kuskov in his reedy voice. 'I have heard it said that the Indians are peaceful there, fishermen mainly. They are called Chinooks.'

'A welcome relief from these Tlingit devils,' commented Prishibeyev.

. 'It is said to be a lovely spot,' said Yankovlevich. 'A friend of mine, one Abrov, the master of the *Dogorska* out of Okotsk, stopped off there once. It is at the top of what the Yankees call the Willamette Valley. There is abundant wood, fresh water, and it is overrun with game. He says the salmon in the rivers are as big as tuna.'

'Break out the brandy, Varya, my buttercup!' roared Luka. 'We must toast this golden goose!'

Suverin's bitter disappointment seemed to dissolve like the froth from freshly poured soda water. Music swelled in his heart and thundered through him.

'I claim this land in the name of His Imperial Majesty, Alexander the First, Czar of all the Russias . . .'

13

Dawn had not yet broken over the Great Plains when the night guards posted outside the tight circle of wagons fired their flintlocks, rousing the camp. The fires of the previous night were coaxed back to life; breakfast – for the most part, bacon packed in barrels of bran to preserve it, or beef jerky – was produced to begin sizzling in skillets. Here and there were also to be seen a precious egg or two. They had been laid in Keys Landing and kept insulated from the dry, dusty air in barrels of cornmeal; eggs now twenty-one days old and nearly four hundred miles from the staging area. There was also bread and ever-present coffee made with river water, so strong one could practically chew it, according to Tawny. But at four in the morning, two gulps snapped her back to consciousness like a shot.

With the day's first meal consumed, the oxen were watered, fed, yoked, and hitched to the wagon tongues. Breaking the circle, the train began to form to resume the trek westward. As it did so, a dozen men sent up a mile-high cloud of dust as they rode out to hunt buffalo.

The sun was barely above the horizon beyond the Big Blue River at their backs when the column moved out, the slowly rolling line stretching nearly a mile in length. No small number of women and children walked alongside their families' wagons. Pausing to pick wildflowers or stroll by the sluggish waters of the North Platte nearby to the left, they were careful to keep pace with the train.

Boyd and Tawny at the reins of their wagon, which for the most part was loaded with necessities only, led the train. He studied the trail ahead, his face darkening with concern. The cloud of dust raised by the buffalo hunters had long since settled to earth behind them. Now, after three hours under a broiling sun climbing the cloudless blue sky, there was no sign of the hunters returning.

'Do you think they've run into trouble?' asked Tawny.

'Either that or they're well off the trail and having a hard time finding buffalo. Which could mean that they've already been herded out of the area.'

'Indians?' He nodded. 'Oh, Boyd...'

'Relax, darling. If we run into them we can deal with them.'

'If? You mean when, don't you?' She sighed, remembering the Osage back home, a few troublemakers in particular that her father had had to deal with, sending them galloping off ahead of a couple of well-aimed shots.

'The trouble is,' went on Boyd, 'if the buffalo are ridden off, most of the antelope will get nervous and run for cover. What we don't want to do is to start in slaughtering the oxen for meat this early in the game.' His tone softened as he patted her hand. 'But don't worry, the boys'll be back. It takes time to run down, kill, and butcher a big bull buffalo. And pack up his hide and tastier parts.'

'All things considered, we're doing well, though, aren't we?' she remarked. 'Yesterday twenty-two miles, today maybe even farther.'

Boyd angled his head, shrugging noncommittally. He glanced out over the landscape stretching to the north, littered with sagebrush and creosote bush.

'It's not these miles we have to worry about, it's those ahead.'

'The Rockies...'

84

At the bottom of Tawny's trunk inside the wagon lay copies of the rough maps brought back by the Lewis and Clark expedition. They were of little practical use to Boyd, but he had brought them along all the same. There were various reference points which could prove of value, particularly near the end of the journey. That expedition's route had carried them north by way of the Missouri River to a point only a few hundred miles below the as-yet-ill-defined Canadian border. They had wintered with the Mandan Indians before proceeding onward, turning directly west early in the spring of 1805. They had crossed the Rocky Mountains by way of the Nez Percé trail following the Clearwater all the way up to the Columbia River. From there they had descended the Coastal Ranges by canoe to eventually reach the Pacific, arriving there in the middle of November. Traveling for the most part by water, as they had elected to do, had added hundreds of miles to their journey.

Long before Tawny, Aunt Lydia, Emily, and Priscilla had even been invited to Marcy Rampling's wedding, Boyd had sat with other officers and employees of the Excelsior Fur Trading Company around their conference table, poring over Lewis and Clark's maps. Certain salient and incontrovertible facts had become clear to Boyd. These he had cited one by one; for the most part the others at the table had agreed with him.

Meriwether Lewis and William Clark's expedition had included twenty-three seasoned soldiers, three interpreters, and Clark's Negro slave, York. Poling a fifty-five-foot keelboat loaded with supplies and rowing pirogues, portaging when necessary over such an incredibly long distance, through such wild, uncharted country, had been more than arduous. Both men upon their return had described it as by far the most trying ordeal of their lives. As Clark had put it, it was as rugged, as exhausting, and as dangerous as being under continual fire for nearly two and a half years.

Clearly there was no way that an expedition which was to include inexperienced civilians and their women and children could hope to duplicate the two heroic explorers' astonishing feat.

85

So it was 'map your own route as you go, travel by land, live off it as much as possible, keep a tight column, keep peace in the family, post sentinels at night, stay clear of Indians if at all possible, and put your faith in the Almighty.'

Boyd Chevrier's assignment would have been difficult enough, all obstacles considered, but added to his shoulder load was the awareness that trusting *his* judgment, relying on *his* experience and leadership qualities, was the greenest group of people ever to set their tender feet west of the Mississippi River. And among them were George Latchford and his daughter Jenny. Happily, Latchford's son, George Junior, proved a quiet, self-effacing boy, nothing whatsoever like his loudmouthed, opinionated father. The same went for Mrs. Latchford and the couple's younger daughter, sixteen-year-old Susan. Nor, as far as that went, did Jenny Latchford resemble her father in his 'holier-than-all-you-thous' attitude toward his fellow migrants, his unbearable pomposity and endless faultfinding.

And yet Boyd would be the first to admit that for all Latchford's simplistic beliefs, his rock-ribbed confidence in God's protection against anything and anyone that might threaten them, in spite of the fact that he considered himself incapable of misjudgment or mistake, he did mean well. He was also civilized and respected by his people.

Daughter Jenny, on the other hand, was uncivilized, as wild as a runaway colt. The fact that she had her pretty green eyes on Boyd and couldn't care less who noticed it rankled Tawny as clutter-brained Marcy Rampling with all her nonsensical boasting and infantile ways never could. Until Jenny made her move, however, there was little Tawny could do about her, without risking Boyd's accusations of schoolgirl jealousy. Busy as he was from dawn until dark, he seemed totally unaware that Jenny was setting her poke bonnet for him. So Tawny was obliged to keep her tongue under control and her suspicions to herself.

'Whatever slows us up along the way, whatever detours we might be forced to take, we've got to make it to the South Pass before the middle of October,' said Boyd grimly.

'That early?'

'Winter comes very early to the Rockies. Some say it never really leaves from one year to the next. We can't build the protection we're going to need against wind and cold in a week, not with this collection of farmers and down-at-the-heel country gentlemen. I'd be willing to bet that half of them have never swung an axe in their lives.'

'How far is it to the South Pass?'

'About eight hundred miles.'

'But at the rate we're going that would only be forty or fifty days. June, July, August at the latest . . .'

'I'm sorry, darling. It may figure out that way at the rate we're moving now, but you've got to take into account how climbing the mountains will slow us down. There'll be days we'll be lucky to log as much as a mile. And even before we come within sight of them there'll be delays, unpredictable things that can happen. I can think of two right off – the Pawnee to the north and the Cheyenne to the south.'

He glanced down at the four oxen moving slowly along under their yokes, their rumps swinging from side to side, their ears flicking away annoying flies, their muzzles caked with dust, heads bowed, instincts committed to the drudgery of hauling the ten-by-four wagon loaded to its maximum weight of twenty-five hundred pounds.

'You woke up on the wrong side today, my love,' announced Tawny. 'Mr. Gloom. It's me, isn't it?'

Up came his head. He stared at her. 'What are you talking about?'

'You, Mr. Chevrier, are having second thoughts about dragging me along with you. Let's get one thing straight. You didn't drag, I volunteered, remember?' She displayed her wedding ring and grinned. 'For worse, so it will eventually be for better. It will be, darling. We'll make it over the highest mountains, we'll get to the Willamette Valley, we'll start our life in paradise. Your men will bring in absolute tons of furs, as Marcy would put it. And, darling, if the valley turns out to be half as lovely and bountiful as that fellow Whitfield claims, all of this and all that lies ahead will be worth it a hundred times over. So buck up, don't let Latchford or the Indians or anything else chew you inside. And for heaven's sakes, don't worry about me. I'm not made of glass, I can take whatever comes.' She paused and laughed.

'What's funny?'

'Speaking of Marcy. I can just picture her in that beautiful bed of hers in a specially built waggon pulled by ten golden oxen. She'd have all sorts of drapes hung up to keep out the dust, and the bouncing and jouncing would put her in a vile temper...'

'Marcy? Marcy who?'

Both laughed and hugged.

The hunters came back into the nooning stop, bringing with them slabs of buffalo meat, which were promptly given over to the women, who set about building fires of buffalo chips, weeds, and sagebrush. Some of the meat would be cooked on the spot; what remained would be cut into strips, dried in the sun atop the wagon bonnets, and preserved as jerky against the days ahead when the weather cooled and the buffalo, antelope, rabbit, sage hen, and other creatures deserted the landscape.

As the flames lowered and the chips and sticks glowed their hottest, skillets were heated and fat was rendered in them. The meat had been fairly apportioned among the migrants by Mrs. Latchford and four other women – the Council of Cooks, Tawny called them. Her own and Boyd's sirloin of buffalo steak she seared on both sides in the skillet; then she propped the skillet up on green sticks about five inches above the coals in order to cook the steak slowly, first one side, then the other. She made gravy, adding a tablespoon of flour to the skillet droppings, cooking it chocolate-brown. Stirring without pausing, she added a cup of milk from the Needhams' cow, the property of the family in the wagon behind theirs in the train. Bringing the milk to a boil and finishing the gravy, she salted and finished cooking the steak.

They had not 'borrowed' the milk. Boyd had announced even before starting out that on the trail 'borrowing' was the straightest route to squabbling. Many had disapproved of this view at the time, pointing out that borrowing was 'merely neighborliness in action'. He had replied that trading was just as neighborly, just as effective, and much less frequently cause for disagreement. For the Chevriers' daily cup of milk from the Needhams' cow Boyd exchanged a small quantity of gunpowder, of which he had brought along no fewer than eight kegs. In fact, it was powder, ball, and beaver and other traps that filled three quarters of the space in their wagon.

Mrs. Needham proved an enterprising sort. Any milk left over after the noon meal was poured into a bucket, which was then hung from the rear axle of the family's wagon, alongside the grease bucket. By sundown the constant shaking of the milk had converted it into butter.

Sitting by their fire eating, Boyd and Tawny were interrupted by Telford Ingersoll, who had gone out with the hunters earlier. Ever one to make on-the-spot judgments, Tawny did not like the look of him. He did not walk, he swaggered, strutted. He too obviously fancied himself cock of the walk, although he had no particular official responsibility or position with the train, not even being a member of the council of ten which represented the entire company.

He was inordinately proud of his strength, having already demonstrated it to the delight of the children, especially, back at Keys Landing, by twisting a horseshoe in a complete circle with his bare hands. Tawny had seen her own father do it a dozen times, drunk and sober, and was not impressed. Moreover, she did not like the way Ingersoll looked at her when he talked to Boyd. Approaching him, the big man excused himself with exaggerated politeness, seized Boyd by the elbow, and drew him aside out of earshot.

'Afraid I got some bad news, Mr. Chevrier. We seed redskins about fifteen mile up the way.'

'Hunters or a war party?'

'War. Scalps on their belts and well armed. Lances, bows, arrers, huntin' knives big as swords. Face painted blood-red an' white . . .'

'No rifles . . .'

'None we could see. We wasn't about to get close enough so's we could, what you might say, inspect 'em. Half an eye could spot the sun bouncing off their knives, though.'

'You're lucky they didn't come upon you butchering.'

'One was wearin' a full bonnet.'

'A subchief. It sounds like a Cheyenne war party. This is their territory.'

Ingersoll nodded. 'I figured the same. What do you 'spect they're up to?'

Boyd knelt and began drawing with his index finger on the ground. 'Here's the river; the Cheyenne have crossed it.' He drew a series of X's on the opposite side of the line. 'The Pawnees are scattered all along this area. They and the Cheyenne hate each other. The only friends the Cheyenne have are the Araphoes. And nobody's friends with the Pawnees. Everybody is afraid of them. From what you saw, it would seem the Cheyenne are putting on something of a show to stir things up. Maybe steal a few ponies. Damned rotten timing for us...'

'We seed 'em early on; they got to be long gone north,' said Ingersoll confidently.

'I doubt that.' Boyd indicated his crude drawing on the ground, in particular the location of the Pawnees. Then he erased his handiwork with the toe of his boot. 'They don't have that far to go before they're into Pawnee territory, and unless I'm wrong there'll be a lot more following them, probably with Araphoes. Our problem is we can't expect the Pawnees to just lay back and defend themselves. They'll be coming out screaming; they'll have a run-in or two to feel each other out...'

Boyd stood up. 'What I'm getting at is, we're heading straight through what could turn out to be their battlefield, this side or both sides of the river. Tomorrow we may find ourselves running a damned gauntlet!'

'We could lay over here a day or so.'

'That wouldn't solve anything. They could fight off and on for a month, for the rest of the summer. We might get through "off", but I'd hate to run into "on".'

Boyd got Ingersoll's solemn word that he would not mention what he and the others had seen. To do so would only raise panic among the migrants. Unfortunately, the man's promise came too late to be worth the breath it took to utter it. By the time he had begun moving down the train to caution his fellow hunters, the news had already gotten out.

Ten minutes later George Latchford and thirty or more others, including the ten members of the council, approached the Chevriers' wagon. With the exception of Latchford, all of their faces were grim.

Latchford lost no time taking over the podium. 'We understand that there are Indians up ahead, Mr. Chevrier.

I, myself, and the other members of the council and these gentlemen want to know what you propose to do to avoid meeting them. My own thought is that we should detour –'

'No detours, Mr. Latchford. That would mean crossing the river, taking the wheels off the wagons, and floating them over. Half of them aren't even caulked for floating. We'd be going to a lot of trouble and labor for nothing. We've got to be practical. We're not going to make it to the valley without running into some Indians.'

'Yes, but this bunch ahead is a war party,' said Robert Needham, leaning against his own wagon and eyeing Boyd with a look that announced that he was testing him for his resourcefulness. 'When we do meet them, what's your plan?'

'Mr. Needham, this is their land we're crossing, their hunting grounds, their battlegrounds, it may turn out. We've discussed Indians before and how we should best deal with them. Now I suggest we refresh our memories and go over a few of the guidelines.'

'You talk, we'll listen.'

'Thank you. As most of you are aware, Lewis and Clark had very little trouble with any of the tribes. They wintered with the Mandans in 1805. They made friends with the Shoshones; they ran into various other tribes. All the way to the Pacific and back to St. Louis, nearly four thousand miles, they lost only one man. And he died of bilious colic.'

'Yes,' interposed a tall bearded older man with one eye, the other lost in an ugly mass of flesh where its socket should have been. 'But they had a squaw with 'em. She done all their palavering for 'em. We ain't that lucky.'

'We have John Tibbets and Lionel Haggerty, two men experienced in dealing with Indians. Mountain men, resourceful, able, and intelligent. Both speak Sioux and other dialects. Besides, we, myself included, can always resort to sign language.

'To be frank, I'm not worrying about the Indians as much as I worry about how the people in this train will react to them when we do run into them. You've all had the same instructions; you know they're like children. We approach them peacefully or greet their approach peacefully, we make known our peaceful intentions right away, make it clear that

91

we're only passing through, we offer them gifts, and they'll leave us alone.'

As well-intentioned and sincere as this speech may have been, it failed to convince Needham, or, for that matter, the majority of those in the group, that they and their loved ones were not in imminent, grave danger. Boyd could understand their apprehension. Talking about Indians and their ways was one thing; meeting them face to face was something else.

'If we behave in a peaceful manner, if we don't start brandishing rifles and other weapons, if some damned fool doesn't accidentally get nervous, lose control, and fire a shot, we can get through wherever we find ourselves, just the way Lewis and Clark did. With help from the Indians, if need be.'

'You sound immensely confident,' said Latchford, staring at him with manifest lack of conviction in his pale blue eyes.

'I am. My wife and I are in this boat too, you know. You don't think I'd take unnecessary chances with her safety, do you? As I said before, they're like children. If any Indian comes up to you, your wife, or your child and touches you... fingers a necklace or a gaudy bit of cloth, anything. Even if he snatches it away, for God's sake let him. Chances are whoever is leading the party will make him give it back. Or offer to trade for it. Better still, if they really want something, other than your rifle or your scalp, give it up. It'll be worth it. It could save your life. You've all been told these things; John and Lionel have stressed them. Whatever you do, don't lose your heads. By this time tomorrow we should be well past the spot where the boys saw those Cheyenne. It's not us they're after; it's not us the Pawnees will be after. Look at it this way – you're home, you're in your house. Two strangers start a fight up the way. You stay out of it because it's none of your business. We're not about to get between these two tribes, because their problems are none of our business.

'We're just passing through.'

John Tibbets and Lionel Haggerty rode horses, and when the train resumed moving Boyd asked both men to ride alongside his wagon. His reasoning was that should they encounter any Indians, the three of them would be able to move out ahead of the others and deal with the situation. Tawny, he politely demanded, was to slip back inside the wagon at first sight of any feathers, whatever the tribe.

Keeping in mind that Boyd had enough to contend with without her adding to his burden, she agreed.

By some minor miracle, promptly attributed by Latchford to 'Divine intervention', the train covered nearly fourteen miles before darkness without sighting a single Indian. The forward point riders reported no sign of anyone.

It was not until three days later, with better than fifty miles of Cheyenne-Pawnee prospective battleground behind them, that they encountered their first Indians.

Sioux.

14

A scout came galloping back to report his discovery. It was late in the afternoon, the sun descending over the distant South Platte twisting northward to eventually join the North Platte, which the train had been following ever since leaving the Little Blue River.

Boyd hastily sent word back down the line, halting the wagons and calling up Tibbets and Haggerty. Moments later they came thundering up, saluting. For a split second Boyd felt as if he were back in the army, dreading the thought and dismissing their acknowledgment of his leadership with a wave.

'John, unhitch my mustang from the tailgate; the four of us are heading out. Indians – they appeared to be Sioux.'

Tibbets frowned. 'Wouldn't you know...' He did as ordered while Boyd handed the oxen reins to Tawny and, standing up on the seat, called back to Robert Needham in the wagon behind.

'Robert, you'll be in charge until we get back. Send down word that the train is to stay put. Don't turn a wheel until we get back.'

'Right, Boyd.'

Tawny threw her arms around his neck. 'Be careful, darling.'

'Don't worry. Just hand me some of that calico and a couple strings of those glass beads hanging up there behind your head. We're going to cheap-buy our way through this one. Relax, it was bound to come sooner or later. All I can say is God bless Lewis and Clark for bringing back all their best tricks of the trekking trade.'

Tibbets brought up Boyd's horse, and seconds later away galloped the four men, including the scout who had returned with word of the sighting. The train brought to a standstill, the drivers and their families got down and began milling about in small groups. Unable to stand the suspense of sitting staring after the now-vanished four riders, Tawny also got down and wandered down by the riverbank. She found her way into a dense thicket of sandbar willow trees, their short, slender, purplish-red branches intertwining at the ends, so closely were the trees bunched. It was cool in amongst them, out of the sun and sultry air. Cool and private and fragrant with the odor of the tiny yellow flowers that turned the branch ends into yellow-and-green woolly caterpillars. She picked one twisting it like a daisy, rapidly, loosening the flowers.

She could hear the river burbling along, although she would have had to push branches aside to actually see it, so dense was the thicket.

Then suddenly, without warning, a man stepped from behind one of the larger trees directly in front of her. Telford Ingersoll. His huge body was bared to the waist as usual, to exhibit his chest and powerful arms to those women and children among the emigrants who were impressed by such a display. His boots were covered six inches up from the heels with mud, as if he had been wading near the bank. His baggy trousers were filthy. They had not, she decided, been washed since the train had left Keys Landing. Nor had their owner.

But it wasn't his body, his trousers, or his boots that caught and held her eyes. It was his eyes, dark blue and rapidly glazing with a lust that chilled her to the bone. He reached out for her, but she shrank from him.

'Don't you dare touch me...'

'Here now, *Mrs.* Chevrier, is that any way fer friends to talk to each other?'

'You're no friend of ours, *Mr.* Ingersoll.'

'I don't want to be no friend o' "ours", just yours. Goddam me for an Injun but you are a beauty! Your face, your skin...' Out darted his hand a second time, seizing a fistful of her high-collared cotton dress and pulling her to him. At the same time, his other hand began loosening his belt, undoing the front of his trousers.

'One sound, beautiful lady, one whisper and I'll snap your neck and toss you in the drink. They'll all think you slipped, fell in, and drowneded...'

'Not with a broken neck.'

He shrugged. 'So I don't break your neck; I just holt you under the water until you stop breathing. The bank's muddy, slippery as a fish. You could tumble in easy...'

He had been drinking. The rum on his breath brought back the horrifying memory of that night in Matthews' Inn eons earlier: the night of the seemingly innocent offer to light her candle, the stranger in the doorway smiling in friendly fashion. And the hideous nightmare that had followed. Her thoughts rushing back to it, she could almost feel the pain, the burning humiliation.

'Don't do it, Ingersoll. My husband will kill you.'

'Your husband is ten miles away, likely getting scalped with the rest o' them jackasses. Besides, you're too good fer him, much too. You need a real man.'

Quickly his hand covered her mouth, clamping so tightly, the edge of it blocking her nostrils, she could not catch her breath. She struggled to free herself, wrenching one way then the other, but he was so strong, unbelievably strong, his arms like steel bands holding her so tightly she feared he would break every rib and snap her spine as well.

Now he eased her slowly down to the ground upon a thin carpet of fallen leaves dotted here and there with the willows' yellow flowers. One hand still over her mouth, he lifted her skirt with the other, wedging himself between her legs, her quivering thighs.

He began to rape her, a lascivious leer twisting his homely bearded features. As she had that night at the inn, she gave

95

up her useless struggling and tried with all the strength of will she could muster to block out the pain. But she was unable to. As agonizing as it was, the harrowing thought that crossed her mind was even worse.

He had been drinking heavily, the stench of him made that evident; but he was not drunk. And he was thinking clearly. What was in his mind she could well imagine. When he was done with her, when he had spent himself, when his lust was appeased, he would make good his threat to drown her. He had no choice but to do so. Were he to let her go, he would be signing his death warrant.

Once more she began to struggle to dislodge his member, to work her slender body out from under his. But each time he thrust she grew weaker and weaker, dizzy, the indescribable pain bringing nausea. Pounding his face with her little fists did not even cause him to blink, let alone defend himself with his free hand. He wasn't human, he wasn't flesh and blood and bone. He was stone, with the strength, the weight, and the insensitivity of granite. His huge body pinning her to the ground made it impossible for her to move anything but her arms. And flailing away at his face and neck only seemed to increase his insatiable lust.

In the midst of his ravaging her he began to laugh, chiding her for her feeble efforts to fight back. After what seemed hours he jerked free of her, pulling himself back up on his knees and for the first time removing his hand from her mouth.

'Now you can yell and scream if you dare. Go ahead, I wants to hear you.'

'Why don't you kill me and get it over with, you filthy animal! Disgusting pig!'

'Ah, but better inside you than that molly-coddle husband o' yourn. Besides, don' be in such a hurry; we're just gittin' started here...'

The last word was scarcely out of his mouth when from behind him, a heavy stick came crashing down, striking him squarely on top of the head. Groaning, his eyes rolling up in their sockets, he fell to one side, unconscious.

To reveal George Latchford standing looking down, the stick still in his hand, his eyes narrowed, his face frowning in disapproval.

'In heaven's name, woman, do cover yourself. Such an unseemly spectacle I warrant I've never seen before. For shame, woman, for shame!'

15

Boyd, Tibbets, Haggerty, and the scout came galloping back all smiles. They had dealt with a Sioux hunting party that had wandered far to the south of their tribe's hunting grounds and were surprised at the appearance of white men, whom ostensibly not one of their number had ever seen before. And they were grateful for the gifts of beads and calico.

Jumping down from his well-lathered horse, Boyd called to Tawny, assuming that she was inside the wagon. But it was Robert Needham who stuck his grizzled gray head out from under his own wagon's bonnet in response.

'She's in here, Boyd. I'm desperate sorry to have to be the one to tell you, but there's been trouble.'

A place had been cleared for Tawny in the wagon bed among the Needhams' belongings. She lay covered up to the neck under a sheet, her face almost as white as it and contorted with pain. Taking both the Needham youngsters by the hands, Mrs. Needham withdrew, marching the boy and girl off toward the river.

'Darling,' whispered Tawny feebly. 'You're all right. I was ... worried so ...'

Vaulting the tailgate, he knelt beside her, taking her hands in his own.

'Her mouth, it's all bruised. Her hair's a mess,' he called back over his shoulder to Needham. 'What happened? Who did this?'

'She's going to be all right,' said Needham crisply, striving for assurance in his tone. He stood at the tailgate, then leaned over it with his forearms. 'Doc Whitelaw's already looked her over. She's in pain –'

'*What the hell happened!*' roared Boyd, cutting him off.

'She...' Needham colored and hung his head like a penitent schoolboy. 'She was taken advantage of. Down in the trees by the river.'

'You mean raped!' snapped Boyd. Suddenly he was livid with rage. 'Who? Tell me his name! *Who?*'

'I don't suppose there's any point in beatin' about the bush. It was the big feller, Ingersoll.'

'Ingersoll. The stinking bastard, I'll kill him for this!'

'Boyd darling,' whispered Tawny. She tried to shift to a more comfortable position under the sheet, but the effort brought pain. Wincing, she drew her breath in sharply between clenched teeth. Bending, he kissed her tenderly, framing her tortured face between his hands, suddenly seized himself by a frustration he had never felt the like of before.

'Rest easy, my darling.'

'She's going to be all right. The doc says so...'

Boyd spun about. 'Get him back here. Fast as you can. I want him to stay with her. I got things to do.' Kissing Tawny one last time, he climbed back down. 'I won't be long, Robert.'

'Now hold on, Boyd, don't be goin' off half cocked!'

Boyd never heard a word. He strode down the train, all eyes fastened on him, some filled with pity, others quizzical, still others unable to look at him, staring, then tearing their eyes away.

'Ingersoll! *Ingersoll!*'

An eerie stillness ran down the length of the train, the emigrants standing and sitting upon their drivers' seats as stiffly as a stand of oak trees. Then a sound broke the silence, the thumping of hooves picking up speed on the far side of the line. Boyd swore and ran to the nearest horse, a powerful-looking bay stallion tied to the side of a wagon.

'Here,' barked a man standing alongside it, 'you can't –'

Boyd ignored him, freed the animal's reins from their hook, threw himself up on its back, and raced off.

Behind him at the head of the line, where Tawny lay still and in unabating pain, Robert Needham stepped to the other side of the train in time to catch sight of Boyd heeling the stallion, cutting between the wagons, and picking up the

98

chase after the big man astride his roan mare kicking up dust half a mile ahead.

'Get him, Boyd, get him and break his back,' said Needham to himself.

The pursuit over the level ground between shrubs and bushes went at a furious pace. Boyd was well over six feet, broad-shouldered and strong, but Telford Ingersoll was a young giant: taller, broader, and outweighing him by better than forty pounds; from neck to calves all sinew and strength. But Boyd had taken a horse fully sixteen hands tall, an extraordinarily powerful mount with a stride that seemed to roll the ball of the world under his hooves with astonishing ease and swiftness. Filling his great lungs with the hot dry air, he charged ahead speedily, shortening the distance gained by Ingersoll on his smaller, shorter-striding mare.

Within fifty yards, realizing that Boyd was quickly catching up with him, Ingersoll drew his double-barreled flintlock pistol and fired one shot, the ball whistling ominously by Boyd's right shoulder. One shot only, saving the second one for when his pursuer closed the gap. Boyd was unarmed, save for the knife in his belt, having in his haste left his rifle leaning against the tailgate of Needham's wagon, forsaking all thought of it in running down the train seeking the rapist.

The man who had raped his wife! Man? Ingersoll was nothing like a man; he doubtless, thought Boyd, had a long record of attacks on defenseless women. The cowardly bastard was in love with himself, with his size, his strength; it mattered not that he was homely as sin and as sinister-looking at times as a cornered rattler. Strutting about bare to the waist, his chest as big as a barrel, muscles rippling. Women looked at him with admiring eyes, children oohed and aahed, feeding his already overfed ego. Tawny had thought him disgusting, had said so more than once to Boyd. Which was undoubtedly the key to this whole loathsome affair. Had she not looked upon him with unconcealable disdain, had she fallen in with the rest of his 'admirers', perhaps she wouldn't have presented the lure of conquest which she unquestionably, albeit unconsciously, had.

99

All this conjecture sped through Boyd's mind as he heeled his horse and continued to narrow the distance separating them. Ingersoll had one ball left. So be it. He'd have to get him in the head or heart to kill him instantly. He, Boyd, would take that chance, even close up. It wasn't a case of avenging Tawny's merciless abuse only: it was to erase the menace of Ingersoll's presence among civilized people forever, for the protection of all the Tawnys to come.

Catch him. Kill him. And catch him he did, whirling around an obstructing clump of sage-brush and coming within ten yards of the speedily tiring mare overloaded with Ingersoll's bulk. Hearing hooves coming up behind him, the big man threw a quick glance over his shoulder, glaring at the sight of Boyd, bringing his pistol around to ready his second and last shot. As he aimed, Boyd dropped, throwing his body down the left side of the stallion, Comanche-style, bringing his face flush against the animal's muzzle. The pistol roared, the shot whizzing under the horse's head, creasing the top of Boyd's left shoulder. Scarlet striped the gray cotton cloth like a slender epaulet sewn front to back over his shoulder as he righted himself. It stung like a branding iron, but fortunately missed bone by a hair. Had it shattered it, it would have rendered his arm useless.

Hammering the stallion's belly with his heels, he caught up to his adversary, riding side by side. Ingersoll struck out at him, his left hand gripping the barrel of his empty pistol. But the distance between them was too wide. Fear filled the bigger man's eyes at the sight of the steely determination in Boyd's own.

Suddenly, as Boyd moved slightly ahead, intent on veering into the big man's mare, sending her to one side to throw her off stride and slow her, Ingersoll, anticipating his move, pulled sharply right.

But too sharply. The mare stumbled, whinnying, and threw him heavily to the ground.

Boyd reined up swiftly. The fall could have broken Ingersoll's shoulder, coming down as hard as he had. Which would have ended the contest then and there. But Boyd had no such luck. No sooner had he himself pulled up and stopped, was down, spinning about and starting for the bigger man, than Ingersoll was up on his feet, cursing, coming at him. All trace of fear had vanished from his face, replaced by a confident smile. Confidence in the fact that now it was to be hand to hand.

Rather, knife to knife. Both jerked their blades from their belts and began circling slowly. Not a word passed between them, until Ingersoll spoke:

'You got this all wrong, soldier boy, you know that...'

Boyd played deaf. It was an old army trick. In hand to hand, if you said nothing it almost always tended to unnerve your opponent. The more he talked, the more he wanted response. And when none was forthcoming it unsettled him.

'It was her, not me. I swear. She tolt me straight out she was headin' down for that thicket. I swear by all that's holy she did.'

They continued circling, tightening the perimeter, drawing closer to each other, the sunlight bouncing off their blades, the air suddenly still, the heat rising from the barren ground and descending from above enveloping them in invisible waves. The crease across Boyd's shoulder stung furiously, but he ignored it.

'Man to man, I ask you,' went on Ingersoll, his voice higher now, his nervousness obviously increasing. 'Why would she tell me she was headin' down thataway if she didn't want me taggin' along? I couldn' hep myself, honest to Gawd. She just stood there smilin' at me, flauntin' her body, workin' her mouth so, drillin' me with them eyes o' hers, beggin' for it. It didn' hurt her, not bad. She drove me to it, she did, I swear. I couldn' hep myself...'

He stopped flatfooted and, whirling like a dervish, a move calculated to catch Boyd off guard, faced him again and lunged, knife forward in the grip of both hands. There was no more than four feet separating the two, and Boyd was hard put to react in time to sidestep the thrust. But he managed to, the point of the oncoming knife catching the side of his shirt, ripping it slightly, missing his rib cage by less than an inch.

They resumed circling, knives held below their respective waists pointing upward. Thrust and withdrawal, thrust and withdrawal, Ingersoll cursing each time he missed. Boyd had yet to utter a word; his heart was so filled with hatred for the giant facing him he could feel it climbing into his throat, all but choking him. In his mind's eye he saw Tawny lying in Needham's wagon, barely able to speak, forcing a reassuring smile for his benefit, wincing, moaning with pain. Inflicted by this overgrown bastard!

God, how he wished he could kill him ten times over, each time more painfully than the last!

Hooves hammering rapidly became audible in the distance, coming from the direction of the train. Fellow migrants coming to interfere, to stop the two of them before death struck one or the other. They'd arrive too late, reflected Boyd determinedly; they'd never get Ingersoll off this hook. Not in the next few moments, not ever!

The sound of the oncoming horses caught Ingersoll's ear; instinctively he turned his head in that direction. Boyd threw himself forward, but slipped on a stone partially buried in the ground. His aim went awry: instead of finding Ingersoll's belly, his blade struck the other's knife, sending it clattering to the ground. The big man cursed, bending to retrieve it. But Boyd was too fast for him. The advantage seized, he lunged forward, at the same time bringing up his right knee sharply, catching Ingersoll under the chin, snapping him straight, staggering him. Boyd then threw his right leg between the other's knee and crooked it, pulling him down. Like a shot he was down on top of him, his knife poised above Ingersoll's face.

'Move an inch and I'll drive it through your skull!' he snapped.

Behind them the men had arrived and were dismounting, shouting at Boyd as they came, trying to dissuade him from killing Ingersoll. His attention wavered. Ingersoll took quick advantage. Batting Boyd's knife hand to one side with his forearm, he rolled him over, stretching his full weight on top of him, his huge hands finding his throat, gripping, tightening. Boyd felt his windpipe about to shatter; then strong hands laid hold of the big man and pulled him off, while others grasped his arms, freeing his hold just in time...

But, lifted erect, Ingersoll somehow managed to free himself from the others' grasp, bend, and recover his knife. Seeing this, they backed away. He came at Boyd. Boyd ducked under the thrust coming straight at his throat and, wrenching to one side, brought both fists hammering down on the back of the crouching Ingersoll's neck. Down on his knees he dropped. Heavily. So heavily his momentum carried him all the way.

He lay flat, immobile. Slowly the others gathered around him. Two men knelt and rolled him over. Somehow, between charging at Boyd's throat and striking the ground, his knife had turned over in his grip. The top of the hilt gleamed in the sun atop his fist. The blade was buried in his belly.

Kicking his left leg once, straightening it, he groaned, his pupils climbed into his head, disclosing the whites of his eyes, and he died.

' "An eye for an eye, a tooth for a tooth",' said a voice behind Boyd. 'Get that knife outta his gut, load him on his horse, and let's head back.'

16

So dreadfully had Tawny been abused, it was fully a week before the bruises and the pain began to disappear, before she could get up under her own power and walk. Even into the second week Boyd was obliged to help her climb into the driver's seat, yielding to her insistence that she sit beside him. She did not talk about her ordeal; it was as if she had summarily dismissed it from her mind. Nor was she curious as to how Ingersoll had died, although Boyd explained what had happened.

The big man had been buried on the trail before the train got under way the morning following his death. One of the two ministers in the company read a brief eulogy of his own devising, words to the effect that in every man born of woman there is lust and that that lust must be kept locked in one's heart. He stated further that an honorable woman is defenseless against it. And he quoted from chapter ten, verse nine of Proverbs:

' "He that walketh uprightly walketh surely; but he that

perverteth his ways shall be known."

'May the Lord in Heaven forgive this man his sin, the child of his lust. Praise the Lord and honor him.'

Neither Boyd nor Tawny nor the Needhams, nor either John Tibbets or Lionel Haggerty, attended the funeral. Tawny was in no condition to do so; the Needhams were too sympathetic to summon up any semblance of forgiveness for Ingersoll and in Mrs. Needham's words would have been hypocrites to attend. Boyd remained at Tawny's side. Other families who did attend came to Boyd later to privately admit that it was nothing more than Christian charity that had compelled them to do so. Virtually everyone's sympathies were with Tawny.

Curiously, George Latchford, despite having saved Tawny's life, was not all that sympathetic toward her. Any compassion on his part seemed to be equally divided between the rapist and his victim.

Following Ingersoll's interment, when the train began moving, Boyd had left Tawny's side to go back to Latchford to thank the man for saving her life. The two did not like each other, but that factor, underlying practically all their conversations and apparent to everyone in the train, had no part in this particular meeting. Boyd made no effort to conceal his immense gratitude, and Latchford accepted it and his compliments graciously.

The older man was clearly taken with himself for having had the presence of mind to follow Ingersoll into the thicket after Tawny had gone in earlier, and did not hesitate to compliment himself. This display of ego completed, he turned abruptly solemn:

'I am deeply sorry for Mrs. Chevrier, her suffering and humiliation,' he said slowly, in a manner that always seems to suggest that the speaker is making up his speech as he goes along.

'She owes you her life,' said Boyd quietly. 'I owe you her life. Again, I thank you, sir, for both of us, and God bless you.'

Latchford stiffened perceptibly. 'You are another matter, sir.'

'I don't understand.'

They had been walking along beside Latchford's wagon,

Lionel Haggerty driving Boyd's at the head of the train. The rumble of wheels effectively drowned out Latchford and Boyd's conversation. This was to prove fortunate for both men.

'You have killed a man, sir,' said Latchford.

'I only wish I had. As it turned out, as you know, he killed himself.'

Shock seized the other's features. 'You say you only wish you had? Then you subscribe to what Thomas Higgins said back there where you and Ingersoll fought – "an eye for an eye ..."'

'Mr. Latchford, I, that is my wife and I, are more indebted to you than either of us to any man in this world. I know how you feel about violence and I respect your point of view. The fact remains, he nearly killed her. He fully intended to. Killing was in his heart, and yes, it was in mine.'

'Ah, but there's a difference ...'

'I don't see ...'

'He's dead, Mrs. Chevrier is alive and will no doubt soon be perfectly right and healthy again.'

'We hope. May I ask you a question?'

'Do so.' Latchford produced a quid of tobacco, offered it to Boyd, who politely declined, then bit off a generous piece for himself and began chewing.

Boyd went on. 'When you hit Ingersoll with that stick –'

'I would call it a club; it was at least two inches thick.'

'What I'm getting at is, you could have killed him. My question is, did you intend to?'

Latchford reflected on this for a moment, screwing his face up in thought, shifting his chew from one cheek to the other.

'In all honesty, I can't say that I recall.' He spat. 'It was instinctive, you see.'

'Of course. But in your heart did you feel as if you wanted to kill him? Had to?'

'My only thought was to stop his brutal and loathsome attack then and there. No, now that I think about it, killing never entered my mind.'

'If it had been Mrs. Latchford he was attacking, would it have entered your mind then?'

'It wasn't Mrs. Latchford, thank the good Lord. It was

105

your wife.' Again he spat, eyeing him archly. 'Who I'm sure you'll acknowledge happens to be a very beautiful woman. Beautiful women are more often than not seductive, in my view. One can only pray that they are as well virtuous. Let us remember Proverbs, chapter twelve, verse four: "A virtuous woman is a crown to her husband: but she that maketh ashamed *is* as rottenness in his bones."'

Fury welled up inside Boyd. 'Are you trying to say that she enticed that bastard? Lured him into that thicket? That she's at fault, not him? Are you actually –'

'I make no judgment. But lest we forget, lust is like the common cold, too easily contracted and shared. After all, sir, we never did get Ingersoll's version of what happened, did we?'

'*You dare ask that!*'

'Please, there's no need to raise your voice.'

'You saw what happened; you were the only one who did!'

'I did not see what preceded –'

'I don't believe my ears. You're a filthy-minded prig, do you know that, mister? We've had our differences, you and I, ever since Keys Landing. Your nose is out of joint because I drive the lead wagon and you don't. That's really what eats you up inside, isn't it? But for you to suggest this – this blasphemy –'

'I can only suggest, sir, that we terminate this discussion here and now. Good day to you, Mr. Chevrier. And my compliments and best wishes for a speedy recovery to Mrs. Chevrier.'

Again he chewed and spat. Turning on his heel, he hurried off, leaving Boyd shaking, suddenly livid. The deeper the man's words sank in, the more he shook. The sanctimonious son of a bitch! The heartless stiff-necked prude!

By the time he got back to the Needhams' wagon, where Tawny lay dozing, Boyd had managed to get a grip on himself. Nevertheless, his disgust with Latchford, his deepening hatred for the man, continued to boil inside him.

Mr. George Latchford, he mused, had better mind his step and where he spat his foul tobacco juice, not because of his twisted interpretation of recent events, but rather his overall attitude in general.

He and his Proverbs. Boyd was no less God-fearing than any other man, but he could just picture Latchford shaking the Good Book under some Cheyenne chief's nose, with two hundred warriors, lances raised or arrows fitted to bowstrings, aimed straight at the company. Give Latchford rope enough and he would get the lot of them slaughtered, and die convinced that it was God's will!

Among his other eccentricities, the man staunchly refused to bear arms. He boasted that he had never owned rifle or pistol, had never fired one and had no intention of doing so for as long as he lived. Boyd laughed inwardly, despite his anger: as long as Latchford lived could be shorter than the man imagined, should he persist with that attitude out in this neck of nowhere. The trouble was that he forbade his son, his whole family, to bear arms. Why he'd seen fit to desert the civilized confines of his native Ohio to drive through hostile territory clear to the Willamette Valley was more than Boyd could fathom. But then, the man's whole philosophy of life was beyond him.

The ensuing three weeks dragged by without incident. Tawny recovered completely; the sun increased its ferocity; a baby girl was born; six oxen died; the dry air of the Plains shrank the wooden wheels and their spokes, and tire irons dropped off by the score. The two blacksmiths in the company worked day and night repairing the damage. Loosened tires were heated red-hot and reset on their rims. As they cooled, they shrank and fit snugly.

On a Monday morning early in July, shortly after breakfast the weather changed abruptly. In twenty minutes the bright blue skies turned gray, clouds rolling in swiftly, blackening, obscuring the sun, and very shortly it began to rain. Within ten minutes it was teeming, as if the gods had seized the river, plucked it full length from its bed, and turned it upside down upon that train.

The wagon bonnets were fashioned of heavy cotton twill, or in rare cases sailcloth; every inch was waterproofed with linseed oil. Held in place by hickory bows set two to three feet apart, the bonnets were well supported. But the downpour was ferocious, and here and there cloth gave way, weakened as it was by the merciless heat pouring down upon it for the past two months. Water poured into the wagons, collecting in the sunken beds, ruining food, drenching clothing and bedclothes, and destroying such precious items as clocks and musical instruments covered too late by their frantic owners.

The deluge persisted for three days straight without letup. Fortunately for Boyd and Tawny, the Needhams, and most of the other families, their wagon bonnets proved impenetrable and their belongings escaped damage.

Their spirits, however, were thoroughly dampened. Fires could not be built, so food had to be eaten cold. The rain slowed the oxen to a pace an old man walking could easily have doubled. However, the downpour did keep the dust down and out of the beasts' nostrils and throats.

But when at last it stopped and the sun reappeared, the river had risen to within inches of overflowing its banks, and the entire landscape, including the trail stretching ahead, had become a quagmire. With the oxen straining under the whip and strong men putting their shoulders to bogged-down wheels, wagon after wagon was freed from the grip of the mud and slowly rolled on.

It took the sun nearly two full days to dry up the land. Tawny had never known such extremes in the weather – from broiling sun to absolute buckets of rain, and back to heat that penetrated every pore and threatened to cook one inside out.

The Chevriers and the Latchfords – all the Latchfords, not excepting the fetching Jenny – discreetly kept their distance from one another. But gossip persistently made its way back up to the Needhams and eventually Boyd that Latchford was growing more deeply dissatisfied with 'young Chevrier's leadership.' The older man seemed incapable of seeing anything but the black side of everything. He was also a born instigator. If Boyd ordered the train one degree on the compass to the northwest, if he suggested that a continuing diet of buffalo meat was not the most digestible nourishment in spite of its succulent taste, if he insisted on rounding the wagons into their night circle as soon as the sun went down instead of pressing onward for another half hour, Latchford would be the first to question his decision – and he would spread his feelings among the others. Tawny suggested to Boyd that the root of the man's problem was his impatience. He had led his people out from the East only to yield his leadership to a man half his age. Once the migrants reached their destination, leadership would pass from Boyd's hands back into his. Boyd would content himself with directing trapping and trading operations; Latchford would be the community leader. As far as that went, Boyd would be more than happy to turn over responsibility for the others' welfare to Latchford, when the time came. Though he would have preferred Robert Needham.

But until that time came he, Boyd, would continue in charge. If disaster caught up with them, if the expedition failed to reach the valley intact, there would be no community. This was a reality that, stomach it or not, Latchford had to swallow. So all he actually could do at present was continue to carp and quibble; he could not countermand Boyd's orders.

There was, nevertheless, nothing in the agreement made between the Excelsior Fur Trading Company and Latchford and his people that said that their temporary alliance could not be dissolved at any time. If, and Boyd was well aware of this, Latchford were to be successful in persuading his followers that Boyd was unfit to lead, they, as a group, could determine an alternate route to their destination and leave Boyd, Tawny, Tibbets, Haggerty, the Needhams, and the few other families since become disillusioned with Latchford and no longer under his spell to stick to the present route.

In Tawny's view, in spite of their loyalty toward Latchford, most of the migrants had faith in Boyd's ability to lead them, and realized that, deprived of his leadership, they would be no match for the difficulties which lay ahead, primarily the Indians.

According to Boyd's calculations, which both Tibbets and Haggerty agreed with, having reached the fork of the North and South Platte rivers, within sight of the Laramie Mountains, they were now only slightly more than three hundred miles from the South Pass. It was the tenth of August. Soon now, as they left the edge of the Great Plains and began to climb, the going would get rougher and rougher with each passing day. No longer would they be able to count on a hundred miles plus a week on average. Once through the Laramies, past Independence Rock and the Ice Slough near the Sweetwater River, it would be less than fifty miles to the South Pass. But each mile up into the Laramies would be harder to make than the one preceding it. If the weather turned foul again they'd scarcely be able to move. Mindful of this, mindful also that over the easiest part of the trail they had come a few miles under halfway in fourteen weeks, Boyd reached a decision – one which, as things turned out, was to have a devastating effect upon the train.

On the night of the tenth of August, with the wagons pulled up in their customary tight circle, the sentinels posted, and the cooking fires bright, Boyd summoned the council, Tibbets and Haggerty, and a handful of the other men and revealed his plan.

Following his instructions, Tawny had drawn a rough map of the trail up into the Laramies and beyond to the South Pass. He laid the map out on the ground where the others could examine it, then went on to explain his changed thinking.

'If we were to keep going to the end of this month and then through most of September we would stand an excellent chance of reaching the South Pass, here.' He indicated. 'Saying all goes well. Our progress would be very slow, slower every day as the trail gradually rises, narrows, doubles back. There will be places we may even have to chip away solid rock to get the wagons through. Either that or empty them, take off hoops and bonnets and wheels, and slip them through sideways, portage them, you might say. Then refit and reload them and continue on our way. All of which would take a great deal of time.

'Up where we're presumably planning to winter there's plenty of yellow pine and spruce fir. We can build sturdy houses, and with all the buffalo jerky and salted-down antelope meat and our dry food we could wait out the worst of the winter and come late May start out again, rested. But summer through where we're heading, up along the Snake River, before we pass the Malheur and John Day rivers, only lasts six or seven weeks.'

110

Everyone, even Latchford, stared at him, listening intently.

'We're all tired, not to mention the oxen, who'll have to do some very heavy hauling up, up, and up day in, day out until we get to the South Pass.'

'They're gonna start dropping like mayflies at dusk,' interposed Lionel Haggerty. 'And if worse comes to worst we could wind up with eight of us pulling each wagon. Oh, ox meat makes for good eating, but they're a darned sight more valuable to us on the hoof.'

'What you're saying is we stop right here,' said Robert Needham. 'We don't even start up into the mountains.'

'Exactly,' said Boyd, looking around at the semicircle looking at him.

'But we're not even halfway,' sputtered Latchford. 'You just said.'

Boyd nodded. The glow of the campfire illuminating the map rosied his face, as it did all the others, but there were no rosy smiles, only disappointed looks and low muttering.

Latchford fixed Boyd with a questioning look. 'If we were to stop here, and I for one am not convinced it would be the smartest thing we could do, what in heaven's name would we use for timber to build winter homes? What would you have us do, hunker down under the sagebrush?'

'There's plenty of scrub oak, piñon, and juniper at the base of the mountains. We could cut it down and build on the spots we've cleared, as close to the base as possible. That way, if we're positioned right, the mountains would protect us from the north wind.

'There isn't a man, woman, or child among us who'd turn down a chance to rest for a week or so, who isn't sick and tired of rolling. And look at your oxen – they're showing more ribs every day, even though they've plenty to eat. Then too, there's always the chance we might not even make it to the South Pass by the end of September. If I had my druthers, I'd want to be there long before that.'

To Boyd's elation, not to mention his relief, his suggestion met with almost universal approval. Even George Latchford saw the good sense of settling down at the base of the mountains to wait out winter's wrath.

But, like all plans, good, excellent, even inspired, Boyd's contained a hidden flaw. By a combination of bald-faced luck and timing the train had yet to encounter any hostile Indians in force. But, like the grains of sand spilling into the bottom of an hourglass, this good fortune was about to run out on them.

They began building, and eight days later, at day's end, the wagons drawn up into their circle under a nearly full moon, the heavens studded with stars as far as the eye could see, with a soft, cooling breeze descending the peaks directly ahead, the emigrants were gathered about their fires relaxing, listening to the whine of two fiddles playing in practiced unison, watching Edgar Thompson, farmer and father of eight, execute a very professional clog, clapping in rhythm for him, applauding at the end of the performance enthusiastically, when suddenly the sound of hooves coming from the north reached everyone's ears.

Indians! Teton Sioux, a party of eight led by one Black Bear Paw, a full chief who was probably sixty and looked closer to eighty, his breechclout draped between his skinny legs, his sunken chest decorated with a necklace of bear claws, his coal-black hair pulled back in twin braids below his war bonnet, his face so incredibly wrinkled the flesh looked as if it had been bunched tightly by somebody's grip.

Boyd, Tibbets, and Haggerty rode out to meet him, joining the two sentinels who had accompanied them to the circle. Dismounting, Chief Black Bear Paw lost no time in getting to the point. He had buffalo robes to trade.

'As many as the round stones in the river bottom. Enough to fill your wagons, every one.'

Marvelous, reflected Boyd, but for the fact that they had neither need for nor room to carry any more buffalo robes. On the trail they'd already collected all they'd need.

The chief's reaction to this response was anything but diplomatic. He insisted loudly that he had hides in abundance. Maybe, decided Boyd, he did, maybe he did not. He tried to read the wily mind behind Black Bear Paw's squinting eyes. Still, whether he was bluffing or not was beside the point. Working cleverly with words and signs and extraordinary patience, Haggerty got the truth out of Black Bear Paw. The Crows, led by their bravest and best, termed

'Crazy Dogs Wishing to Die' by the other tribes, had been warring with Black Bear Paw's people all summer long. Losses had been heavy on both sides, heaviest on the side of the Crows, according to the chief.

'He's lying in his rotting teeth,' murmured John Tibbets warily. 'Look at his face; look at the way the others are hanging their heads. They've been getting their hides beat off.'

'Ask him what he wants,' said Boyd evenly. 'As if I didn't know.'

To inquire as to what Black Bear Paw did not want would have been the easier question.

He wanted rifles, powder, and ball. Not all the migrants could spare – all they had. In exchange he would give them 'enough buffalo robes to fill every wagon'.

There was no way they could strike a bargain. Boyd could not afford to give up so much as a single pistol, even as a gesture of friendship, asking nothing in return. Calico, a skillet or two, all the glass beads they had, every harmonica in the train, and a dozen other catalogue luxuries – but no rifles, no ammunition.

Black Bear Paw became very angry, then incensed. His rage set him stomping about while his entourage stood staring stonily at Boyd, at the others, killing them with their eyes. The chief raved, ranted, carrying on generally in imitation of a demented buffalo. But he failed to frighten anyone, least of all Haggerty, who came precariously close to laughing in his face. Presently, running out of breath, Black Bear Paw waggled a threatening finger at Boyd and each of the others in turn, mounted his pony, and ordered his men to do likewise. Off they rumbled.

'Now we're in for it,' said the night guard resignedly. 'That there sumabitch ain't about to take no no for no answer.'

'Lucky thing we're already circled,' said Tibbets.

'Well, let's not stand here deep thinking the thing,' remarked Boyd. 'Let's get back inside and get ready to defend ourselves.'

Time dragged, wracking everyone's nerves to the snapping point. The migrants watered down their wagon bonnets, overcame their initial panic, wholly ignored

George Latchford's suggestion that a party ride to intercept the Indians and talk further with them, and readied their weapons.

A half hour passed, during which Boyd, Tawny, and Lionel Haggerty visited each wagon in turn for a few words of caution and encouragement, a cursory inspection of rifles, and parting advice to the defenders to keep down and covered as best they could.

It was now forty-three minutes since Black Bear Paw and his braves had wheeled about and ridden off into the night.

Back they came, their war cries shrilling down the wind, faintly at first, rapidly becoming louder, more chilling, supported in sound by the steady pounding of hooves. The migrants readied their rifles. Every man, every woman, every boy twelve years or older – with one family excepted, the five Latchfords – poked rifles through wheel spokes, around corners, and under wagons. And thundering back, screaming to stir the stars, came the Teton Sioux. Boyd estimated that there were at least three hundred of them. This set the odds at between four and five to one in favor of the savages against the grown men of the train. To make bad matters worse, some of the attackers carried rifles. How much ammunition they carried, how much the Crows had left them after their long summer of dispute, Boyd and the others would soon know.

Circling the circle, pushing their ponies at a frantic pace, the Indians got off fewer than ten shots, then, for fully two minutes, not one more. Boyd and the others sighed in relief. The few rifles had to be props only, waved high, brandished menacingly, designed to strike terror into the hearts of the defenders. But they were now useless. Little wonder Black Bear Paw was so enraged when his demands were politely but firmly declined.

His braves' lances posed even less of a threat than the few shots his riflemen had managed. The migrants' steady, well-aimed fire kept the attackers fifty to seventy-five yards away, but for an occasional warrior who took it into his head to ride straight at the barrage in a vain effort to break up a clutch of particularly effective defenders.

The Indians' attack was potent nevertheless: consistently well-aimed arrows came winging through the night by the

114

score. And took their toll. Fire arrows aimed high plunged downward, striking the dampened wagon bonnets. In spite of the cloth being thoroughly wet down, as the hostilities wore on a few bonnets caught fire. A squad of women was ready, however. Boosted up onto wheels, they extinguished the flames with wet blankets before serious damage could be effected.

But the savages' accuracy with bow and arrow continued remarkable. And despite the fire fighters' heroic efforts and their men's steady fire, wagons began to catch and burn. In a voice booming over the noise of the gunfire Haggerty remarked to Boyd, next to whom he lay prone, that any one of the braves, even riding as fast as they were and shooting sideways, could 'knock the eye out of a prairie dog at fifty yards'. This, Boyd was not about to dispute.

A thick pall of smoke hung over the encircled train. The din of battle continued, and the screaming and yelling, both inside the ring and out, was chilling.

Suddenly Tawny grabbed Boyd by the arm, directing his attention across the circle to the wagon opposite their own. The two of them froze at the sight of George Latchford, hitherto seated on the ground, his back to the action, reading his bible aloud to himself. Now he was standing, exposing himself almost completely to the enemy's arrows, waving his bible high and exhorting the Indians:

'Desist from this madness. Rein up your horses, lay aside your weapons and we shall lay aside ours. Let us meet in peace like brothers and –'

He was never to reach the end of his sentence. An arrow stopped it in his throat, the shaft passing cleanly through his windpipe, the head emerging from the nape of his neck. Screaming, his wife, Susan, and George Junior rushed to his aid. Boyd, Tawny, Haggerty, and a dozen others looked on in horror as Latchford stood momentarily statuelike, his bible tumbling from his hand. In rapid succession two more arrows found their mark, striking him full in the chest. He was dead before he hit the ground.

Bending over him, groaning pitifully, unwittingly exposing her back, his wife took an arrow between her shoulder blades. George Junior and Susan also thoughtlessly exposed themselves in their concern for their father

115

and mother; both were hit and died within seconds.

Jenny Latchford was nowhere to be seen.

The attack continued for less than an hour. The Indians were beaten off, leaving the ground strewn with their dead and their dying. And within the circle of wagons a hundred and thirty defenders were dead or seriously wounded, sixteen wagons burned beyond repair, and at least fifty animals – oxen, horses, including John Tibbets's, and mules – slain or stolen.

The carnage that met Boyd's and Tawny's eyes as they began moving from wagon to wagon was indescribable. Nearly half the group had been wiped out.

17

The *Saint Nicholas* was only two days out of New Archangel and already subaltern Nikandr Suverin was as bored as he'd ever been back at the fort: with the endless panorama of scattered greenery rising above the dark blue water, the daily dullness of life aboard the galliot, the same faces, the same hearty greeting from Captain Prishibeyev every time the two of them met on deck, the two mash-faced Aleut squaws who looked like twin sisters, the sort whom when in the grip of *ryabinovka* he, Suverin, had not been averse to bedding down, to his shame and regret the morning after. It was claimed that one could catch all manner of vile diseases from Aleut women; fortunately for him, he had yet to contract anything in spite of his frequent depredations upon their persons.

Everyone else on board – Captain Prishibeyev, the men, even the captain's wife, Natasha, who continued to taste Suverin with her ever-staring eyes and enticing mouth – seemed in high spirits over the expedition; just getting away from the fort appeared sufficient to lift their morale. Though not his own.

He stood at the rail watching the icy water slide slowly by as the wind rounded the short-headed mainsail and stretched the jigger, the small aftermast sail, and the bow of the vessel dipped and rose in its progress southward.

His thoughts went to Natasha. He had yet to bed her, although the two of them would have liked nothing better. She had never given him anything so obvious as a verbal hint; all her invitations came by way of her eyes and her mouth. He answered in kind. To be sure, the problem remained that she was the captain's wife, Prishibeyev being at least fifteen years older than she, and in bed, Suverin would have willingly bet his last ruble, about as effectual as a fresh corpse. If only Prishibeyev and everyone else on board would have the decency to magically vanish for an hour or so, he and Natasha could go for a rousing roll. Give him the chance to prove his manhood, she'd be his on the side forever. No question about that. 'What woman wouldn't be?' he asked aloud.

More realistically perhaps, when they reached their destination, began building the new fort near Cape Disappointment, and occasion demanded Prishibeyev's presence aboard the ship, Natasha, by that time become as bored as this subaltern, would go for a walk with him in the woods. Something splendid could be made to happen on a bed of pine bough needles. One thing was certain – once he had taken Natasha he'd never touch another Indian as long as he lived.

The colonel had given him express orders to march his seventeen charges, including the four obedient but absurdly unsoldierly Aleut men, around the deck six times daily to keep them fit, their legs in shape for the rugged labor of clearing the forest and erecting the fort upon arriving. It had to be up and completed before winter set in.

Once it had been raised the fort would be stored with the supplies stuffing the hold of the galliot and full-scale trading would begin with the friendly Chinooks.

Were the Chinook squaws and daughters any better-looking than the Aleuts or the Tlingits? wondered Suverin, running a hand through his handsome hair under his cap and smoothing his mustache. Probably not – all the Indian women he'd seen looked pretty much alike, but for their beads and styling of bear-greased hair! Thank the holy saints for Natasha.

They headed south-southeasterly down the coast for Queen Charlotte Island. Captain Prishibeyev's orders were to work his way through the Dixon Entrance near Prince Rupert and pursue a course down the Hecate Strait, keeping his ship close to the mainland. As the captain had predicted, the weather was holding uniformly depressing, rain and fog, mist and fog, the sun seemingly vanished from the sky forever. Gone back to Saint Petersburg and civilization, surmised Suverin.

In the Hecate Strait north of Queen Charlotte Sound they sighted totem poles and, in line with orders, hauled sail, anchored, and fired the falconet. Moments later the Haida Indians, who had been watching them pass, came out to greet them in their huge seventy-foot canoes. They exchanged hides for cloth, pots and pans, trinkets, and more useful items. Like the Tlingits to the north and the Kwakiutl to the south, the Haidas displayed tall totem poles rather like signposts designating their territory. Also to be seen were shorter posts with their warriors' victims' heads perched atop them.

The more picturesque and less gruesome totem poles stood in front of the Indians' heavily framed houses and represented coats of arms of the respective tribal families.

Captain Prishibeyev, however, had developed some concern over the weather, 'smelling', as he termed it, a heavy storm in the offing, so he decided to anchor offshore to trade with the natives on only two occasions, preferring, as he explained to Suverin and the others, to cover the nearly twelve hundred miles to their destination with all possible speed. One other reason prompted his change of heart.

He, Natasha, Suverin, and Sergeant Torskovich sat in the damp little cabin one night after dinner and Prishibeyev, having spread his maps out on the table, anchoring them in place with the others' glasses of tea, made known his plans.

'I realize that our orders are to put in at sight of every group of totem poles, but such step-by-step trading makes for slow progress, and I have decided that it has to come second to our main objective – to get where we're going and begin building the fort before cold weather sets in. Do you agree, Nikki?'

'I do indeed, sir.'

'Snaking our way down through these offshore islands adds a good hundred to a hundred and fifty miles to our overall distance. What the colonel fails to realize is that we can do just as much trading with the Chinooks down below as we can with these isolated tribes along the way. If we're lucky, and the wind holds and the storm doesn't develop, we can make Cape Disappointment in less than a month.'

Everyone present sipped his tea and followed the captain's finger tracing their route out of Queen Charlotte Sound toward the west coast of Vancouver Island, nearly three hundred miles in length down to Juan de Fuca Strait.*

But that night, within two hours of their after-dinner conference, the wind died, and for the next four days, although the weather cleared to some extent, the intermittent fog lifting seemingly for good, not so much as a whisper of breeze caressed the sails. They hung at their masts as limp as wet laundry, and the *Saint Nicholas* sat like 'a painted ship upon a painted ocean'.

The delay infuriated the usually mild-mannered captain. Suverin, though at first annoyed and beginning to become disgusted with the entire venture, seeing it as merely a transfer from one ice prison to another, took to his quarters, assuming the temporary role of monk. Bored as he continued to be, and growing increasingly frustrated with the presence but inaccessibility of Natasha, he bridled his lust and curled up in his bunk with a copy of Denis Ivanovich Fonvizin's *Universal Courtiers' Grammar*, determined to improve even further his already exemplary character, with an eye to deepening his impression upon Natasha. Fonvizin's work made for insufferably dull reading, but it was the only book on board other than the captain's log. The lieutenant's reading reached a point where he began to welcome the periodic interruptions for the daily keep-fit marches around the deck.

In the early evening of the fourth day, the wind emerged from its retirement and filled the sails, and they proceeded on their way. They speedily arrived at a point within half a day's distance of the entrance to the Juan de Fuca Strait, passing it during the night, the wind still with them. It

* Near present-day Victoria.

119

continued to bear the galliot directly southward until before the week was out they arrived within sight of the Willapa Hills just above where the Columbia River discharges its mighty waters into the Pacific.

Cape Disappointment on the map became Cape Disappointment in actuality. They were within scarcely half a mile of land when, with astonishing swiftness, the heavens turned black and disaster struck.

18

The storm that arose seemed to boil up out of the sea beneath the *Saint Nicholas*, as if a submarine volcano were erupting. The rain came down in torrents, but failed to calm the turbulent waters. The sails were down before the worst of the storm hit, the captain ordered all three anchors thrown out, Natasha huddled in a corner of the cabin engrossed in her prayer book, the men rushed about battening down everything that might go over the side, and the *Saint Nicholas* embarked upon the severest test of her durability she could possibly face.

'In thirty years at sea I've never seen such powerful currents!' bellowed Prishibeyev above the roar of the storm as he and Suverin, bundled up in foul-weather gear, crouched side by side at the top of the companionway stairs, watching the sea throw up mountainous waves and carve great channels between them, the water cascading over the decks but by some miracle failing to shatter the naked masts.

Their hearts in their throats, the two watched and waited. Eventually deserting prayer for their companionship, Natasha came running up the stairway to seize both men's arms. She was terrified, her lovely eyes saucering. But her husband and her admirer did their best to calm her.

'It can't last long at this rate, my dear,' remarked Prishibeyev hopefully. 'We'll ride it out, love, never fear.'

His words had little effect; she feared. Mightily. As did he, as did Suverin, as would any man with a brain in his head. One after another the anchor chains snapped like rotted twine. Down came the foreyard, and like a toy boat flung against the side of a tub by a child the *Saint Nicholas* shot straight for the shore, sliding up on the rocks, her bow coming to rest between two enormous trees. Had it struck either one it would have been smashed to chips. As it was, the hull was heavily scraped, seams burst, and holes appeared in a dozen places. Fortunately, the incredible power of the wind and a timely wave fully forty feet high had thrown the ship almost completely out of the water.

No lives were lost, no one aboard her came out of it worse than shaken up and closer to his Maker, except for one of the Aleuts, who suffered a broken forearm. Nor was any of the ship's cargo ruined.

Nevertheless, the ship itself would take the better part of a month to repair. Captain Prishibeyev thanked God for their deliverance; Natasha thanked her prayer book; Suverin thanked the wave that had grounded them.

The storm gradually lessened in intensity and presently calm was restored, the skies overhead brightening, the sea settling. The *Saint Nicholas* sat at an awkward, a thoroughly absurd angle, her masts snapped off, her seams burst here and there, two discouragingly large holes gaping just above her keel on her starboard side. Holes big enough for a grown man to scrunch his way through. Fortunately, both were clear of the water even at high tide. Other, smaller holes were also to be seen.

Despite their deliverance and the salvaging of the ship's cargo, Captain Prishibeyev was plunged into despair. For the first hour after the storm had abated Suverin consciously feared that the man would lose hold entirely and put a bullet through his head, so utterly downcast was he.

But he gradually came around. Camp was made on the rock-strewn beach, half in, half out of the woods, and guards were posted in the event any curious Chinooks or Cowlitz Indians came around with thoughts of pilfering or worse.

Hunting with the aid of the four Aleuts, the men were able to bring back deer meat. Fish were even more plentiful, salmon, eels, steelhead, and sturgeon. Food, therefore, promised no problem. In full charge, now that the party had landed, Suverin set about searching out the best location for the proposed fort, and work was begun on repairing the *Saint Nicholas.*

The biggest problem confronting the company was the fact that now not one but two difficult jobs had to be completed before winter set in. The fort had to be built, the galliot repaired. In its present location it could be shattered to kindling by the winter storms.

The fort was to be modeled after the one at New Archangel, although this one was to be only two thirds the size of the other, fifty by forty feet at the base, with the upper story flush with the lower structure rather than jutting outward an additional two feet. Watchovers would be needed at the two front corners, but these could wait until the following spring. There would also be no need to put up a separate cookhouse, blacksmith's workshop, or other outbuildings until later on.

But before they began clearing a space to build the fort a party of Chinooks appeared, and from them the Aleuts learned that a fort already existed, less than ten miles from where they were presently situated. It developed that some years earlier Americans had erected an installation for the same purpose the government in Saint Petersburg had in mind, as a trading post for dealing with the Chinooks and other tribes. But for some reason the fort had since been abandoned.

Taking two Aleuts and four of his own men with him, Suverin set out with one of the Chinooks acting as their guide. They headed through the woodland straight for the northernmost reach of the Willamette Valley, a broad tract of prairie and timberland south of the Columbia River, dipping between the heaven-bound spine of the Cascade Range to the east and the coastal mountains to the west.

On this trek, however, Suverin and his party failed to reach the valley, coming upon the Americans' fort before they did so. The very idea that a fort already existed so close to where the storm had beached them had excited Suverin. But the Chinooks in their conversation with his Aleut interpreter had never gotten around to describing the condition of the fort. First sight of the place had practically dealt the lieutenant a stroke.

There was no gainsaying the fact that it was indeed a fort,

122

or rather had been one. However, since being abandoned by the Americans it had been plundered by the savages in the area – the peaceful Chinooks among them, no doubt, Suverin reflected – practically laid waste from wall to wall.

'Holy saints,' he growled to Sergeant Torskovich. 'What a mess. We'd be better off burning it to the ground and starting over.'

'If I may say so, sir, we'd be wasting our fire. This is not the best place for any fort. Look . . .' He pointed to the left and upward to a hill that rose almost to the tops of the tallest trees. 'Six braves standing up there could wipe out a whole company with fire arrows.'

The Aleut understood and was quick to agree.

'These Americans,' groused Suverin. 'I have heard in Saint Petersburg that they are the strangest people on earth. Brilliant and stupid and everything in between. Courageous fighters, shrewd businessmen, unscrupulous as boyars. But with all the breeding and good manners of Turks.'

'Well, they sure don't know where to build a fort,' said the sergeant airily.

Inside, the second floor had collapsed to cover the first; absolutely nothing was salvageable. The Indians had picked the place as clean as a fish, as the sergeant put it.

The party returned to camp with the unhappy news, and the next morning ten men under Suverin's supervision began clearing a spot for the fort. The lieutenant personally stepped off and measured the dimensions while the remaining men went to work restoring the *Saint Nicholas*. Captain Prishibeyev pitched in to help.

Natasha and the two Aleut women, meanwhile, set about preparing food for the present and stripped and sun-dried deer meat and gutted and cleaned and salted down fish for winter stores.

Whipsaws, adzes, and axes resounded through the forest; trees came crashing down, were trimmed, their trunks cut to length, ends notched, and the walls of Fort New Kiev began to rise.

19

Behold, the Lord thy God hath set the land before thee: go up and possess it, as the Lord God of thy fathers hath said unto thee; fear not, neither be discouraged...

And they turned and went up into the mountain, and came unto the valley of Eshcol, and searched it out.
                                    – DEUTERONOMY, 1:21,24

Two hundred and fifty-two people had set out from Keys Landing in sixty-six wagons, each drawn by four oxen, with mules and horses in addition. Shortly before the train's departure a baby had been born. During the long and arduous journey to the South Pass two more women gave birth.

But long before reaching the South Pass the following spring, the battle with the Teton Sioux had initiated a seemingly unending chain of difficulties, dangers, and privations. One hundred and eighteen had been killed, or subsequently succumbed from their wounds in the attack. Sixteen wagons with their contents had been destroyed by fire arrows; forty-six oxen and horses had been killed.

The company, reduced to a hundred and thirty-five souls – adding to the death toll the demise of Telford Ingersoll earlier – had built shelter and wintered at the base of the Laramie Mountains, but the following spring's trek over the mountains and in time over the Rockies beyond had exacted an additional heavy toll on man and beast alike.

Since Boyd and Tawny's wagon was one of the very few carrying only two people, Tawny – in full knowledge and in spite of Jenny Latchford's all too evident feelings for Boyd – invited the girl to join them. With the others in Jenny's family killed by the attacking Indians, it was, in Tawny's opinion, the Christian thing to do. Jenny proved to be extremely grateful. With the resiliency of youth, she eventually recovered from the loss of her loved ones, but her feelings toward Boyd became, if anything, stronger. Inviting Jenny to join them may have been the mistake of her life, reflected Tawny more than once, but in her heart she felt secure; her marriage was built on the firmest possible foundation. She persuaded herself that no other female, including Jenny Latchford, was capable of stealing his love and affection from her.

Tawny *knew* Boyd, the fiber of his character, his self-respect, his ingrained loyalty, his dependability, his love. With Marcy Rampling's defection she, Tawny, had filled a need for him, not out of convenience, but rather conviction, love, and devotion. Theirs was a happy marriage, in spite of the hardships. And they looked forward to their future in the Willamette Valley with the eagerness and anticipation with which children look forward to Christmas morning.

Deep down, Tawny pitied Jenny. In spite of her remarkable rebound from the disaster which had befallen her family, there were times when a heart-wrenching sadness got a grip on the girl and held fast for hours. There were nights when she cried herself to sleep, and as time went on Tawny's heart went out to her, in spite of Elvira Needham's friendly warning to 'keep a close eye on her'. And to sit between Boyd and Jenny on the driver's seat.

The irony of the situation, nevertheless, did not escape Tawny. To have the one eligible female, a very fetching female at that, with an amorous eye for Boyd, actually join them in their wagon was beyond anything Tawny could have imagined upon their starting out for Keys Landing.

For his part, Boyd was sympathetic, warm-hearted, and generous with conversation designed to rebuild Jenny's shattered morale. But he never failed to behave like the gentleman that he was, and never encouraged her innermost feelings toward him. What the girl really needed, decided Tawny, was neither consolation nor even their friendship: rather, a beau. Hopefully, when the train arrived in the valley one of the unattached young men would get to know Jenny and become friendly with her.

The Willamette Valley. Boyd's friend Wells Whitfield with the Lewis and Clark expedition had exaggerated its length by some fifty miles. It proved actually closer to one hundred and fifty miles long by forty wide. But Whitfield had in no way exaggerated the valley's beauty. By the time the train had come within sight of it in early August of 1808, the land was at the zenith of its beauty. A navigable river as clear as polished crystal ran through the entire length of the valley, with a number of branches emerging from either side. The smaller branches rose in the foothills, the larger ones descended from the mountains, thickly covered with forests. The part-timberland, part-prairie valley also offered countless springs.

In the Willamette River flowing down from the Cascades to join the Columbia opposite Fort Vancouver swam white swans and other water birds. Seals cavorted in the river's tidal currents; wolverine, deer, and grizzly bear roamed the deeper forests; quail and grouse nested in the brush. And every tributary along with the river itself was alive with trout, salmon, and sturgeon.

The August heat here in no way compared with that of the Great Plains, was not in the least oppressive. Nor, promised Boyd, would the winter to come be nearly as cold as that they had spent in the foothills of the Laramies. A small amount of light snow would fall in January and February, but mostly during the winter months there would be rain, beginning in late October and continuing off and on until spring. This dampness would penetrate the soil gradually, which would prove a blessing to the farmers, irrigating their fields, keeping them fresh and productive.

As a result of the rigors of crossing the mountains, the migrants' total number following the previous winter had been reduced by eleven. They were now down to one hundred and twenty-four, forty of whom were grown men. The train's other unhappy loss was a large number of oxen. The company reached the valley with barely three dozen of the beasts surviving out of a starting total of two hundred and sixty-four.

No sooner had they arrived than a temporary camp was set up and plans were devised by the council, with Boyd's suggestions, for laying out the tiny community. A single large building would serve as a church, schoolhouse, and community center, with individual cabins grouped about it in close proximity. For protection against marauding

Indians, a stockade fence was to be erected around the entire site.

Indians... The Southern Molalas, who were as blood-thirsty and predatory as the Teton Sioux.

20

Fort New Kiev had been completed, watchtowers and all, some weeks before the survivors of the Excelsior Fur Trading Company wagon train led by Boyd Chevrier arrived in the Willamette Valley. The spring and most of the summer had been devoted to bartering hides with the friendly Chinooks. The arrangement was proving highly successful, beaver, otter, seal, wolverine, even bear hides filling the hold of the *Saint Nicholas*. Repaired and once more seaworthy, it had already returned to New Archangel to unload and come back to Fort New Kiev for a second holdful.

Meanwhile, as the summer wore on, Lieutenant Nikandr Suverin's ideas for establishing Mother Russia's permanent presence along the Pacific Coast began to flower in abundance. The previous year's trek southward, guided by the Chinook, which had brought them to the plundered shell of the ill-fated American fort, was responsible for sowing one of the seeds in the young officer's mind.

'Why not build a second, even a third fort down the line southward?' he asked Captain Prishibeyev, Natasha, and Sergeant Torskovich. 'Three forts that would in time increase to a dozen or more! Not on stupidly chosen sites like that American fiasco, but in ideal spots, say fifty or sixty miles apart?'

'You would need an accessible harbor for each of them,' advised the captain. 'I'm sure there would be many, though. Good thinking, Nikki, my boy.'

'I heartily agree, sirs,' interposed Sergeant Torskovich. 'That is an excellent idea. But to put the men back to work building even a second fort after the way they practically killed themselves putting up this one, not to mention repairing the galliot, well...'

'Suppose you let me finish!' snapped Suverin, the triumph that can come only with genuine inspiration setting his eyes gleaming. All four sat at a rude table in the main dining-meeting-peltry-bartering-storeroom of Fort New Kiev, finishing a dinner of fresh steelhead trout, wild onions, berries with brown sugar, other wild fruits, and tea or vodka, depending upon the diner's preference.

'Why not create a work force using our friends, the Chinooks?' continued Suverin.

Sergeant Torskovich discreetly suppressed a smile, ever mindful that his superior had little sense of humor, and no capacity for accepting criticism, particularly from one beneath him in rank. Still, Suverin's suggestion was absurd, and what the sergeant had on his chest he had to get off.

'May I be so forward as to remind the lieutenant that the Chinooks are hunters and fishermen, not carpenters.'

'He has a point,' said the captain. 'Hand one a hammer and he could smash his own hand to a pulp.'

Suverin dismissed this argument with a cursory wave. 'Leo,' he said to Torskovich, 'any man can become anything you want him to be provided the incentive is there.' He threw a characteristically patronizing look at Torskovich. 'Hunting and fishing takes up barely half their time. And still they fetch in hides by the hundreds...'

'Thousands. We'll be heading back to New Archangel to transship another load again within a few days,' said the captain, seizing Natasha's hand and squeezing it affectionately. 'And we'll be back again next spring as fast as the wind can fetch us.'

Natasha's eyes drifted to Suverin's, catching and holding them. The look on her face appeared to be one of hope that her husband's impulsive gesture of affection in no way offended the lieutenant. But Suverin had too much on his mind to be concerned about husband or wife, despite catching her glance. His vision saw a whole line of forts springing up like mushrooms down the Oregon and California coastlines. A vision he was realistic enough to recognize that his superiors in Saint Petersburg already had firmly in mind. Nevertheless, were he to take the initiative, the feathers in his cap would rival the war bonnet of the Chinooks' chief, Concomley.

He would, however, be sorry to see Natasha leave; if his ego was not crushed, it was, he confessed to himself, somewhat bruised at the recollection that with so much to do and so few to do it during their months here, not to mention the presence of the lady's husband, he, Suverin, and Natasha never had gotten the opportunity to test each other's sexual prowess.

'Why don't you come back up with us this time, Nikki?' asked Prishibeyev out of the blue. 'The sergeant here can handle things while you're gone. And you could use a change of scenery.'

The salty old devil, thought Suverin. He'd love to run back, not for the trip certainly, but for the change. And to see Varya and the colonel.

'I'd like that, Captain,' he said. 'Very much. Sergeant, do you think you can handle things while I'm gone?'

'Certainly, sir,' said Torskovich, 'now that you've set everything up to run so smoothly.' The compliment was called for, of course. Verbalizing the thought racing through his mind was not, reflected the sergeant. *By St. Gregory, let him run the show for two months or so and he'd do a job that would make Suverin look like a recruit in comparison. And earn himself a lieutenant's bar into the bargain, he'd be willing to wager!*

That afternoon, supplied for an overnight stay and leaving Sergeant Torskovich in command of the fort, Suverin and six other men set out heading south, passing the rotting remains of the American fort and entering the Willamette Valley. Two hours' march into the valley brought them to a scene of carnage the like of which the lieutenant had never imagined possible. One glimpse drained the blood from his face and brought a loud gasp to his lips.

A wagon train had been completely destroyed. Charred bodies lay about, men and women scalped, throats cut, knife wounds crimsoning their chests and stomachs.

From all appearances the massacre had taken place barely hours earlier. From all appearances there couldn't possibly be any survivors.

Nearly four hours earlier the migrants, having arrived, were in the process of preparing their temporary camp when out of the trees rushed a horde of savages wielding tomahawks and screaming like maniacs. Falling upon the astonished settlers, they began massacring them. The men of the train hardly had time to attempt to defend themselves and their loved ones before they were overwhelmed by the blood-thirsty braves.

As luck would have it, Tawny and Jenny Latchford had left the lead wagon to go to a neighbor's to help the family unload, the contents of Boyd and Tawny's wagon consisting mostly of powder kegs and ammunition and being too heavy for either of the women to lift.

The migrants were able to get off fewer than a dozen shots, no more than two or three finding their targets. The killing of these few attackers served only to rouse the Indians' fellow braves to even greater fury. The onslaught was too sudden, too overwhelming, the issue too obviously decided within minutes. The wagons had not even been drawn up into their protective circle. Worse yet, many of the emigrants, women and children especially, had wandered a short distance away to look over their new surroundings, and in consequence were easy prey for the savages lurking in the trees, watching the train arrive.

Tawny and Jenny found it impossible to get back to their wagon. Boyd was nowhere to be found, nor was Tibbets or Haggerty, who had been working with him. All four Needhams had already been killed, Robert dying with his unfired rifle in his hands, his scalp taken, blood pouring from his head and from his heart, where his murderer had first stabbed him.

Hand in hand, Tawny and Jenny continued to race about wildly, searching for Boyd. The shrill cries of the attackers, the screams of the dead and dying migrants went on without interruption. While a number of the Indians were busy knifing and scalping their victims, others were setting fire to the wagons and running off into the woods, leading the surviving oxen and horses and carrying everything in the way of loot they could manage.

Two braves, vicious-looking older men, their tomahawks

130

raised menacingly, singled out Tawny and Jenny and came rushing up to them as they stood petrified with fear in the center of the unabating slaughter, screaming for Boyd, neither knowing which way to turn. There was simply no avenue of escape. Jenny fell to her knees, collapsing in a dead faint; Tawny dropped down to help her. At that moment the two braves stopped short, each seizing one of the women by the hair, preparing to scalp them. Twisting about, Tawny was able to avert the downward swipe of the tomahawk and wrench free of the Indian's grasp. Shooting to her feet, she began to run, not daring to look back, fearful of what she might see happening to Jenny, lying prostrate and defenseless.

Tawny ran and ran, hearing the brave she had escaped closing the gap separating them. Still she screamed Boyd's name, looking in every direction for him – save behind her. For some inexplicable, wholly unwarranted reason she had gotten hold of the thought that Boyd was somehow managing to survive, that they would find each other, he would kill the Indian bent on scalping her, and they alone would escape.

All of this wishful thinking was filling her mind when suddenly she tripped and fell, hitting her forehead sharply on the ground and losing consciousness, a black pit whirling like a maelstrom yawning wide, drawing her swiftly down into its depths.

21

Lieutenant Suverin and his men wandered about the scene of the slaughter for fully ten minutes, examining bodies for signs of life, however slight. They found none. Some of the Russians, despite being hardened campaigners in their time and accustomed to the butchery of battle, still could not restrain themselves from vomiting at the sight of so many scalped heads.

Wisps of smoke still rose from the burnt-out wagons, and

under the hot sun soon, by the third day, the corpses would begin rotting.

'We cannot leave them lying here like this for the wolves and bears to pick over,' observed Suverin to Corporal Andrutsake, who had temporarily replaced Sergeant Torskovich as the lieutenant's second in command.

Andrutsake, a slightly built, unusually scholarly-looking fellow for a noncommissioned soldier, wearing glasses and the merest suggestion of a reddish-blond mustache, nodded and crossed himself. He then tore his eyes away from the sight of the Needhams, scalped and lying together at his feet. As he looked away he covered his mouth with one hand.

'There are no shovels that I can see, sir,' he said. 'No tools of any kind. Whoever did this killed and looted and ran away with everything they could carry.'

'We can get shovels back at the fort,' said Suverin quietly. 'Who did this horrible thing, I wonder? Certainly not the Chinooks or the Tillamooks. The Tills are too lazy for the physical effort required of butchery. Besides, they'd only scalp the men; the women and children they would take as slaves. No, not the Tillamooks and not the Tualatin or the Northern Molala. Who?'

'If I may be so bold, sir, does it matter a wooden kopeck to these poor souls now?' asked Andrutsake.

'It matters to us, Corporal. This was no small wagon train. Possibly two, even three hundred braves attacked them. Such savagery, brutality... even the Tlingits aren't up to this.' He glanced about the area. 'One thing seems certain, whoever it was used knives and tomahawks only, no bows, no arrows, evidently no firearms.'

'I have yet to see any tribes this close to the ocean with firearms, sir,' piped up another man.

'And you have seen them all, of course,' countered Suverin sarcastically, bringing a flush of embarrassment to the man's hairy cheeks.

A trapping party comprised of nearly twenty men emerged from the trees directly ahead of them. Chinooks. Out working for their Russian 'business associates', as it happened. Suverin recognized the leader of the group, an Indian called Yellow Wolf. Like most Chinooks, he was easily identified as a member of the tribe by the shape of his head, deliberately flattened at birth, a custom shared by a few other tribes, notably those from around Puget Sound and to the north up the coast and inland. Shortly after he was born, the Chinook baby was placed in a cradle lined with moss, with the head end slightly raised. A pad of cedar bark was placed on the infant's head and over this a strip of skin was securely laced to the wood of the cradle. As the baby's head grew over the next year, the press caused it to elongate. The child's eyes would bulge with the pressure, but the Chinooks claimed that he suffered little pain, and whatever he did experience would serve to make him a more courageous warrior. At the end of the year the pressure was removed, leaving the head properly flattened, never to revert to its original shape.

Apart from the shape of his head, Yellow Wolf was an impressive-looking, handsome brave, tall, much more slender and erect in his posture than the others gathered behind him. He was also, Suverin had learned early, intelligent, wise not only in the ways of the forest, but in his dealings with the 'white skins from the north', as the Chinooks called the Russians. It was Yellow Wolf who had been chosen by his chief to handle the peltry bartering with the white man.

One look at the carnage bloodying the lush green grass of the area and Yellow Wolf knew at once what had happened. No, the butchers had not been Chinooks or Tillamooks or Northern Molalas, or any other tribe which Suverin had ever seen or even heard of. According to the Chinook, responsibility for the slaughter lay with the Southern Molalas, a particularly cruel and barbarous and, unfortunately, fairly large tribe, in comparison to most of those living in and near the northern reaches of the valley.

It seemed that every so often the Southern Molalas would take it into their hot heads to venture north for the sole purpose of killing everyone they met. They considered the Willamette Valley their personal hunting ground, every inch of it, even though their main location was far to the south. According to Yellow Wolf, the Southern Molalas rarely took slaves, a practice pursued by practically all the northern tribes, not excluding the Chinooks themselves.

To Suverin all of this was very enlightening, but at the

133

same time discouraging. Despite having rifles and plenty of ammunition, which no tribe with arrow, spear, and knife could possibly match, to fulfill his ambition and build forts down the line straight through Southern Molala territory would seem to be begging for trouble. The Russians' only purpose in being there was to trade, not convert souls to Orthodox Catholicism or to war against the natives. And the first rule in trading was to maintain peaceful relations with one's suppliers. As they maintained with the Chinooks and the few Tillamooks who occasionally showed up at the fort with the wolf hides.

'Every one of these poor people slaughtered,' commented Suverin, shaking his head.

Yellow Wolf too shook his head, his handsome face grim with pity.

'Not all,' said a brave behind him, a stumpy little man with scars lacing his bare chest and a number of beaver pelts under one arm. 'We passed their camp the long way around, as I told you, Yellow Wolf. What I did not say was that, being on the right with my brother and closer to the camp, we could make out that they had taken slaves. Two of them.'

'Are you sure of that?' asked Yellow Wolf in a surprised tone.

The man nodded, as did another coming up behind him, whom Suverin took to be his brother.

'But how could you tell if they were taken from here?' asked the lieutenant.

'Both were white women, both young, both dressed like the woman at the fort.'

'Mrs. Prishibeyev,' mused Suverin aloud, rubbing his chin thoughtfully. 'My, my, this puts an entirely different light on the situation. Corporal...'

Andrutsake stepped forward, saluting. 'Sir?'

'Take two men with you and get back to the fort fast as you can. Come back here with at least ten men. Plenty of arms and ammunition.'

Yellow Wolf studied Suverin with a perplexed look. 'The women are Americans, not of your country...'

'They are nevertheless women,' responded the lieutenant. 'And if we can save their lives we shall do so. Well, Corporal, what are you waiting you? You have your orders.'

Andrutsake saluted, clicking his heels for additional emphasis, spun about, pointed at two of the five other men who had accompanied them, and off they went on the double.

'Fast as you can!' called Suverin after them. He turned to Yellow Wolf. 'We will effect the rescue after nightfall.'

'You will be greatly outnumbered, rifles or no rifles.'

'I would hope your people would arm themselves and join us,' said Suverin.

Yellow Wolf shook his head. 'Chief Concomley would frown on such a venture. We Chinooks war only if we are attacked; this –'

'I understand. Nevertheless, odds or no odds, we will rescue those poor women. And take forty or fifty of those butchers with us to their deaths. Would that we might wipe them out completely. Under cover of darkness, with surprise on our side, employing useful strategy, it should not be difficult.'

Yellow Wolf nodded agreement, but it was a gesture of politeness only, deference to the white lieutenant's confidence in himself, a character trait with which the Chinook was all too familiar.

In his heart, however, he considered Suverin not so much courageous as foolhardy. He sighed inwardly. When, he thought, the Molalas got finished scalping these would-be rescuers the complement at the great fort of logs would be reduced to two or three men.

The future of the peltry-trading business was beginning to look bleak indeed.

22

It was well after ten o'clock, darkness enshrouding the valley, but the sky was brighter than Suverin would have wanted it to be had he a choice. The Chinooks were not about to help them, as Yellow Wolf had informed the lieutenant. They did, however, agree to bury the wagon train's dead.

Andrutsake had returned with more men and arms, bringing the company, including the four Aleuts, who were superb marksmen, up to fourteen. Hardly a match, as Yellow Wolf had reminded Suverin earlier, for three hundred bloodthirsty savages, but with him Corporal Andrutsake had brought something else that could prove very helpful to the would-be rescuers. And would certainly bring down the odds. It was a case of hand grenades – French pomegranates, as Colonel Luka Poplova back at New Archangel called them. An excellent device for throwing panic into the midst of the unsuspecting savages, scattering them to the four winds long enough to free the two captives, in clear view, tied to seven-foot-tall stakes in the center of the camp near the main fire.

Tawny and Jenny Latchford stood naked, their clothing long since ripped from their bodies, their breasts and stomachs and legs crisscrossed with slash marks, the result of switches bunched in the hands of the Molala squaws like besoms and used to whip the captives. Both women's hands were tied above their heads, their legs were spread, their ankles staked to the ground. The reason for this position was not lost on Suverin and the others sneaking up to the edge of the trees surrounding the camp.

'The braves stand in lines and ravage them,' said one of the Aleuts to the lieutenant. Suverin suddenly felt sick to his stomach.

'Wouldn't you think their squaws beating them would be enough? Will you look?' he whispered, pointing. 'The way they're hanging their heads they look half dead.'

At that moment a dumpy little squaw came up to the prisoners bearing a large gourd, and while other squaws held up both women's heads, she fed each of them water. Suverin watched, boiling inside with anger. He could see that the shorter of the two, bound to the stake on the right, was unable to swallow the water, or whatever it was being fed her, letting it dribble down her chin onto her exposed breasts.

But the other captive, half a head taller and with beautiful wavy, cinnamon-colored hair, slender and full-busted, twisted free of the squaw's grip on her hair defiantly, drank, and spat into the fire, setting up a loud hissing. This simple act might have been nothing more than temptation to defiance on her part, but it was an insult which her captors did not take lightly. Almost at once she was set upon by three squaws who began flaying her with single switches, setting her screaming with pain.

'The filthy animals,' gasped Suverin, looking on.

'She should not have defied them so,' said Corporal Andrutsake.

'How could she not? She's quite obviously a woman of great pride, courage, and resolve. She knows what lies ahead for her. I give her credit – she's made up her mind that if she is to die she will do so with dignity.'

'They won't kill her,' interposed one of the Aleuts. 'She will be useful as a slave. And one their squaws can take their anger out on.'

'She'll try to escape, that one,' said Suverin. 'If she fails some headstrong buck will stick his knife in her back.' The lieutenant shook his head, lowering his eyes to the ground. 'I can't watch any more of this.'

'They will be going to sleep for the night soon,' suggested Andrutsake. 'If we wait an hour or so, maybe less, we could sneak in and –'

'We're not waiting another minute!' burst Suverin irritably. 'Hand me four of those grenades. The rest of you carry one or two. Don't leave any in the box. We're going to encircle the camp, each of us counting to fifty. By then we'll be well spread around them. At fifty we throw one grenade. Aim at those directly in front of you. Throw from prone position. Fortunately for us, the two women are in the center. Holy saints, be careful, don't anyone throw into the damned fire. Shamonah!'

'Yes, Lieutenant,' responded one of the Aleuts.

'You and I will run in and rescue the women. Have your knife ready; I'll have mine. Cut them loose, bring them back here. If I am right, the braves who survive the grenades will chase after us. You, Andrutsake, and two or three of the rest of you will flank our avenue of escape. Your job will be to protect our backs. Once we've passed you, with whatever you have left, grenades, rifles, even your pistols, see that you cut down any braves pursuing us. Clear?'

'Clear, sir.'

'Let's go. On your feet, all of you. Stay within the cover of the trees and move out. We start counting . . . now! One . . .'

The first grenade landed dead center of nine warriors gathered in a tight bunch, examining the rifles taken from the wagon train. An earsplitting concatenation followed, throwing the Molalas into absolute consternation. On their feet, the survivors ran about wildly, bumping into one another, screaming, their screams cut off sharply as bullets found their hearts and heads, killing them instantly.

Suverin and the Aleut, Shamonah, made straight for the stakes, speedily freed the two women, and started back toward the cover of the woods carrying them. A brave ran up, tomahawk upraised, to strike Suverin, but a bullet out of nowhere caught him squarely in the throat, killing him. His weapon fell from his hand, the flat of the razor-sharp flint blade glancing harmlessly off the lieutenant's shoulder.

Not a single Molala saw fit to pursue the rescuers. This in no way deterred the Russians surrounding the site from continuing to pour rifle fire at the survivors, their supply of 'French pomegranates' now exhausted.

Tawny and Jenny Latchford were wrapped in blankets and carried like small children through the woods to a prearranged rendezvous point, where the rest of the Russians and the three Aleuts assembled within a quarter of an hour.

Taken by surprise as they had been, their numbers decimated by the grenades and rifle fire, the Molalas' camp bore a striking resemblance to the wagon train massacre site. The only distinctions between the two slaughters were the absence at this one of charred wagons and the fact that the dead and dying Indian braves' scalps remained intact – this last by Suverin's order, much to the disappointment of the Aleuts.

Tawny was delirious, able to mumble one word only over and over again. 'Boyd, Boyd, Boyd . . .'

Jenny Latchford was nearly dead; like Tawny, bleeding from dozens of gashes. Both women's bleeding was stanched, but on the way back to Fort New Kiev, even before the party reached the site of the abandoned American fort, Jenny died.

Her slender bruised and beaten body was carried to the Russian fort, and before dawn it was wrapped in a piece of sailcloth and buried alongside that of one of the company's two Aleut women, who had died of pneumonia the previous winter.

Tawny remained delirious for a week, during which time the *Saint Nicholas* was loaded and final preparations were made for her return to New Archangel. Natasha proved an angel of mercy, giving her own bed to the suffering survivor and tending to her needs night and day.

Suverin had been very concerned about her delirium from the first. Taken by her courage, her defiance, pitying her immensely, and certainly not indifferent to her beauty, he hovered about Natasha hour after hour as she sat by the girl, caring for her.

Natasha, perceptive by nature as she was, could easily see that Suverin's interest in her patient went well beyond sympathy. But Natasha was not in the least jealous. To see the girl recover mind and body was more important to her than any feelings she and Suverin had for each other. Getting her patient well and on her feet again was a challenge she could not have accepted more eagerly had the girl been her own flesh and blood. Then too, dear Nikki would always be available.

Over and over again he would ask the same question:

'Do you think she'll recover her mind? Do you?'

'For the hundredth time, why ask me? I'm no nurse. Give her time, why don't you? She's been through a living hell. And kindly stop hovering over us like a thirsty vampire. I promise I'll keep you posted on her progress. Now be a good boy and leave us.'

The *Saint Nicholas* set sail, and four days later, as the sun prepared to lower itself into the blue waters of the Pacific off the port beam, Natasha was feeding Tawny hot broth when Tawny, propped up against three pillows, gently pushed her hand away, declining the next spoonful. She spoke:

'Where am I? Who are you? Is this a ship? It is; it must be, I feel the rocking motion. My husband, where is he?'

Natasha beamed and squealed for joy. Cinnamon Hair's mind had come back! She answered her questions as best she could.

Suverin knocked and entered the little cabin without waiting to be asked. At once, merely glancing at Tawny's eyes, he realized that she was no longer delirious.

'What is your name, my dear?' asked Natasha.

'Chevrier. Tawny Chevrier. My husband, Boyd...'

Suverin's face clouded. 'He was with you in that wagon train?'

'We led the train out here from Missouri. You found him? He's on board?'

Suverin sat down dejectedly. 'I am deeply grieved to have to be the one to tell you, but you, Mrs. Chevrier, are the only survivor.'

Tawny gasped. 'That's not so!' she burst, tears leaping into her dark eyes. 'It can't be. Boyd –'

'We, my men and I, met a trapping party of Chinooks. They assured us that every man, woman, and child in your train had been murdered by those disgusting animals. All except you and the other woman, the dark-haired girl –'

'Jenny!'

'She died before they could get her back to the fort,' said Natasha solemnly. 'Was she your sister?'

'No. She's dead, you say?' Tawny's hand went to her forehead. Suddenly she felt faint. It was all too much to accept. 'But my husband isn't. He can't be. He must have gotten away. He was with Lionel Haggerty, you see. Up unloading our wagon. Both know the Indians, their ways and all. Boyd was sure that if there was trouble I'd be captured but they wouldn't kill me.'

'You being young and so lovely,' said Natasha.

'Well, a woman can be useful to them. We were all warned even before we crossed the Great Plains. Boyd knew that; I'm sure he was counting on it. Not that he *wanted* us to be captured, not at all. But he'd never have deserted me or Jenny. He was coming back to rescue us, I'm sure. Naturally he had to find a place out of sight of the Indians. The trouble was Jenny and I were right in the thick of things. It would have been impossible for him to reach us. But in time. Oh, he was coming back, coming back...'

She was striving desperately to convince herself of that, of all she was saying. But regardless of how convincing she tried to make it sound, her eyes and the pained expression on her face told both her listeners that in her heart she was only talking wishfully. She nevertheless refused to let go of the last slender strand of hope.

'I just know he escaped, he's alive! Where is this ship heading?'

'New Archangel. Up in Alaska, up beyond Queen Charlotte Island,' responded Natasha, glancing at Suverin and looking back at Tawny, her eyes suffused with sympathy.

'Tell the captain to turn around. Please, you must. We have to go back. We've got to find my husband. The poor darling – not finding me, he must think I'm dead!' She was becoming more and more confused; realizing this herself, embarrassed by it, she flung the covers aside and tried to rise. But Suverin caught her by the shoulders and gently pushed her back against the pillows, Natasha replacing the covers.

'Now,' said Suverin, 'please try to understand and accept it. We searched that whole area; the Chinooks, too. I give you my word – on my solemn oath, there were no other survivors.'

'You're wrong! You must be.' Tawny paused, staring from one to the other, looking for lies in their eyes. And as suddenly as she'd raised the subject, she dropped it, as if it were too disturbing to discuss, especially with these strangers, neither of whom, for all their kindness toward her, offered her any encouragement.

'Your accents,' she said, 'you're not Americans.'

'We're Russians,' said Natasha, pleased at the change of subject. 'But yes, we speak English. I know it from my husband, the captain of this ship, Captain Prishibeyev. He speaks a number of languages fluently. Lieutenant Suverin here, who risked his life for you...' Suverin blushed like a schoolboy. 'But you did, Nikki!'

He shrugged. 'I had plenty of help.'

'I'm very grateful,' said Tawny. The words sounded woefully weak considering what he'd done, but she could think of nothing else to say at the moment. Perhaps when her head cleared completely...

He was talking: 'My English comes from where my French comes from,' he said. 'The training school for officers in Saint Petersburg. You'd be amazed at how much English is spoken at court, almost as much as French. I was stationed there three years before being reassigned to New Archangel.'

The three of them talked for another hour before Tawny's eyelids began drooping. Natasha noticed this, and she and Suverin retired from the cabin to let her sleep.

But Tawny could not sleep, rather would not permit herself to do so.

Boyd, my dearest darling, where are you, what have they done to you? What am I doing sailing north on this strange ship? And poor, poor Jenny...

She was half tempted to pinch herself in the hoped-for belief that it was all a nightmare, so much so terrible had taken place almost from the moment the train had reached the valley. In the whole tangled sequence of events she could discern one bright spot only: she herself had somehow managed to survive, thanks to Lieutenant Whatever-his-name-was. Still, she did not want to be on this ship heading north to Alaska, every passing moment taking her farther and farther away from Boyd.

She glanced about the little cabin. The ceiling was so low that were she to stand she'd probably have to bend like an old beggar to keep from bumping her head. It was sparsely and rudely furnished as well, with only the bed, a washstand, and a small armoire fastened to one wall. Not even a mirror above the stand. Then she noticed that Natasha had left behind a small hand mirror, setting it to one side of the washbasin. Natasha had also left behind the overpowering scent of eau de cologne, as if she'd bathed in it so as to deliberately leave the fumes in the little cabin as a reminder to Tawny that, despite her having been through so much for so long, deprived of the feminine fineries of life, there still existed such things as sweet scents, clean sheets, a comfortable bed...

Dear Natasha; Tawny hardly knew her, but somehow got the feeling that they had been friends for years, though the captain's wife had to be at least eight years older than she, close to thirty if not past it.

She tried to get up to get to the washstand and the mirror for a look at her face, dreading what she would see. She

142

tried, but never made it. No sooner had her bare feet found the cold floor than her head began whirling and she sank back against the pillows.

She was wearing a nightdress, too short and somewhat bulky for her slender frame; one of Natasha's, no doubt. Lying flat on her back with the covers thrown down, she was able to gather the nightdress and bring it up to just below her breasts. Her body was a mass of welts, slash marks, and bruises. But it had been a week since her ordeal, and most of the marks were beginning to fade. She could only hope that every one would soon vanish.

Trying to get up and failing even to stand brought home to her the worrisome realization that although she might no longer have been delirious she was far from recovered.

An assumption well founded. She was to continue feverish on and off for the next ten days. She also suffered a bone-wrenching chill for a full two days, despite Natasha's piling blanket upon blanket over her. There were also occasional periods when she all but went out of her head with grief, lying there thinking about Boyd. Had it not been for Natasha keeping her almost constant vigil by her bedside she might very well have gone back into delirium.

Hour after hour, day after day Natasha talked soothingly to her, nursed her, fed her, brushed her hair for her, and did all the other seemingly trivial but all-important things every woman confined to bed needs.

And yet, despite everything Natasha was able to do for her, she continued seriously ill and in the grip of an anguish that threatened to become permanent.

Boyd, Boyd, my darling Boyd . . .

23

Even before Suverin and his men encountered Yellow Wolf and the other Chinooks, Boyd and Lionel Haggerty had begun their search for the captured women. During the Molalas' attack, while Tawny and Jenny had been wandering about calling for Boyd, he and Haggerty had been trapped inside the lead wagon, fighting off savages attempting to climb in over the tailgate and the driver's seat at the opposite end. When finally both men were able to get past their attackers, out of the wagon, and begin looking for Tawny and Jenny, it was too late. They were just in time to catch sight of the two women's abductors carrying them off into the woods.

Yelling loudly, they raced after them, both by sheer luck avoiding any more personal encounters with the Indians. In the woods, however, losing sight of Tawny and Jenny and the two braves, neither Boyd nor Haggerty knew which way to turn. For hours they wandered about, moving farther and farther from where the massacre had taken place. Their search was fruitless. They had no idea which direction the savages had come from, since they had launched their attack from all sides. There was also no way of identifying the tribe. Knowing who they were, they might, with the help of other Indians, locate their main camp, to which Tawny and Jenny were undoubtedly being taken.

Haggerty early perceived the hopelessness of their situation and the futility of further search, but he was nevertheless deeply moved by Boyd's reaction to the capture of his wife. All the fight so clearly evident in the many tense and dangerous situations which the train had run into en route to the valley seemed to have deserted the man. He appeared completely crushed.

They searched unsuccessfully for hours, until darkness fell and any further effort would have been useless. Unable to find their way back to the site of the massacre, they made camp by a stream, caught two trout in a weir skillfully fashioned by Haggerty, cooked and ate the fish, and retired for the night, sleeping under the stars, few of which were visible through the thick foliage above their heads. Haggerty slept; Boyd did not. He lay awake staring at the branch directly over him, placing himself on trial in the courtroom of his conscience, citing the evidence pro, mostly con, and speedily declaring himself guilty.

Chevrier, you are hereby found guilty of gross negligence, of incredible stupidity in failing to reach the two of them before those bastard savages vanished into the woods. God only knows where they've taken them. And only He knows what's to become of them . . .

'I swear by all that's holy, if they kill her I'll butcher every Indian in this valley!'

'Go to sleep, Boyd,' said Haggerty, his tone an appeal that came perilously close to pleading. 'You need sleep. We both do. Tomorrow, somehow, some way, we'll find that tribe's main camp. We'll get them both back. But we can't do anything now, and lying awake isn't going to do anything but drive you out of your head. Go to sleep, please . . .'

All the next day they wandered the woods, Boyd falling deeper and deeper into depression, in spite of Haggerty's unceasing efforts to keep his spirits up. Toward dusk they ran into a Tillamook hunting party loaded down with deer. The leader proved friendly, for some reason not in the least surprised at the sight of two white men wandering through his tribe's trees. Haggerty could not understand the Tillamooks' language, but, using sign language and drawing on the ground with a stick, he and Boyd were able to learn a number of important and helpful and disheartening facts.

According to the Tillamooks, the attacking tribe had been the 'Tribe of the Crazy Dogs', the Southern Molalas, as distinguished from the Northern Molalas, who in contrast were as peaceful as the Chinooks.

'Crazy Dogs kill everyone, everything!' said the leader, his face filling with fear.

Haggerty was able to get across to him that the Molalas had taken two white women prisoner. In response to this he and Boyd were calmly informed that both had been raped and their throats slit.

'How can he know that for sure?' asked Boyd.

Haggerty shrugged and put the question to the Tillamook.

'He says one of his men saw it happen. Or knows somebody who did.'

'Doesn't that sound a little vague to you?' asked Boyd in exasperation.

Haggerty shrugged. 'Maybe. But why would this one say such a thing if it wasn't true? Everything else they've told us seems to make sense.'

'I don't care who saw what, I don't believe Tawny's dead!

Jenny, maybe, but Tawny's too shrewd, too resourceful.'

'Be realistic, Boyd. How resourceful can anybody be up against a half-crazed savage with a tomahawk in one hand and knife in the other? Particularly a female...'

'I don't care; she's alive. I know she is. I know *her*. It wouldn't surprise me if she turned the tables on the bastard who grabbed her and killed him with his own tomahawk!'

'I hope she did,' said Haggerty, with nothing like conviction in his tone. He scratched his beard and his neck, swatted away a gnat, and thought. Then he asked the Tillamook leader the whereabouts of the Molalas' camp. Boyd and he were told that the tribe had set up a temporary camp and were given directions to it. It lay to the south near the 'big river', which had to be the Willamette River. The Tillamook leader spread his huge hands two feet apart, indicating how far the sun would rise from the horizon during the time it would take the two men to cover the distance to the camp.

Darkness fell and the night was overcast, neither the moon nor a single star showing. The two had little choice but to spend a second night by the river, rise with the sun, and follow the Tillamooks' directions to the Molalas' temporary camp.

This posed a problem which Boyd pointed out to his friend shortly after the Indians went on their way.

'If that camp is temporary, considering we've already wasted a day and a half, who's to say they'll still be around when we get there?'

'Let's just eat and sleep and hope for a break,' rejoined Haggerty.

They found the Molalas' temporary camp, the clothing on the corpses scattered about easily recognizable, not to mention the goods stolen from the wagon train. But Boyd's fear was immediately realized. Not a living soul was to be seen. The fires were cold. Those who had survived whoever had attacked the camp had either played dead and run off later or had fled into the woods during the fighting. The two men counted well over a hundred corpses, braves and squaws.

Two tall stakes stood side by side near what appeared to

have been the tribe's council fire, its ash-filled bed much larger than those of the other fires.

Pieces of rawhide cut with a knife were found at the foot of each of the stakes. On the rawhide was dried blood. It could also be seen on the stakes themselves. Switches lay about the ground, and one of the dead squaws still held a number of them bunched in one hand.

'I hate to say it,' said Haggerty quietly, 'but in practically every tribe I've come across the past dozen years, scouting, trailblazing, guiding, the men tie up white women prisoners and let their squaws beat 'em with willow switches or whatever else comes in handy.'

'I know all about it,' said Boyd morosely. Kneeling, he examined the parted pieces of rawhide. 'This blood has to be Tawny's and Jenny's.'

'But it's cut, Boyd,' countered Haggerty, his green eyes brightening. 'Don't you see, somebody cut them loose. Freed them . . .'

'Yeah.' Boyd stood up, tossing the two pieces of rawhide he had been examining to one side. 'The question is, before they died or after?'

'Jesus, man, don't talk like that.' Haggerty swept his arm around the area. 'Look at all these bodies. Nothing but redskins. Not a white man or woman among 'em. Look.'

'I see.'

'It seems to me like somebody attacked these bastards, maybe under cover of darkness, just before they bedded down for the night. Attacked 'em and rescued your wife and the Latchford girl.'

Boyd's eyes lit up. 'You think that's possible?'

'Put it all together; think it through. Somebody, God knows who, jumped this bunch just the way they jumped us back up the line. And massacred them.'

'Not the Tillamooks.'

'No.' Haggerty's face darkened in thought. 'That's what puzzles me. Who? Like that bunch o' Tillamooks said, these Southern Molalas are the Crazy Dogs of the valley. Every other tribe, from the Tualatins, the Yamhills, the Santiams, Lakmiuts, the whole kit and boodle – even this bunch's northern brothers – hate and fear 'em. So if no other Indians wiped 'em out, who could have?'

'Who knows? I don't muchly care. If anybody ever had it coming . . .'

They wandered about as they talked, exchanging conjecture. Boyd's spirits might not have suddenly begun to soar, but they were definitely uplifted. If Tawny and Jenny had been rescued, and it certainly looked like it, Haggerty's curiosity was on the mark. *Who had done it?*

The answer to this question came from a most unexpected source. In midsentence Boyd stopped abruptly, both men freezing at the sound of a low moan. One of the 'corpses' stirred, raising a muscular left arm feebly, beckoning to them. They ran to him.

He was a young brave, barely out of his teens. He showed bullet holes in both shoulders and through the left side of his rib cage. He had lost a great deal of blood. Clearly his rugged build, combined with an iron constitution, had enabled him to survive, at least up to now.

He asked for water. Boyd searched about, found a gourd half full of stale water well heated by the sun, and fed it to him. In the man's eyes was death, coming slowly, stealing up on him. But he still managed to speak.

Haggerty signed the question. 'The two white women slaves your people took from the wagon train north of here. They were tied to the stakes?'

The man nodded ever so slightly and opened his mouth, begging for more water. Boyd gave it to him, although most of it never reached his throat.

'Who took these women from you?' asked Haggerty.

Lifting his hand with great effort, the brave pointed at first one eye, then the other.

'White eyes?' asked Boyd.

Again a barely perceptible nod.

'He's delirious,' said Boyd, 'either that or lying. We had no survivors. I know for a fact there are no other Americans here anywhere in the valley.' The question was repeated. The answer was the same. Boyd frowned and dug into his memory. 'There *was* an American fort built here some years back by men who came up the coast in a whaler, crossed the mountains, and tried their hand at fur trading. But according to what I heard at our briefing, for whatever reason, Indians, illness, who knows, that fort was abandoned years ago. Before Lewis and Clark came out.'

'White eyes, white eyes,' said Haggerty, thinking aloud. 'Wait a minute, Boyd, Americans aren't the only white eyes in the world.'

Boyd was with him on the instant. 'The Russians! They've been trading for furs up and down the northern coast for years. Now they've come down this far; I'd bet my life that's the answer! Douglas Prescott told us all about them. They built a big installation up in Alaska, what they call New Archangel. Yankee whalers have been up there.'

Haggerty nodded. 'I've heard the Russians trade for hides up and down the Alaskan coast. The Hudson Bay Company is up in arms about it, but of course there's nothing they can do to stop them.'

'Short of Canada declaring war,' said Boyd.

'But why would they come this far south?'

'To get a foothold, why else? Nobody has any real claim to this territory, not us, not the British in Canada. Maybe the Spanish down below, but nobody else. Lionel, it's wide open, all of it, here for the grabbing. Douglas claims the Russian government has its eye on the entire coast.'

'Chinooks,' whispered the brave.

'Listen to him,' said Boyd excitedly. 'The Russians – they must trade with the Chinooks, right?'

They got what they could out of the man before his eyes rolled up into his head and it fell to one side.

'That's that,' said Haggerty, getting to his feet.

Boyd tossed away the gourd and closed the dead man's eyes. 'Lionel, we've got to find us some Chinooks. If they're dealing with the Russians they'll have all the rest of the answers we need.' Impulsively he grabbed Haggerty by both arms and whooped loudly. 'Lionel, they're safe, the two of them. They were rescued and they're safe! I know it ...'

'You feel it in your bones.' Haggerty half laughed. 'To be honest, so do I. Come, let's head back up the way we came. The Chinooks have to be a good twenty to thirty miles to the north. With any luck we might run into a trapping party.'

Each of them took a rifle and ramrod, patches, and leather

belt bags of powder and balls. They started north, leaving behind a scene of carnage rivaling that of their own ill-fated wagon train camp.

In the midst of life there was just too much death, reflected Boyd ruefully as they gained the trail and followed it northward.

The following morning they ran into a party of Chinooks, and they reached Fort New Kiev later that same day. Sergeant Torskovich welcomed them and, with one of his men acting as interpreter, answered all their questions. He pointed out Jenny Latchford's grave alongside that of the Aleut squaw's and cautioned Boyd that his wife had been delirious when they had taken her on board the *Saint Nicholas*. But he quickly added that she was in the captain's wife's capable hands and assured both Boyd and Haggerty that Tawny would recover.

'How do you propose to get to New Archangel?' asked Torskovich. 'The *Saint Nicholas* will not return here until spring.'

'I'll find a way,' said Boyd resolutely.

'Wrong,' interposed Haggerty. '*We'll* find a way.'

A way could be found; any American ship sailing up to New Archangel from Yerba Buena* would take them. The problem was time. By the time the two of them crossed the Coastal Ranges and covered the roughly eight hundred miles down the coast to Yerba Buena, it would be late in the year. Too late for even the most daring Yankee whaler or seal-pelt hunter to challenge the notorious Alaskan winter.

24

By the time the *Saint Nicholas* reached home port at New Archangel, Tawny was on her feet and well on the way to full recovery. It would, however, be months, possibly years before the last scars of the slash marks inflicted upon her

* Present-day San Francisco.

helpless body by the Molala squaws would disappear. If all of them ever would.

Varya Mihailovna Poplova welcomed her like a daughter after Natasha had explained her presence and detailed the horrifying experiences to which Tawny had been subjected. Varya's husband, the colonel, was likewise warm and receptive toward her, at once adopting a benign, fatherly attitude. Tawny was given her own room and repeated assurances by Lieutenant Suverin:

'If you're able to put up with our company through the winter, you can be sure the first American ship that puts in here come spring will give you passage to wherever you wish to go.'

'In the meantime,' said the colonel, 'you must consider yourself our honored guest. Apart from being our only guest.' The men laughed; the women, accustomed to the commander's rather weak attempts at humor, only smiled.

'It's barely the beginning of October,' said Tawny, eyeing the colonel with a friendly smile. 'Is it possible any American ship might show up before winter sets in?'

'That, I'm afraid, is very doubtful,' interposed Captain Prishibeyev. 'Winter comes to us very early up here. Even if a vessel could make it through the first crop of ice floes, it would be too cold for the whalers or seal hunters to work outside, you see.'

The entire group was gathered around the dining-room table, the most pleasant and cheerful collection of strangers Tawny had ever met, so unpretentious, so genuine and considerate when she compared them to Uncle Aldous and the other Ramplings in St. Louis.

And yet, despite the Russians' continuous efforts to buoy her spirits, to keep her occupied and relieved of the boredom they themselves suffered now and then by engaging her in seemingly endless conversations and asking hundreds of questions about America – 'Mee-soor-ee' – and the long journey from Keys Landing, there was nothing any of them could do to lighten the weight of the stone which had settled in her breast where once her heart had been.

But hard as she tried to avoid admitting it to herself, it seemed useless, even absurd to go on pretending that Boyd was still alive. Lieutenant Suverin had been very explicit in detailing what he and his men had found, their conversations with the Chinooks, with whom all the Russians at Fort New Kiev had become very close, and the Indians' wholehearted agreement that among those in the wagon train, she and Jenny Latchford only had escaped with their lives.

Sitting across from her at the dinner table sipping *ryabinovka*, which Tawny had been encouraged to try, only to find it not to her taste, Suverin could not take his eyes off her. She was, he had decided, the most beautiful woman he had ever seen, in spite of her wretched condition, the bruises, the slashes and battering she had been suffering when he and the Aleut had rescued her and the unfortunate Jenny Latchford. Indeed, she made Colonel Zorodoff's wife, Yermolay Alexeyvich's deliciously endowed red-haired mistress, and every other woman at court look fully as fetching as Polish milk cows. Long before their return he had lost all of his on-again, off-again interest in Captain Prishibeyev's wife. With Tawny's arrival, Natasha had suddenly become much too old for him. Worth a smile and a kind word daily, to be sure, but that was as far as he'd ever go with her now.

To his surprise, Natasha took her relegation to second best with grace and nothing resembling jealousy toward Tawny. The two had become too close. As close as Varya Poplova had every intention of becoming, it appeared. Tawny proved to be the daughter neither woman had ever had.

Suverin could hardly deny to himself that Natasha's reaction to his ignoring her obviously bothered her not in the least. Could it be possible she was never serious about him in the first place? Could it be that she was merely playing games with him? No, the very idea was ridiculous. Every woman who'd ever met him had practically fallen at his feet!

Still, considering the situation realistically, he really ought to be grateful to Natasha for behaving so sportingly. A chill crossed his shoulders: could it possibly be that he was losing some small portion of his enormous appeal to the opposite sex?

No. Impossible! Unthinkable! His mirror daily denied

such a ridiculous suggestion.

But his life had turned a corner. Women, he suddenly had no desire for. One woman. One only. The one sitting across from him, her eyes so dark and deep, her lips so full and inviting, her hair the most beautiful he had ever seen, her body ... But at all costs, he must handle the situation with the delicacy of a surgeon performing a difficult operation. He had to be extraordinarily careful – friendly, solicitous of her health, attentive without overdoing it. Be her big brother. Until all thoughts of her dead husband buried themselves too deeply in her mind ever to rise again. Then and only then would he, Nikandr Alexis Raymonovich Suverin, begin to lay siege to her heart. How was it Yermolay Alexeyvich, His Imperial Majesty's chamberlain's nephew, put it? 'Bring her to heart, to heel, to headboard. In that order.'

Patience. A month, perhaps even two, but the idea was to make her come to him, make himself so attractive, so irresistible to her that she could not help but fall in love with him. No question, the prize was certainly worth the waiting.

Before the year was out she would be his, even if, God forbid, he had to marry her. But what a catch, what a beauty! He could just picture the faces of his friends back at court when he introduced her to them. Their eyes, their jaws sagging in astonishment.

'Nikki!' Colonel Poplova broke into his thoughts so abruptly that Suverin came perilously close to spilling his drink.

'Sir?'

'What are you dreaming about, my boy? You're ten thousand miles away. Is that not so, Varya, my dear? Natasha?'

Mind your own damned business, Colonel Big Mouth, reflected Suverin, striving to keep from coloring.

'Where do you come from in America?' Varya asked Tawny.

'A tiny little place in the Osage Indian country of Missouri. It's called Titus Forks, after the man who founded it.' She went on to tell Varya about her father and his business and her hope that now, widowed as she was, she might return to Missouri as soon as possible. Captain

Prishibeyev proposed her the choice of taking ship down to Yerba Buena, then traveling cross-country or the long voyage around Cape Horn, up the east coast of South America to the Gulf of Mexico and New Orleans.

'That way you could travel up the Mississippi River to St. Louis,' he added.

It was a thought that had not occurred to Tawny, but the length of such a voyage notwithstanding, it seemed practical.

To her. Not to Suverin. He was beginning to wish in earnest that his commanding officer and Prishibeyev would concentrate on minding their own and not the girl's business. The more ideas they jammed into her lovely head, obviously the harder it would be for him in Saint Petersburg, in Kiev, anywhere in Russia, not this Titus Forks. She might not realize it at the moment, but that part of her life was over forever. The book closed and sealed.

If it was to be the last thing he did in his life, by the holy saints he'd see to that!

25

To Tawny that winter in New Archangel was interminable, the cold outside insufferable, but the warmth of her new friends and rescuer boundless. Everyone treated her like a princess, and with her health completely restored, life began to look brighter than it had in ages. Hardly a day went by that Suverin did not repeat his promise that the first Yankee ship to show its sails in the harbor once the ice broke would carry her back to her people.

In the meantime his admiration for her was displaced by a love so deep-seated, so heart-wrenching, he found himself hard put to disguise it. Never in his life had he been in love before, but he was now, head over boot heels. In Varya's words she could see it from a 'verst* away'.

---

* Approximately two thirds of a mile.

The colonel's wife trapped her husband's favorite subaltern in the latter's quarters late one afternoon shortly after Suverin had come back from making rounds of the sentries, a daily chore which he, as second in command, had little heart for, but as well little chance of avoiding.

'Every time she walks into the room you shatter into little pieces,' Varya said, grinning impishly and waggling a finger under his nose. 'Confess, Nikki, you're desperately in love with her. You adore her!'

'Nonsense. I've never been "desperately in love", as you choose to put it, not with any woman. And never will be. In my code, any soldier who hands his heart over to a woman becomes a detriment to his unit. My uniform is my love.'

'To say nothing of your ambition...' Varya threw her head back and laughed.

'Duty really does come first, Varya Mihailovna.'

'Nonsense. As if you were overburdened with duties in this tropical paradise.' Clapping him on the back playfully, she laughed again. 'Good luck to you with her, Nikki. You're a catch and so is she, even if she is a foreigner. I like her, she has spunk, and she's as lovely as a garden in spring. Bright, too. She's picked up more Russian in two months than could any linguist. But, you naughty boy you, you see that you do the honorable thing.' Again the waggling finger. 'You're to marry her. If you don't I promise you by the saints I'll make Luka take your grade away and reduce you to private.' Again she laughed. And, to his relief, left him in peace. Hardly peace of mind, but at least alone.

So it had become that obvious, had it? Staring into his mirror, pinching the ends of his mustache, he shook his head. Holy saints!

Suverin's falling in love with Tawny, and her own seat on the sidelines watching, was the biggest and certainly the most entertaining event to occur in Varya Mihailovna Poplova's life since she and the colonel and the others had landed at New Archangel. But being a woman, and knowing Suverin as well as he knew himself – or so she fancied – Varya felt constrained to warn Tawny. Taking her aside shortly after Christmas and the beginning of the New Year, celebrated with great ceremony and considerable drinking at the fort, the two had a long, private talk, the substance of which was a friendly warning from the older woman that Tawny be on her guard.

The two were in Varya's bedroom with the door locked against possible intrusion. The colonel's wife sat Tawny on the edge of her bed and got right into her mother-to-daughter lecture.

'He's in love with you.'

'I've suspected as much.'

'How do you feel about him?'

'I like him very much. After all, he saved my life. And he's been very kind, a perfect gentleman.'

'If one of the Aleuts, one about sixty-five, saved your life, would you fall in love with him?'

'I said I like Nikki very much. I didn't say I love him,' said Tawny evenly. This early into the conversation her cheeks were already beginning to redden.

'Ah, but you will fall in love with him. Just you watch...'

'I doubt that.'

'Doubt it all you please, you will. And because you will I must warn you that even though he will profess to love you with all his heart and soul, and will believe that sincerely, he has another love.' Tawny's eyes widened, more in puzzlement than surprise. 'Not a woman; you're the only woman in his head, in his heart. I'm talking about the service, the army. You or any other woman who lines up with our Nikki for life must be prepared to... how shall I put it, contend with that reality. Thousands upon thousands of us do.'

'I'll keep it in mind,' said Tawny dryly, smiling and patting Varya's chubby hand.

'You don't think you'll fall in love with him?'

'No, I do not.'

'You will. I can see that rascal Cupid hovering about. I'm never wrong when it comes to matters of the heart.'

'There's always a first time. The problem here is that I haven't the slightest desire to fall in love. Actually, it's the last thing I want to do. Not with one foot practically on board an American ship and heading for home.'

'We'll see...'

*

Late in April Tawny fell ill with a cold and sore throat. Varya and Natasha put her to bed, over her protestations. Meanwhile, Captain Prishibeyev and his men were preparing the *Saint Nicholas* for her first run down the coast to Fort New Kiev, where Sergeant Torskovich had kept the flag flying all winter long. They would leave as soon as the supply ship put in.

Suverin visited Tawny daily while she was confined to the covers and obliged to swallow some foul-tasting brown medicine which Varya Mihailovna swore by all the saints would douse the fire in her throat, stop her hacking cough, clear her lungs, and get her back on her feet.

A Russian barkentine, the *Sviostoloff*, come all the way from the Motherland, put into the harbor, crunching her way through the slowly melting ice to anchor while Tawny lay abed. It came to drop off supplies, new men, and to pick up the hides gathered the previous summer and fall. More importantly, at least to Suverin, to his absolute astonishment, included in the *Sviostoloff*'s captain's leather order packet was a signed transfer for one Lieutenant, now elevated to Captain, Nikandr A. R. Suverin. Not a second captain, but a full senior!

The Russian army was not unlike every other military force in the world, bound up in red tape, commanded by the usual pack of misfits, malingerers, and muddleheads, and in its day-to-day operations, in peace or war, as unpredictable as the weather. Earlier, before the long voyage down the coast to Cape Disappointment, Suverin had been praying for a transfer to arrive reassigning him to his original unit, stationed in Saint Petersburg. No such transfer had been forthcoming. Now, when he least expected it, here it was, handed to him by Captain Boleski, commanding the *Sviostoloff*, along with four shoulder straps replacing his lonely one!

Suverin was given his two surprises on the deck of the *Sviostoloff* in the presence of Colonel Luka Poplova only, who proceeded to congratulate Nikki heartily, throwing one arm about his shoulder and all but dancing a jig with him.

Captain Suverin's heart beat wildly; his head spun. The three men stood at the bow of the ship, the two older beating their chests with their arms against the cold. Suverin's commanding officer eyed him fondly.

'I'll be sorry to lose you, Nikki,' said the colonel, in what for him was a dramatically serious tone. 'This surprises me as much as it clearly surprises you.'

'Well, you two no doubt have much to talk about,' interposed Captain Boleski. 'I confess this cold is getting to be too much for me. Besides, I have work to do. If you'll excuse me, I'm going below to check on the loading and see if I can lend a hand to Captain Prishibeyev. I've brought him some equipment he requested for the *Saint Nicholas*. I shall see you both later.'

No sooner had the captain vanished down the companionway than Suverin closed in on his colonel, all but grasping him by the lapels of his fur coat while addressing him in a voice decidedly conspiratorial in tone.

'Colonel, I must ask you a great favor, the biggest favor you can possibly grant me.'

'You want to take the woman home with you...'

'I would give my right arm to.'

The wind came up, whining loudly through the shrouds above their heads, flapping the canvas. They stepped back into the entrance to the companionway to avoid the icy blast.

'Don't talk nonsense. Your right arm you'll need, my boy, to hold her close.' He winked slyly. 'The question is, would she be willing to go with you? All I hear from her is talk of getting back to Missouri.'

'Before, yes. But she's no longer brooding over the loss of her husband. Nor is she homesick for this Titus Forks. On my honor as an officer and a gentleman, I would be a good husband to her. The best. I am and would continue to be devoted to her. She knows that.'

'Maybe I shouldn't say it, but nothing would please me more than seeing the two of you tie the knot. You'd make a fine couple.'

'Then we have your blessing?'

'Let's put it this way – I like you too much to stand in your way.'

'I appreciate that, sir, more than I can ever put into words. The thing is, the women mustn't know about this. As far as that goes, nobody else should know.' Suverin tapped the yellow envelope in his left hand with his index finger.

'This ship arrives, loads, and leaves. Only nobody ashore knows I'll be going along.'

Colonel Poplova tilted his head and eyed him gravely. 'My boy, what you're really talking about is kidnapping.'

'I love her. I intend to marry her. I will be the best husband on the face of the earth.'

'I have no doubt you'll try. The question remains, does she love you?' Suddenly the colonel was having second thoughts. Suddenly Suverin felt nervous.

'She's very fond of me . . .'

'I, too, am very fond of you, but I don't love you.'

'Sir, I'm deadly serious. I've never been more serious in my life.'

'You need an accomplice in this conspiracy that's boiling up inside your brain, is that it?'

'If I can get her on board tonight and we sail with the tide before dawn, nobody at the fort will realize she and I have gone until it's too late. I mean, Captain Prishibeyev wouldn't be about to chase after us in the *Saint Nicholas*, would he?'

The colonel laughed. 'You're a two-tailed devil with three sets of horns, you know that, Nikki? When you set your sights on something you really go all out. What's your plan? Do you intend to knock the poor creature over the head, bundle her in a sea bag, and carry her on board under cover of darkness? And by the time she wakes, this tub will be past Kodiak Island and within sight of the Alaska Peninsula? Would it be something like that?'

'I love her, Luka.' He had never called the colonel by his first name before in all their years together. He would never have been so presumptuous. He did so now, of course, only to impress Poplova with his seriousness. It was necessary, and superbly timed. He had the colonel in his corner, and was not about to let him slip away. Suverin knew very well that the older man couldn't have been fonder of him had he been his own firstborn.

'All right, all right. Handle it any way you like, just don't tell me the details,' said the colonel. 'If Varya Mihailovna ever gets wind of it she'll skin me from eyes to ankles.'

'I'll handle the whole thing, in the most delicate way possible.'

'One thing you have to keep in mind. Your wife-to-be is bedridden.'

Suverin shook his head. 'I was with her less than an hour ago. She's rid of her cold and sore throat. She'll be up and around tonight.'

'Listen to me, my amorous friend, you take good care of her, you hear me?'

'I'll treat her like a princess; you know I will.' He studied his superior's eyes. 'But I can count on you – you will go along with me? You won't whisper a word to the others?'

'I've agreed to close my eyes. What would you have me do, sign a paper in blood?'

'Thank you, my colonel.' Suverin paused. 'One thing amazes me.' He held up the envelope. 'Why did this show up now, do you think? Out of the blue?'

Colonel Poplova shrugged. 'Somebody in Saint Petersburg likes you. Who knows why? This is the army, Nikki, there's never any logic, any reason for promotion. Not in my experience. Back home they don't even know what you accomplished down at New Kiev. My boy, don't question it, just accept ... Captain.'

Two army officers appeared on deck, both close to Suverin's age, one portly, the other as slender as a totem pole and very nearly as tall, at least six foot eight. Side by side, approaching them in the company of Captain Boleski, they looked comical.

Both were lieutenants; they and a dozen non-commissioned officers and men had been reassigned to New Archangel, with half of their number eventually destined for duty at Fort New Kiev. This information, imparted to the colonel and Suverin by Boleski, went in one of Captain Suverin's ears and speedily out the other. He couldn't care less about replacements.

His thoughts were fully occupied with something of much greater importance.

26

The three-masted barkentine, *Sviostoloff*, was loaded by sundown, and Captain Boleski and his crew were invited ashore for a sumptuous dinner prepared by the colonel's wife, Natasha, and two Aleut women helpers. Tawny appeared at the table, looking fit and rosy-cheeked, for the first time in four days. She was greeted by everyone with applause and was introduced to the visitors from the Motherland, all of whom congratulated her on her progress in learning their language.

She ate heartily. Suverin was edgy; he nibbled at his food, exchanging occasional glances with Colonel Poplova, who to the new captain seemed to be taking their plot much less seriously than Suverin would have liked. Just before dinner, while Varya was busy in the kitchen with the other women, Suverin had slipped into the Poplovas' private quarters and pilfered a small quantity of a soporific which the colonel sometimes took when he suffered insomnia.

Suverin knew exactly where to look for the small bottle containing the pale brown liquid; his co-conspirator's directions had been explicit.

After dinner, after a delicious *groosh** pie and a *froo'ktaf peero'zhnaye*, † both prepared by Natasha, which practically everybody save Tawny and the tall, slender, newly arrived lieutenant stuffed themselves with, bottles of *kvass* and vodka were produced, Captain Boleski presented gifts to the ladies, and after-dinner drinking and smoking were initiated in earnest by the men.

The principal topic of conversation during and after dinner was naturally the news from home, primarily what was going on at the capital and in the court, the state of His Majesty's health, and politics.

* Pear.
† Fruit cake.

Tawny retired early. Suverin stopped by before she blew out the lamp to share tea with her, a welcome nightcap to aid the digestion and keep away the cold of the wintry April night sneaking through the slender crack alongside her window, which had been repaired repeatedly, but appeared determined to reopen every so often.

She finished her glass of tea, congratulated him again on his elevation in rank, permitted him to kiss her good night in brotherly fashion on the cheek, and he withdrew. She would sleep tonight deeper than she had ever slept in her life, he reflected, bidding her good night and closing the door behind him. There was no lock, only a latch, easily lifted from the outside with the blade of his pocketknife.

When Tawny awoke, it was to discover herself in a bunk bed in a cabin slightly larger than Natasha's aboard the *Saint Nicholas*, but much more comfortably furnished. It was also remarkably clean, not so much as a speck of dust anywhere to be seen. Although she had no way of knowing it upon awakening, the *Sviostoloff* had wound up her fore and aft anchors and swung about, and was heading back the way she had come.

And had already been at sea for nearly three hours.

Sitting up in the narrow bed, Tawny was able to look out a porthole and see a sight so dazzling it caused her to wince: mountains of ice and dark blue water filled with large bergs. She could hear the flapping of canvas directly over her head; it was not until this sound reached her ears that she was conscious of a slight headache and a furry feeling covering her tongue.

She lay back down and thought a moment. Her first impulse was to scream, get whoever happened to be closest to her door inside, and demand an explanation of where she was, how she had gotten there, where the ship was heading, and answers to a dozen more questions.

But why bother? She could hardly run to the tiller, swing the ship around, and sail it back to New Archangel. Calming herself, getting a grip on her nerves, she got up, fighting off her headache, planting her bare feet on the floor, only to discover pretty pink wool slippers on the floor and a fur cape neatly folded lying at the foot of the bed.

Rising, pushing her feet into the slippers, she bundled the cape about her and started for the door. She was preparing to open it when a gentle knock sounded.

'Tawny?'

'Nikki!' She wrenched open the door. 'What the devil –' she began.

'Before I start,' he cut in, 'you have my permission to claw my eyes out, to rip my cheeks open, to do whatever you wish. Just don't go so far as to kill me. To explain this honestly, I have kidnapped you. Yes, Tawny, my darling, unfortunately that's the only suitable word to describe it. We're on the *Sviostoloff*, homeward bound. My home, which will become ours. I love you, I'm taking you home with me; we will be married –'

'You're insane,' she gasped. 'Totally mad, drunk, I have no idea which, nor do I care. This can't be happening . . .' Her fingertips went to her temples. She reeled slightly, grabbing the doorjamb for support. He caught her; she shook free and searched his eyes. 'You wouldn't dare. This is monstrous . . .'

'Must I repeat it all? Call me a scoundrel, dress me down properly, curse me, if it will help, but it was something I had to do! I say again, I love you, I want you, I need you more than the blood in my body. Yes, I confess I have deceived you –'

'*Deceived me!*'

'Ssh, I beg you –'

'You're not insane, you're nothing but a damned fool! A schoolboy who's stolen something that doesn't belong to him. That never could!'

'Tawny –'

'What in the world ever gave you the idea that I loved you? Did I ever suggest such nonsense? Ever even hint it?'

'Must we stand here in this doorway discussing it? You certainly don't hate me, you can't. And you can't make me believe you don't have any warm feelings toward me . . .'

He was beginning to feel like the fool she had accused him of being. He had known from the beginning that such an incredibly rash strategy – if that was what one could call it – could prove risky at best. But what choice had he? The first Yankee ship to show its colors in the harbor of New

163

Archangel would have signaled the beginning of the end. Its captain would have taken her aboard and she could have been lost to him forever. What was he to do? Just stand by and let her leave, give up the one he loved? The one he adored . . . couldn't live without? Wave good-bye to her forever from the water's edge while she stood at the rail of some accursed whaler waving back?

Thank you for saving my life, but love? Marriage? You're joking, you must be . . .

No, with the colonel's blessing, at least his indulgence, he had taken this boldest of bold steps. Here she was. He'd expected that she would be furious with him. But that didn't bother him; she'd get over it.

It was a long way to Saint Petersburg, half-way round the world. Her anger would subside; her disgust with him, with his deceit, could and would gradually lessen. It was up to him to see that it did. Let her carry on, let her get the shock and frustration out of her system. In a week, perhaps less, she would have simmered down and they would be able to discuss things rationally.

Any woman would feel as she did now, anyone with her spine and spunk.

But eventually she'd see the light. Of love.

27

After Tawny had slammed the door in Suverin's face she returned to the bed to sit down and calmly assess her predicament. Before the last of her patience had deserted her the new captain had told her that her clothes, which she and Natasha and Varya had made during the winter, were in the chest given her by Colonel Poplova upon her arrival at New Archangel; it, and thus everything that she owned, was on board. He had also stressed that she could expect to be treated as a lady and that her privacy would be respected. This last promise, uttered with the utmost gravity, proved the snapping point. If kidnapping her was his idea of respecting one's privacy then he had a good deal to learn regarding basic social conduct. And she told him so, in far less socially acceptable terms.

But for some inexplicable reason, in spite of her anger and frustration she felt a small measure of sympathy for her rescuer-abductor. Clearly he was passionately in love with her – that much she didn't need Varya or Natasha to tell her. The man was no more able to conceal his true feelings than a cloudless sky could hide a full moon.

Still, he might have behaved honorably about it. He could have made an effort to court her and, like any real gentleman, formally request her hand in marriage. On second thoughts, he could hardly do that: despite his massive ego, his overweening confidence in himself, he obviously didn't have the nerve to risk being turned down. Besides, why take the chance when he could spirit her away as easily as a bad little boy steals a penny candy from an unsuspecting storekeeper?

Saint Petersburg. Good Lord! She'd heard of the place, of course; for hours on end it had been the chief topic of conversation at the dinner table in New Archangel. The capital was touted by one and all as the garden spot of the country, the Paris of the East, according to Natasha. And with Alexander I on the throne, the court was the center of luxury, of endless balls, state dinners, parties galore ... Of course, absence does wonders to people's imaginations, and perhaps the city and the court were not nearly as marvelous as Varya, Natasha, and the others so fervently claimed them to be.

Good, bad, or middling, she would make no plans to stay. She would never even see Saint Petersburg if the opportunity arose to make her escape on the overland journey to the capital, necessitated by the ship's putting in well north of there.

Her heart sank even lower when later in the day Captain Boleski invited her to his tidy, dully furnished little cabin for a glass of tea and, in answer to her query, began tracing the *Sviostoloff*'s route westward, around the corner of the Alaska Peninsula, up through the Bering Sea, changing direction toward the northwest, passing inside Wrangel Island and farther on inside the New Siberian Islands through the Laptevykh Sea, past Cape Chelyuskin, continuing along the northernmost Siberian coastline, down into the Kara Sea.

'From here to there we cover close to fifteen thousand miles.'

'Fifteen . . .'

Boleski nodded, his gleaming bald head showing lonesome wisps of white hair that caught the sunlight through the port glass and turned silver.

'We have, dear lady, a good six months' journey ahead of us. Possibly less, but I doubt it. Less only if the wind holds steady and doesn't begin battering us and pushing us all over the waters.' He sighed wistfully. 'What I wouldn't have given to lay over in New Archangel for a week. Just one. Just long enough to feel ground under our heels instead of wood. We've been at sea for such a long time.'

'Where do you head for when you leave the Kara Sea?' asked Tawny, placing the tip of her finger at the precise spot Boleski had lifted his own from.

He took hold of her finger and moved the tip slowly in a southwesterly direction. 'Past Vaigach Island to port, Kolguev Island to starboard, around Kanin Point, and down into the White Sea. We dock at Belomorsk.'

'But that's even a thousand miles farther!' she burst, noting the mileage scale in the corner of the map and making a rough comparison.

'More or less. In Russia we have a saying, my dear: "When one travels, distance is nothing if one packs patience in one's portmanteau." '

Engrossed in the map, she only half heard him. 'I'm curious, how could you possibly follow this route in the winter? It must have been ice-locked . . .'

'It is completely impassable, and we didn't follow it. We came up to New Archangel from the Persian Gulf, from Basra.' He indicated a diagonal line through the Indian Ocean, up through the Netherlands Indies, continuing toward the north-east, bisecting the north Pacific Ocean to Alaska. 'About fifteen thousand miles.'

'Why not go back the same way?'

'Very simple. Your and Captain Suverin's ultimate

166

destination and that of our cargo is not Basra, it's Saint Petersburg. Putting in at Belomorsk brings us close to the capital. There is another way – directly across to Nikolaevsk here, in the Sea of Okhotsk, north of Japan. That's only about seven thousand miles. But upon landing you would have to journey no less than eight thousand more across the country. Better sails over one's head than wheels under one's feet, I always say.'

'This geography lesson is all very interesting. The problem is I shouldn't even be here on board!'

He laughed.

'I've been kidnapped.'

He stopped laughing. 'You're joking.'

'Do I look as if I were? Do I sound like it?'

A shocked look further wizened the captain's already deeply furrowed features.

'I was aware of no such thing. Upon my word as a Christian. And I am a religious man. Colonel Poplova himself requested a cabin for you. In two hours I had my sister's own private cabin readied.'

'Sister?'

'My late sister, Alishka. She, like you, was a widow; after her husband died she traveled all over the world with me. She herself died last year.'

Pity welled up in Tawny at the look in the man's eyes.

'I never married, you see.' He stared at his desk, at the map, then caught himself. 'New clothes, clothes she never even got to wear, hang in the armoire in your cabin. I keep them there because the place is never used and their presence, well, it's as if she were still with us. They're yours to wear if you wish.' He sized her up. 'My poor Alishka was as tall as you, but slightly heavier. Not much. Her things should fit you with a little taking in, if you're handy with needle and thread.'

Tawny was genuinely touched, but aware as well of the need to follow up the evident advantage Boleski's shocked reaction had given her.

'Kidnapped by Suverin. A hanging offense in my country,' she said pointedly.

The captain seemed confused, actually mystified. 'Colonel Poplova told me that you and Captain Suverin are to be married. The colonel even asked me to perform the ceremony here on shipboard.'

'Colonel Poplova is at best a romanticist, at worst a liar. He's as much responsible for this disgusting affair as Suverin himself. If it weren't for him Suverin never would have been able to get me on board, I'm sure.'

Boleski nodded. 'He does treat the captain like a young prince.'

'The very reason he couldn't refuse him when Nikki asked for his help.'

'Nikki?' Up went Boleski's left eyebrow.

'Suverin, Nikki, Captain, what difference does it make what I call him? As Poplova probably told you, Suverin saved my life. I'm curious – what does that mean in your country, among your people, that I'm automatically obligated to marry him?'

'Not at all.'

'I will never marry him; nor will I be his mistress, if that's what's crossing your mind...'

'Dear lady, you misjudge me. I was thinking no such thing.' Captain Boleski blushed furiously.

'I'm sorry, I shouldn't have said that. I'm... very upset.'

'Yes, naturally. Who in your position wouldn't be? Don't be afraid, though, your door locks and bolts from the inside.'

Again her eyes strayed to the map. 'If you went back through the Pacific you could drop me off at any one of a dozen ports. I'd get back to the mainland one way or another.'

He shook his head. 'I only wish I could help you, but we have a schedule. The Company is waiting for our cargo. See for yourself, the Pacific is much the longer route. We'd also run the risk of being becalmed down here past the Hawaiian Islands...'

The captain rubbed his bald head vigorously and wrinkled his brow in thought.

She concentrated, wringing out her mind, examining every possibility. 'Are you scheduling any stops between here and Belomorsk, any at all?'

'I'm afraid not. And even if we were forced to lay over, by bad weather or for whatever reason, there'd be no place you'd want to get off. Even during midsummer the settlements along the coast here are tiny, populated by savages or whalers and sealers put ashore by their commanders for insubordination or worse crimes; a hard-drinking lot. They'd welcome the sight of a white woman, all right, but you wouldn't welcome the sight of them. No, I regret to say there'll be no stopping off if I can prevent it until we reach home port.'

Tawny walked to the porthole, shading her eyes from the bright white sun and the powerful glare. All she could see in every direction was ice and snow, as if the entire world had been encrusted with it.

But she no longer had the sinking feeling in her heart that had depressed her so after she'd slammed her cabin door in Suverin's face. She turned to face the captain.

'If you can't let me off, all the same there is something you can do.'

'Name it.'

'Stand by me. You alone have the authority to marry us. Refuse to do so, however much he urges you to, whatever he may offer you as a bribe.'

This last suggestion was uncalled for. The reaction on Boleski's face showed how deeply the very idea offended him. He averted his eyes.

'Please forgive me. You're obviously not a man to be bribed.'

She must mind her words, she thought. Here was a good, decent man, one who could be not only a dependable friend when most she needed one, but her father-protector as well. Were matters to come to that necessity.

'He will work on you,' warned the captain. 'From the little I've seen of him he's subtle and he's clever. And far from shy – he'll do everything in his power to win your hand. Without snatching it from your wrist, if you follow my meaning.'

'I do. Still, he hasn't a chance. I don't love the man; it's that simple.'

'You still love your husband.'

'Captain, this may not be easy to accept, but my being widowed has nothing to do with Nikki and me. If in my life I had never even met my husband I still seriously doubt if I would ever marry Nikki. My gratitude toward him for rescuing me doesn't extend to love. He knows that; he just refuses to accept it.'

'He's crazy about you. A blind man could see that at the dinner table at the fort last night.'

'Perhaps.'

'No "perhaps" about it.'

'I've done nothing to encourage him.'

'Most men don't need encouragement. Just a little opening to sneak through.' He sobered. 'You must be furious with him over his sorry business. I only wish I could put about and bring you back, but we've come too far, and besides . . .'

'Orders are orders, I know.'

'Do you think that given time you could learn to love him?'

'Not in a thousand years. A lot of people have a lot of misguided ideas about love. They think because one loves another ardently, passionately, the other can't keep himself, or herself, from being won over. I suppose that sort of thing does happen occasionally, but not to me.'

'One certainly knows one's own heart.' The captain nodded.

'In my whole life I've only been in love with one man, Boyd Chevrier. He felt love for me, I felt it for him. At the same time. Almost the same moment, like two matches striking as one. That's the way it works; at least it did for us. Neither of us had to persuade the other, neither had to reach out and touch the other's heartstrings, as it were.'

'It just happened.'

'Exactly.'

'Interesting. What I myself don't know about love would fill volumes. Still, you may find, having already been happily married, that the single life can be very lonely. My poor sister Alishka did.'

'Please don't misunderstand, I don't dislike Nikki. Oh, I could strangle him for pulling this stunt, but he's always treated me respectfully.'

'Why not take a bit of unsolicited advice from one who would be your friend? Deep down you may feel something for the captain and not even realize it. Not at the moment, on the heels of this stupid kidnapping. But you may feel more kindly disposed toward him as time goes on. All I'm saying is don't batten down your true feelings.

'Don't deny yourself happiness just to punish him.'

A week went by. Suverin discreetly left her alone; he did not sneak about peeking around corners at her. To avoid him she requested and was granted the privilege of taking her meals alone in her cabin.

He did not ask to join her. Whenever they passed each other on deck, which was rare due to the biting wind, he would touch the bill of his cap, bow slightly, and greet her. This she would acknowledge with a nod and a whispered greeting. They never stopped to talk, although he did make an attempt to do so once or twice; she merely silenced him with a withering stare and walked on.

Her aloofness, her insistence upon eating alone so as to avoid him, the ice floe that fashioned itself and was rapidly rising into a small iceberg between them, did not seem to bother him, however. She could easily guess why. The voyage would take half a year to complete. If ever time was on anyone's side . . .

Alishka Boleski's wardrobe was unusually attractive, considering that the bachelor captain's sister had spent most of her time since her husband's passing traveling about the seas rather than mixing in the social whirl of a fair-sized city in competition with other women of taste.

Still, indulging one's taste in attire brings a unique satisfaction to the wearer, personal pleasure that needs no compliments to sustain it. One's audience is only part of the game. In the armoire Tawny discovered some perfectly exquisite things: there was an afternoon dress of jaconet muslin with long sleeves finished with a puff at the top, drawn up by a narrow tape in a casing. The skirt itself was narrow and trimmed with row on row of corded tucks and hemmed-in scallops. There was also a gown of sage-green China crêpe brocade in stripes, with a wide border in the same design on the hem. Above the hem was a series of fine tucks.

171

Tawny also found a gown of yellow gauze with a raised spot of velvet, as well as a green China silk pelisse lined with pink cambric.

There were bonnets, a beehive, one of celestial blue crêpe with antique front, edged and ornamented with honeycomb trimming also of crêpe, and a perfectly lovely turban of gray *chambrai* thickly frosted with silver.

A small chest sitting at the bottom of the armoire was opened to reveal drawers, petticoats, and waistcoats made of real Spanish lamb's wool, not-unwelcome underclothing on chilly days.

There were also cosmetics, Pear's soap, which Tawny hadn't seen since St. Louis, and loved, powder, rouge, lip paint, even some jewelry, which she bridled at wearing but which Captain Boleski insisted she put on. The best of the lot was an emerald necklace linked with dead gold.

The dresses could easily be taken in. The bonnets fit. Only Alishka's slippers proved useless, miles too large. Included among them was a pair of pea-green slippers of fancy kid, which she fell in love with but could only admire.

The second week went by, and the third. She kept herself busy sewing and trying on clothes before a full-length mirror obligingly provided her by the captain, his own, taken from his quarters, which, despite her protestations, he insisted she keep.

But one can only spend so much time sewing and admiring the results in a glass. The weather continued cold into the fourth week, severely curtailing opportunities for long walks round and round the deck.

There was nothing to read, nothing in English, and her Russian, although good and getting progressively better orally, was useless when it came to deciphering the Cyrillic alphabet. *There* was a mystery, she had long ago decided, that called for instruction in unraveling practically from the cradle.

The monotony increased daily, in spite of Captain Boleski's long and friendly chats, his stories about his life at sea, his description of Saint Petersburg with its incomparable collection of palaces and churches built by the czars. Natasha had called the capital the Paris of the East; the captain termed it the Athens of the North. And proudly quoted Voltaire:

'"The united magnificence of all the cities in Europe could but equal Saint Petersburg."'

For all the captain's efforts to inject something of interest into each day, the days grew depressingly longer. The *Sviostoloff*'s commanding officer insisted that Tawny's continuing to take her meals in her cabin was becoming nothing more than self-inflicted boredom. Punishment, Boleski termed it. He was right and she knew it. So she began eating with the others. Including Nikki.

As time went on they were becoming more pleasant toward each other; that is, she consented to converse with him more often and at greater length. Once or twice for a fleeting moment it struck her that, given his conduct toward her before the kidnapping and since, they would be infinitely closer now. But the fact remained, he had abducted her, and even though it was, in everyone's mind, clearly the impulsive act of a man in love, it would be a long cold winter in Saint Petersburg before she could ever forgive him.

Still, deep down she confessed that whether she accepted the fact or not, he was wearing away her resistance.

They talked one day on deck, a particularly beautiful day, sultry for spring, the wind filling the sails, but not sending men reeling down the deck like drunkards with its customary fury. Nor forcing her to grip the railing with one hand and her shawl over her head with the other, like some old gypsy. Perish forbid she wear a bonnet on deck with the wind up. Ribbon tied snugly under chin or not, the last she'd see of it it would be flying over the bowsprit and on ahead!

Nikki looked very handsome, as always clean-shaven, in marked contrast to the other men on board, not excepting the captain, who had taken to growing a beard. Nikki's mustache was neatly trimmed, his eyes were as absorbing as ever, his smile was wistful rather than beaming. A smile he had developed, she was sure, solely for her benefit. But she continued too preoccupied with thoughts of Boyd to be impressed, to care in the least.

For what must have been the eighth time Nikki told her all that he knew regarding the wagon train massacre.

'But you never actually saw him dead.' They stood at the taffrail out of earshot of the helmsman, watching the whitecaps fleck the dark blue water like so many white fur pieces momentarily laid out lengthwise, vanishing and popping up elsewhere. 'I've described him to you; you know exactly what he looks like.'

Suverin sighed. 'When a man is scalped, Tawny, it's not that easy to define and recognize his features. Besides, all the men in that train were dressed pretty much the same, isn't that so? Another thing – he was in the first wagon with his friend; they had to have come looking for you; that stands to reason. But doing so would have exposed them, as it exposed all the rest of your people. All killed, needless to say.'

'Perhaps Boyd and Haggerty couldn't get out of the wagon, I mean with the savages trying to get at them. That delayed them, and when they did get out and saw Jenny and me being dragged off they chased after us.'

'They didn't catch up with you.'

'Because they were too far behind.'

'Possibly, but once into the woods, out of the line of fire, they could have followed you. They would have, wouldn't they, to see where you were being taken? And would have tried to rescue you. Before we were lucky enough to.'

Tawny sighed. 'I want him to be alive so much, you can't believe...' Tears filled her eyes; she turned away.

'Of course you do...'

'Still, even if by some miracle he did survive and come to rescue me too late, he has to think *I'm* dead by now.'

What she neglected to point out to Suverin, the words shouting soundlessly in her heart, was that she had arrived at the inescapable conclusion that it was hopeless. Wanting, praying that Boyd was still alive couldn't make it so. Even worse, he and Lionel Haggerty had probably never even gotten out of the wagon alive. Which had to mean both had died believing she was already dead, knowing that if she wasn't, a fate worse than death awaited her.

'He had such high hopes for the Willamette Valley,' she said quietly.

'It's a beautiful place, but it's the Indians', the Chinooks',

174

the Tillamooks', the Molalas'... it's just too savage for settling; it's too early. Given another twenty or thirty years, maybe, but not now.'

'You built a fort there.'

'Not in the valley itself. And the American fort that was closer to the valley was destroyed. Fort New Kiev was well north of it and close to the water, where we could have gotten away by ship if we'd had to.'

'It was Boyd's dream, and that of his company. That of a lot of fine, decent, courageous people.'

'Dreams are like china, Tawny, the best of them can shatter so easily.'

'So it seems.'

'Tawny ...'

'Yes?'

'What I did to you I know now was reprehensible. It was the act of a coward, really.'

'You're no coward. I'd be the first to testify to that.'

'I could have proposed to you back at New Archangel. With everyone's blessing. How many times Varya Mihailovna told me you and I were the perfect match. The apple-cheeked lady... I miss her, I miss them all.'

'I do too.' There was a trenchant pause. The wind whipped the sails, the ship creaked wearily, the sea slapped against the hull. 'You could have proposed,' she went on, 'but I would have turned you down.'

'I would have bet on it.' He lowered his head sheepishly. 'That's the only reason I did this to you.'

'Nikki, please, the wistful smiles, examining the toes of your boots, that pathetic tone of voice. You really are acting out a role. I'd much prefer you didn't. It makes me feel uncomfortable.'

'I only did it because I knew I'd lose you forever!'

'I know, you've said that before. Let's talk about something else.'

'As soon as we land, as soon as you get the chance, you'll run off, won't you?'

'I said I don't want to discuss it.'

'Very well.'

28

The days followed one upon the other with a sameness that gradually became nerve-wracking. She and Nikki continued to talk; Captain Boleski had the good sense to stay out of it. She almost wished he'd begin pleading Nikki's case for him, extolling his virtues, emphasizing what a great future he had, reminding her that a truly devoted husband, or wife for that matter, wasn't the commonest commodity on the market. But Boleski said nothing.

She lay abed at night waiting for sleep to come, turning the whole business over in her mind like a prospector examining a newly found diamond, with, to be sure, less enthusiasm, but fully as much concern for possible flaws. Discouragingly few presented themselves. But deep in a corner of her mind, no larger than the head of a pin, a thought persisted. Nagged. What if Boyd were still alive? He could find out from the Indians where she had gotten to. He'd turn the whole Pacific Coast upside down looking for her; he'd search the world.

'Oh God . . .' she said aloud to the darkness.

Why did she persist in clinging to that straw? Why couldn't she make herself accept reality? The way her father accepted it when her mother had killed herself? The way Captain Boleski accepted the death of his sister?

She certainly wasn't brooding anymore; all it was was this tenacious suspicion that the picture was incomplete. Only because she had never actually seen poor darling Boyd lying at her feet dead. She had only Nikki's word for what had happened. No, that was not altogether true; she herself had been there. She'd seen. And he was right about one thing – if Boyd had seen her being dragged away with Jenny he would surely have followed; _he_ would have been the one to have rescued them, not the Russians. As far as that went, even if he had been unarmed, lying waiting and watching in the woods, once Nikki and his men had freed them Boyd would have shown himself. At that stage there certainly would have been nothing to prevent his doing so.

The next day another side of the diamond showed itself, unflawed and gleaming. Her cabin door had a lock and a bolt. But when Nikki knocked, she did not hesitate to let him in. Despite his boiling with frustration in his desire to possess her, he had kept Spartan control of himself. This said more for him than anything out of his mouth.

She was walking alone on the deck one day when she happened by the after hatch, saw that the cover was partially removed, and could hear two men below in conversation.

'... because he's a damned fool, that's why...'

'But she lets him into her cabin. I've seen 'em through the porthole window, her sitting on the edge of the bed, him standing or sitting in the chair, both talking away a blue streak...'

'I know, and he doesn't lay a hand on her.' There was amazement in the voice.

'He *is* a damned fool. What a beauty she is, that body's enough to take a man's breath away. Them breasts, riding high and firm, just... by the saints, I can't even talk about her without seeing her and wishing I had ten minutes alone with her – five!'

'Do you think he's a fairy? The army's full of 'em, you know.'

'He's no fairy, he's just stupid. A gentleman. La-de-da. Christ, if I was in his boots I'd bolt that door and fill her fulla me so fast. Bet your life I would...'

'Me too, who wouldn't, eh?'

'I wonder how long he'll be able to hold out?'

'Not for the next four months.'

'I don't know. I couldn'ta done it for four hours, for four seconds once she let me into that cabin. You'd think she was a saint up on a pedestal, you would...'

'It's more'n I can figure.'

She walked on. And thought about Nikki. Lately, she reflected, she couldn't keep from thinking about him. The walls of the fortress Crystal Taunton Kinross Chevrier were beginning to crumble. Pretty soon down it would come, ramparts, towers, and all.

'Nikki, Nikki, Nikki, what am I to do with you?'

What if she were to give in and marry him? Varya Mihailovna's words came back to her, the business about the army being his life, his 'first wife', his ringed wife his second. Apple Cheeks might have been right, for her. Married to Luka as Varya was.

But Nikki was not the colonel. Not that New Archangel's commanding officer was a bad sort; the only thing she could brand him guilty of would be his conspiring with Nikki to abduct her. That and spoiling Nikki shamelessly. It was just that Varya's Luka, although good-hearted and generous to a fault, even-tempered, and possessing a dozen other laudable traits, lacked the capacity for affection that Nikki possessed in an abundance equal to Boyd's. To be honest. Not to mention Nikki's frankness in admitting that his only reason for 'stealing' her was out of fear that he was about to lose her forever.

'Nikki, Nikki, what are you doing to me? What am I doing to myself?'

29

Boyd Chevrier and Lionel Haggerty sat at a small unsteady table, its surface sticky with spilled liquor and blotched with the burn marks of cheroots and pipe tobacco ashes, both men downing rum in the company of a heavy-set older man whose white beard failed to cover his pockmarked cheeks. The stranger's false teeth, fashioned of hickory, clicked when he talked, but this ostensibly embarrassed him not at all. He was extremely garrulous; he was a mother lode of information. His name was Willis Fentown – 'with a "w".' Fentown was first mate on the *Phoenix*, a Yankee sealer that regularly ventured to the Aleutians, to Attu and Near Islands in particular, at the tip of the Alaska Peninsula, which thrusts itself well out into the Bering Sea under the Pribiloffs. There the *Phoenix* took seal and sea otter: 'before the savages snatches 'em all.'

The table around which the three sat was close to a corner of a large rectangularly shaped room crammed with men and the combined stenches of their body odor, tobacco smoke, and sundry other smells. Haskell's Mariners' Bar on the waterfront was located not far from the Franciscan mission of San Francisco de Asis, on the Laguna de los Dolores near the north end of the peninsula of Yerba Buena. Haskell's was *the* gathering place for most of the northwest coasters who fetched a living of one sort or another out of the placid waters of the Pacific. The crew of the *Phoenix* was well represented in the crowd.

Boyd and Haggerty had arrived in Yerba Buena two months to the day after departing the valley, arriving in the mist-shrouded little port all but completely broke, having been forced to sell their rifles on the way. The long journey over the mountains and down the coast to the little settlement had reduced both men to a tramplike existence. They had reached their destination with their clothing practically in tatters and their boots displaying soles and heels reduced to the thinness of paper and threatening to fall off their feet. But all the mild winter long they had been odd-jobbing up and down the waterfront, saving their earnings, investing in new clothes and boots, and in the meantime inquiring of everyone they met as to the possibility of signing on to work their passages north to New Archangel come spring when the ice broke.

Boyd's story that his wife had been taken there by well-meaning Russians who thought that he had been killed by the Molalas along with the others in the Excelsior Fur Trading Company wagon train had reached Fentown's ears, and it was he who had approached Boyd and Haggerty in the street, leading them into Haskell's to discuss the situation.

At this, possibly the blackest time of his life, Boyd was to hear the crushing news that Tawny was no longer in New Archangel, but instead on her way to Russia. Fentown himself had not been anywhere near New Archangel, admitting as much. This, despite his obvious sympathy for Boyd, his willingness to help him find his 'missus', along with his sincerity and apparent trustworthiness, cast immediate doubt on the mate's story. Until he clarified what he had learned:

'The *New Bedford* stops at New Archangel regular. Her first mate, Andy Totter, a cousin of mine, told me straight out just this noon that there was no American woman living up at the fort there. That is, there was, but she'd sailed away on a Russki ship that was taking hides back to Belomorsk for shipment to Saint Petersburg.'

Haggerty drank and eyed Fentown with a glint of suspicion in his bloodshot eyes.

'How come you went out of your way to ask about Mr. Chevrier's wife?'

'I didn't. I was told. You two been here in Yerba Buena, asking questions all winter long. It seems to me I come up with the answer you want. Which means the rum's on you, right?'

'I wonder how the two of us missed bumping into this cousin of yours ourselves,' ventured Boyd.

'That wouldn't have been easy, Buck. His ship, the *New Bedford*, wintered in Vancouver to be the first up to the sealing grounds and New Archangel and just got back from there early this morning. Like I say, I spoke to Andy this noon.'

'Russia!' Boyd slammed his cup down, sloshing what was left of the contents over his hand and the table. 'Why in God's name would she leave for there?'

'Think about it, Boyd,' said Haggerty. 'I mean put yourself in her place. She has to think you're dead. That all of us were killed. Those Russians who rescued her and the Latchford girl had to be just as convinced. That soldier we talked to at Fort New Kiev said so.'

Fentown nodded his approval of this logic. 'If she fancies herself a widow, like the man says, maybe she hadn't the heart to go back home. Maybe she was afraid, being all by her lonesome . . .'

'There's another thing,' said Haggerty. 'That soldier in charge at Fort New Kiev told us when they took her away to New Archangel she was delirious.'

'He also said she was in good hands, the captain's wife's.' Boyd set his jaw firmly and stared into his empty cup. 'Tawny's strong and healthy; she wouldn't stay sick for long.' He shook his head, unwilling to accept the contrary. He glanced from one to the other.

'But you're both right about one thing, she's certain I'm dead. Why else would she sail off to Russia?'

180

'I hate to say it,' said Fentown solemnly, 'but with you dead, I mean her thinking you were, sure of it, maybe she found herself a new man. If she's as pretty as you've been describing her to everybody...'

'Oh God, that can't be!' burst Boyd.

'Take it easy,' said Haggerty, patting him on the shoulder as Boyd lowered his head between his hands.

'Saint Petersburg. My God, that has to be a million miles away.'

'You mean to go chasing after her?' asked Fentown, his tone tinged with surprise.

'What do you think?'

'Since you ask, I think myself it'd be more like chasing a wild goose than a woman.'

'Not just *a* woman, Mr. Fentown, my wife! Besides, I've cut all ties here. I sent a long letter to my employers back in Missouri explaining what happened to the train, to Tawny. And resigned my job. With no one outside of Lionel here to work with me, there was no more job...'

'We could work our way across the Pacific easy enough, couldn't we?' Haggerty asked Fentown.

The first mate nodded. 'It's getting up to Saint Petersburg that might be the hard part, traveling through Russia. It's not like England or France, you know. They're a strange lot, the Russkies; they don't take kindly to Canadians or Americans strutting about their country, marching into Saint Petersburg. That's because we're their biggest competitors in the fur trade.'

'I can't worry about that.'

Fentown downed the last of his rum and thought a moment, squinching his bright blue eyes tiny and crevassing his forehead so that it brought his hairline halfway down to his bushy eyebrows.

'If you really are hell-bent on getting to Saint Petersburg I can give you a bit of advice that might turn out helpful. Working your passage around Cape Horn and up the Atlantic into the Mediterranean is a far better way of getting there. It shouldn't be hard. Where to land is the big question.'

'As close to Saint Petersburg as we can get,' said Haggerty.

Fentown frowned. 'Please, this calls for very exact planning. Now it happens I have a close friend who knows more about that part of the world than any of us.'

Rising to his feet, Boyd tossed a paper dollar on the table. 'Let's go out of this hole and go find him,' he said.

'He' turned out to be Thomas Squires, a rigging rat, a former schoolteacher who had found the dreary confines of the classroom less to his liking than travel on the open seas. He was a slender, bright-eyed, intelligent-looking man in his mid-thirties, living in a single room in the only hotel in Yerba Buena, the Bluenose, a room which more resembled a well-stocked library than a residence. Squires was between vessels, as it were, fortunately for Boyd and Haggerty. The man's forte was history, but his knowledge of geography was by no means limited.

Introduced by Fentown, Boyd told his story of the catastrophe, Tawny's disappearance, and how he and his friend had come to be in Yerba Buena.

'So you see why I've got to get to Saint Petersburg.'

Squires cleared a small table of dirty dishes and, digging among a number of rolled-up maps in a large box, came up with an up-to-date map of Central Europe. His initial advice was for both Boyd and Haggerty to get work as deckhands on the first ship they could find bound for Italy, preferably. Wherever the vessel landed, with great good luck hopefully on the Adriatic side of the boot, they would then make their way to Vienna.

'War is about to break out again over there. Before the end of this year, I should think. France is openly threatening Austria. The Austrian army needs all the help it can get. If, as you claim, you're an experienced soldier, they will welcome you with open arms.' Squires nodded at Haggerty. 'And you as well. Anyone who can fire a rifle will be welcome.'

Boyd reacted, mystified. Neither he nor Haggerty could understand how their joining the Austrian army would get them to Saint Petersburg. Squires smiled indulgently and tapped his temple. He was once more back in the classroom instructing students:

'One step at a time, Mr. Chevrier. Once you are in the army, hostilities between the two countries should be on the verge of ending. You see, Austria is no match in the field for Napoleon. She will petition for peace and probably end up giving up everything but the Vienna Opera House to get it.

'The big blowup is still to come. When that takes place, Mr. Chevrier, you must make your move.'

Before explaining precisely what that move was to be, Squires provided his listeners with some background on the existing situation. It was all incredibly complicated. Europe was a cauldron continually simmering with the threat of war, a stew seasoned with intrigue, with duplicity, and lumped with alliances made and broken virtually overnight. And when the cauldron boiled over into war, which it very often did, events took place with astonishing swiftness. Leaders who were friends woke up in the morning to find themselves enemies. Ministers were dismissed, reinstated, imprisoned, released ... diplomatists were held as hostages, then traded for those of the other side. Napoleon had formed a somewhat shaky alliance with Mother Russia. There was more. Squires mentioned other names, some familiar to Boyd, some not – Klemens Metternich, the brilliant archconservative Austrian statesman, friend, now enemy, of Napoleon, friend to Napoleon's foreign minister, the famed Talleyrand. And still others busy stirring the cauldron – the emperor's ambitious sister, Caroline Murat, Alexander I, Czar of All the Russias, even Pope Pius VII.

Squires discussed the names and the events occurring and anticipated with the ease of a housewife imparting the ingredients of her favorite recipe to a friend.

'To sum up,' he went on, 'late in the year, as I see it, Metternich will be on good terms with Russia, after she and France have their falling out. Being on good terms he'll be sending a diplomatic staff to Saint Petersburg. Your job, Mr. Chevrier, will be to ingratiate yourself with your superiors so that you'll be able to apply for a position on that staff.'

'Can we do it, do you think?' asked Haggerty, still, from the look on his face, in a quandary as to what Squires was talking about.

'Not both of you. One, possibly, particularly since you're to be a volunteer, Mr. Chevrier, a patriot for pay, to be sure, but a man who showed up when he was needed and to whom the Austrians and Metternich should be deeply grateful. As long as Austria is not at war with Russia she'll keep a diplomatic staff there. And a diplomatic staff member in any foreign country has considerable freedom of movement.'

'You're saying I could come and go as I please,' said Boyd.

'Within reason, yes. And something else – you'd be invited to a great many state functions; you'd get around. You'd meet people, important people.'

'I speak no Russian.'

This Squires dismissed with a toss of his lean hand. 'Practically everybody in Saint Petersburg speaks French. With a name like Chevrier you must know some French.'

Boyd brightened. '*Mais oui, monsieur.* Mr. Squires, I have to hand it to you. You think of everything so fast . . .'

'There's just one thing,' interposed Fentown gloomily. 'It all sounds like a great good time if he doesn't get killed in the fighting beforehand.'

Squires shook his head negatively. 'You'd be too valuable to stick in the front lines,' he said. 'Were I your commanding officer, I'd set you to work training the less experienced men. I doubt if it'll turn out that much of a shooting war anyway; most of the ammunition will be words and more words. Table pounding, threats and suddenly peace.'

'You could probably get a ship inside of a week,' offered Fentown.

'That's good news,' said Haggerty.

'For me, Lionel, not you.' Boyd placed his hand in comradely fashion on Haggerty's shoulder.

'You don't for a minute think you're going into this without me, do you?' Haggerty glared, his feelings obviously hurt.

'I certainly do. And I am.'

Haggerty eyed Fentown and shook his head. 'Now there's gratitude for you. Here we've marched through hell together and come out with our skins intact, and now he wants to turn me out to pasture!'

'You've risked your life for me,' said Boyd. 'I can't in conscience ask you to keep risking it until you lose it. She's my wife, Lionel . . .'

184

'It's none of my business,' said Squires, 'but to me "turning you out to pasture", as you call it, would be the honorable thing to do. There's no small amount of risk involved in this business.'

'Exactly the way I see it,' said Boyd evenly.

'You go,' said Haggerty, 'I go. No arguments.' He bristled. 'I won't argue with you, Boyd. What I will do is stand toe to toe with you, and the winner gets to make the decision.'

'Oh sure, I'd be apt to fight you.' Boyd shook his head. 'Lionel, you've told me a dozen times if you've told me once on the way out from Keys Landing and over the mountains from the valley down to here that a hundred yards out to sea gets you so seasick you turn blue.'

'I'd have made it up to New Archangel. I can make it anywhere.'

'Old friend, this isn't anywhere. We're talking about –'

'Twenty-odd thousand miles,' said Fentown.

'Now that you mention it and I think about it,' said Squires, 'hold everything just a shake.' Taking out a map of the world, he spread it over the map of Europe. 'There'd really be no need to go all the way down and around Cape Horn. What you could do is get down to Mexico, get across the narrowest point, here.' He indicated. 'And sign on with a ship out of, say, Vera Cruz, one headed for the Mediterranean.'

Fentown nodded. 'Much better, much much better. That'd be half the distance.'

'*If* you don't have to sit in Vera Cruz waiting for your ship,' remarked Squires. 'You'll need luck and timing, but heaven knows after what you've been through up to now you're due some luck.'

'We've been through nothing compared to her,' said Boyd quietly, a faraway look in his eyes.

All three shook hands with Squires and thanked him. The hour being late, they invited him to join them for dinner and a drink or two or three at Haskell's. The seaman from the classroom agreed, rolling up his maps, restoring them to their box, and putting on his jacket and cap.

'When do you and me get to slug it out?' asked Haggerty of Boyd as they left the room.

'Let's talk about if after dinner, okay? I'm hungry. I don't like fighting on an empty stomach.'

Fentown and Squires laughed. Haggerty scowled and said nothing.

30

'So then I now pronounce you man and wife!' intoned Captain Boleski brightly, beaming as widely as his face, tightly netted with lines, would permit. 'Captain, you may kiss the bride.'

Nikki took Tawny in his arms and kissed her, delicately, almost tentatively at first, then with more pressure, working his mouth with hers warmly, passionately. Oddity of oddities, in all the months they had known each other this was only the second time he had kissed her on the lips – rather, that she had allowed him to. The first was the evening before, when he had proposed. Then he had taken a small, very old-looking blue-velvet-covered ring box out of his pocket, opening it and showing her a perfectly lovely pear-shaped diamond, three carats set about with smaller stones, all supported and interlocked in gold. It had been his mother's and his grandmother's before hers.

And it was now Tawny's.

For an instant, despite the warmth of his kiss, the sight of the ring, the unmistakable look of love in his eyes, she wondered why she had surrendered, given up the fight and consented to be his wife. The *Sviostoloff* was only a week out of Belomorsk. The summer had dragged by, each day longer than the previous one; it was now approaching mid-September. She had become sick to death with the tedium, the ceaseless boredom of life aboard the ship.

And in her heart she yearned so to be loved.

There he was, within summoning distance, frequently all but at her elbow. Not pestering her, certainly; for that she had to give him credit. But always there, prepared to all but prostrate himself at her feet, he adored her so.

It wasn't nearly as complicated as she tried to make it, though, so lonely was she, loveless, desperately wanting and needing love, embracing, and a heart devoted to her. To continue the course she was pursuing, practically fending him off, seemed senseless. Nothing more or less than self-inflicted punishment, as Captain Boleski had termed it months earlier.

Widowed at twenty-two, one doesn't stay a widow the rest of one's life. Better to change one's religion and become a nun. Some things go on inside that one simply has no control over. Latent in her a fire smoldered that begged to burst into flame. And blend with Nikki's own.

All of this raced through her mind as the captain and his men raised their glasses of vodka, toasting the happy couple, cheering loudly, downing their drinks and smashing their glasses against the corner of the cabin.

Then the singing began, and each man took turns whirling Tawny about briefly while the others stood in a semicircle clapping accompaniment. She was on the brink of collapse when Nikki rescued her.

'You need a drink, my darling,' he said quietly, proffering a glass of vodka.

She waved it away with a good-natured smile, gasping for breath, fanning herself with one hand. 'No thank you. Just sipping that stuff burns the lining of my throat so smoke practically –'

'Comes out of your lovely nose!' He laughed and downed the glassful with one swig, to the lusty cheers of the onlookers.

She had never seen him so happy; or was part of it relief? Would she herself be happy? she wondered, reaching down and smoothing a wrinkle from the front of her lovely lace-cuffed and -collared mauve silk gown. Yes, she decided on the spot, *they* would be happy. In Saint Petersburg, in New Archangel, in New Orleans, anywhere. After all, happiness is where one's love is; geography has nothing to do with it. Wherever they found themselves, as long as his arms were within reach, his lips, his body . . .

What would her daddy think of Nikki? How would Jack Kinross take to him? Much too formal, he'd declare at first glance, Nikki's uniform, his posture, his concern with his appearance. Still, vanity in a man wasn't the worst trait; it ran far behind mistress-keeping and chronic drunkenness and a host of other threats to happiness.

Jack Kinross and Nikki were complete opposites; fortunately, they would never meet.

The months rolled back swiftly to that impossible coach ride with Aunt Lydia, Priscilla, and Emily, the night of horror at the inn, St. Louis, where she had learned how full the force of fury could be. Boyd and she had found out that morning at the bottom of the stairs with Lydia and the Ramplings hurling invective and vases down at them!

Boyd. Poor darling. Poor dear man. Not even to be able to place flowers on his grave seemed to underscore the unfairness of it all. They'd never had a chance, not really. Why, because she'd stolen him from Marcy? Had the fates elected to punish the two of them for that? To travel all that way under such exhausting and demanding conditions, to meet with disaster almost within minutes of arrival...?

No, they'd never had a chance. But Nikki and she had one now, better than a chance. The world lay at their feet. She would make him a good wife, a wife his friends would marvel at...

By the bed in her cabin that night, with the porthole drapes discreetly closed and fastened, the door locked and bolted, they stood face to face and undressed. Starting at the top, undoing each button of his tunic in turn, sent a small tremor through her body, and when at length he stood naked before her in the dim glow of the candle, beholding his perfect, ideally proportioned body sent her rushing to him to press her cheek against his chest and run her hands down it.

He disrobed her, so carefully, so very effortlessly, with such sensitiveness she was scarcely aware that his fingers were touching her. Her clothing seemed to fall away garment by garment until she too stood naked. And began shivering.

'Are you cold, my darling?'

'No, no,' she said quickly.

Taking her slowly in his arms, he pressed her to him, running his hands down her back to her firm buttocks, hands that felt as if they were gloved with silk, so smooth were they. Bending slightly, he lifted her, bearing her to the bed, turned down and awaiting their presence. He knelt over her and her fingers reached up and touched his cheeks, moved around his dark eyes, caressed his forehead, and wandered slowly through his hair. Touching him was magnificent; she felt like a mortal touching a god, Adonis, the god of manly beauty. Her Adonis, hers alone. Forever!

He touched her in turn, with such tenderness, with such delicate control, that within minutes that seemed like eons she was all but consumed with desire for him. All but screaming for him to take her. To feel him inside her.

When at last he mounted her and they began, it was too glorious to believe. She had never dreamed, never fleetingly imagined it could be so beautiful, not after that hideous experience with the savages in the valley. But his foreplay, their mutual play, and his making love to her now blocked out all memory of that frightful black day. They clung to each other, each reluctant to so much as move a hand; they clung entwined and he moved within her.

Slowly at first, agonizingly so to her, then gradually increasing the pace, faster, faster...

And with the stars and moon and the eyes of the gods shut off from their lovemaking, the captain and most of the crew deep in dreams, the men on watch nodding at their posts, Belomorsk drew closer.

31

The overland trip by coach from Belomorsk to Saint Petersburg totaled a little over four hundred miles, but stops to rest and refresh the horses and change teams every hundred miles, as well as to rest and refresh Captain and Mrs. Nikandr Suverin, were blessedly frequent. And there were she thought, smiling inwardly but at the same time owning to some relief, no Indians.

The trip took ten full days, but the weather, though brisk to windy cold, was pleasant, the scenery in early autumn, particularly before they came within view of Lake Ladoga, lovely. Emerging from the forests of the north, they reached the farm country east of the lake, where, according to Nikki, potatoes and vegetables were raised. Beyond this area near the southeast corner of the lake were more farms, devoted to dairy cows and livestock.

Saint Petersburg, founded by Peter the Great more than one hundred years before, stood on a delta through which the dark blue waters of the Neva River flowed. Marshes and forests covered nearly half the area, and although the bays of Kronstadt, Koporya, Luga, and Larva offered good anchorage, the coastline at the head of the Gulf of Finland was made up mainly of reefs and sandbanks.

They entered the city at twilight. The traffic was heavy, and there was activity everywhere she looked. Nikki pointed out that Saint Petersburg was home for more than two hundred thousand people. For all of this number, adding the two new arrivals, it was also chilly and somewhat damp, a condition that persisted for most of the year before and after the depressingly short summer.

The capital was set out according to a plan which was surprisingly simple. The largest sector was situated on the mainland on the left bank of the Neva and boasted the better streets, the bigger shops, bazaars, and markets. Here too were to be seen most of the various czars' palaces, the cathedrals and theaters. Three unusually long streets, the main arteries of the capital, radiated from the Admiralty. These were Prospekt Nevskiya, the Gorokhovaya, and the Prospekt Vosnesenskiy. Their coach moved at a brisk pace down the first-named thoroughfare, which ran nearly three miles straight east-southeast until two thirds of the way along it it began curving toward the south. The Prospekt Nevskiya was filled with traffic moving sluggishly in both directions. To Tawny the street started out far more picturesque than any in St. Louis or even those streets in the larger cities of the eastern United States which she had seen pictures of. The shops were delightful-looking; one wanted to jump out of the coach and run inside and browse, so inviting did they appear. The throngs and the many and infinite variety of vehicles created a stimulating and exciting scene, but as they rode on she began to see that the buildings

190

bordering the area were, for the most part, homely and neglected. They passed the cathedral of Our Lady of Kazan; Nikki pointed it out with enthusiasm and pride. She complimented it, but thought it ugly. Still uglier was the Gostiniy Dvor, a two-story building divided into cheap little shops, which Nikki agreed was an eyesore. Next came the Anichkov Palace, which looked to Tawny more like an enormous barracks than any palace.

There were bright spots, to be sure, elegant, spacious squares filled with fading flowers and profusely adorned memorials to former rulers. There were many parks as well, and the magnificent mansions of the boyars living in the city proper. All of these homes had been built during the reign of Elizabeth, fifty years earlier; all were decidedly imposing, with their colonnaded porches and artistically proportioned windows reflecting the orange of the dying sun. But by far the most interesting building pointed out by Nikki proved to be the Hermitage of Catherine the Great, who had died only fourteen years before.

Nikki had been inside the Hermitage twice. Lower-ranking officers rarely frequented any of the palaces, he added with a chuckle. He lauded the Hermitage as Saint Petersburg's most impressive building. Finer than the Winter Palace itself or the Chepelev Palace, situated next to the Hermitage. He spoke enthusiastically of 'Czarina Catherine's pride', describing the great carpeted staircase, the malachite pillars supporting the ceiling, the spacious halls filled with echoes of the past, the statuary, the paintings, the exquisite pieces of fashioned ivory and jade assembled from all parts of the world.

They took a three-room apartment on Varonski Street close to Military Headquarters, which would allow Nikki to walk to Headquarters daily, even on an occasional Sunday, he explained, should duty demand it. The place came completely furnished, even to a shiny new samovar, reminiscent of Varya Mihailovna Poplova's in New Archangel.

Tawny set about unpacking; even though the hour was growing late, Nikki was obliged to report at once to Headquarters. There he was to be given new orders, outfitted anew from shako to boots in keeping with his

191

promotion, and in general begin sending his roots down now, returned as he was to 'home base', as he put it.

Minutes after he had kissed her good-bye and was out the door and she'd waved to him from the front window, a knock sounded at the door. She opened it to Nikki – rather, a woman, a few years older than she herself, with Nikki's eyes, his coloring, his mouth, and the identical curly dark hair. Framed in the doorway, she wore a velvet pelisse over a pretty high-waisted bombazine-and-crêpe dress. Her hand extended, she introduced herself.

'Mrs. Suverin? Permit me, I am Olga. Olga Marie Kovakin. Suverin-Kovakin, Nikki's sister. His one and only sibling.' Tawny's surprised reaction brought a smile to the woman's face. 'You don't believe me? Of course, knowing Nikki, he just never got around to telling you he had a sister, isn't that so? Your landlord, who by chance happens to be an old friend of our papa's, sent word around – I live just around the corner and two blocks up – that you two were back from the Arctic, so I thought I'd ... may I come in?'

'Please do.'

Olga Marie Kovakin, whose husband, she informed Tawny, was 'fairly highly placed' at the Academy of Sciences, proved witty, charming, as warm as the Missouri sun in July. And filled with information, with a lengthy and elaborate answer to every one of the dozens of questions Tawny flung at her. They brewed tea and sat among the partially unpacked luggage and talked and talked and talked.

'I simply can't understand why he never told me he had a sister,' said Tawny.

'Nikki likes to pretend I don't exist.' Olga smiled mischievously over the brim of her glass. 'I'm not, as you may have noticed, a closemouthed person,' she went on. 'Let's be honest, I'd rather talk than breathe.' She laughed, then sobered. 'And Nikki is very private about some things I don't give two pins about keeping secret. What good is any secret anyway if at least one other person doesn't know about it?'

Tawny did not altogether follow this logic, but refrained from commenting. 'What sort of secrets?' she queried. 'Does Nikki have a poisonous past I'm not supposed to know about?'

Olga bobbed her head and grimaced. 'No worse than any other serviceman. He's sowed his share of wild oats, if that's what you mean. He's a full captain now, I hear. I wonder what company the Horror will give him, in what regiment.'

'The Horror?'

'That's what we civilian Petersburgers call General Araktcheiev. Wait until you meet him. He stands like a toad with a stick thrust through him from feet to neck. He's squat like a toad, though; his hair looks very like a man's brush turned upside down; the heads of spikes look softer than his eyes, his nostrils are forever quivering, he sweats like a miner, he's the most disgusting sight you've ever seen. He talks like this.' She tightened her voice and spoke brusquely, barking three- and four-word orders. 'Unfortunately, repulsive though he may be, he's brilliant, or so everybody says, and the czar has made him Minister of War and Inspector-General of the Artillery *and* Infantry. Which gives him absolute control of the army.'

'And Nikki. Does he know Nikki?'

'He'll get to, now that Nikki's a captain. Remember the name, Araktcheiev. You'll hear it in this house often enough. His second in command, a homosexual named Zoropkin, will be the one to reassign Nikki, though.'

Olga talked through six glasses of tea, jumping from subject to subject with the agility of the toad with whom she had compared Araktcheiev.

Daddy and Mother Catherine were dead. That much, and very little more, it turned out, Tawny already knew. Olga and Nikki were the Suverins' only children. They had been left some money, which Nikki had promptly squandered gambling; this indiscretion on his part proved to be the main reason for the break between brother and sister. Olga had never really forgiven him; for his part, he elected to ignore her.

This proved the shell of the nut of the Suverin family history. But Olga, by nature forgiving, and with her brother absent so long, was anxious to see him and be 'family' and close to him again.

The more Olga talked, the more Tawny liked her. Although she looked nothing like her physically, Olga had all the fine traits of character of Varya Mihailovna. Thank heaven for a new friend so soon, she mused.

The topic of conversation was switched to the city, the capital.

In Saint Petersburg, Alexander I sat upon the throne, Czar of All the Russias. It was he who had set Araktcheiev upon the 'throne of the army'. The Horror was not the worst choice, in Olga's view, except for the fact that he was so repulsive-looking even his closest associates snickered behind their hands at him. And his ridiculous pomposity was the talk of the city. The man was also a notorious lecher, whose preference leaned toward girls a third his age, which was fifty-eight. As for Alexander himself, he was, to Tawny's surprise, only thirty-two, a man of many contradictions. He had inaugurated his reign eight years earlier, in 1801, after the brutal murder of his father. Alexander had come to the throne an avowed liberal, dedicated to weakening the power of the all-powerful boyars and bettering the lot of the merchants, officials, the middle class in general, and the serfs.

'The way to hell is paved...' began Olga, smiling sardonically.

Alexander, a confessed mystic, was called by Napoleon in print a 'shifty Byzantine'. Which was a most apt description of the czar, according to Olga.

'Russia today, sad to say, is totally corrupt,' she continued. 'And the blame for that lies at the czar's feet. For all of Alexander's pretensions to liberalization, the boyars are still in complete control.'

'What exactly is a boyar?' asked Tawny. 'I've heard Nikki use the word.'

'An aristocrat, the parasites the Corsican got rid of when he took power in France. One step down from the ruling princes. Garbed head to toe in privilege. The boyars were supposed to have been officially abolished by Peter the Great long before either of us was born. But some animals refuse to stay killed. Like sharks.'

They talked well into the night. Tawny grew more and more worried about Nikki.

'He's meeting old friends, making the rounds,' said Olga. 'Don't expect him back before midnight at the earliest. Come, let's go out and get something to eat. Then we'll come back here and I'll help you finish unpacking.'

32

Nikki came home shortly after two in the morning, hours after Olga had left, talked out, promising to see both husband and wife soon. The family soldier finally showed up slightly more than drunk, but looking, nevertheless, resplendent in his newly issued full captain's uniform. He wore a white felt shako with a black leather peak and gold chin strap, tilted at a rakish angle (as a result, she surmised, of his condition). His almost absurdly high collar was supported by stocks; he wore a long-tailed green coat, impeccably white, although somewhat wrinkled, leather breeches and boots that gleamed like glass. By his right side hung his gold-hilted saber.

'You look absolutely beautiful,' she said, throwing her arms around him and kissing him lovingly. Abruptly she took away her lips and stepped back. 'But your breath, my darling.'

'Not beautiful,' he said, slurring his words. 'Dashing ish the proper wor'...'

'And what regiment did they put you in, the one you hoped for?'

'The one they wanted me in, the pigsh... The Twen'ny-fourth Infantry, jush back from fightin' the Turksh. As miserable-lookin' a bunch ash you'll ever she... but I'll whip Company B into ssssshape, never fear.'

'I think you need a good night's sleep to whip Captain Suverin back into shape.'

'I think I'm gon' be ill. How very un... undignifi'. You will 'scuse me, my darling, I mush go an' relieve my guts of sishty-odd toash...'

'Sixty?'

'When ol' frien's reunite.' He waved one hand high, staggered. She caught him and helped him to the bathroom.

He snored like a grampus that night, as she'd never heard

him before. But then, she'd never seen him so drunk before. Nor so sick after.

It took very little time for Captain and Mrs. Nikandr Suverin to settle down to life in Saint Petersburg. Each morning, save an occasional Sunday, Nikki would leave the apartment shortly before eight o'clock, invariably casting a glance about the front room, voicing complaint regarding its smallness. (The entire apartment was twice the size of the Kinross family cabin back in Titus Forks; she adored it, it was so bright, cheerful, and warm as winter began.) Off he would go, to come home at various hours; she decided very soon that she could never plan dinner. If he said six o'clock, it would surely be eight; if eight, surely ten or eleven. The later he returned, the tipsier he generally was.

Still, there were daytime visits and shopping tours with the indefatigable and talkative Olga, just the two of them or occasionally with Olga's friends. There were parties, to which Tawny wore her best, looking her most radiant. Nikki delighted in showing her off, reveling in the stares of friends and strangers alike. It reached a point where she began to feel more like a comely mannequin in a shop window than his wife.

But her heart continued to remind her that she had fallen hopelessly in love with him, his 'official' neglect notwithstanding. When he hadn't had too much to drink he made love with all the attentiveness and tenderness he was capable of. And she reciprocated in kind.

But Nikki's unpredictable hours, his drinking, and his admitted gambling vexed her, and every so often they would squabble, and not speak for a time. Only to patch things up in bed. His argument was that as an officer it was required of him to drink with his fellows and his superiors; and later and later late-night meetings at Headquarters or at Saint Peter and Saint Paul Fortress were becoming increasingly common, for good reason, as December arrived and the snow mantling the city deepened.

There existed the Franco-Russian Alliance, to be sure, established at Tilsit in East Prussia two years earlier. But rumors abounded that Napoleon was preparing to drop his guise of amity and invade Russia. In such an event Saint

Petersburg, being so close to the western border, presented a highly vulnerable target.

Furred, mufflered, and muffed, Tawny and Olga walked to the Haymarket one particularly blustery afternoon to a little corner jewelry shop where Olga was having the clasp on a bracelet repaired. They entered the shop to a dazzling array of glass cases under which pearls and precious stones were displayed on various colored velvets, the diamonds – rings, bracelets, necklaces, and pendants – on black. And stunning!

The man behind the counter was young, pasty-faced, and unprepossessing-looking. Dropping his book, he leaped from his stool if they were his first customers of the day. Behind the rear counter a drape blocked their view of the workroom, and when the young man had greeted them and Olga had identified herself and shown him a pasteboard receipt, it was through this drape that he vanished after excusing himself with great ceremony.

He came back almost at once, his face sagging with disappointment.

'I am terribly sorry,' he said in the tone of a lackey who had committed some grievous indiscretion, 'but your bracelet is not yet repaired. If I may prevail upon you to wait just a few minutes, the work will be completed. I really must apologize again; we have been inundated lately . . .'

Tawny glanced about the shop. Through the windows facing the main and side street it was obvious that very few of the passersby were even looking at the window displays, let alone considering coming in.

'We'll wait,' said Olga.

'You're very kind. It shouldn't be long. If you will excuse me, do feel free to browse. We are fortunate in having the very finest jewelry in all Saint Petersburg.' Nodding, he retired to his stool, retrieved his book, and pretended to resume reading, though it was easy to see that he was keeping an eye on the two of them. A very practiced eye.

Olga pointed to a diamond ring. 'Look, pear-shaped. Almost identical to yours,' she said. 'It's so beautiful. Yours, I mean, with those little stones all around. And the gold setting.' Tawny laughed. Olga looked confused. 'Did I say something funny?'

197

'You make it sound as if you'd never even seen my ring before.'

'Before what?'

'Really. It *was* your mother's and your grandmother's.'

Olga stared. 'Nonsense. Our mother's ring is on her finger in the grave.'

It was Tawny's turn to stare. 'He lied to me! Why?'

'He actually told you that?'

'Your mother's *and* your grandmother's.'

'I swear by all that's holy I never saw it before in my life. He must have won it gambling, payment for a debt. One of the few times he came out ahead,' she added dryly.

An old man hastily buttoning his vest with one hand, holding up Olga's bracelet with the other, came out from behind the drape, his rheumy bespectacled eyes beaming. The repair work was paid for, and Olga and Tawny left the shop.

Pursuing the subject would add nothing to it, and Olga was sufficiently sensitive to recognize that doing so would only embarrass Tawny. As for Tawny, her first impulse was to confront Nikki with his lie the moment he walked in the door that night. But within minutes, as she and Olga made their way through the bustling Haymarket, she changed her mind. Accusing him would only implicate Olga; Nikki was no fool, he'd know where Tawny had gotten her information. Relations between brother and sister were not exactly strained, but in spite of Olga's efforts to improve them after Nikki's long absence, they were not that good. Nikki had little use for Dr. Paul Kovakin. This Olga resented; more than anything, or so she frequently averred, she wanted her husband and her brother to be closer.

'But the only way that would come about would be for Paul to join the army.'

The threat of the Corsican Ogre might have put the military at the ends of its collective nerves, but Saint Petersburg's civilians, in particular the ladies, were much more concerned with an extraordinary social event soon to take place. One which Captain and Mrs. Suverin, Olga and her husband, and others on the upper rungs of the social ladder could look forward to taking part in. The town, customarily quiet and bourgeois, would be crammed with nobles, ambassadors, marshals, ministers, princes and princelings, chamberlains, and their ladies. And the czar would be in his glory.

Olga and Tawny were walking through Tsarkoe Selo Park two days later when Olga sputtered forth the news:

'Dear me, I must be getting old, I completely forgot to tell you. The King and Queen of Prussia have been invited to Saint Petersburg!' she burst excitedly. Sleighs glided softly past them in both directions. Children were building a snowman nearby. The holiday spirit was in their eyes and in the air.

Olga began elaborating: 'There will be thirty thousand armed men for the honor guard. Perhaps Nikki's regiment.' She stopped short. 'Why the sad face when I mention him? Has he been treating you badly? Has he? I must know. Tell me, my dear.'

'Not badly, not well. More like not at all . . .'

'He's neglecting you.'

'Olga, I can confide in you because I trust you. It's getting so the only time he pays the slightest attention to me is when we're in bed. A woman needs something besides sex; this one does. Dear God, what I wouldn't give for a simple Sunday-afternoon stroll through this park. Two hours of conversation back to back. Once a month even.'

'You go to tons of affairs, galas . . .'

'He escorts me, yes, and then I spend the whole evening dancing with creaky old generals and admirals. Rarely anybody under sixty. That Araktcheiev, I can't escape the man. He looks at me with those eyes of his like he means to rape me right there on the dance floor in full view of everyone. He rubs himself against me; he's ten times as repulsive as you described him to me weeks ago.'

'And where is your loving husband while all this goes on?'

'He seems to disappear into the woodwork. Oh, he shows up every so often with a drink for me and half a waltz. I suppose to prove that he hasn't run out the back door. He drinks, he gambles; there seems to be less and less money.'

'That's Nikki.'

'Do I sound like a complaining spoiled brat?' Tawny stopped short, eyeing Olga worriedly.

Olga patted her arm. 'Nonsense. If anybody's spoiled, it's Nikki.'

'The worst of it is I'm not his wife anymore, not really. I'm just a ... a display piece.'

'You're very beautiful, unusually beautiful. Russian women are so pudgy and cowlike, except a few of the younger ones. And they look positively nauseating in beautiful clothes. While you ...'

'I know, you said.'

'You *are* beautiful, Tawny.'

'So is a diamond. But I don't fit around a finger. I'm not a toy, Olga, nor a mannequin. God in heaven, how I wish he'd retire from the army. Get into some business or something, anything that would let him keep regular hours so that we'd have some time together.'

'An army wife is a neglected wife.'

'So I've heard.'

Olga sighed. 'I'd talk to him ...'

'Please, not a word. Promise!'

'Oh, I wouldn't. He wouldn't listen to me anyway. As I say, Nikki is very spoiled, very self-indulgent. His way is the right way, wrong though it may be. He can be incorrigible.'

'He's changed completely from what he was on shipboard. His whole personality seems different.'

'Back to what it was before he left for New Archangel, I'm afraid. Nikki ought to have been on the stage, my dear, he's that good at pretending.'

'He doesn't pretend when we make love. If he does, I can't complain.'

' "Incorrigible", that's the word for him, all right. Let's talk no more about the stinker; it only upsets us both. The King and Queen of Prussia, can you imagine? She's supposed to be enchantingly beautiful. They'll be here in just a few days now. They say that at least two thousand men have already gone to work removing the choicest furnishings from the Imperial residences and transferring them to Chepelev Palace next door to the Hermitage. Just to make them comfortable while they're here.'

Frederick William and Queen Louise would arrive in Saint Petersburg on the eleventh of December, to stay as the guests of the czar until the twenty-first. That evening Nikki returned to the apartment surprisingly early for him, shortly before seven.

Tawny was astonished; she had never seen him so excited. He was like a little boy about to burst with good news. One would have imagined he'd been promoted to general. She assumed that, as Olga had suggested earlier, his regiment had been selected as the visiting royalty's honor guard.

She was mistaken. Seizing and kissing her passionately, he held her close, swaying the two of them slowly back and forth.

'My darling, my dearest, beautiful darling, you'll never guess what's happened. That is, what's going to . . .'

'Is it –'

'Ssh.' He broke from her. 'Oh, by the way, to celebrate we're eating out tonight. The finest restaurant in this tired old city – it has to be!'

'We don't have the money, Nikki. You don't get paid until the twentieth.'

'Bother the money, I can charge it. Let me speak, my darling, let me tell you. There is this regiment, the Nineteenth Infantry; their commander, Druzovich, is an old soldier – oh, a good man, ferocious against the Austrians in '87 and '88, but ready to retire.' He chuckled. 'If he doesn't die first. The man has to be a hundred and one. The point is, guess who may be offered three stars! Will be!'

'Three?'

'A lieutenant-colonelcy, second in command to old Druzovich's replacement, whoever that may be. Who cares? From captain to lieutenant-colonel in one jump! Can you imagine? It's unheard of. It's like a dream; I can't believe it; I have to pinch myself!' He began swinging about the room, roaring gleefully. 'Lieutenant-Colonel Suverin! Lieutenant-Colonel Suverin! Lieutenant-Colonel Suverin!'

'How marvelous for you, Nikki.'

He stopped twirling, his joy vanishing instantaneously. 'You don't sound very enthusiastic . . .'

'If it's what you want and you get it.'

'No "ifs", it's mine, all right. It's better than double the money, it's a whole new world. It's heaven! Yes, by the holy saints, that's exactly what it is. Do you realize I shall be the youngest lieutenant-colonel in the entire military? Twenty-seven and a lieutenant-colonel! Twenty-seven. Aren't you proud of me? I can tell you I'm damned proud of myself, damned proud!'

'Hadn't you better count your chickens *after* they hatch?'

'They're as good as hatched, my darling. And the fox is dead in the woods. All the foxes.' His voice had taken on an edge she did not like, his eyes narrowing and his handsome face darkening almost evilly. Rank and the power that went with it was what he wanted. It was all he wanted. Not her, not her love or respect or loyalty. Not friends, not even money. Only the hand of rank and the power that gloved it.

'Come, get your things. Hurry, I'm famished, I'm thirsty, I'm high as the sky. So high I can scarcely breathe.'

He helped her on with her coat. She put on her hat and muffler and got her muff down from the front-room closet shelf.

'Shouldn't I change into evening wear? Something formal?'

'Nonsense, why waste the time? You look beautiful, radiant, my radiant Tawny!'

They started out the door. 'Slow down, Nikki, people in the street will take you for a madman!'

'Who cares about the trash in the streets? We'll hail the first sleigh by and go straight to Kovetsky's near St. Isaacs Square. They say their *pelmeni** is magnificent. We'll have French wine and caviar. We must have caviar, a kilo apiece. Oh, I almost forgot, there's something else – we've been invited to his estate for this weekend by one of my superiors. It's near Luga.'

'Oh?'

'Yes, Friday night through Monday morning. We'll have an absolutely delightful time. It'll be one continuous party, I promise. A rehearsal for the Prussians.'

'Whose place is it?'

'General Zutroff.'

'Do I know him?'

'You've never met him. But he's a very likable fellow. He's actually a duke. Which, my darling, makes my

---

* Light boiled dumplings filled with meat and served with sour cream.

becoming a lieutenant-colonel even a greater triumph. My blood is no more royal than the shopkeeper's on the corner. And here I am, Nikandr Alexis Raymonovich Suverin, Lieutenant-Colonel, Nineteenth Infantry. Let's have three huzzahs!'

33

They enjoyed a perfectly delightful, if scandalously expensive, dinner. Nikki stayed on his best behavior throughout the evening, although continuing to carry on about his good fortune for the benefit of everyone within earshot. And their lovemaking that night proved sheer ecstasy.

Later, shortly before dawn, while he slept beside her, one arm flung across her breasts, a smile spread across his face, she dozed and thought about the two of them and their relationship. He was a decidedly different Nikki from the one she had married on board the *Sviostoloff*, but there was, she conceded, still a lot of the old Nikki left in him, the traits that had persuaded her that loving him, accepting his ring, wherever it came from, were not to be regretted. If he stayed out late and drank a little too much and gambled, he was no different from his fellow officers. Besides, there was obviously no way to change him; taking him as he was, accepting his faults with his good points, seemed the wisest course. Fortunately, or unfortunately, she did love him.

On Friday they engaged a sleigh for the weekend in the country. The temperature had dropped well below zero and the two horses clopping along the narrow road sent great clouds of vapor curling up into the bitter-cold air. The sky was mother-of-pearl, rapidly darkening to slate, but sitting alongside Nikki, below and behind their driver, cuddling close, she felt no winter inside. Only love and pride in his achievement-to-come. Soon now, he assured her, before the end of the year was the latest word.

They drew within sight of the general's estate. It

appeared that they were the first arrivals; no other sleighs were to be seen. The house resembled a feudal castle, mostly granite, with towers assaulting the sullen sky and the turrets of the chimneys, of which she counted no fewer than eight, resembling cannon aimed at the heavens.

It was only four-thirty when their driver pulled up at the front door, but already it was beginning to get dark, as if the day were giving it up early in the knowledge that it could never show the sun. Lights appeared in the downstairs windows. For all its forbidding appearance, close up the place took on an inviting look, and she imagined it to be cozy and beautiful inside, with great roaring fires, magnificent furnishings, all the trappings of wealth and position.

'Is General Zutroff married?' asked Tawny as they got out and the driver set about taking down their luggage and stacking it in the snow.

'Who?'

She laughed. 'Our host, idiot!'

He grinned. 'You mustn't call a lieutenant-colonel of the Imperial an idiot. It is expressly forbidden.' Nikki nodded toward their driver, who pretended not to have heard a word.

A subaltern, the general's aide, Tawny surmised, greeted them at the door. The place was a palace! As they entered and surrendered their outer clothing to servants who rushed up to them and she surveyed the ceiling, it appeared to be a hundred feet above their heads.

A balcony supported by dark brown marble columns with Roman Corinthian capitals crowned the main hall, and on the walls beneath hung enormous paintings, all battle scenes. Bronze busts of Russia's former rulers stood about like ladies- and gentlemen-in-waiting. The floor was marble, lighter brown squares with the central section inlaid with a circle of sabers creating a sort of military sunburst. At the far end the fireplace was huge, fashioned of white marble, above it a lovely Chippendale-style mirror with matching candle-holders on either side. Simply swinging her eyes from one end of the room to the other took Tawny's breath away. The one room made Aldous Rampling's entire home look as unimpressive as the rudest shack in Titus Forks.

'Well, well, well, here we are. Here we are . . .'

A general in full uniform had appeared at the railing above. He leaned over it smiling down, or rather leering at her. Tawny's blood froze. That bristling hair, that ramrod figure, that squat body... she shivered, feeling his arms around her, hearing the orchestra playing.

General Araktcheiev!

34

The Horror greeted them most cordially, hanging on to her hand much too long for Tawny's liking, bowing and scraping to her like one of his own servants, welcoming them over and over, each time merely changing a few words in his greeting. It was as if he were deliberately trying to keep them from catching a train.

She was livid. And it showed; it had to. Her cheeks felt as if they were burning to cinders, her throat had constricted, shortening her breath, her heart slammed against her rib cage. She could kill Nikki. Kill him!

'If you'll excuse me, General Araktcheiev, it's been a long ride. May I go and freshen up?'

'By all means, how thoughtless of me. Anna!' A large woman with heavy Germanic features, an unsmiling slit of a mouth, and unhappy gray eyes came marching briskly forward. 'Anna... oh, my dear Madame Suverin, may I introduce Anna Fritsch, who will be seeing to your every need during your most welcome stay here. Anna, Madame Suverin wishes to see her room.'

'Yes, sir. This way please, madame...'

Tawny started off following the woman. She was seething, absolutely furious. Stopping at the foot of the stairs, she turned.

'Nikki...'

Engaged in jovial conversation with their host, Nikki looked her way. 'Yes, my dear?'

'Excuse me, General.' Tawny started back toward the two of them, leaving Anna standing with a perplexed look on her doughy face. Tawny took Nikki by the arm.

'May I steal him from you for a few minutes, General?' she asked in the sweetest voice she could muster.

'Go along, my boy. I shall see you both in the conservatory shortly. You'll want some tea to warm you up. And, madame, again if there is anything you require, anything at all, if we don't have it we'll send out for it. I want this weekend to be the most enjoyable, the most memorable of your lifetime.'

'I'm sure it will be. Come, darling...'

Anna Fritsch was dismissed at the bedroom door, much to the woman's surprise.

'Come back in ten minutes or so, won't you?' asked Tawny sweetly. With this she gripped Nikki by the sleeve and all but shoved him into the bedroom, closing the door and locking it in Anna's face.

'You talk, I'll listen,' hissed Tawny.

He reached for her to take her in his arms, but she backed away.

'Don't touch me, you pig, you filthy liar. General Zutroff, was it? Well, are you just going to stand there gaping at me like a schoolboy caught with his hand in the cookie jar?'

She barely saw his hand rise from his side, flick forward with the speed of a striking snake, and slap her hard. So hard she staggered backward, nearly falling onto the bed.

'Bitch, hold your bitch tongue! And listen. Number one, you don't talk to me like that. Ever!' He raised his hand threateningly. In spite of herself, her anger, she cringed. 'Or next time you'll get this.' He made a fist, then slowly lowered his arm. 'And worse. Don't talk, just listen. I can appreciate the fact that our esteemed host is no Apollo and old enough to be your grandfather, but he also happens to be the second most powerful man in the country. My country, *our* country, wife! He finds you immensely attractive. To be blunt about it, the old fool adores you.'

'Nikki, I want you to listen to me. If you ever lay your hand on me again...'

'You'll what? Tell me.'

She failed to suppress a sigh. There was no answer to that; they both knew it. He smirked at her. God, how she hated him!

'Would I be overstepping my bounds if I asked a few simple questions? On second thought, why bother? Why don't I give you the answers? We're his only guests this weekend, isn't that so?' Nikki nodded, the smirk frozen on his face gradually fading. 'This weekend is your lieutenant-colonelcy. He wants me and you've offered me to him. You needn't bother denying it, I see it in your eyes.'

'Who's denying it?'

'Dear God in heaven, I don't believe this!'

'It's a harsh world, my love. I could be fifty before I move up to such a level.'

'And this is the way promotions are "earned" off the battlefield. Officers unhesitatingly hand over their wives, the women they love, to their superiors. My, my, such generosity . . .'

'I made a promise, my love, and all you're going to do is help me keep it.' He paused, fixing her with a questioning look. 'You amaze me, you really do.'

'I amaze *you!*'

'Please, lower your voice. Try to behave like a lady. Yes, you amaze me. I would think you'd be willing, even eager, to make a small sacrifice to assure my promotion. After all, don't the two of us benefit?'

'Small sacrifice? Did I hear you right?'

He shrugged and turned from her. 'Very well, now that everything's out in the open and we have it all straight, will that be all? We shouldn't be rude and keep our host waiting, should we?'

'I won't do it, my "love". I won't let him touch me. Not so much as his hand on my arm going in to dinner.'

Nikki spun around, facing her. His eyes were suddenly onyx-hard, his voice as cold as the frost on the panes.

'Oh, you're sadly mistaken on that score. You'll let him touch you. You will let him do anything and everything with you that pleasures him. And whether you enjoy it or not, if you're as intelligent as I give you credit for being, you'll make him believe you do.

'Because, my darling, this is not just for the weekend; I'm afraid it's a permanent arrangement.'

35

Within twenty minutes Nikki had fled the house. For where, Tawny had no idea, nor was she the least bit interested. Moments after he was gone a sleigh arrived bearing her trunk with all her things.

She was no longer angry, nor stunned by Nikki's revelation. That shock had rapidly worn off, to be supplanted by fear. More than fear, much more: she suddenly felt herself in the vise of positive terror. For a moment she envisioned herself lost in, groping about in, a dank and dark multichambered cave with some scaly monster blocking her way to freedom. Her dread was well founded; that night, if nothing else, was destined to prove without question that General Araktcheiev's nickname, the Horror, was most appropriate. The night she was raped by the animals at Matthews' Inn on the way to St. Louis, Telford Ingersoll's cruel and abasing attack, the savages ravishing her in the Willamette Valley paled in comparison to the living hell he so eagerly created for her with his perverted ideas of what a man and a woman should share in the privacy of the bedchamber.

Conventional sex held no appeal for the Horror. From the moment he forced her inside the room and began systematically ripping her clothing from her body it was clear to Tawny that she would have no defense against him, that she was at his mercy. But that mercy was a thought that could never enter his twisted mind. Trembling, fairly writhing with fear even before he started, she could clearly see that he was no man, nothing like a man, but a devil, evil incarnate, and that he intended to use and abuse her in ways no human being worthy of the definition should even think about, let alone practice.

She was not wrong.

To protest was useless. His quirt stopped every utterance before it became sound as he repeatedly slashed her across her naked buttocks. And he was deaf to her pleading, her supplications for mercy; oblivious to everything save his overpowering need to satisfy his lust. The unspeakable acts he forced her to perform, his sadistic delight in the pain, suffering, and humiliation they caused her, seemed to increase as the night wore on. Had there been a knife or scissors within reach, she would have killed him. Or herself. But gradually his bestiality and her more and more docile submission to it achieved a point that moved her past caring any longer whether she lived or died.

And in his lovely, warm, expensively furnished bed-chamber, near and upon an extraordinarily beautiful silk brocade bed, by the dim light of twin Etruscan lamps set on matching fruitwood side tables under the brooding eyes of the czar portrayed in the uniform of an admiral, she surrendered to the Horror's every viciously perverted whim and desire until at long last he exhausted himself and fell asleep.

And for the first time in her life, Tawny, catching her breath, stumbling bruised, battered, and naked out of the room to make her way to her own, was besieged by the conviction that her mind was going the way of her mother's.

Down into the black and bottomless pit of madness.

Anna Fritsch came to her as she lay abed the next morning, aching furiously all over her body and filled with a sense of desperation she had never known the like of before. Not even as a prisoner of the Molalas, for then she harbored the hope that Boyd would save her and Jenny. Poor dear darling Boyd...

Anna brought her breakfast on a tray. 'The general has gone back to Saint Petersburg, but will return this evening.'

'Dear God...' gasped Tawny, as her memory opened and a panorama of the more terrifying scenes of the night before came flooding forth.

Setting the tray down on the bedside stand, Anna fluffed up Tawny's pillows and helped her to pull the edge of the coverlet up to her chin to hide her nakedness.

'Was it terrible, child?'

'Ghastly. Oh God... God...'

The woman shook her head and clucked sympathetically.

'There's toast and marmalade and honeycake, and the coffee is piping hot.'

Tawny was repelled by the mere sight of the food. 'I'm not hungry, thank you.'

'You must eat, child, to keep your strength up.'

'What strength?' She glanced at the ceiling in despair. 'And to keep it up, for what, so that I'll last one night longer?'

'He's a monster, I know.'

'You don't. Nobody who hasn't gone through what I went through last night in that torture chamber he calls a bedroom could know.' She lowered her eyes and they brightened as she stared at Anna. Realizing for the first time what she had heard her say.

'He's gone for the day? Thank God in heaven . . . I must get away. You'll help me. Please, I beg you, help me . . .'

Anna turned from her to escape her eyes, then looked back pityingly. 'I only wish I might.'

'You must! I can't stay another night under this roof. I'll die, he'll surely kill me. He's not human, he's an animal!'

'All the same, you can't leave. It's freezing out; it must be twenty below. Worse, if one of us were to so much as lift a finger to help you escape, we'd be shot. I've seen stable serfs stood against the wall and shot for trying to prepare a horse for one of you poor creatures. No, sad to say, there's no getting away. When he's done with you, when he tires of you, then and only then.

'But you're so beautiful, I'm afraid he won't tire of you for a long, long time.'

'And what does he do with those he tires of, have them shot?'

Anna sat on the edge of the bed and began gently brushing Tawny's hair back from her forehead. Then, turning to the tray, she poured half a cup of the coffee, added cream, started to add sugar when Tawny shook her head, stirred, and handed the cup to her. Tawny scrunched upward a few inches to keep from spilling when she drank.

'I don't think he goes that far. A free woman isn't a serf . . .'

'Free? That's a laugh.'

'I believe that in the past they've just been sent away.'

'Where?'

Anna shrugged. 'Who can say? He certainly never talks to me about it. Drink. Slowly, it's hot.'

It was, piping. And delicious. Tawny sipped and nibbled at the toast, but had no taste for it, even after Anna had spread a slice with the orange marmalade.

'And why do you stay?' asked Tawny. 'He'd have no reason to harm you if you wanted to leave.'

'But where would I go? I'm fifty-eight years old, no husband, no family.'

'Fritsch, that's not Russian...'

'Prussian. My father was a Prussian uhlan, my mother was Russian. From Tula, south of Moscow.'

Tawny lowered the cup and stared at her appealingly. 'Please listen. I don't know how – I can't think, I ache so, my head is in a muddle – but I have to leave this place before he comes back. I beg you...'

Anna stood up, flinging her hands out in a gesture of helplessness.

'How? Nobody would dare to help you. Even if you bundled up and walked, if he comes back and finds you gone he'll go wild.' She lowered her voice, as if afraid that someone was listening outside the door. 'There are times, many times, I think he's demented.'

'You think? Anna, I know!'

'Anyone seeing you try to leave would stop you. Would have to for his own protection. Let you go and whoever it was would be committing suicide if one of the others saw or heard. To a man they all kiss his boots.'

Tawny thought a moment.

'I don't want to hurt any of you, or put you in danger, but I can't stand this, the pain, the degradation, the not knowing from one minute to the next whether or not he's going to lose all control and... I'm only flesh and blood, Anna, I can't take much more. You say you think he sends us away when he tires of us. I don't. I think every other girl has died in that room, just given up the ghost to be free of him and his viciousness.'

'There's one bright spot – he's only here weekends. You'll be alone from Monday to Friday.'

'To what, recover?' responded Tawny.

'And next weekend shouldn't be at all bad. King Friedrich' – she gave it the German pronunciation – 'and Queen Louise of Prussia will be here, and you and he will be back in Saint Petersburg!'

Tawny nodded. 'You're right, I'd forgotten.' Her wan smile faded. 'Unluckily for me, there are still bedrooms in the city. Anna, do this much for me. Get a letter out of this horrible place to a friend of mine.'

'I wish I could. By all that's holy I do, but if I were caught . . .'

'You can't possibly be. All you need do is slip it in with the rest of the mail that goes out of here. Surely he or the servants, even you write letters.'

'The post comes at noon, usually. But don't you see, whoever you write to would try to do something for you and they couldn't do anything but raise a fuss and –'

'And you'd be in the middle, is that it?' Anna nodded slowly. 'You needn't worry about that. If what I try backfires, I'll take the full blame. I'll confess to slipping it into the mail pile; I can actually do it.'

Tawny sat up, carelessly letting the coverlet drop, revealing her bruised and swollen breasts. Anna gaped, covering her mouth with the back of her hand to stifle reaction.

'*Ach du lieber . . .*'

Tawny quickly covered herself. 'Get me pen and ink and any kind of paper. Hurry, please. And you can take away this tray, I'll just finish the coffee.'

She wrote to Olga, explaining Nikki's perfidy, the heartless, insidious agreement he had made with Araktcheiev, and detailing her plight. Signing the letter 'Yours in desperation', she placed it in its envelope, sealed it, and addressed it. Finishing, affixing the stamp given her by Anna, she sighed audibly. Dear sweet Olga, she would move the Hermitage off its foundation to help her, if she could.

That was the crux of it – what could she possibly do? What could anyone do for her? Nikki had said it all: the Horror was the second most powerful man in the country. What earthly chance did she have to escape him?

Thinking about it, she then slowly, mechanically tore the

letter in half. Then into bits, collecting them on the edge of the coverlet, cupping one hand and filling it, making a mental note to toss them into the fire when she got up.

What was the use? She could only hope that someday, in some manner, Nikki would be made to pay. The thought of revenge against anyone who had wronged her had never occurred to her before that moment. No, stopping to think about it, not once in her entire life. Not even against Telford Ingersoll. But she wanted it now. Badly. Anyone who would deliberately place her in such a situation, imbue her with a state of mind wherein she found herself wishing she were dead in order to escape it all, deserved the harshest possible punishment.

And by all the gods, if she lived through this she'd see that he got it!

36

Frederick William was both feeble and fatuous, a weak king with enough weaknesses of character to disserve any three men. He was stunted, he stuttered, he was physically awkward. He was every inch a misfit, born and ruling under a luckless star. He was also honest, sensitive, dignified, and well meaning. If ever a wife was ill suited to the man she married, Queen Louise was she; she was brilliant as well as beautiful – dark-eyed with classic, delicately contoured features, graceful, charming, irreproachably virtuous, and as loyal to Frederick William, despite his many failings as a monarch and a man, as any wife could possibly be.

In the court circles of Saint Petersburg it was well known that Alexander felt genuine compassion for the two of them and in company with the rest of the world blamed no one but Napoleon for their plight, for the Corsican Ogre had dismembered and all but destroyed their once proud kingdom. Indeed, so destitute had Prussia's royal couple become that it was necessary for the czar to help them 'keep up appearances'. Upon arriving at her apartments in the

Chepelev Palace, Queen Louise was to find a toilette set in massive gold, a dozen dresses – one embroidered with pearls said to have cost at least a hundred thousand rubles – and a perfectly beautiful collection of Persian and Turkish shawls.

The state banquet of welcome hosted by His Imperial Majesty was held at his temporary home, the Tauris Palace, the first in a series of entertainments on a scale not seen in Saint Petersburg since the days of Catherine the Great. In attendance were the two czarinas (Maria Louisa of Baden and Alexander's mother, Maria Federovna), the grand dukes, the wealthier boyars, and the nation's highest military personnel. General Araktcheiev escorted Tawny, in the interim, since their first night together, having to some degree curbed his sadism, permitting her to recover so that she would be certain to look her best.

The banquet was to be followed by a ball to which more than seven hundred other important officers and citizens and their ladies had been invited.

The table seated no fewer than one hundred and seven guests in addition to the king and queen, their host and hostesses. Under four glittering chandeliers a veritable Lucullan feast was set out upon the royal plate with the entrée freshly killed pheasant.

Sitting alongside her escort looking her loveliest in a plain robe of white satin without pearls or jewels or any ornamentation save a small bunch of fragrant stephanotis stuck in her cinnamon hair, Tawny barely tasted her caviar, preferring to let her eyes drift over the assembly, noting Queen Louise's beauty, in contrast to the somewhat plain, even mannish-looking czarina. As for His Highness, this was Tawny's first opportunity for a close-up look at Alexander. Her initial impression was that of a troubled-looking man striving his best to make his unfortunate royal guests feel at ease. He was, she had heard, a simple man, although 'simple' was the last word that would have occurred to her to describe the present setting.

Alexander was slender, fit-looking; he was also sur-prisingly good-looking, with blue eyes, finely chiseled features, a straight nose, and light brown hair. It was said that he had had a great many mistresses in his thirty-two years. As this recollection crossed her mind, as if feeling her eyes upon him, he glanced up from his plate and stared at her without any expression whatsoever on his face.

She could feel her cheeks tingle as she looked away. Araktcheiev covered her hand with his own.

'Enjoying yourself, my dear?'

'Yes . . .'

'Excellent. It makes me happy to see you happy.'

Olga and her husband were not socially important enough to be invited to the banquet; hopefully, mused Tawny, she would see her later at the ball.

If only she hadn't torn up the note she'd written to her! She could pass it to her, then perhaps they could sneak off together later. Olga would find a place to hide her if anyone could. The temporary softening of his treatment of her notwithstanding, she had to get away from the Horror. Once the king and queen departed for home, back to his place she would go, back to resumption of the humiliating depravity and degradation he so delighted in subjecting her to.

Dinner seemed to drag on for hours, course after course being thrust in front of her, soups and salads and pheasant and more pheasant. And wine by the tun. She ate and drank very little, having no appetite whatsoever. Having had none for days now. For the most part, with the exception of the czarinas and a handful of others, most of the ladies also seemed to be nibbling and picking at their food while the men gorged themselves, the Horror cramming pheasant into his maw at such a rate one would have imagined it was to be his last meal ever.

If only that could be true, reflected Tawny wistfully.

Nikki was nowhere to be seen. Evidently even lieutenant-colonels weren't high enough in rank to share pheasant with Their Majesties. Tawny doubted she would see Nikki at the ball, either. Not that she cared to. If he did show up she just might lose control, fly at him and scratch his eyes out, bother the occasion and its significance!

Conversation rumbled up and down the table, which seemed to stretch almost out of sight. She and Araktcheiev sat two down from Czarina Maria Federovna and her escort, the Polish ambassador. At the distant end sat most of the Horror's staff, including General Zoropkin, whose gestures clearly announced his sexual preference, as Olga had told

215

her when they had first met back at the apartment.

Tawny sighed inwardly; at the moment that seemed ages ago.

A few minutes before eleven the eating came to an end and one and all arose from the table. They filtered slowly down the corridor and down the winding stairs to the enormous ballroom on the first floor. The orchestra was already playing a waltz *à trois temps*.

Tawny entered the room on Araktcheiev's arm; he was in his glory, nodding to everyone they passed, his ugly face frozen in an apelike grin. They danced; he held her too close as usual, and, having had just enough wine to rekindle her spirit, she very politely asked him to ease his grip. To her surprise, he hastily did so.

Fluted columns of black marble supported the massive, slightly domed ceiling, from which hung thirty-six chandeliers, flooding the room with light. Between the heavy velvet drapes, each individually decorated with the royal crest, the windowpanes were opaque with frost. Dimly seen through the frost the lights of the city glowed an eerie bluish-gray. But it was as warm inside as it was cold out, as thirty musicians filling a stage against the center of one wall provided music for those already dancing.

To find Nikki's sister and her husband in such a mob seemed hopeless, particularly since Tawny could not be absolutely sure they had even been invited.

But they had been. She spied Olga in the doctor's arms, whirling around a pillar near the orchestra. She managed to catch her eye, prompting a smile of recognition and a little wave. Tawny's response was the very grimmest look she could put on her face, and over the general's shoulder she nodded in the direction of the corridor. For a moment Olga failed to understand, then she caught on and nodded.

The music came to an end, applause ensued.

'Will you excuse me for a moment?' asked Tawny. 'I must freshen my face.'

'Your face looks as fresh as your flowers to me, my dear,' said Araktcheiev.

'You know what I mean.'

'Of course. But do hurry back...'

She found Olga waiting in the corridor and explained as

briefly, as quickly as she could. Olga's face became ashen.

'Nikki!'

'Ssh.' Tawny glanced warily about. A handful of couples had drifted out of the room and were standing talking. Inside, the orchestra resumed playing, offering a quadrille.

'The stinker! The rotten –'

Tawny cut her off. 'You must get me out of here, away from that beast.'

'I can get both our coats and hats and things and meet you just inside the main doors. We'll head straight for our house.'

'What about Paul?'

'I'll explain to him. He'll vanish; he's very clever, resourceful. He'll play along, I promise.'

'When then?' asked Tawny breathlessly, hope rising, seizing her.

'In five minutes –'

'No, that's too soon. Don't you see, I've already gone to the powder room this once; we shall have to wait at least an hour for a second time. Better an hour and a half.'

Olga nodded and consulted her lapel watch. 'It's eleven thirty-two. Let's say a quarter to one. Remember, just inside the main doors. I'll have all your things.'

'Oh, Olga, I'm so grateful.' Tawny kissed her. 'You can't imagine . . .'

'Never mind the details, we can do all our talking after we're free of this mausoleum.'

The next hour and a half seemed to creep by. Each passing minute on the alabaster clock on the mantel over the blazing fire seemed like five. Tawny had to force herself to keep from glancing at the hands for fear that the ever-alert Horror would question her interest in the time.

At last the clock showed seventeen minutes before one. Abruptly she stopped dancing, breaking from him. Leaning against a column, she touched her forehead.

'My dear . . .'

'It's nothing, I just suddenly feel a little faint. I think I need a glass of water.' Araktcheiev lifted his hand toward a full colonel gliding by with his partner, but Tawny took hold of the general's arm.

'That's all right, I'll just go to the powder room and get it myself. Then I can sit for a few minutes.'

'I told you you should have eaten more.' He seemed genuinely concerned. How ironic, she thought: he could all but abuse her to death in the bedchamber, but when she became slightly dizzy on the dance floor it actually seemed to alarm him!

Excusing herself with a purposefully wan smile, she made her way through the throng to the corridor, hurrying. Olga stood waiting, holding her things. Seeing her coming, she smiled.

'Hurry, it's bitter out. We'll walk to the corner and get the first sleigh by,' she whispered.

Tawny buttoned her coat, put on her hat, and wound her muffler around her neck. 'I don't care if it's ninety below; I'd walk out of here naked to get away.'

They approached the doors. The uniformed and bewigged doormen opened them for them, both staring puzzled, neither saying a word, ostensibly neither daring to. Outside the cold hit them like a whip snapping. They started down the sanded steps. The front gates were wide open; music and the muffled sound of voices could be heard coming from the ballroom. The city slept. A subaltern stood by the gate pillar to the left, swinging his arms and stamping his feet against the cold. He turned their way as they approached. He was very young, with a round, red face and stupid-looking eyes. Tawny had never seen him before.

He held up both hands. 'That is far enough, ladies.' Tawny's heart sank. 'General Araktcheiev's orders. His wishes are that you' – he nodded at her – 'madame, do not leave the palace.' He snapped to attention, clicking his heels and bowing. 'Now, if you will be so kind as to turn around, I shall be pleased to escort you back inside.'

37

Extending his hands, the general beamed as he welcomed her back at the entrance to the ballroom. She had been brought back alone, Olga going on her way, being summarily ordered to do so by the subaltern.

'Here you are, my dear,' said Araktcheiev warmly. 'I was beginning to think we'd lost you. Feeling better? No more...' He twirled his index finger.

A chinless man of medium height wearing a wild-looking carrot-red mustache, his face and the backs of both hands peppered with freckles, stood beside him. He seemed strangely embarrassed. Whether he was or not, Tawny could not care. The Horror thought of everything; now he was even reading her mind! Hadn't Olga said that he was brilliant? They hadn't even gotten past the gate, and what made the whole grisly business even worse was that now he knew that there was at least one person in Saint Petersburg willing to try to help her get away from him. And Olga and Paul would be lucky to get off with a reprimand for their part in the abortive attempt.

How she hated this. And feared it. Tonight, when he got her alone... God, she could not make herself think about it.

'My dear, allow me to present His Imperial Majesty's private secretary, Dr. Novossiltsov.' Novossiltsov bowed ever so slightly. Araktcheiev also bowed, drew the back of her hand to his lips, and kissed it. 'I shall bid you good night. You will go with Dr. Novossiltsov. You will oblige me by doing precisely as he tells you to do, is that clear?'

She nodded wordlessly. He nodded to the red-mustached one, turned, and strode off.

'Follow me, if you please,' said Novossiltsov stiffly. She did so, back up the winding staircase, past the dining room, where servants were still busy cleaning up, up to the third floor, down a long corridor, turning left, then right, coming to a blue door inlaid with gilt.

219

Producing a key from his belt pocket, Novossiltsov unlocked and opened the door, stepping aside, gesturing her inside.

'Tonight you will sleep here.'

'But –'

He continued without permitting her to interrupt.

'You will find it most comfortable. Everything you'll require, including attire for sleep, has been provided. You need merely pick out what you like from the armoire.'

'I don't understand.'

'You will.'

'May I trouble you for the key?'

He shook his head negatively, bid her good night, closed the door in her face, and locked it. She tried the handle; it refused to budge. Turning, she surveyed the room. The mantel of multicolored marble was Louis XIV. The wood in the grate was unlit, awaiting the n   touch of a taper. The fauteuil and chaise longue before it were Louis XV. The walls were paneled, painted in a soft gray and light blue matching the door. The bed looked enchanted, it was so beautiful, a Louis XV *lit à Polonaise* lavishly draped with yards upon yards of pale blue gauze.

Light in the room emanated from four wall sconces. Trying the door one last time, giving it up, she sighed heavily, crossed to the armoire, selected a nightgown of India muslin embroidered with silver, disrobed, and put on the gown. Blowing out each candle in turn, she got into the bed. It was deliciously comfortable, as soft as a warm breeze, but jet-black in the room, so dark that even minutes later, when her eyes should have become accustomed to it, she could not even make out the canopy draping at the foot of the bed.

She was becoming more and more fearful now as time slipped by. She would not be sleeping tonight with the Horror, for that she could give prayerful thanks, but what the next hour would bring she dared not guess.

In spite of her dread she was so exhausted she could not stay awake. She had no way of knowing how long she had been asleep when she woke, sitting up, sensing that someone had entered the room. Light flooded the bedcovers briefly.

220

Then a shadowy figure closed and locked the door.

'Who is it?'

She asked a second time, but no response came out of the darkness. She could hear him remove his clothing, and presently he got into bed.

'Please don't hurt me . . .'

Still not a word, nothing but soft steady breathing and the rustling of the sheets. He was above her now, lifting the covers with his back and reaching up under her nightgown. His hands were ice-cold, and she could feel her flesh tighten and begin to creep.

'Please . . .'

He was awkward and fumbled, but was gentle. Remarkably so. But there wasn't a sound out of him other than his unhurried breathing. Now she could feel his member slipping slowly between her trembling thighs; she wanted to scream, to protest and batter him with her fists, but his silence was so ominous, and her surroundings so dreadfully dark, she was afraid to.

Without a murmur, while his cold hands gripped and held her breasts, she submitted, feeling him inside her, working his member. Slowly at first, then faster and faster still . . .

38

Novossiltsov had come by early in the morning, her visitor having departed before dawn, after taking his pleasure with her a second time. Dressed and served breakfast in an out-of-the-way room, she was then given into the charge of the subaltern who had stopped her from leaving the Tauris Palace the night before. Two hours later he deposited her at the front door of General Araktcheiev's mansion, bid her farewell, and, snapping the reins over the horses' flanks, swung the sleigh about and started back toward the city.

On the way out she had pleaded with him to drop her off at any one of the three villages through which they passed.

His refusal to do so, to even discuss it, was understandable, even if disheartening. Obviously the man was just as fearful of the Horror as she was. Araktcheiev had not yet returned from the capital, according to Anna, giving Tawny a welcome, if short-lived, reprieve from his certain wrath. She could not make herself believe that he was the sort to overlook or excuse her attempt to flee him. His ego would never allow him to do either.

She stood with Anna in her bedroom, discussing the futility of her plight.

'I might as well kill myself and be done with it,' she said bitterly. 'To go on like this, passed from one to another like some popular doxy.'

Anna put her arm around her, then drew her close. 'You mustn't talk so; it's not the end of the world.'

'I wish it were!'

Releasing Tawny, the older woman set her chin in her hand, put on a thoughtful expression, and began pacing up and down alongside the bed.

'I have been thinking. You say your former husband's sister knows all about this business?'

'Yes, but she can't help me. Not now. She tried and failed because I was stupid. Because I never stopped to think he'd have men covering every exit from the palace.'

'Don't despair, child, your chance will come. And during the king and queen's stay in the city. You'll see. You'll be going back there tonight or tomorrow. If you can get away from him you must make your way to the wharf at the west end of Vasilievski Island. You can catch a sleigh in the street and instruct the driver to take you there.' She raised one finger ceilingward solemnly. 'Most important, the next time you leave this accursed place you shall go prepared. I have money. You'll need it.'

'I can't take your money, Anna.'

'You can and you will!' It was a command that brooked no argument, delivered with set jaw, tight lips, and piercing eye. 'What good is money to me?' continued the older woman in a milder tone. 'I almost never get outside these walls, let alone to Saint Petersburg. Up until the end of the year when the big ice floes begin setting into the harbor there are ships coming and going from Kotka and

222

Helsingfors* in Finland for Stockholm in Sweden. Once you are clear of Russian territory he can't lay a hand on you.'

'You make it sound so easy. Getting out of whatever palace the next affair is held in will be impossible.'

'You'll find a way. And money talks very convincingly. His subalterns are not all that well paid. A few rubles can turn one's eyes away . . .'

The Horror did not return that night. Late in the afternoon, as the sun settled into frozen Lake Peipus like a great grayish-white ball of ice, a sleigh drew up to the front door bearing a carton with a note attached to the lid. It was addressed to Tawny. She could not read the Cyrillic writing, so Anna translated it for her:

'My dearest one:
      There are to be troika races on the Neva tomorrow afternoon, great fun, to be followed by a *bal de masque* in the evening at the Winter Palace. This costume should fit you, but if any alterations are needed Mrs. Fritsch will see to them. A sleigh will pick you up at noon. Do not forget your costume.

                                                            Fondly,
                                                                 A.

P.S. When next we talk you must tell me the name of the woman who so rashly attempted to spirit you away last night. That was very naughty of you both. You will tell me her name and address.'

'I'll never tell him,' said Tawny soberly. 'He can beat me to death.'

'Hush, such talk. Let's have a look.'

The costume proved to be a full-skirted fairy princess ensemble complete with blue-sequined top, matching blue slippers, a tiara, a wand, and a domino mask.

'It's beautiful,' commented Anna, lifting it out and holding it against Tawny. 'And should fit you.'

Tawny displayed little interest in the costume but at

* Present-day Helsinki.

Anna's insistence tried it on, and with a tuck or two taken about the waist it was made to fit.

The Neva had been frozen since early November, and would continue in that state, according to Anna, until April or even May. But the Gulf of Finland and the Baltic Sea, being salt water, remained open, although as a result of the ice floes rapidly building up, the former would become all but impassable for any ships save solidly stemmed icebreakers until spring. Still, for the next two weeks the wharves would be as busy as usual.

The troika races were exciting, but a painful spectacle to Tawny, reminding her as they did of the horse races back home in Missouri. Reflecting on Titus Forks and her father, she found herself imagining that he and the house and stable were no longer part of the world but on another planet entirely, off somewhere in space. Tears misted sight of what proved to be the closest and most exciting of the six races.

The Horror was in a mood astonishingly affable for him, smiling and waving at everyone. Even when she had been brought to him by two of his men to his temporary box near the royal boxes on the riverbank and declared in response to the first words out of his mouth:

'I never saw the woman before in my life. And that is all I can tell you.'

He had smiled with uncharacteristic tolerance and self-control, giving Tawny no way of knowing whether he believed her or was simply not in any mood to bully Olga's name out of her at the moment, confident that he could do so at his pleasure at some later, more opportune time.

The czar's Winter Palace was huge, more a complex of individual palaces than a single one. It stood only three stories high, but covered practically an entire city block. The façade was distinguished by a series of Roman Corinthian crowned columns on two distinct levels, a type of architecture Tawny had already become bored with seeing during her relatively brief time in the city. What set the Winter Palace apart from the various other palaces, aside from its immensity, were the statues and other embellishments standing like chess pieces along the edge of the roof.

The ballroom was half again the size of that of the Tauris

Palace, accommodating more dancers, nearly a thousand according to the Horror, and its stage a larger orchestra. Everyone was costumed, including His Imperial Majesty, who came as Charlemagne, and his wife and mother, who appeared as Joan of Arc and a fairy princess, respectively. Tawny counted more than twenty fairy princesses, which, if nothing else, gave her the satisfaction of knowing how little originality Araktcheiev was capable of displaying when it came to selecting *bal de masque* costumes. He himself was attired in a Roman toga with a crown of pasteboard laurel leaves. He introduced himself to everyone as Emperor Hadrian, probably the most capable emperor, apart from Julius Caesar, Rome had ever boasted. Tawny thought Nero more appropriate, or possibly Caligula, but made no mention of either.

Unlike the previous ball, throughout which the Horror permitted her to dance with others on only two occasions, here, since everyone else seemed to be changing partners with each dance, he graciously allowed an endless parade of partners to cut in and whirl her about the floor – ministers, fellow officers, the Austrian Ambassador, Novossiltsov, even Alexander.

Most of the guests wore domino masks; there were as well a smattering of various animal costumes. Tawny did not see any sign of Nikki, nor were Olga and Paul Kovakin there. The latter discovery inspired an audible sigh of relief. Domino masks provide little disguise. Were Araktcheiev's conscientious subaltern lingering about, he would have little difficulty recognizing Olga.

Tawny had excused herself a number of times in order to sit and rest, and felt worn out by ten-thirty. Chairs lined one entire wall for the convenience of the dancers, although not a single man sat.

She was sitting resting when the Horror brought her a glass of wine. He stood hovering over her stubbornly, unwilling to be the first man to take a chair.

'You're the loveliest fairy princess on the floor,' he said solemnly. 'I'm so proud of you. Drink your wine.'

Tawny was tempted to decline and explain that it could very well put her to sleep, but didn't dare. He rambled on, complimenting her, his good fortune in 'discovering' her.

Lord in heaven, how she despised him, he was so arrogant, so cocksure! She nodded and now and then said something, to make it appear she was interested. But there was nothing, there never could be anything he had to say which would hold her attention.

She let her eyes drift past him and roam the dance floor, couples swinging by. The rhythm of the music had picked up considerably from the previous song.

Her eyes stopped at sight of a man standing alone by a window diagonally opposite the orchestra stage. He was well over six foot; his hair was black and unusually curly. He was disguised as an ambassador among, ironically, any number of bona fide ambassadors, his red sash of office slanting down his shirt front. His posture struck her as a bit stiff, as if he had been too long in the military, in spite of his being a young man. Perhaps his mouth could have been wider and the lips firmer-looking; she could not see his nose, but knew instinctively that under the mask it was a trifle small.

Her heart seemed to swivel in her chest, turning upside down, and it took every ounce of willpower and singular presence of mind for her to stifle a gasp which would have been followed by a shriek of joy.

It was Boyd.

39

Dear Lionel:

By the time you read this I'll be on my way. I know you're going to be furious, I can close my eyes and picture the red rising in your bull neck, your jaw pushing forward, the fire filling your face, your eyes. But before you start dressing me down as an ingrate, a madman, and all the rest of the kind words, think a bit and you'll realize that what I've been trying to drum through your thick skull is right, that because she's my wife this part of it has to be my responsibility. Mine alone. I can't in conscience bring you or anyone else along. Some things a man has to do on his own.

If I get all the luck of a lifetime into the rest of this year I'll make it. I'll find her, and bring her home. Look us up in Titus Forks a year from now – May, June, who knows? I can't put a date on it, I have too far to go and too many obstacles to get over or around. But have no fear, I'll make it.

We made it to the Willamette Valley, God save those poor people's souls, and we two made it to Yerba Buena, so I've had all the training in hardship I need. Anyway, here I go. Curse me for a traitor, get it all out of you, simmer down and wish me the luck of the Irish, Mr. Haggerty. I'm off on my journey into hell to bring back an angel.

Your friend forever,
B.

Haggerty had been adamant, staunchly refusing to let Boyd even consider leaving without him. They argued on and off for days. Finally Boyd was forced to resort to his deceit, accomplished with the help of the ever-helpful Willis Fentown. Boyd and Haggerty had planned to leave on a south-bound vessel on Thursday, but, unbeknownst to Haggerty, another ship, a Mexican freighter, unexpectedly put into Yerba Buena to pick up a cargo of redwood. Its itinerary would carry it home to Salina Cruz, which, according to the captain, would place Boyd about 260 miles south-southeast of Vera Cruz across Mexico's slender southern reach.

He had worked his passage down the coast doing every filthy, dangerous, back-breaking job on board, from clubbing rats in the hold to minor repair work aloft in a fairly stiff breeze to unloading the cargo. But the *Victoria* covered the nearly three thousand miles in thirteen days, and in that brief time he earned enough, combined with the money he had saved odd-jobbing about Yerba Buena during the winter, to invest in a horse, a feisty mustang to carry him overland to Vera Cruz.

In the days following the meeting with Thomas Squires he and Lionel and Fentown had managed to pick up additional information regarding the American woman the Russians had taken to New Archangel. It was, after all, the sort of oddity that might be expected to relieve any seafarer's boredom, and so became the talk of the settlement. The problem for Boyd lay in separating fact from fancy. He had left Yerba Buena knowing this much for certain: Tawny had spent the winter at the fort in New Archangel. She had been delirious, she had recovered and had sailed away on a ship bound for Saint Petersburg, to be married on board to one Lieutenant-become-Captain Nikandr Suverin. Obviously she was by this time convinced that Boyd was dead with the others. There was little chance that he might be misinformed on any of this; half a dozen ships had stopped at New Archangel on their way back from Alaskan waters, and officers and men were eager to talk of the tall, slender cinnamon-haired beauty who had been the Russians' guest.

By the time he reached Europe she would be in Saint Petersburg. And no longer a 'widow'. Making his way across the flat, dusty, unseasonably hot plain of Oaxaca toward the state capital gave him a good deal of time to think and to plan. He had a map given him by Squires; the former teacher's history lesson had been interesting, but his suggestion that Boyd join the Austrian army had seemed a trifle farfetched, not to mention overly complicated. It had become more of both since. If Boyd had learned anything in the U.S. Army, it was that the simpler the strategy, the better the chances for success. And the simplest strategy he could come up with to deal with this problem had to be a frontal assault. So, jettisoning Thomas Squires's plan, he decided that, once arrived in New Orleans, instead of seeking work on a ship bound for the Mediterranean he would head for England, landing wherever he could there, and after reaching the eastern coast locate a fourth ship, this one heading into the Baltic Sea, hopefully for Saint Petersburg.

He would stroll down the gangplank, search the city, find Tawny, and get her out. Get the two of them aboard the same ship heading back. Any ship, whichever one was leaving first and would take them. Simple? He could make it appear so on the screen of his imagination, but in his heart and that part of his mind which demanded a realistic,

228

practical approach to all dangerous ventures he knew it would be anything but simple.

He waited only four days in Vera Cruz for a ship to New Orleans. But once in the Crescent City, situated, ironically, less than a thousand miles from Titus Forks, he waited most of the summer for a ship that needed one semi-able seaman and was heading for the British Isles. Any British Isle, he told himself in mounting desperation. It was the middle of September before he signed on as a bullworker with the *Falcon* out of Southampton and returning home. He worked like a man possessed, like a man grateful for the job, which he unquestionably was, and added better than a hundred dollars to his savings en route. Arriving in England, he made his way by begging rides and public coach to the east coast and Great Yarmouth. There, two weeks later, he took passage on his fourth ship, a Swedish barkentine heading home for Malmo.

In Malmo luck was with him. Prowling the docks, he found a vessel heading up the Baltic into the Gulf of Finland. Destination: Saint Petersburg.

He also found one Ivan Kurzhentshev, a young giant imbued with the warmth of a winter fire and, as later events were to prove, a sense of loyalty on a par with Lionel Haggerty's. Ivan spoke eight languages semifluently, among them English, poorly, but Russian impeccably. The two men speedily became close friends, Boyd telling his story, Ivan listening with sympathetic ears and immediately pledging assistance to the cause. Once arrived in Saint Petersburg, they would work together to find Tawny. During the long bitter-cold nights, as the winds mercilessly thrashed the rigging over their heads and the ice-studded seas hammered at the *Magnus Stenbok*'s stem bar, Ivan taught Boyd basic conversational Russian, which, with Boyd's French, could not help but be useful once the two of them debarked and began their search.

The *Magnus Stenbok*, carrying cotton, woollen goods, and tobacco, dropped her anchors at the western docks of Vasilievski Island early in December, shortly after sundown of the night of the grand ball welcoming the King and Queen of Prussia on their state visit.

Nothing could be done that night, Ivan all but forcibly restraining Boyd from rushing ashore and beginning to comb the city, searching for Captain Nikandr Suverin's residence. The two men worked with the rest of the crew emptying the holds of their cargo, slept the remainder of the night, and early the next morning began their quest. They stopped first at the Saint Peter and Saint Paul Fortress and were told that Captain and Mrs. Nikandr Suverin's last known address was an apartment on Varonski Street, but Boyd was advised that the two were no longer living together. 'The lady has moved out.'

He and Ivan nevertheless went straight to the address obligingly given them, and approached the landlord. He was standing in the lower hallway in the shadow of the stairs in conversation with a pretty, dark-haired, well-dressed woman, who, Boyd noted, seemed extremely upset about something. The two were talking so fast he couldn't make out a word.

But whatever the landlord told her seemed to satisfy her, and she thanked him and started for the door. They exchanged nods with her as they passed. Ivan approached the landlord and inquired where he might find Captain Suverin's apartment. His question was delivered in a normal tone and was easily heard by the woman heading out the door. It stopped her and she turned around.

She proved to be Olga Kovakin, who had come to find 'that rapscallion of a brother of mine!' she explained to a speechless Boyd, unable to believe the suddenness of the lightning that had struck, dropping the gold of luck at his feet. To be speedily followed by the dross of misfortune.

He was told, through Ivan, of the two women's unsuccessful attempt to leave the dance at the Tauris Palace the night before, and that Tawny was with, had been given to a General Araktcheiev, better known as the Horror, handed over body and soul, like a birthday gift of a bottle of vodka, according to Olga.

She, Ivan, and Boyd took a table in a nearby tea shop, where Boyd learned all that she knew of the unhappy situation into which the helpless Tawny had been thrust by Suverin. Hearing this set Boyd's blood boiling and put finding the captain before any attempt to rescue Tawny.

'I'll find him and kill him with my bare hands,' he muttered tightly. 'I will!'

They were sipping tea brought by a waiter too long in service, too unsteady of hand, spilling a little from each steaming glass as his trembling hand set it down, begging their respective pardons for his clumsiness, and shuffling off. The place resembled Haskell's Mariners' Bar in Yerba Buena in size and layout, but the bar was missing, the clientele considerably more genteel in appearance – only seven others being present – the furnishings were more modern, and it was cleaner than Haskell's had been on the day it opened.

Ivan and Olga dissuaded Boyd from losing his perspective. Rescuing Tawny held priority over any vengeance he might plan against Nikki. Bringing him to account wouldn't do a thing for Tawny in her present plight. It was at this point in the conversation that Olga began to tell them about the masked ball on the schedule of events, expressing her feeling that if Tawny was to be rescued, that event seemed to offer the best opportunity.

'A word of warning. Don't do what she and I tried to do. You're better off working up a clever scheme and sneaking her out.'

'Time it so we rush her to the *Stenbok* just before she weighs anchor and sails,' interposed Ivan, by this time as deeply involved as Lionel Haggerty would have been had he come along. Then and there, lowering their heads and their voices in the manner of dedicated conspirators, using Olga's knowledge of the layout of the Winter Palace, they devised an escape route, a disguise of sorts for Tawny, and a way to get her out.

Boyd's heart beat faster. To come so far, to endure so much, to follow the faint star of hope to this point where within a relatively few hours he would come face to face with her, filled him with unreinable optimism.

He'd get her away from the Winter Palace. Out of Saint Petersburg. Once the *Magnus Stenbok* was out into the Gulf of Finland, into international waters Sweden-bound, no Russian, regardless of rank or influence, could stop them!

40

He saw her from across the room, angling his head, striving to peer through the horde of dancers swinging by to the strains of the music and intermittently blocking sight of her. He started over. Araktcheiev stood with his back to him, continuing to babble, pausing to sip his wine, resuming regaling her with his meaningless opinion on Napoleon's recent war with Austria, ending in the mid-October surrender of the latter nation. An eventuality anticipated by all of Europe.

Boyd came up to them. Was his heart beating as fast as hers? she wondered, avoiding his eyes for fear her expression might betray that he was no stranger. The Horror was unusually perceptive. The briefest glance, the slightest change in the eyes, the bending of the ends of one's mouth invariably seemed to ignite his supicion.

'I beg your pardon,' said Boyd in Russian. 'General, may I have the pleasure of a dance with your lovely wife? Madame?' Clicking his heels absurdly, he bowed, seizing her hand and kissing it.

Araktcheiev gave her away with a wave and an apish grin that carved deep creases in his homely face. A moment later she and Boyd were whirling about in a waltz.

'Smile, talk, be animated,' said Boyd softly. 'We're two strangers having a pleasant conversation. He's over there watching our every move.'

'How in heaven's name did you find me?' she asked breathlessly. 'Oh, my darling, it's really you! Alive!'

'Tawny, control yourself, for God's sakes. Never mind the how and when and where and why. Not now, not here. We'll have plenty of time to talk later. For now we've only got to the end of this song. Listen. Interrupt if you like, but remember everything I say. I'll escort you back to your Roman emperor. You'll sit, and when you do, start counting. You'll have to, there's no clock in here. Count one thousand one, one thousand two, and so on, up to two hundred and seventy. At two hundred seventy, four and a half minutes, excuse yourself, get up, and go to the ladies' room.'

'Darling –'

'Once outside in the corridor, turn right. Walk past the ladies' room to the front of the building. Turn right again and walk to the far end, the side door.'

'You don't understand. I've already tried to get away from him. It's impossible. He has eyes everywhere.'

'We'll take care of his eyes, great good care.' He frowned in spite of himself. 'I wish we could get out the back some way, but we can't. The river comes right up to the building all along the back. So it has to be the side door. There's only one.'

'He'll catch us, he'll have you shot. My God, I'd rather we never see each other again than you killed!'

'Ssh. Don't raise your voice. And keep smiling, even laugh. Remember, out to the front, turn right, the length of the building to the side door. You'll find a linen closet almost directly opposite. It's unlocked. Look for a bearskin robe on the third shelf. Wrap yourself in it, go to the door, wipe the fog from one of the panes and look out. You'll see me with my friend, Ivan. When I signal, you come out. Walk straight to me, don't run.'

'It'll never work, not now, not since I've already tried and failed. His men will be crowding every entrance.'

'I've counted fourteen entrances to this place. It's twenty below zero out there. Anybody assigned to watch for you isn't going to be standing around.'

'So they'll stand inside. What's the difference?'

'We can handle anybody in our way, Tawny. We've got to. I've come too far for this night, for these precious few minutes and you. I'm going back the same way. With you.'

Her forced smile began to fade. 'If I don't get out of here tonight we'll never see each other again as long as we live.'

'Exactly. Smile, my darling, and keep smiling. All right, I'll see you in less than six minutes. Get to the closet, get the robe on, over your head so you can fold the sides over your face.'

'Boyd.'

'No more talking, just dance.'

They danced. The song ended; the dancers applauded enthusiastically. He returned her to the Horror, thanking her, once again clicking his heels, bowing, and withdrawing. By this time she was on the verge of a heart seizure. Any second now, she was sure, her heart would thunder its last. It had to! It seemed to be pounding at twice normal rate, hammering her breast, threatening to burst. She felt as weak as water and told herself that she would never make it to the side door. She hadn't the strength; she'd surely collapse in the corridor, to be found by well-meaning guests, brought around with smelling salts, and hurried back to Araktcheiev.

She'd never see Boyd again. It seemed so cruel, so utterly heartless. To taunt her with the knowledge that by some miracle as yet unexplained to her he was alive and well and here in this frozen hell. She had actually seen and talked with him. Only to lose him. It was almost as if he'd risen from the grave to visit her, only to vanish as suddenly, as unexpectedly, as he had appeared.

But he was no phantom. He was flesh and blood alive; and he was right. This was to be their first and last chance. She must trust him to deal with whatever obstacles might lay in their path to freedom. Hadn't he proven his courage and resourcefulness in that regard any number of times on the way out to the Willamette Valley? How could she be so negative when he was so determined, so optimistic? How could she let fear of failure chain her and hold her back? How would she ever live with herself if she did?

'Did he say who he was? He never introduced himself.' Araktcheiev handed her back her wine-glass.

'Count Somebody or other. Swedish, I think he said,' she lied.

'Handsome fellow. Did you enjoy his company?'

'Not really. I'm afraid I'm too exhausted to dance, especially the waltz.'

Araktcheiev clucked sympathetically. All she could think of was a maiden aunt commenting on some minor crisis in her niece's social life.

'Tonight you'll get a good night's sleep. I shall see to it. I'll make arrangements for a room here in the palace. You need your sleep; we mustn't let that beautiful face take on a haggard look. That would be criminal.'

She nodded without listening, closing her mind to his words, concentrating on her counting, reaching two hundred, offering rejoinder to make him think she was paying him attention, allowing ten counts for it and resuming. She got to four and a half minutes. Now.

She rose from her chair. The song had ended, and immediately the orchestra struck up another waltz.

'Shall we dance?' he asked, offering his arms.

'The next one. Please excuse me, I must go to the ladies' room.'

He dropped his arms, his face sagging as he did so. 'I shall count the seconds until you return.'

'I won't be long.'

For some unfathomable reason she impulsively reached out and pressed his arm. In consolation. He beamed, and for an instant she imagined he was going to leap into the air with joy. To him it was a sure sign that he was making headway in winning her affection. A sure sign. She shouldn't have done it, she reflected; it was the last thing she should have done, only she was so grateful to him for letting her go, rather than narrowing his eyes mistrustfully and refusing her permission by merely taking hold of her and starting to dance.

The end of the corridor loomed miles away. She felt a bit faint as she started toward it, walking fast, but not too fast. Her overworking heart now seemed to be draining her of the last of her energy. She made it to the end, though, and turning right found herself at the linen-closet door.

Praying the robe would be there, she opened it slowly. Without protection she couldn't set foot outside. It was there; quickly she bundled it around her. It was huge, and heavy. It must weigh a hundred pounds, she thought as she pulled it around her head and shoulders, all but buckling her knees. Moving to the outside door diagonally opposite, she rubbed away the steam with the heel of her hand in a slow circular motion, dreading what she might see. Holding her breath and peering out, she recognized Boyd, bundled in a fur coat and cap, talking to an officer and a soldier, the three of them halfway down the entryway to the sidewalk. Beyond the short posts supporting the ends of the iron grillwork that fenced the way a sleigh was parked at the curb. Two horses stood at the pole, impatiently pawing the street whitened from curb to curb with frozen snow leveled by the day's continuous traffic back and forth across the Neva. The horses shivered under their blankets, and slender white clouds rose from their nostrils. Hunched up on his seat, reins in hand, the driver glanced expectantly at Boyd. And waited.

For what? Until Boyd got rid of the Horror's men she didn't dare open the door. Immediately, as if Boyd had read her thought and was acting accordingly, the soldier saluted and left him and his superior and walked back to the sleigh to speak with the driver. The driver leaned down, evidently to answer his question; Boyd turned to look at them, turned back, and, bringing up his right fist, struck the officer hard in the jaw, crumpling him in a heap. At the same time, down from his seat leaped the driver, arms outstretched, hands closing around the unsuspecting soldier's throat, pushing him over backward into the snow. Straddling him, he knocked him out with two well-placed punches. Then each man picked up his man and, looking up and down the way, deposited them in the sleigh, laying them crosswise on the floor. Opening the door, she hurried out.

The night air was a hundred needles jabbing at her unprotected eyes. The city was black as the pit to the left across Dvortsovaya Square to Saint Isaac's Cathedral and beyond. She could faintly hear the orchestra playing deep inside the palace. She was running. Standing beside the sleigh, Boyd urged her to move faster, reaching out for her, practically pulling her off her feet to him. Into the sleigh they climbed, resting their feet on the unconscious officer. Away they flew. Seconds later they had crossed the Neva to within sight of the not-yet-completed Stock Exchange. Now the driver was urging the horses to greater speed and turning sharp left to follow the embankment.

On and on they rushed, swinging right into Lini Street so abruptly the sleigh threatened to topple over. To the corner and left onto Bolshoi Prospekt, which would take them straight out to the western docks. The wind rose, lifting powder from the snow, twisting it into gigantic white wraiths dancing wildly.

'Satisfied?' asked Boyd, grinning like some furry devil.

'Oh, Boyd, I don't believe this. I don't believe it.'

'So pinch yourself, my darling. It's no dream. Oh, allow me to introduce my friend and fellow kidnapper, Ivan Kurzhentshev, a mere stripling, as you can see, whom I've turned to a life of crime. Ivan, may I present my wife.'

'My pleasure, madame.' He touched his cap deferentially and smiled down.

'No, Ivan,' she said somberly. 'Mine, all mine.'

Her heart continued to pound, but a sense of relief was beginning to loosen the knot of nerves at the back of her neck as the shadowed immensity of the Winter Palace faded into the darkness. Nevertheless, they were not yet out of the woods, she thought, and wouldn't be until they sighted the coast of Sweden. Only then would she feel truly safe. She huddled close to him, his arm around her protectingly. The soldier at their feet slept on, but the subaltern under their feet stirred. Regaining consciousness, he turned his head and looked up at them. And spoke. Boyd glanced up at Ivan.

'What's he saying?'

'That we must stop the sleigh at once. At once, do you hear? Turn around and head straight back to the Winter Palace,' said Tawny.

Boyd laughed. 'Ivan, would you be so kind as to tell him what we planned to tell him?'

Ivan addressed the officer, who by now was sitting up and gingerly rubbing his jaw. The soldier alongside him stirred and opened his eyes. The wind rose higher, shrilling painfully.

Tawny got the gist of Ivan's speech to the subaltern. In more words than she could understand he advised him to reflect upon his and his man's situation. Back at the Winter Palace General Araktcheiev had probably already satisfied himself that the lady was missing and had summoned all those assigned to cover the many entrances. To note that these two were missing:

'He can only suspect the obvious, no? That you have willingly accompanied the lady wherever she's going.'

'Nonsense,' said the subaltern tightly.

'Anything but,' rejoined Ivan. 'What it comes down to is you two let her get away. And now there'll be hell to pay.'

Pulling up the horses, stopping the sleigh, he bent down, glowering first at the officer, then at the soldier. 'This is your stop. You've got ten seconds to get out. Go back and report, if you dare. If you, Lieutenant, want to lose your precious stripe and you, Private, your freedom for a few months. If not a good deal more.'

'Out!' snapped Boyd, grabbing the officer, who was sitting up, jerking him to his feet and pushing him out of the sleigh. The soldier quickly followed of his own accord.

'Go back and report like two good tin soldiers,' said Ivan, snapping the reins and bellowing to the horse. They started off.

Tawny looked back at the two standing gaping after them. Their expressions mingled confusion and fear. Of Araktcheiev's wrath, what else, she mused.

'Rest assured,' said Boyd, 'if they know what's good for them they won't report back right away. They'll take the time to think up some cock-and-bull story to protect their hides. Which time we three will make good use of.'

'There's no way they can protect their hides,' ventured Tawny. 'Not against the Horror.'

Boyd shrugged. 'That's their problem.'

'Darling, how were you able to separate them the way you did? Get the soldier to go over to Ivan?'

'I merely asked the lieutenant for a cheroot. When he said he didn't have any, which I suspected – officers, according to Ivan, being forbidden to smoke on duty – I told him Ivan had half a dozen. Forbidden or not, he couldn't pass up the chance to smoke in this bitter cold.'

'I just remembered,' interjected Ivan, 'I don't have any smokes.'

Boyd and Tawny laughed, then sobered. He took her in his arms and kissed her warmly, her eyes, her cheeks, her chin, her mouth, pressing hard, then softening contact, working her lips with his own lovingly, setting her quieted heart thumping again.

'My darling, my darling,' he whispered. 'Just a little farther and we'll be at the docks and aboard the *Magnus Stenbok* heading back for Malmo. Your nightmare is over, my love.'

She sighed. 'It's marvelous, Boyd, simply marvelous. To

come back to life. Yes, back from the dead. To feel your arms around me, your kiss, your love. Hold me, darling, and promise you'll never let me out of your sight again . . .'

'I promise.'

41

According to Boyd's watch they had less than twenty minutes to reach the wharf and the waiting *Magnus Stenbok*. More than enough time under ordinary circumstances, but the weather this night was beginning to prove anything but ordinary. No snow fell, but the wind was threatening a gale, thundering down from Karelian to the west of the White Sea above the city. When at last the sleigh drew within sight of the harbor they saw that it was frozen over, strewn with cracked ice and heaped with floes and floebergs. Tawny gasped at the eerie sight, and her heart sank.

'How will the ship ever get through?'

'As easily as slicing cheese,' bellowed Ivan above the roaring wind. 'Now and for the next week or so. After that the harbor, practically the whole Gulf of Finland, closes up tight. To get to Helsingfors you'd need a dogsled.'

The sky doming the harbor looked sinister, packed solidly as it was with fat black scowling clouds massed together by the wind. Its power was such it almost toppled the sleigh, and it burned Tawny's eyes so they dimmed with tears. All three got down, Ivan handing the reins to a man waiting by the gangplank. At once the two began haggling over what Tawny took to be final payment for renting the team and sleigh.

The *Magnus Stenbok* was held fast to the wharf along the vessel's port side by four six-inch hawsers.

'Two anchors hold her starboard fore and aft,' explained Boyd, as they lowered their heads against the gale and mounted the gangplank.

All sails were safely furled and no one was on deck, no one anywhere to be seen on the wharf, save for the man arguing with Ivan over the horses and sleigh. Stepping inside the companionway, waiting and listening, they finally heard him come stomping heavily up the gangplank. The wind was becoming stronger by the minute, threatening to develop into a full-scale squall, if not a storm.

'She's got to be forty-five knots at least,' commented Ivan worriedly. 'If Captain Swenson knows what's good for him he'll run up the red lights. We're spoiling for a blow like I've never seen . . .'

'But won't we be leaving?' asked Tawny hopefully, drawing the bearskin robe snugly about her. 'Can't we run out from under it?'

Sneaking a glimpse of the sullen sky, Ivan grunted and shook his head.

'Not at this rate.'

'We'll be lucky to hold fast where we are,' said Boyd, nodding.

'But, darling, we've got to get away. They'll be coming after us.' Suddenly a note of desperation had crept into Tawny's tone; her eyes widened with fear.

'I wouldn't worry about that,' said Ivan. 'Nobody in his right mind will step out his door in this blow. Listen to that wind. Cross your fingers we don't lose any yardarms, even a mast. Cross your fingers and pray the hawsers hold!'

'You don't know Araktcheiev,' persisted Tawny. 'He'd send a search party out in a hurricane. And, Boyd, he's got to know we headed here . . .'

'Those two tin soldiers won't tell him,' responded Boyd.

'But common sense will. Where else would we go?'

Ivan shook his head in disagreement. 'It's a big port, four ports in one. There have to be thirty or forty ships anchored.'

'There could be four hundred, he'd have every one searched. I have to have a disguise; all three of us should disguise ourselves.'

Ivan shrugged. 'Whatever you want.'

'We can certainly borrow you a cap and jacket and trousers,' said Boyd to her. 'Still, if a search party does board us, you've nothing to worry about. Nobody else on board knows anything about this.'

'Captain Swenson's got to know,' said Ivan. 'It's his neck

that'll be on the block if anything should . . . you know.' He lowered his eyes sheepishly.

'You think he might not want to take her along?' asked Boyd. 'That's ridiculous. If there's any chance of that then we'll just have to smuggle her out!'

Tawny cut in. 'No, Boyd, he's making sense. We have no right tricking the captain or anybody else into hiding me. If I was found by Araktcheiev's men it could put him in a terrible fix. It wouldn't be fair.'

'Leave Swenson to me,' said Boyd. 'I'll talk him into taking you.'

'You can start now,' said Ivan, his eyes fixed, staring over Boyd's shoulder. Boyd and Tawny turned to look.

Approaching them, coming up the narrow way, was a man wearing a three-quarter-length otterskin coat and the cap of his command. Captain Gustavus Swenson looked more Latin than Nordic to Tawny, with dark hair curling out from under his cap, swarthy skin, and eyes as black and as restless as a ferret's. He was of medium height, but blockily built, powerful-looking even under his heavy outerwear. He greeted Ivan and Boyd with a frown.

'I was beginning to think you two would never get back here,' he muttered. He then glanced in puzzlement at Tawny.

'Captain, this lady is my wife.'

'Your wife?' Astonishment flooded Swenson's features.

Boyd explained briefly. The captain listened, covering the lower half of his face with one hand. His second and third fingers were missing down to the palm.

'Madame, you two, I must ask you to come back with me to my quarters.'

Behind his cluttered desk hung a barometer. Circling the desk upon entering the cabin, he approached the barometer and studied it, indicating the level of the mercury with his index finger.

'It appears we'll have plenty of time to talk; she's still dropping. We'll have to pass up this tide.' He raised his dark eyes ceilingward. 'Let's hope the lines hold. Please sit, madame.' He turned to Boyd. 'Now what is all this about? What is your wife doing here, of all places? I mean Saint Petersburg?'

Boyd started to reply, but Tawny cut in and poured out the story from the landing in Belomorsk on.

'Ah, so the Minister of War is part of it, is he? The Horror... ye gods, he could board us with fifty men, and when they found you, madame, I could kiss my papers goodbye. I'd never be able to discharge or lade cargo here again as long as I sail. Which wouldn't be all that long once the owners got wind of this. I'd be lucky if he didn't jail me, madame, or either of you two. I can sympathize with you. But stop and think what you're asking me. To his way of thinking I'd be harboring a fugitive.' Up came his hands, stopping both men's interruptions. 'Yes, yes, I can imagine what he and his bunch put her through; I know him by reputation. As everybody does. Still, you're asking me to risk my skin, my ticket, my cargo, my ship.' He shook his head as he prattled on, defending his reluctance to become involved. Tawny's imagination put Captain Boleski in his place, in his coat, under his cap, which now lay on the desk in front of him. Boleski too would know the Horror; the difference was he would willingly take the risk. And risk there was, although patently slight were she to disguise herself as a seaman. There'd be no need to hide, just be hard at work with the others.

The two men Boyd had thrown out of the sleigh could recognize him and Ivan, so surely they would be assigned to the search party. Still, Boyd and Ivan would have time to disguise themselves. They might even flee over the side and hide behind the nearest mass of ice studding the frozen surface of the harbor. They needn't be out exposed to the gale very long. She might even hide with them.

These and a dozen other thoughts flashed through her mind like a volley of darts before Captain Boleski changed back into Swenson. In the meantime his square jaw had pushed forward a good inch, indicating that his mind was made up. She was not welcome aboard the *Magnus Stenbok*, not as long as he was master.

The discussion stopped before Boyd could get out so much as a single word of argument. The howling wind was beginning to loosen shards of ice. Like gigantic daggers they clattered across the harbor, piling against the wharves, now and then slamming and shattering against the unprotected side of the ship. Tilted one way then the other by the blast, she struggled to free herself, straining at her lines. The one forward wharfside was the first to give way, with a sharp twang like a bullet ricocheting, the vessel jerking, all but upsetting the four of them.

'Christ!' bellowed Swenson. 'Give way there.' Brushing by Boyd, he leaned out the door. 'Mr. Johansson, topside on the double with some hands. Set another line to replace that one, set two! You, Kurzhentshev, you too, Chevrier, get up there and lend a hand. Move!'

Too late. The wind howled fiercely, the death song of the spheres; the ship skewed crazily, the three remaining wharfside lines and both anchor chains snapping like kite strings before the first man could gain the deck. The *Magnus Stenbok* hurtled away from the wharf, crackling through the ice sheet, careening before the blast. Swenson, Ivan, Boyd, and Tawny ran up the steps to the head of the companionway, gripping the stair rail and peering out. Other ships had broken loose, one, a brig, toppling over, her masts crashing through the ice, her deck throwing a dozen hands clear. Neither Johansson nor any of those he'd summoned, all of whom came up behind them, dared venture forth.

'This is it!' bellowed the captain, his dark face draining of color, turning ashen before Tawny's startled eyes.

From somewhere forward a man had made it to the helm. All four watched in wonderment as he unlashed the wheel and began steering the ship. But he slipped on the icy deck, his feet went out from under him, and the wind slammed him against the pillar box. The wheel, released, began spinning wildly. Boyd and Ivan vaulted out of the companionway, racing to it, grabbing it from both sides, clinging with all their strength as the wind struck again, then let up briefly, permitting them to bring the prow about, setting the bowsprit seaward.

'Boyd!' screamed Tawny. Swenson had to grab her by the arms to keep her from running out to join them.

'It's all right, two can hold her. They can.' The man who had been blown off the wheel was up on his hands and knees, catching his breath. Suddenly a sloop out of control came sliding by, narrowly missing the *Magnus Stenbok*'s stern, smashing midships against a huge jagged floe with a sound like the cracking of a cane over a man's knee. Swenson cursed under his breath, his face graying a shade deeper; then a quick glance out into the gulf actuated a look of surprise.

'Look ahead,' he shouted. 'Open water!'

He was right. And fewer floes were visible. Most of them seemed to have collected in the harbor. Tawny looked back at the wharf: they had already covered better than half a mile, slipping between the masses of ice and nearing the open water.

Still the ship continued to groan under the relentless buffeting, threatening to split apart in a hundred places, her masts stabbing the blackness overhead, tilting back and forth, sending first the port gunwale then the starboard dangerously close to submerging.

Boyd and Ivan held fast to the wheel, until the first man gained his feet and managed to secure it, holding their course outward bound.

They made open water, running out from under the worst of the wind into bone-chilling cold. With a loud cheer the crew poured out of the companionway, scampering up the ratlines, spreading over the yards, unfurling canvas. The *Magnus Stenbok* was a barque, square-rigged on the fore and main but fore-and-aft on the mizzenmast. Within minutes all sails were set and sheeted, clew lines, leech lines, buntlines, and spilling lines made fast.

Captain Swenson had long since let go of Tawny. The two of them now up on deck, she looked back at the dark jagged outline of the city under the swiftly moving clouds. Then her eyes met his.

'It appears we're sailing on this tide like it or not, madame.' He smiled, touching the bill of his cap in salute. 'May I be the first to welcome you aboard?'

I would hasten my escape from the windy storm and tempest.

Destroy, O Lord, and divide their tongues: for I have seen violence and strife in the city...

For it was not an enemy that reproached me; then I could have borne it: neither was it he that hated me that

244

did magnify himself against me; then I would have hid myself from him:

But it was thou, a man mine equal, my guide, and mine acquaintance...

The words of his mouth were smoother than butter, but war was in his heart: his words were softer than oil, yet were they drawn swords...

But thou, O God, shalt bring them down into the pit of destruction: bloody and deceitful men shall not live out half their days; but I will trust in thee.

PSALMS 55:8–9, 12–13, 21, 23

EPILOGUE

In somewhat battered condition, in light of its unexpected but timely departure from the Vasilievski wharf, the *Magnus Stenbok* arrived in Malmo, Sweden, one week later. From there three separate ships in turn took Boyd and Tawny to Ostend, on the coast of West Flanders, San Juan, Puerto Rico, and New Orleans. They reached Titus Forks early in June the following year. There Boyd joined his father-in-law, Jack Kinross, in breeding and trading horses. In the years that followed, as the business flourished, Boyd and Tawny built a beautiful home overlooking the Osage River. Four children were born of their union: Boyd, Jr., John, Lionel, and Crystal Anna, after Anna Fritsch.

It was not until four years later that Lionel Haggerty came to Titus Forks, spending two weeks there, recounting old times with the Chevriers.

Shortly after the *Magnus Stenbok* was swept away from Saint Petersburg by the storm Nikki was informed that his anticipated promotion to lieutenant-colonel would not be forthcoming after all. Within three months an even worse dilemma befell him: he was mortally wounded in an *affaire d'honneur* stemming from a dispute with a fellow officer over a woman. He died of internal bleeding before sunset of the day of the duel. At the time of his death his age was officially listed as twenty-seven. His sister, Olga, and her husband, Paul Kovakin, lived a long and happy life in Saint Petersburg, for the most part untouched by the political unrest in Russia over the course of the next fifteen years.

Czar Alexander I's rule lasted until 1825. On the first of December, at Taganrog, following a long and debilitating siege of malaria compounded by exhaustion, Alexander died. His body did not leave Taganrog until the tenth of January, 1826. The accession to the throne of his successor, Nicholas I, precipitated a series of pocket revolutions, delaying Alexander's burial for nearly four months. It was not until March 25 that the coffin was interred in the Fortress of Saint Peter and Saint Paul.

General Araktcheiev, become Count Araktcheiev, as Alexander himself put it, 'Vice-Emperor', clung to power until the death of his patron. But even before Nicholas assumed the throne a relentless police machinery had taken over nominal control of the government, suppressing, regulating, and crushing all freedom in Russia. Espionage flourished. Asiatic despotism backed by Prussian militarism shackled the Empire. General Benckendorff replaced Araktcheiev as head of the military and grand inquisitor. On April 26, 1826, lacking the support he needed to sustain his career, the Horror resigned all of his other offices and retired to Carlsbad. There he died on April 21, 1834.

Marcy Rampling married unsuccessfully three times and was preparing to take her fourth husband when he summarily broke the engagement. Priscilla and Emily Cutshaw married men from Titus Forks, both families residing not far from the Chevriers.

Aldous and Helen Rampling died in 1832. Tawny's aunt, Lydia Cutshaw, died the following year.

Tawny and Boyd both survived well into their eighties, enjoying their children, grandchildren, and great-grand-children.

Sit tibi terra levis*

---

* May the earth lie lightly upon thee.